THE FINISHING SCHOOL

ALSO BY MICHELE MARTINEZ

Most Wanted

THE

SCHOOL

FIC
MAR
05/04

MICHELE MARTINEZ

wm

WILLIAM MORROW
An Imprint of HarperCollins*Publishers*

HarperCollins books may be purchased for educational, business, or sales promotional use. For information please write: Special Markets Department, HarperCollins Publishers, 10 East 53rd Street, New York, NY 10022.

FIRST EDITION

Printed on acid-free paper

Library of Congress Cataloging-in-Publication Data

Martinez, Michele, 1962–
    The finishing school / Michele Martinez.— 1st ed.
      p.   cm.
    ISBN-13: 978-0-06-072400-9
    ISBN-10: 0-06-072400-5 (alk. paper)
    1. Women lawyers—Fiction.   2. Public prosecutors—Fiction.   3. Preparatory schools—Fiction.   4. Manhattan (New York, N.Y.)—Fiction.   I. Title.

PS3613.A78648F56   2006
813'.6—dc22   2005043415

06 07 08 09 10 WBC/RRD 10 9 8 7 6 5 4 3 2 1

FOR MY HUSBAND,

my partner in all endeavors

ACKNOWLEDGMENTS

I am deeply indebted to my agent, Meg Ruley, for being my counselor, cheerleader, and friend. She's the best. I am also indebted to all the other wonderful people at the Jane Rotrosen Agency for their assistance and support.

I still can't believe how fortunate I am to be edited by Carolyn Marino, who combines tremendous insight and skill with the lightest, most gracious touch. All of the incredible people at William Morrow and HarperAudio are a delight to work with. I am especially grateful to Michael Morrison, Lisa Gallagher, and Dee Dee De Bartlo, and to Jennifer Civiletto for all her help.

The following people read this book in manuscript form and gave me terrific comments: Don Cleary, Christina Hogrebin, Nicole Gruenstein, and Randy Dwenger. Many thanks also to the one and only Cass Adelman for the excellent Manhattan doggy and girls'-school details.

THE FINISHING SCHOOL

EVEN THE MOST dedicated prosecutor hates the sound of a pager shrieking at two o'clock in the morning. Melanie Vargas barely slept these days anyway. In the middle of a divorce, with a baby daughter who was spending the winter sick with one thing or another, Melanie hardly needed that terrible screeching coming from her dresser top. But duty called. She scrambled out of bed and immediately slammed her hip into the sharp corner of the bedside table.

"*Shit.*"

Just as the pager stopped wailing, her one-year-old, Maya, who'd fallen asleep in bed beside her after fussing half the night with a double ear infection, woke up and started to howl.

"Okay, okay, shush," Melanie whispered, digging under the pillows surrounding Maya. Her fingers touched soft plastic, and she popped the pacifier into her daughter's mouth, then raced across the room to grab the pager before it went off again. Squinting at the readout, she saw her boss's home phone number glowing bright red in the darkness. *Damn!* This was only getting worse. Her boss gave her agita under the best of circumstances.

"Well, it's about time!" Bernadette said, picking up on the first ring. Bernadette DeFelice, chief of the Major Crimes Unit of the New York City U.S. Attorney's Office, did *not* like to be kept waiting.

"Hey, Bern, it's Melanie—"

"I *know* that, for God's sake, I just paged you. Listen, I've got two dead rich girls in James Seward's apartment on Park Avenue. You know who he is? That Wall Street guy running for Senate?"

"Of course. Did *he* kill them?"

"No, nothing like that. It's his daughter and a friend of hers. They OD'd. Looks like heroin. Right before Christmas, too. Hah, teenagers. And people wonder why I never had kids."

It was Monday night—strike that, Tuesday morning—and Christmas was a week away.

"Wow, the poor parents." Melanie looked over at Maya snuggled under the covers and thanked God her own little one was safe and sound.

"Okay," Bernadette said, "the plan is, find the drug supplier right away and make an example of him." She chuckled cynically. "Some Dominican kid selling dime bags in the Heights isn't gonna know what hit him. I need you to get over to Seward's ASAP."

"Bernadette, it's two o'clock in the morning, and my daughter's sick."

"Is that my problem? This is a *real* job, girlfriend, not the fricking DMV. You're meeting up with Vito Albano from the Elite Narcotics Task Force. And you'd better damn well impress him. I've been trying to get business from him for a long time, but the Special Narcotics Prosecutor had a lock on him. This is our big chance. That squad does amazing cases."

"Bern—"

"Do you *realize* how lucky you are to get this call? This case is gonna generate huge press. Both girls are from prominent families, and they went to— What's that fancy girls' school? Miss Holbrooke's?"

Melanie tried to muster some enthusiasm, not easy to do at this hour. "It sounds really great, but—"

"Albano *asked* for you by name, Melanie. All right, technically, he asked for Susan Charlton, but when I told him she was on vacation, he was happy to take you. Apparently he's heard about your penchant for getting . . . shall we say 'overly involved' in your investigations. Which reminds me, no cops-and-robbers stuff this time. That's an order."

"Bern, I really can't—"

"Do you *understand* what this means? Do I have to spell it out for you? You're developing a solid reputation with the movers and shakers, so don't blow it. I told Vito you'd be there in fifteen minutes. Don't make me look bad." Bernadette rattled off the tony address and hung up.

MELANIE HAD REACHED Steve Hanson—her ex-husband, or soon-to-be ex anyway—not at his apartment but on his cell phone at 2:00 A.M., with music and laughter in the background. Up to his old tricks, the *desgraciado*. She tried not to think about it and just be glad that he agreed to come over and stay with Maya.

By the time she'd brushed her teeth and pulled on black pants and a turtleneck, Steve was at the door of the apartment. She turned on the light in the foyer and peered through the peephole. Seeing him gave her a jolt. Mmm, too bad he still looked so good. Tall, lean, blond in a rugged sort of way, always dressed like a million bucks. *Watch out for this man,* she reminded herself, unlocking the dead bolt. *Plenty of other women like what you like.*

Steve seemed to sweep into the foyer on a wave of fresh, cold air. Snowflakes still clung to his eyelashes and on the lapels of his charcoal gray cashmere overcoat.

"Hey, Merry Christmas, baby," he said, grabbing her shoulders and kissing her full on the mouth. She couldn't help it, she started to kiss back. The guy knew what he was doing, and she was kiss-deprived. But then she tasted alcohol and, beneath that, whomever he'd kissed last. He smelled of perfume, definitely. She pulled away.

Steve looked her in the eyes. "I'm glad you called, Melanie. I've been missing you. Families should be together at the holidays."

She turned her back, opening the door to the coat closet so he wouldn't see the emotion in her face. Steve knew how to push her buttons, knew about her own childhood Christmases, without her father. She saw through the manipulation. If they reconciled, like he claimed he wanted, nothing would be different. Just smell the man and you could tell that.

"Hand me your coat," she said, holding out her hand, her voice neutral.

"Wow, look at that tree! How'd you do that?" Steve stood at the threshold to the living room gazing at the seven-foot-tall Douglas fir, which was decked with popcorn and cranberry garlands she'd strung herself late at night when she couldn't sleep.

"Hector the doorman helped me get it up here. It looks nice, huh?" She felt proud of it, of how she'd managed without him.

"Yeah, it looks beautiful. So do *you*, at two-thirty in the morning." He walked over to where she stood and gazed down at her with sleepy hazel eyes. "I take that back. You look *hot*. Like throw-you-down-and-jump-on-you hot."

"I have to go." She twirled away just as he grabbed for her.

Ay, de mí, the guy was good-looking, but she refused to let him get to her. He was drunk and horny after a Christmas party, and she didn't even take him seriously sober. Her marriage, she'd decided, had been more about sex and stability than soul love. There was another man she dreamed of nights.

"Maya's in our room," she said, the "our" slipping out before she realized it. "She can have Motrin again at four if she needs it," she said, opening the front door. At the sight of the elevator, her mind flashed ahead to the gruesome scene that awaited her at James Seward's apartment. Two young girls, having died terrible deaths, lost forever to their parents.

She hesitated and turned back. "Christmas morning," she said.

"What?"

"Christmas morning. It would be okay if you wanted to come over. Help Maya open her presents. I could make some scrambled eggs."

His face relaxed into a smile. "Okay," he said. "That would be nice."

She straightened her shoulders and marched out the door.

2

MELANIE HAD TO FIGHT her way through a throng of reporters camped out in front of the Park Avenue building. Moments later, the mahogany-paneled elevator discharged her directly into the foyer of the Sewards' penthouse. Her gaze traveled upward—taking in enormous oil paintings in gilded frames, ornately plastered thirteen-foot ceilings, and a glittering crystal chandelier—before settling back on the man standing in front of her. Dressed in slacks, a checked shirt, and a loud tie, he looked to be in his late forties, and he was in the process of finishing a cigarette. His thinning dark hair was carefully combed over his bald spot, and a small pot-belly protruded like a melon from his tall, lanky frame.

"Vargas? I'm Albano. You're late."

"Sorry. I got here as fast as I could. I just—"

"All right, all right. You're here now, let's go."

He took a deep drag, then crushed out his cigarette in a delicate-looking porcelain planter and took off through an archway to the left. Melanie hurried after him, down a wide hallway past enormous, dark-ened rooms, each more elaborately decorated than the last. They turned a corner and headed toward the back of the apartment, passing a gleam-ing kitchen, all white tile and stainless steel. A tuxedoed man sat at the kitchen table talking urgently on his cell phone. Melanie recognized him from having seen him on the news.

"Seward?" she asked Albano under her breath as she raced along beside him.

He nodded. "What'd your boss tell you?"

"That his daughter and one of her friends OD'd and that we're supposed to track down the supplier and get a warrant for his arrest."

"It was Seward's stepdaughter, not his daughter. His wife's kid from a previous marriage. But yeah. Seward calls the commissioner instead of 911, you believe that? Prick's been on the phone nonstop since I got here, so we haven't interviewed him yet. I'm gonna let you and the case agent do that, but come take a look at the bodies first."

Albano halted before an open door at the far end of the hallway, turning toward her so her view was blocked. A hum of activity emanated from the room, and the faint perfume of decaying flesh sailed out to her on a blast of cold air.

"By the way," Albano said, "your boss. Is she that redheaded girl with the nice, uh, the nice . . . voice?"

"She has red hair," Melanie said, smiling. Not natural, of course, but undeniably red.

"Yeah, I think I met her at a conference last year."

"Oh, is that why you called us? I know you usually work with Special Narcotics."

"Ah, that's just a money thing. Nothing personal. Special Narcotics has a budget for buying cops equipment, you know."

"No, I had no idea."

"Uh-huh. I'd love to take more cases federal. You get heavier sentences. But funding being what it is, I can't afford to dis a prosecutor that wants to buy me cars and radios."

"So why call us *now*?"

"Seward insisted. He wanted the feds called in, and the guy has the juice to do it. The mayor, the commissioner, everybody's bending over backwards. I'm under orders to solve this thing fast enough to squash the press coverage, you believe that? Like we can lock up the supplier by sunrise and go for pancakes." Albano reached into his pocket and took out a pack of Rolaids, shaking his head, tossing three into his mouth at once.

"I get the sense you don't think that's likely," Melanie said.

"You have any idea how many mopes there are in this town selling dime bags to high-school kids? Needle in a fucking haystack. You want my opinion, this case is a nightmare. Seward's a major pain in the ass, and the press is watching our every move."

"Yeah, the tabloids must be drooling. Seward's stepdaughter OD'ing, and both girls went to Holbrooke. You know, the fancy finishing school? That's news in itself," Melanie said.

Miss Holbrooke's School, known simply as "Holbrooke" among the initiated, was one of the oldest and most famous private schools in Manhattan. Melanie had grown up in the city in a rough neighborhood and gone to public school, but she knew Holbrooke all right. She'd learned about it when she got to Harvard and discovered that the lunch tables in the Freshman Union were ruled by a clique of Holbrooke girls with famous last names, wearing just the right expensive jeans. They looked like models, were mean as cats, and hadn't gotten in on their SAT scores.

"Did you talk to the doormen?" Melanie asked Albano. "Any evidence of anybody in or out of the building tonight who could've delivered the drugs?"

"Useless. Four guys on duty—two doormen, two porters. Nobody saw a fricking thing. There was a holiday reception for a hundred people happening on the twelfth floor. They were so distracted with that, King Kong coulda walked in and they wouldna noticed."

"What about household help? These people must have a maid or something."

Albano pulled a small notebook from his back pants pocket and consulted it. "Uh, there's usually a live-in housekeeper, but she's in

Manila for the holidays. Rest of the staff consists of a day maid, cook, driver, and—get this—laundress–slash–ironing lady. Last person left at about six-fifteen tonight. None present on the scene when any events of interest occurred." He put the notebook back in his pocket. "So . . . ready to take a look?" Albano asked.

Melanie drew a breath to steel herself for viewing bodies but just ended up with a noseful of death smell. As if an animal had died in a damp basement, except more so. No point in hesitating. Not like they would smell any better if she waited.

"Let's go," she said, and stepped through the door.

3

THE LARGE CORNER BEDROOM was crowded with cops and bitterly cold. The windows lining its two exterior walls had been thrown open to the freezing night air. Melanie clapped her hand violently over her nose and mouth. Even with the cross-ventilation, the room reeked of vomit, feces, and spoiling meat.

The ghoulish face of the girl on the bed drew Melanie's eyes like a magnet. She'd collapsed half sitting against the headboard, her skin mottled and blue, her eyes open, bulging nearly out of their sockets. Vomit spilled from her slackened mouth, yet her long blond hair and classic features suggested she'd been beautiful in life. She was clad only in a skintight sweater and tiny thong panties, her long legs bare but rigid and inert.

"The other one's here," Albano said.

Melanie stepped around the bed. A pretty brunette lay splayed out stark naked on the floor near the bathroom door, her head turned sideways and her vacant eyes staring right at Melanie. Her cheek rested in a pool of congealed blood and white foam. Melanie took a step closer. A familiar-looking fleshy pink object lay in the pooled blood on the floor.

"What's *that*?" she asked through her fingers.

"Tongue," Albano replied matter-of-factly. "She bit it off. You can actually see a perfect impression of her teeth if you look close."

"Thanks, I'll take your word for it."

"The blonde on the bed is Whitney Seward, the bigwig's step-daughter. This one's Brianna Meyers. Her mother's some famous interior decorator," Albano said, practically rolling his eyes. "Oh, lemme introduce you to the case agent. Ray Wong from DEA. Ray-Ray, c'mere."

A short, muscular guy with close-cropped hair and a military bearing came over and shook Melanie's hand. She forced herself not to wince at his powerful grip.

"Ray-Ray's one of the best, if you don't mind your people wound a little tight," Albano said. "First guy through the door on every raid. Every now and then, we just take his gun away for a few days to make sure he don't hurt nobody, right, Ray?" Albano punched Wong on the arm and chuckled, but Wong didn't look amused.

"Do we know why these girls are undressed?" Melanie asked. "Is there some sexual aspect to this?"

"Did you talk to that black girl from the M.E.'s office yet?" Albano asked Wong, gesturing at a young woman in cornrows and funky glasses who was conferring with some Crime Scene detectives.

"She's been occupied, sir."

"Let's ask her," Albano said.

Shavonne Washington, the investigator from the Office of the Chief Medical Examiner, was speaking to Butch Brennan from Crime Scene, a cheerful old-timer whom Melanie knew from other cases. Melanie greeted Butch warmly, then turned to Shavonne.

"What's your assessment?" she asked.

"I'm not allowed to certify cause of death without an autopsy unless it's natural causes, but I *could*," Shavonne said. "This one's a no-brainer. All the classic signs of narcotic drug overdose. You got vomiting, loss of control of the bowels. You smell *that*, right? Nasal and lachrymal discharge. Severed tongue on the brown-haired girl, who's also got white powder under the nostrils, indicating nasal ingestion. No visible track marks on the arms, but that's no surprise. Kids in this socioeconomic bracket are squeamish. Shooting up's too street for them—they prefer it up the nose. So I'm gonna say with ninety-nine percent certainty heroin's the culprit here."

"You're sure it was heroin? Why not cocaine if there's white powder under the nose?" Melanie asked.

"Cocaine ODs are pretty rare," Shavonne explained, "and they usually happen because the victim had some undetected cardiac problem. With cocaine you never see people OD'ing simultaneously like this. Whereas with heroin, if the stuff's powerful enough, it's not uncommon to get a couple bodies at a time just from snorting. More, even."

"One's nude and the other's half undressed. Any signs of sexual abuse?" Melanie asked.

"No visible trauma consistent with defensive wounds. But the autopsy'll look for evidence of recent sexual intercourse, forced or consensual. If there *is* evidence, we'll take swabs and DNA-test the semen. That's probably not why the bodies are naked, though. It's normal for ODs to be missing some clothes. They rip 'em off while they're freaking out."

"Did we find the missing clothes?" Melanie asked Butch.

"The brunette's are in a pile on the bathroom floor, so that looks consistent with what Shavonne's saying. The blonde's skirt and sneakers were in the kitchen. Why there, is anybody's guess."

"Did we recover any heroin from the scene?" Melanie asked.

"Looks like they snorted it all before they kicked off," Butch said. "But we found the empty glassines, so the lab'll test for residue. Take a look."

Butch handed her two clear plastic evidence envelopes that had already been heat-sealed and dated. Each one in turn contained a tiny pouch made from waxed paper with a fold-over flap, precisely sized to hold an individual dosage unit of heroin. Known as glassines or "decks" in cop parlance, these particular pouches had been stamped with the word GOLPE, in bright red ink.

"The decks were found right next to 'em, like they snorted the junk one second and keeled over the next," Butch said. "One was found on the bed next to the blonde's right hand and the other on the floor next to the brunette's right arm."

"Hmm, that's odd," Melanie said.

"Why do you say that?" Butch asked.

"If the dark-haired girl snorted the heroin and fell over in a seizure the next second with the glassine still in her hand, why are her clothes all the way in the bathroom?"

"Maybe she snorted more than one deck," Butch offered.

"Then we should've found another empty, right?" Melanie examined the glassines. *"Golpe,"* she intoned, giving the word its Spanish pronunciation.

"You recognize the stamp?" Lieutenant Albano asked.

"Stamps" were the brand names of the drug trade. Knowing the brand name would make tracking down the supplier a whole lot easier, since certain gangs tended to specialize in certain brands of heroin.

"No. Just that it's Spanish. It means 'slap' or 'punch.' In this context it's more like 'hit,' a hit of dope. The Spanish name is unusual, don't you think?" she asked.

"Well, no offense there, Counselor, but the major heroin distributors in this town are all PR or Dominican. The Spanish sell the shit, so they put it in a language they understand."

"Not true, Lieutenant," Melanie said, struggling to keep her tone polite. "Spanish-speaking drug dealers typically use English brand names. They reach a larger customer base that way. To me the Spanish stamp means these drugs were intended for a Spanish-speaking market. That could help us narrow things down."

"We'll get on it, run the stamp through the databases," Ray Wong said.

"What about fingerprinting the glassines?" Melanie asked.

"We're dusting everything. We'll need to print the bodies for comparison, though," Butch said.

"No problem. The bodies are still fresh enough to get prints, especially with this cold air slowing decomp," Shavonne said, gesturing toward the open windows.

Bodies. Melanie hated the sound of that. They weren't just bodies. They were human beings, young girls with names and personalities, somebody's children. Or at least they *had* been.

"How old were the victims?" Melanie asked.

"High-school juniors, so you gotta figure sixteen, seventeen. Everything ahead of 'em," Albano said, shaking his head.

"*They* should be our focus," Melanie said. "Who were they? Who were their friends? Where did they go in the past few days? We need to get to know them. That's the way to solve this case."

4

THE OBVIOUS FIRST STEP in learning more about the victims was interviewing Whitney Seward's stepfather, in whose apartment they'd drawn their last breaths, and who'd apparently discovered their bodies. Speaking to Seward's wife, Charlotte, would have to wait, since she was under sedation and unable to talk.

Melanie and Ray-Ray found James Seward seated at a marble-topped table in the lavish kitchen, speaking to his campaign manager on a cell phone. His gray-blond hair, lashless pale eyes, and aristocratic nose were familiar to anybody who watched the six o'clock news. Seward was now in the process of trying to buy himself a Senate seat, which was turning into an expensive and messy proposition. He was one of many candidates in a crowded primary field. Allegations swirled around him—from questionable trading practices on Wall Street to fund-raising scandals during his tenure as state party chairman—and he was trailing badly in the polls. Melanie recognized that she had a preexisting impression of this guy as slippery and dangerous, so she warned herself to keep an open mind.

Seward ignored their presence for as long as he possibly could, then put his hand over the mouthpiece irritably. "*Yes?* What is it?"

"Melanie Vargas from the U.S. Attorney's Office and Special Agent Raymond Wong from DEA," Melanie said as they both flashed their credentials. "We need to ask you some questions, sir."

"I'm busy right now. Phone my campaign headquarters in the morning," he said.

Melanie and Ray-Ray looked at each other. Was this guy kidding?

"Sir, we're investigating federal narcotics violations that resulted in two deaths. If you don't cooperate voluntarily, we'll subpoena you to the grand jury and place you under oath," Melanie said.

Seward's pale eyes seemed to focus on her finally. Something in their expression changed subtly, and he got off his phone call.

"Do forgive me, Miss— What did you say your name was?" he said after hanging up.

"Vargas. Melanie Vargas from the U.S. Attorney's Office."

"I'm under terrible stress tonight, as you can imagine. My step-daughter is dead. My wife is devastated. And the press is all over me, screaming for blood."

"We'll do our best to keep this brief."

"Thank you. I would very much appreciate that. It's been a difficult night."

"You have my deepest sympathy. I'm a parent, too." From what Melanie had observed so far, Seward wasn't exactly overcome with emotion, but who knew? The guy was an uptight WASP. Maybe this *was* grief-stricken on him. He certainly looked haggard anyway.

Seward took them to what he called his library to get away from the bustle of emergency personnel in the main part of the apartment. It was a large, paneled drawing room with lots of lavishly upholstered sofas and shelf after shelf of the type of gilt-edged books that decorators bought and nobody actually read. A desk sat in one corner, big and shiny as an ocean liner. Seward settled himself behind it in an imposing leather chair.

"Please, have a seat." He nodded toward two high-backed, uncomfortable-looking wing chairs facing the desk, and Melanie and Ray-Ray sat down. Ray-Ray opened his notebook, pen poised.

"I'll be happy to tell you anything I can," Seward offered.

"Let's start with the basics. What time did you discover the bodies?" Melanie asked.

"It wasn't actually me who discovered them. It was the building super, Luis Reyes. He has a master key, and he'd come up here looking for his daughter, who's a classmate of Whitney's. I wasn't home at the time. Charlotte and I were at a benefit at the downtown Guggenheim."

"Oh! I was under the impression you'd found the bodies yourself," Melanie said.

"The police may have assumed that, since I was here when they arrived. But I never said so. You're the first person who directly asked me whether I discovered them or not."

"But it *was* you who called the police?"

"Oh, yes. Not just the police. The *commissioner.*"

"I'm surprised Mr. Reyes didn't just call 911 when he found the bodies. That's the usual reaction."

Seward hesitated for a millisecond. "Yes. Well. You see, I told him not to. Frankly, I didn't trust Luis to handle things properly. Given the sensitive nature of the situation, I preferred to pursue it with my own contacts at a . . . uh, *higher* level. Many of the 911 dispatchers take money to feed tips to the tabloids, you know."

"I see. All right, we'll speak to Mr. Reyes also. He's here?"

"No, he went downstairs to his apartment. In the basement. He was quite upset, so I told him to go lie down."

"You told him to leave the scene before the police arrived?"

"Yes. I hope that's not a problem. I can get him right back up here if you like."

"That won't be necessary. We'll go downstairs and speak with him after we're finished interviewing you. But I'm curious as to why you didn't tell the police that Mr. Reyes was the one who discovered the bodies?"

"I guess I just didn't realize it was important. I apologize if I've caused any confusion."

Seward's pale eyes gazed at Melanie steadily. There was nothing that odd in what he was saying. It hardly surprised her that someone like him would choose to pull strings rather than let the building custodian dial 911. He obviously felt 911 was for the little people. Still, she got a strange vibe from him.

"Do you know what time Mr. Reyes found the bodies?" she continued.

Seward drew a slim silver cigarette case from his jacket pocket and extracted a European-looking cigarette, lighting it with steady hands. He was neither uncooperative nor nervous, yet his pauses before answering were odd, as if he were buying time to think. Then again, give the guy a break. It was almost four in the morning, and his stepdaughter was dead.

"I wouldn't want to speak for Luis. Best you ask *him* that," Seward said finally.

"Your point is well taken, Mr. Seward. When did Mr. Reyes first call *you*, then?" Melanie asked.

"I'm not exactly sure when he first called," Seward said, exhaling calmly. "It was loud at the benefit. I didn't hear my phone ring. When my wife and I were leaving, I realized I had a voice-mail message. I listened to the message, then immediately called Luis back. That's when he told me Whitney and Brianna were dead."

"What time was that?"

"Quite late. Perhaps midnight."

"What did you do next?"

"I rushed home, naturally."

"At what point did you call the police?"

"Once I got home. I met Luis at the door, checked in Whitney's room to see exactly what it was we were dealing with, and then I called the commissioner. From this very phone, in fact," he said, nodding toward the telephone on his desk.

Melanie saw that Seward was watching her reaction carefully. *He's worried his behavior looks fishy,* she thought.

"Is there a reason you didn't call the police immediately? As soon as Mr. Reyes told you he'd found the bodies?"

Again Seward paused. "Ye-e-es," he said slowly. "I knew I wanted to deal with this through my personal contacts, and I didn't have the commissioner's number with me. It's unpublished, you see."

"But weren't you worried that the girls might have needed medical attention, that perhaps they were—"

"Still alive? No. If I'd felt that was a possibility, naturally I would have acted differently. But Luis made it quite clear they weren't breathing. I felt there was nothing I could do except try to minimize the fallout from the situation for myself and my wife."

"How long did it take you to drive uptown?" Melanie asked.

"Holiday traffic was awful. All the tourists looking at the tree. It took half an hour at least."

"You waited over half an hour after hearing that Whitney and Brianna were dead before you called the police?"

Seward sighed. "To an outside observer, I understand that might seem cold. But put yourself in my shoes. I knew the second the press heard about this, they'd descend on us like a plague of locusts, and I was right. You saw what it was like downstairs, didn't you? My wife is a very fragile woman, and she'd just learned of her daughter's death. I couldn't subject her to a horde of flashbulbs in front of the building, especially not when it was *my* political career bringing them to our doorstep. So I did what I had to do to ensure our privacy. I knew the girls were already dead, so I didn't think it would matter. Please. Try to understand."

Melanie's instincts were clanging like a fire alarm. She realized she suspected Seward of something. But what? When she thought about it, there was nothing here. Anything strange James Seward had done, he'd

just told her about himself and provided a perfectly plausible explanation. Like most people, Melanie distrusted rich, arrogant politicians.
She'd better be careful not to let that personal prejudice color her
judgment.

"Look," Seward continued, reading the ambivalence in Melanie's
expression, "I may not have done things perfectly, but I'm in a very difficult position. I'm trying to be as cooperative as possible. In fact, if
we're finished with the preliminaries, I'd like to tell you where Whitney
and Brianna got the drugs that killed them."

"You *know*?" she asked. Ray-Ray looked at her in astonishment.

"I can't know definitively, since I wasn't there. But I have my suspicions," Seward said.

"Please, by all means, tell us what you think," Melanie said.

"Carmen Reyes, the super's daughter, is—or I should say *was*—a
classmate of Whitney's at Holbrooke. She got in on a College Bound
Kids scholarship. I had a hand in arranging that, and now I'm kicking
myself. Because Carmen was here right before Whitney and Brianna died.
The whole reason Luis used his passkey to get in is that Carmen hadn't
come home when she was supposed to, and he was looking for her."

"You believe that Carmen Reyes gave Whitney the drugs, Mr. Seward?"

"Yes, it's obvious, isn't it? Carmen was here earlier tonight, right before this happened, and now she's gone. Disappeared."

"She hasn't returned home?"

"That's correct. And it's . . . what? After four o'clock in the morning?"

"So you think Carmen—"

"Of course. She gave them the heroin, then she saw the terrible results of her actions, and she ran away. Carmen Reyes is the answer to
this whole thing."

5

FOR THE FIRST MINUTE after she woke up, Carmen was sure she was dead. Everything was black. Something was weird with her breathing, like she was choking. And her arms and legs were numb. She'd seen what he'd done to Whitney and Brianna. The terrible way they'd died. It probably felt like this. Maybe he'd done the same to her?

The next minute her brain started to function again. It interpreted the signals from her body more precisely. Carmen felt the pressure against her eyes and realized that it was dark because she was blindfolded. Her tongue told her that she was choking on a rag stuffed in her mouth. And the sparks that shot through her arms and legs when she moved let her know that she was tightly bound and stuffed into a confined space.

The minute after that, Carmen screamed. A hoarse sobbing sound through the gag. She screamed again and again, till her throat burned. She felt like screaming forever, until she lost her voice or suffocated on the rag or went totally insane. But at some point, when she drew breath, her mind registered utter quiet all around her. Wherever she was, she was alone. There was nobody to hear her screams, so she forced herself to stop.

Wherever *he* was now, she knew, he'd be coming back. Probably soon. That thought immediately calmed her—the calm one feels on the verge of death. She wanted to live to see her family again. Papi and

Lulu. She *had* to. The three of them were so close since Mami died. They wouldn't be able to handle another loss, couldn't go on without her. Right that moment she swore she'd make it, for their sakes. And, having seen what this man was capable of, she'd better conserve her energy. Surviving would take everything she had.

6

MELANIE'S NEXT STEP was to interview the super who'd discovered the bodies. She and Ray-Ray took the service elevator down to the basement of James Seward's Park Avenue building. In contrast to the exquisite mahogany car that had ferried them to the penthouse, the service elevator was painted industrial gray and smelled like garbage. Directly across from where it let them out, a grimy door bore a small nameplate reading L. REYES, SUPER-INTENDENT.

Ray-Ray pressed the buzzer. They waited. A darkening at the peephole told them someone was looking out.

"Yeah? Wha' you want?" said a gruff voice from the other side of the door. The accent threw her back years, to her father's English. Her father had lived in New York for two decades, but his English never made it beyond passable.

"Señor Reyes, Melanie Vargas. Soy de la oficina del fiscal."

The door swung open immediately.

"Prosecutor? Yes, I been waiting!" The short, balding, coffee-skinned man who stood before them looked like he'd walked through hell. His eyes were puffy and red, his face haggard, yet he smiled at her and pumped her hand excitedly.

"This is Special Agent Raymond Wong from the Drug Enforcement Administration," Melanie said.

"Good, come in, come in," Reyes said, relief in his voice.

He led them into a sparsely furnished living room with concrete walls and floors. An electric heater in the corner did nothing to dispel the basement chill. Exposed pipes punctuated the ceiling, their sickly green paint peeling off in strips. Even the small Christmas tree pushed up against the far wall looked like it was struggling.

"Here. Sit down, and I get you her picture. You need that, right?"

Melanie and Ray-Ray exchanged uneasy glances. Should they tell Reyes they weren't exactly here about his daughter? The fact was, they *did* need to find Carmen Reyes. She might know something.

"Well, actually—" Melanie began.

"I'm glad you change your mind. Three times I call the police, and they keep tell me missing-person report you can't file for twenty-four hours. But Carmen is a very good girl. She never go out at night. She never go *anywhere* and not tell her *papi*. Look at this picture. You see how good she is? This from Great Adventure last summer."

He handed Melanie a framed photograph of a tall, skinny girl standing in front of the sign for the Nitro. She wore pink sunglasses and a huge grin that showed her braces. Her hair was pulled back into a demure ponytail, and her T-shirt read ROCK THE VOTE. No question, she looked like a dream teen, sweet and studious. On the other hand, appearances were often deceiving.

"Is this the most recent picture you have of Carmen?" Melanie asked.

"Yes. My wife die from cancer four years ago. Since then is only the three of us, and we so sad we don't take too many pictures." Tears flooded Reyes's eyes. How could Melanie possibly tell this man that James Seward had just accused his daughter of supplying the heroin that killed her classmates? She decided she wouldn't. Not yet anyway, not until she knew more.

"Mr. Reyes," she said gently, "please, have a seat. I'd like to ask you some questions." She nodded at Ray-Ray, who opened his notebook.

"Of course. Whatever you need, you tell me. What she wearing, when I last see her. I remember."

"We'll get to all that. But first tell me about Carmen going to visit Whitney Seward tonight."

"Yes, I think it's connected, right? Could be some drug dealer give Whitney the stuff, and he kidnap my Carmen so she don't tell! *¡Ay, Dios!*" Tears began falling from Reyes's eyes, and he buried his face in his hands. "I don't know what I gonna do if sonthing happen to her!" he cried. His stocky frame began to heave and shake with sobs.

"Let me get you a glass of water," Melanie said.

She went into the adjacent galley kitchen and flipped on the overhead light. The shadows of dead cockroaches stood out in bold relief inside the plastic light fixture. New York was strange, the way extremes of wealth and poverty coexisted so closely, even in the same building.

After he drank the water, Reyes seemed calmer.

"About seven-thirty, Whitney call Carmen and say can she come upstairs and study for the math test. My Carmen a genius with numbers. They got her working in the office at Holbrooke because she so good with math. She could make a lotta money in business someday, but she say she wanna be math teacher instead, work with kids."

"So it was Whitney who called Carmen, not the other way around?"

"*Sí.* I thought was strange, because Whitney never call here. Whitney and Carmen, they were not friends."

"No?"

"Whitney is very fast. Carmen's afraid of her. Besides, Whitney is very mean to Carmen, because she rich and Carmen is poor. You know, Carmen don't got the right clothes, like that."

"Why did Carmen go upstairs if she didn't like Whitney?"

"How we gonna say no? Mr. Seward is the *jefe*. The boss. He run the co-op board in this building, so he hire and fire the staff people. And he get my girls in good school so they go in college. Not just Carmen but Lourdes, too. Lulu, we call her, my little one. So if Whitney ask for help to study, you bet Carmen gonna help her."

"So Carmen went upstairs to the Sewards' apartment?"

"Yes."

"What time?"

"Right away when Whitney call. Maybe seven-thirty, seven forty-five."

"What was Carmen wearing?"

"Her school uniform. Plaid skirt and navy sweater. She didn't have no coat. I hope where she is now, she not too cold." Reyes began to cry again, covering his eyes, his shoulders shaking. After a moment he pulled himself together and looked up.

"I know this is difficult, Mr. Reyes. You're doing a good job."

"I'm trying. Help my Carmencita."

"Let's stay focused on the details of what happened, okay? I think it'll be easier that way. How long was Carmen upstairs before you discovered the bodies?"

"After maybe two, three hours, I say, Wha's happening? Is taking too long. So I call up there, and nobody answer the phone. I wait little bit more. Then about maybe ten-thirty, I worried, so I go up and knock on the back door. No answer. I try front. Same. So I go in with my key and look around. And I find this terrible thing." Reyes drew a ragged breath and looked up at the ceiling with reddened eyes.

"Tell me where you found the bodies."

"Whitney on her bed. The other girl on the floor near the bathroom. Carmen nowhere."

"What were they wearing when you found them?"

"Whitney got on a top and underpants. The other, nothing."

"Did you touch or move anything in the room?"

Reyes looked alarmed. "No. I know better. You get in trouble for that, right? I see a lotta cop shows on TV."

"Why didn't you call the police right away, when you discovered the bodies?"

"I call Mr. Seward first, because it's his daughter, his house."

"And he told you not to call the police?"

Reyes looked alarmed. "Tell me? No. He never say nothing like that."

"James Seward didn't tell you not to call the police?" Melanie asked, confused. Hadn't Seward already admitted that to her?

"No, I tell him, please, *señor,* you call. I don't speak too good, you know. He never tell me not to call."

"Okay." Melanie paused, intending just to note this minor discrepancy and move on. Yet something about the timing here bothered her. "Mr. Reyes," she couldn't help asking, "your daughter was missing, right?"

"Yes."

"And you'd found her two classmates dead?"

"*Sí.*"

"Well, I guess I'm just surprised you wouldn't call immediately yourself."

Reyes flushed red, his eyes leaking tears again. "Yes. Of course I *wanna* call right away, because Carmen is gone. I *want* to."

"So why didn't you?"

"You know, I very confused. Mr. Seward say he gonna call for me."

"But I thought you just said it was *your* request that Mr. Seward call."

Reyes started to sob noisily. "Yeah. I dunno. Is very confusing," he choked out.

Jeez, this guy was a mess. Maybe there was nothing here. Anyway, she'd better get the basic facts down.

"Okay, I don't want to get hung up on this detail. Mr. Reyes, please." Melanie gave him a tissue from her bag. "Are you okay to talk?" she asked after he'd blown his nose and wiped his eyes.

"Yeah, okay."

"Now, do you remember what time it was when you first called Mr. Seward?"

Again Reyes looked alarmed. "Time? No, I can't say."

"Any idea? You said it was probably around . . ." She paused, getting confused herself now. "Ray-Ray, what time do we have that Mr. Reyes entered the Sewards' apartment?"

Ray-Ray flipped back to the preceding page in his spiral notebook. " 'Witness states daughter went upstairs around seven forty-five. Witness further states he became concerned when daughter had not returned after two to three hours.' "

"So at the latest it was ten forty-five when you entered the apartment," Melanie said to Reyes.

Pain and panic raced across Reyes's face. "I don' know times, okay? I'm not looking at my watch. All I know is, I wanna find my Carmen. You gonna help me do that or not?"

"Yes, of course. We just need to hear what happened. We have to get the facts."

"Look, I don't know the time, okay?" Reyes snapped. "I call for a while and don't get no answer. Finally I reach him, he say he gonna call the cops himself. So I wait for him to come home. Mr. Seward tell me do sonthing, I listen, because I need my job."

Melanie nodded. Whatever Seward's motives, Reyes's motives for obeying seemed authentic. "So what happened next?"

Reyes sighed deeply, his face scrunching up. For a moment Melanie thought he might cry again. But then he began speaking very quickly, the words spilling out in a rush. "Around midnight Mr. Seward and the missus come home. He check the bodies, very fast. He call the police. The rest you know. So let's talk about sonthing else."

She looked at him searchingly, wondering why he was so determined to change the subject, but then decided to let it go. This man was obviously upset. She had enough to do to solve this case without imagining credibility issues where there were none.

"Tell me about Carmen. How she spent her time, where she went. Anything that might help us track her down."

"Mostly she go in school, she work, she go in church. She very quiet girl."

"What about her friends? Was there anyone Carmen associated with who might have been involved with illegal drugs?"

"A kid calling her a lot. Him, I don't like. Maybe you gotta check him out, see if he know sonthing."

"Of course. Tell us about him." She looked over at Ray, who nodded and continued to take notes.

"Carmen meet him in church. A real *cholo*."

"Cholo?"

"You know, a gangster. He's from El Salvador." Reyes scrutinized Melanie closely. "You *puertorriqueña, ¿sí?*"

"Yes, I'm Puerto Rican. So you don't like the boy because you think he's in a gang or because he's Salvadoran?"

"He's a gangster, and he don't got no papers. I tell Carmen, La Migra gonna deport this one any minute. I complain to the priest about my daughter meeting *ilegales* in the church, and you know what he say to me? Jesus don' care about papers!" He shook his head with disgust.

"Was Carmen dating this kid?"

"No, I never let her. She teaching him to read, from the church program. But he call her too much. So I tell him no call here no more." Reyes shrugged. "I don't know, maybe is sonthing. Maybe he get mad."

"What's the boy's name?" she asked.

"Juan Carlos Peralta."

"Do you know how to get in touch with him?"

"Carmen had his *número de celular* in her book."

"We'd like to see Carmen's address book."

"Okay. Is in her room. You come."

Reyes led them down a small hallway and pushed open a door at the end. Two narrow beds and a dresser filled the tiny room. A young girl sitting on the bed nearest the door looked up at them, startled. Presumably Carmen's younger sister, Lulu. She'd been staring vacantly into space, fiddling with a silver peace sign that hung around her neck on a cowhide string. She was about thirteen or fourteen, with enormous brown eyes just like Maya's and dark hair in a ponytail. And she looked scared.

Reyes took Carmen's address book from a table between the twin beds and handed it to Melanie.

"Thank you. Is this Lulu?" Melanie asked, her eyes on the girl.

"Yes. Lulu, you be polite. Say hello to the prosecutor who gonna find Carmen for us," Reyes said.

"Nice to meet you," Melanie said.

Lulu stared back at her silently. Melanie couldn't decide if the girl was sullen, in shock, or just sizing Melanie up before she decided to open her mouth.

Melanie sat down on the bed next to Lulu. "I can see you're upset. I'd like to introduce myself and tell you what I'm trying to do, because maybe you can help me. Okay?"

Lulu shrugged. "Whatever."

"You go to Holbrooke, too?"

"Yeah."

"She's in eighth grade," Reyes said.

"You know two Holbrooke girls died tonight from snorting heroin?" Melanie asked.

She finally had Lulu's attention. "No. Papi didn't tell me that. Who?"

"Whitney Seward and Brianna Meyers."

"Whitney was into drugs." Lulu nodded, unsurprised.

"How do you know that?"

"Everybody knew."

"Does your sister do drugs?"

"No way. Never."

"Does she hang out with kids who do?"

"Carmen doesn't hang out with anybody."

"Do you have any idea where Carmen might have gone? Do you think she ran away?"

Again Lulu looked at Melanie with that strange, steady gaze. There was a lot going on behind her brown eyes. Melanie almost thought Lulu was weighing whether or not to talk. She seemed old beyond her years; yet there was something in her gaze that Melanie recognized from her own childhood, from that dark time after her father was shot in a robbery, after he went back to Puerto Rico and left them alone to face life in their bad neighborhood. It was fear.

"Who knows? Maybe she did run away," Lulu said finally, sighing.

"No!" Luis Reyes burst out, slamming a fist against the bedroom wall. "That's crazy, Lulu! What you saying? You making me very sad. Carmen no run away, never! Since Mami die, all we got is each other. Carmen never do that to us!"

Reyes began to sob again, and Lulu lay facedown on her bed and put her pillow over her head. This interview was going nowhere fast.

Melanie pulled a business card from her bag. "I'm leaving you my cell and office phone numbers, Lulu," she said to the girl's back. "If there's anything else you think I should know, you call me. It could be a matter of life and death for your sister."

Lulu just lay there silent as a stone. Melanie handed a card to Luis Reyes as well. Reyes then escorted them to the door of the basement apartment, crying the whole way. As Melanie was about to leave, he grabbed her by the arm.

"You gonna find her, right?" he asked urgently, eyes streaming tears.

Melanie looked into the man's desperate face and found herself wishing her own father had cared this passionately about *her*.

"Yes," she said gently, vowing to herself to make it happen. "I will find your daughter. I promise."

7

COLD PINK LIGHT from the rising sun bounced off windows on the west side of Park Avenue as Melanie and Ray-Ray emerged from the building and headed for his car. While the Crime Scene guys finished up, they'd check out leads on Carmen Reyes. Bernadette had called a team meeting for 9:00 A.M. sharp. Melanie planned to have some answers by then.

As he drove, Ray-Ray radioed Carmen's description to the DEA dispatcher for relay to other law-enforcement agencies. Melanie kept her mouth shut when he called it in as "subject wanted for questioning" rather than as a missing person. Her goal was to find Carmen, and describing the girl as the subject of an investigation might actually generate a meaningful response. It was better than calling her a runaway, certainly. Teenage runaways were a dime a dozen. With no evidence of foul play, the most the cops would do was put in a few perfunctory calls to hospitals and the morgue.

Melanie went through Carmen's address book and read out the location where they could expect to find Juan Carlos Peralta. This early there was practically no traffic, and they whizzed across the Fifty-ninth Street Bridge. The East River below glittered cold and black, and the silver towers of midtown stood out like knives against the morning sky. In mere minutes they were cruising the mean streets of Queens looking for Peralta's building.

"Okay, I have a gut feeling about this," Melanie said, unable to keep silent any longer.

Ray-Ray said nothing, staring out at the street signs, fingertips drumming restlessly on the steering wheel. He didn't seem the type to follow a hunch.

"Maybe Carmen's getting a bum rap," Melanie continued. "To me she reads like a nice, studious girl from a decent family. Plus, her little sister seemed really scared of something."

"Think I like locking up Chinese people, ma'am?" Ray-Ray said, taking his eyes off the road long enough to give Melanie a disapproving look. "But I do it if I got the evidence. This girl is most likely involved. Or else why split?"

Ouch. Maybe he was right. On the other hand, maybe he was wrong. Imagination did not appear to be his strong suit. Melanie kept silent for a few minutes, leafing through Carmen's address book, tiny, with a flowered cloth cover and worn, gilt-edged pages. There was nothing of interest in it other than the Salvadoran boy's cell-phone number and address. Just a few relatives in Puerto Rico and a pen pal in Wisconsin named Heidi.

"Okay, forget Carmen. What about her sister? Didn't she look scared to you?" Melanie asked.

"Scared?"

"Yes."

"No. Not particularly."

"Oh, come on, Ray-Ray, she definitely did!"

"She looked upset, ma'am. Natural reaction under the circumstances. You asked if she knew anything about her sister's disappearance, and she replied negative. In fact, from what I observed, the younger sister believes this is a runaway situation."

"She never said that."

"She implied it. To my mind anyway. Granted, that doesn't necessarily equal the Reyes girl supplying the drugs. There's about a million reasons a teenage girl might run away. Maybe she just didn't like being told not to date this Peralta kid."

"What about Seward and Reyes? Didn't you think there was something off in the timing there? Who called the police—and when?"

He shrugged. "Seward's a rich asshole pulling strings. Reyes is your average member of any minority community. Doesn't like the cops, worried about his job, so he lets Seward call. Nothing unusual as far as I can tell."

"Yeah, well, I think there's more here than meets the eye. We should look beyond the obvious."

"Honestly, ma'am, I've never found much call to do that on this job. The obvious generally works pretty well."

Ray-Ray slowed down and scanned the numbers on a series of run-down tenements. He pulled up across the street from one of them.

"That's the place," he said, jerking his head toward the building. "What do you advise we do?"

Melanie checked her watch. It was seven o'clock in the morning. "He's probably inside. You knock and announce, then ask to interview him. If he says no, I run back to my office and type a quick subpoena while you sit on the house to make sure he doesn't go anywhere."

"Sounds like a plan," Ray-Ray said.

They got out of the car and crossed the street. Plows had gathered last night's snow into ugly gray mounds, now decorated with intermittent streaks of bright yellow dog pee. Ray-Ray tried the door, plate glass embedded with chicken wire, with a huge crack across it. It was unlocked. They climbed three flights up a steep, poorly lit staircase to Peralta's apartment. It wasn't lost on Melanie that Ray-Ray kept his hand on the gun at his waistband. Normally Melanie didn't ride along like this. The agents went out, located the witnesses, and rendered them safe—translation: disarmed them—before bringing them back to the sterile sanctuary of her government office to be interviewed. But with an investigation this urgent, there wasn't time for such niceties.

The door of Peralta's apartment boasted a tattered poster of the blue-and-white Salvadoran flag. Ray-Ray raised his fist and rapped loudly with his knuckles.

"¿Quién es?" asked an old woman's faltering voice after a pause.

"Drug Enforcement Administration. We're here to speak with a Mr. Peralta, ma'am," Ray-Ray said.

"La Dea!" the old lady shouted.

From inside the apartment came the sound of pounding footsteps, followed by the screech of a window being thrown open. Ray-Ray lowered his shoulder to hurl himself against the door. Melanie grabbed his arm.

"Exigent circumstances!" he barked, looking at her accusingly.

He was right. They could hardly afford to wait for a warrant. A young girl was missing, and someone who might have information was escaping out a window.

"Go!" she yelled.

Ray-Ray threw himself against the flimsy door several times in quick succession until it burst open. Inside, curtains flapped in the wind as a dark head disappeared from view down a metal fire escape.

Ray-Ray blew into the room and out the open window. Melanie raced after him, leaning out the casement in time to watch him clamber down the fire escape in hot pursuit of his quarry. The dark-haired kid reached the end of the metal railing and jumped the remaining six feet or so, hitting the ground and rolling. Ray-Ray leaped right behind him, scrambled to his feet at the same instant the kid did, and lunged for his legs, yanking them out from under him. In a second Ray-Ray had the cuffs on him and looked up at Melanie with a huge grin on his face. She saw what Albano meant. Ray-Ray lived for this shit, you could just tell.

Melanie turned back to the room. They were entitled to search anything in plain view, incident to what was, if nothing else, a lawful arrest on immigration charges. Unfortunately, the only things she saw were a gruesome painting of Christ on the cross, a table with a half-eaten breakfast of cold tortillas, and a squat, prune-faced *abuela* in a shapeless polyester dress.

The old lady glared at Melanie. "Why you bother my Juan Carlos? He no sell drugs. He good boy."

If there was one thing marriage had taught Melanie, it was that you could live with a person for years and still not have a clue what they were up to.

"Well, if he's such an altar boy," she replied, "why did he just jump out the window?"

8

MELANIE RUSHED INTO the big conference room carrying her Starbucks and muffin, only to find she was stressing out for nothing. Ten past nine, and nobody else had arrived yet. Ray-Ray Wong must still be where she'd left him fifteen minutes earlier, when she decided she couldn't possibly survive this meeting without caffeine—sitting in one of the interview rooms on the sixth floor with Juan Carlos Peralta. Peralta had signed a waiver of speedy arraignment and agreed to talk. And they had plenty to ask him about, starting with the twelve glassines of heroin found stuffed in his sock at the time of his arrest. That would be the first order of business as soon as the meeting ended.

Much as Melanie sympathized with Luis Reyes, maybe this whole thing was cut-and-dried, after all. She didn't want to believe it. Carmen had looked so sweet in that picture, and Melanie couldn't help identifying with her. *La raza* and all that, being a poor girl in a rich kids' school. But facts were facts. Carmen's boyfriend was undeniably a heroin dealer. Carmen wanted to hang with the cool girls, and she'd found the ticket. It made sense.

The second Melanie dropped into a chair, it hit her how much she missed that little *niña* at home. Maya would've woken up by now and found her mommy gone. Melanie glanced around the empty room, then jumped up and hastily dialed her house from the telephone on the credenza. Sandy Robinson, her baby-sitter, reported that Steve had just left and that Maya's fever was down. The medication was working this time, *gracias a Dios.* Sandy held the receiver up to Maya's ear, and Melanie talked baby talk into the phone. Bernadette glided in, caught her doing that, and looked at her like she was crazy. People with no kids didn't get it. Or maybe it was just that Bernadette didn't. Melanie hung up fast and took her seat before she got yelled at.

Bernadette was even more heavily made up than usual, wearing a tight crimson pantsuit with gold buttons that matched her brightly colored hair and showed off her chest. She sat at the head of the table.

"So, what do you think?" she asked. "Great color for TV, right?"

"You'll stand out," Melanie said diplomatically.

"You, on the other hand, look like something the cat dragged in."

"Gee, thanks. Maybe you forgot, but I've been up all night."

"Honestly, girlfriend, one late night and you're toast. It takes stamina to play with the big kids."

Ray-Ray Wong strode in and shook hands with Bernadette.

"By the way, two new agents are coming to this meeting," Bernadette said as Ray sat down next to Melanie. "Vito and I agreed it's worth staffing up so we can resolve this case quickly. One is a detective named Bridget Mulqueen, who's on your squad already, I understand, Ray-Ray."

"Jeez Louise! Not Gidget!" he exclaimed.

"That's more emotion than I've seen from you since we met, Ray," Melanie said. "What's wrong with her?"

"Nepotism hire," he muttered.

"Oh, come on, that's an exaggeration," Bernadette said.

Ray-Ray fixed her with a withering stare.

"All *right,* maybe," Bernadette conceded after a moment. Melanie was impressed. Not everybody could stare down Bernadette.

"Her one previous assignment was IAB," Ray-Ray said, "and *they* wouldn't even keep her. We got her because the lieutenant owed Jimmy Mulqueen a favor. This chick is wicked connected."

"Bridget does happen to come from a family that has quite a few members on the job, including Deputy Commissioner Mulqueen," Bernadette conceded.

"Who's her father," Ray-Ray put in.

"If you want to be the one to tell him his little girl isn't good enough for this case, be my guest. There's a nice traffic post in Queens that needs filling. You want my advice, keep your mouth shut and give her some rap sheets to run. Meanwhile, I'm making it up to you with the other new team member."

"Who's that?" Melanie asked, taking a sip of her Starbucks.

"You've worked with him before, Melanie. Dan O'Reilly from the FBI."

Ray-Ray and Bernadette both stared at her as she choked on her coffee, turning bright red, unable to catch her breath.

O F COURSE, Dan had always taken her breath away, from the very second they met. But that was something she'd been trying to put out of her mind.

The phone on the credenza rang, and Bernadette got up to answer it. Ray-Ray turned to Melanie, who was still wheezing.

"You okay?" he whispered.

"Yuh," she managed through her choking fit.

"This guy incompetent, too?"

"No, no. He's very good. It's just . . ." She trailed off into another round of hacking.

Ray-Ray nodded as if he understood. "Got it. Hate the fuckin' Feebs myself. I was hoping they were off narcotics permanently, post-9/11, but now they sleazed their way back in with this narcoterrorism BS."

Bernadette returned to the conference table.

"Okay," she said, sitting down, "they're here. They'll be up in a minute."

A *minute*? Melanie was nearly hyperventilating. Bernadette couldn't know what she'd done by assigning Dan O'Reilly to this case. In fact, her boss probably thought she was doing Melanie a favor, had doubtless handpicked Dan precisely because she thought he and Melanie worked well together. What a disaster! Little did Bernadette know.

It was months since the two of them had seen each other, but Melanie still had it bad for this man. The second they met, she'd felt like something big was going to happen between them. And it started to, but then it got all mucked up. She sobbed herself to sleep some nights, regretting that she'd ever let him go, longing for him, wondering if she should try to call. Here she was divorcing Steve, the father of her child, and yes, she was sad about that. But it was Dan she cried for. And the worst part was, it was her own fault.

*D*AN HAD ARRIVED *before the baby-sitter. It was their first real date, and he brought her flowers. Melanie took them, nodding her thanks, then put them down distractedly on the hall table. She was on the phone with the pediatrician, still in her bathrobe with hair wet from the shower. Maya was in her arms, burning with fever. Her ears again, the third time in a month. She screamed so loudly that Melanie could barely hear the doctor on the other end of the line.*

"Sorry," Melanie mouthed to Dan. "What can I do, Doctor? Please, she's really bad right now." Watching her daughter suffer, Melanie felt more helpless than she ever had in her life. Dan's presence, which she'd been so looking forward to, now seemed like an unwelcome distraction.

"I don't like to do it, but I'll phone in a stronger antibiotic tomorrow. Give her the Motrin and the ear drops, and bring her in in the morning," the doctor said.

Melanie hung up and turned to Dan, meeting his eyes desperately over Maya's writhing body.

"I'm really sorry," she said, "but I can't go out. I already sent the sitter home."

His face fell. "I'm so disappointed I made a reservation at a real nice place. Julian—"

Maya wailed even louder, causing Melanie's blood pressure to skyrocket. Melanie was about to lose it, big time. Amazing, the physiological impact of your child's cries.

"This isn't a good time," she snapped. "You should just leave."

From the expression on his face, you'd think she'd punched him. Okay, maybe her tone was a little harsh, but didn't he understand that Maya had to come first? What kind of mother would she be if she left Maya sick with the baby-sitter so she could go on a date?

"Isn't there some way we can work this out?" Dan said. "Maybe we just go for a quick bite to—"

"You're not listening. Don't you see how bad she feels? How can you ask me to leave her?"

"You want to postpone till tomorrow night?"

Melanie put her hand on Maya's forehead. The poor little thing was burning up. "I can't make any plans," Melanie said flatly.

"Ever?" He was beginning to sound annoyed, which in turn annoyed Melanie.

"I don't know. Don't pressure me."

Dan's eyes flashed with anger. "I'm not pressuring anybody. You don't feel the same way I do, fine. I can take a hint."

"Dan, I have responsibilities you don't! I have to put my daughter first. It's not about you and me. I don't have room to fall in love right now."

HE'D WALKED OUT, and that was the last she'd heard from him. Oh, she'd left messages, at first trying to make light of the situation, later apologizing profusely. But he'd never called back, so eventually she gave up. She had her pride. Now that she was about to see him again after so many months when he'd loomed large in her mind, she had to remind herself that nothing had changed. Underneath that all-American face, behind those crystalline blue eyes and easy smile, Dan O'Reilly was still a person of tremendous volatility. He wanted everything from her, wouldn't settle for less, refused to compromise. If they had to work together, Melanie told herself, she'd better keep a safe distance. Or else she risked losing her balance completely.

She tried to pay attention to what Bernadette was saying.

"—upside of a big group in front of the cameras is, it looks like we're devoting resources."

"My personal opinion, ma'am. We could be getting real work done, instead of standing there like window dressing. We made an arrest this morning, and I for one would prefer to continue debriefing the prisoner," Ray-Ray said.

"*What?* An arrest? Why didn't you tell me this, Melanie?" Bernadette said.

"I paged you, but I never got a callback," Melanie said. Which was true.

"So who authorized you to intake the arrest, miss?"

"Joe Williams. He's acting deputy chief with Susan on vacation, right?"

Bernadette crossed her arms and opened her mouth to say something nasty. Melanie knew she'd done nothing wrong, but that never stopped Bernadette from reaming her out—especially in front of people, which was one of Bernadette's favorite pastimes. Luckily, just then Lieutenant Albano strode into the room, wearing a satin Yankees jacket and trailed by a young woman carrying a tall stack of three-ring binders. Presumably Bridget Mulqueen. Melanie looked past her at the open door, but Dan was nowhere in sight. Bridget dumped the binders onto the conference table so haphazardly that their contents flew out and scattered everywhere.

"Evidence. Who needs it?" Ray-Ray said, deadpan, rocking back and forth in his chair.

Bridget threw him a nasty look as she bent down to clean up.

"Everything I do, this one has to make a remark. Like you never dropped anything, knucklehead?"

Ray-Ray just smirked at her. Bridget looked like somebody's bratty kid sister—mid-twenties, maybe, with short, scruffy blond hair, a pixieish face, and a flat-chested, powerfully haunched jock bod. She wore jeans and a down vest. Melanie felt sorry for the kid and thought about getting up to help her, but she just couldn't muster the energy.

Albano walked up to Bernadette and pumped her hand warmly. "I haven't seen you since . . . what? Fort Worth a couple years back on that Juarez cartel thing? You're lookin' good, lookin' good."

"Great to see you, too, Vito. I want you to know I'm very grateful that you brought us this case. We'll justify your confidence in us, promise."

"Make sure you give it your personal attention, huh, hon?" He winked at her.

"Absolutely. I just *know* this is the beginning of a beautiful relationship."

Bernadette smiled flirtatiously and winked back. Sex appeal was a perfectly legitimate tool for bringing in business as far as she was concerned. She'd even advised Melanie to dress sexier and keep a fresh box of doughnuts on her desk to attract the cops, and much as Melanie tried to laugh off the heavy-handed tactics, she had to admit they worked. There were so many prosecutors' offices vying for the good cases in New York City—state, federal, special task forces, all divided up into different districts and boroughs with overlapping jurisdictions— that it took somebody with elbows as sharp as Bernadette's to keep them at the forefront.

Melanie continued to watch the door. Where was Dan? Did she hallucinate Bernadette saying his name?

Then, suddenly, he was standing there, and she wasn't ready for him. She probably never would be.

9

DAN O'REILLY WAS OUT running on the Rockaway Beach boardwalk at 6:00 A.M. when his pager went off. He decided to ignore it till he finished the route, despite the 811 after the callback number. The 811 code meant urgent; 911 you only used in life-or-death situations. But his boss was a little too free with the 811s, and Dan didn't like to cut short his run for some bogus emergency. It was five below with the windchill and pitch-dark out, but still he stuck to his routine. That was how he kept going in life. He didn't believe in sparing himself for weather, although he did let his dog sleep in today. Guinness was getting old. Poor guy's paws couldn't take the salt on the roads.

The pager went off twice more before he finally gave in and headed back.

Five minutes later he walked through the green door of the 100th Precinct building, told the girl behind the desk he was with the Bureau, and asked to use the phone.

"Sure," she said, following him with her eyes as he pulled off his knit cap and shook the sweat out of his dark hair. She was a beat cop, thirtyish, alone out front here. She flipped open the barrier and motioned to him to come back.

"Aren't you gonna ask to see my shield?" he asked.

"Nah, I believe you. You look like a cop. Besides, I seen you running out there sometimes. I can't believe you go in this weather."

"You should be more careful " he said, flashing the shield anyway. Accept a favor and next thing they were offering to cook you dinner. It made him feel bad, saying no all the time, so he tried not to let it get to that point. Life was strange. All these women beating down his door, and he couldn't feel a thing. Instead he gets hung up on a woman who made it clear she had no room for him in her heart. Nothing he could do about it either. She'd reached him somehow, that one, so much that he just couldn't shake her.

He dialed his boss from the nearest desk.

"Yeah, Mike, what's up?"

"Danny Boy. Listen, I got a request this morning for one of my best men to sign on for a real quick TOD. Naturally, I thought of you."

You could always count on getting a stroke job with this guy. Dan missed his old boss, who'd retired last year. This one was a headquarters flack who talked out of both sides of his mouth. Still, Dan was curious.

"Tour a' duty?" he said. "Overseas?" Things in this town had been so bleak for him lately that the idea of going far away, someplace dangerous, had an appeal.

"Nah, nothing like that. We'd detail you to the Elite Narcotics Task Force just for a few days. They got a pretty straightforward case they want worked real fast by somebody with a background in retail heroin. I remembered you did those Blades cases a few years back."

There had to be a catch. It wasn't like his boss to be generous.

"What's in it for you, Mike?"

"Political shit. You know this motherfucker Vito Albano?"

"Sure. Heard of him anyway. He's supposed to be pretty good."

"Yeah, well, he's up my ass. Turf-battle crap. I got a bunch of targets with clear terrorism links, and he's claiming they're straight drugs so we gotta keep our hands off."

"Does Albano have dibs? Who dexed 'em first?"

"Well, okay, *he* did, but that was before we knew the background, see. Anyway, I'm engaging in a little bridge building, if you will. I'd really like your help, Dan."

Mike walked on eggshells with him. He asked instead of ordered. Dan had the respect of the other guys on the squad. Mike didn't, and they both knew that.

"What's the case?" Dan asked, not committing yet.

"Two girls OD'd this morning. One of 'em's the daughter of—"

"Yeah, that guy Seward. I heard it on the news. You want me to work an OD case, with the shit we're juggling now? You got to be fucking kidding me. That's just jerking off a rich guy, far as I'm concerned."

"It's only for a couple days. Develop a relationship with Albano, and it could really help us out in the long run. I'd owe you. They got a meeting set for nine over in the U.S. Attorney's Office."

Dan felt suddenly short of breath, with a strange prickling sensation on the back of his neck. He knew, he just knew.

"Who's the AUSA?" he asked, his voice hoarse.

"Hold on, I got the roster right here. Uh, AUSA's a female. Melanie Vargas is the name. Oh, and you got a Raymond Wong and a Bridget Mulqueen from ENTF. So whaddaya say?"

A minute went by, then another. Dan forgot that his boss was on the other end of the line, waiting for an answer. He couldn't believe the coincidence: getting offered a case with Melanie, when she was on his mind from sunup to sundown and every minute in between. And the dreams. Those were the worst, because in his dreams he was with her again, and he was so fucking *happy* it was pathetic. Now all he had to do was say yes, and he'd see her.

He told himself he should leave things how they were. He'd ended it for a reason. He saw how it was gonna go, just like with his ex-wife, and he couldn't handle another relationship where he cared more than the other person did. If he had any doubt, he only needed to remember what he saw that time he watched her house. Melanie'd been calling him, and he was wavering. She sounded sad, like she was really hurting over the way they'd left things. So he broke down. He went by, planning to ring the buzzer. Even had some flowers in the car. Then he saw 'em, coming back from the park. Her and the husband, Melanie pushing the stroller. Dan felt like he was gonna choke, the way they looked like a family. He read the guy in a second, from his walk, his clothes, the tilt of his head. An Ivy League smart-ass in a fancy suede jacket, thinking he ruled the world with his twenty-dollar words. And the worst part was, by the way she looked at the asshole, the way she laughed at what he said, Dan had to think there was something still going on between them. Not that he blamed her. Who the fuck was he to go after the likes of Melanie Vargas anyway? A woman like her, with those looks, those smarts, deserved better than a cop's salary, better than some hack whose idea of the good life was a patch of lawn to mow, some pizza and a cold one in front of the TV on a Saturday night. Still, it killed him the way that asshole treated her. One thing Dan would say for himself, if she belonged to him, he'd be faithful till the day he died. He had no choice. He couldn't look at another woman if he tried.

"Dan?" his boss said.

Hell, maybe he should just go for it. He'd been numb since the last time he saw her anyway. Felt nothing. Might as well be dead.

"Yeah. Nine o'clock, you said?" he asked.

"Yup. So you'll do it?"

"I'll be there," Dan said, and hung up.

Moth to the flame. How fucking stupid could you be?

10

DAN HAD ACKNOWLEDGED MELANIE with a curt nod right when he first walked in, and now he wouldn't meet her eyes. He sat at the far end of the table, with a few empty chairs between him and everybody else, flipping absentmindedly through one of the evidence binders Bridget had brought. Melanie made herself pretend he wasn't there.

"Vito, were you aware these two made an arrest this morning?" Bernadette was saying.

"Yeah. Ray-Ray beeped me an hour ago."

"Oh, so I'm the only idiot in the dark here? Thanks a lot. Good communicating, Melanie."

"Take it easy, Bernadette," Albano said. "Give the kids a break. This pinch looks real promising. Salvadoran kid. Grabbed 'im with twelve decks in his sock, right, Ray-Ray?"

"Yes, sir."

Bernadette raised her eyebrows, seeming appeased. "Really? Well, that *is* good. It's fabulous, in fact. We'll have something to report at the press conference."

"I don't think you should announce this to the press yet," Melanie said. She could imagine the headlines—the tabloids screaming that Carmen Reyes had scored heroin from her gangster boyfriend, given it to the other girls, watched them OD, and then fled. She kicked herself for not warning Carmen's father of the possibility.

"Press relationships are my domain, Melanie, but I'll hear you out. Why don't you think it should be announced?" Bernadette asked.

Everyone turned to look at Melanie. She felt Dan's eyes on her, but if she met his gaze, she wouldn't be able to think straight.

"It's premature, and it could burn the investigation," she replied, looking only at Bernadette. "This Salvadoran kid, Juan Carlos Peralta, may have been dating the daughter of the superintendent in Seward's building, whose name is Carmen Reyes. Carmen was a classmate of the two girls who died. She's missing. We need to establish the link between the two of them and confirm that he gave Carmen the heroin. *Then* we'll have a case."

"But there's a major countervailing consideration. With an arrest this quick, we look golden, don't you see? Wait even one day and we lose that impact. Believe me, I understand how the media works."

"Bern," Melanie said, "there's a strong possibility Carmen ran away last night. That she's out there right now, cold and hungry, thinking about coming home. If she finds out her boyfriend is in custody, she may decide to keep running and not look back. Then we lose a critical link in the chain between Peralta and the dead girls."

"We arrested him with twelve glassines. How is that not a case already?" Bernadette demanded.

"Right now all we can charge him with is those glassines, and they don't even add up to federal weight. Plus, they aren't the same stamp the girls ingested last night. Let's do the legwork to tie him to the heroin that killed the girls. Then we can charge distribution resulting in death. *That* has teeth."

"How long do you need to establish the connection?" Bernadette asked, crossing her arms and looking doubtful.

"Hard to say. If Peralta talks, or if we find Carmen this morning and she gives him up as the supplier, not long at all. If we have to pound the pavement, then a bit longer," Melanie said. She paused for a moment, then added, "We should probably pound the pavement anyway."

"No substitute for shoe leather," Albano said, nodding.

"Whatever we come up with will be useful down the road if we take Peralta to trial," Melanie noted.

"What steps are you thinking about, specifically?" Bernadette asked.

"We start with the victims," Melanie said. "Whitney Seward and Brianna Meyers. We should subpoena their cell and landline telephone records right away. Who knows, maybe they called Peralta directly."

"Okay, I see your point. But don't lose the forest for the trees. Stay focused on charging the ODs, and don't worry about pulling every last toll record. Oh, and I assume this is obvious, but skip the records on James Seward's home phone. Too many political implications to that."

"Bern, we need those!" Melanie protested.

"Nobody gets treated with kid gloves on my watch, Bernadette. Fair's fair," Albano said.

"You're asking for trouble, Vito. Seward's extremely well connected. I don't need to get in hot water over pulling his tolls and finding some phone-sex line or something," Bernadette said.

"Who gives a shit? Long as we don't leak it, how's he even gonna know?" Albano said.

"Of course he'll know. Anybody in his position has spies. If I subpoenaed your phone, you think somebody wouldn't snitch to you?"

"Okay, maybe, but *so*? It's a normal investigative step to take. The dickwad gives you trouble, talk to me, and I'll take it up with the commissioner," Albano said.

"I can call the commissioner myself. That's not the point. I want to keep you happy on this case, Vito, but I have to think of my other interests, too. Why stir up a hornets' nest for nothing?"

"It's not for nothing, Bern," Melanie put in. "There's something screwy about the timing of Seward finding out about the ODs and calling the police. I can't put my finger on it, but it bothers me. I think we should take a closer look at him."

"Please, spare me the far-fetched theories," Bernadette said, rolling her eyes. "He's the victim's stepfather, and he should be treated with respect. Understood?

"I follow the trail wherever it leads," Albano insisted, puffing out his chest. "That's the way I work. You and me need a private meeting to talk about rules of engagement here, Bernadette. Okay?"

Bernadette locked eyes with the lieutenant. *Albano's a dead man,* Melanie thought, and waited for her boss to explode. But instead, after a long moment, Bernadette smiled girlishly.

"That's probably a good idea, Vito. Maybe we can do it over lunch later."

Albano flushed slightly. "Sure. Sounds good."

"Um," Melanie said after an awkward pause, "so I have the green light to pull Seward's tolls?"

"All right," Bernadette said. "But obviously grand-jury secrecy rules apply. No leaks."

"Course not," Albano agreed, still looking at Bernadette. "Code of silence. By the way, Melanie, we picked up the girls' cell phones from the scene last night. You might be able to get the numbers right off 'em." He nodded at Bridget Mulqueen, who sifted through the evidence binders and pulled out two heat-sealed envelopes, which she passed down the table to Melanie. The first contained a small silver Motorola flip phone, the second a shiny pink Nokia with a screen.

"The silver one was in Brianna Meyers's backpack," Albano said. "The pink one was on the bedside table, so we're assuming it was Whitney's."

"The pink one is a camera phone, right?" Melanie asked, examining it.

"Yeah, that tiny hole there is the lens," Albano said. "We haven't checked the memory for stored photos yet, though. We wanted to ask you—"

"If you need a search warrant?" Melanie said, finishing his sentence for him. "It depends. If the phones are registered to the victims, no, because their privacy rights died with them. But these girls were minors, so the phones are probably registered to their parents. I'll write up warrants this afternoon, just to be safe. While I'm at it, I'll include their computers, too, so we can get their e-mails and the Web sites they visited."

"All right," Bernadette said. "Does anybody have anything else before we break?"

"One quick question," Dan said, looking up from the binders. Melanie caught her breath. Those eyes. How was she going to get through this?

Dan pulled an eight-by-ten crime-scene glossy from its plastic sleeve and held it up for everyone to see. It showed Whitney Seward's bedroom, looking toward the wall where her desk was, in the opposite direction from the bodies on the bed.

"What about it?" Albano said. "That's just the Crime Scene guys documenting the room."

"Just out of curiosity," Dan asked, "anybody know who opened all the windows?"

11

ROUNDING THE CORNER after collecting a legal pad and her briefcase from her office, Melanie didn't see Dan O'Reilly standing by himself at the elevator until it was too late. She stopped in her tracks, feeling unprepared for the encounter. But he turned and saw her, so she walked up to him as naturally as she could manage.

"Hey," she said, forcing a bright smile, feeling like she'd been punched. Too many things came rushing back. The rough caress of his voice as he whispered in her ear, the taste of his mouth. She kicked herself for that time she'd made out with him in his car. If they'd never kissed, it wouldn't hurt like this now.

"Hey, yourself. How you been?" He smiled down at her with the bluest eyes she'd ever seen, tinged with sadness. Who was she kidding? She'd be hurting no matter what. This wasn't just a sexual-attraction thing, never had been.

She feigned a nonchalant shrug. "Hanging in. You?"

He nodded. "Same."

"Okay. Good."

"You cut your hair," he said. Her raven hair, which just skimmed her shoulders now, had been longer when they last saw each other. Dan's arm twitched, as if he wanted to touch her but wouldn't let himself.

"I cut it a while ago. It's easier to manage this way." She smiled again, looking down at her boots, heart pounding.

"Your boss is in fine form," Dan offered after a pause.

"Yeah. It's called '*Hello,* I want to be a judge.'"

"Oh, is that it?"

"Definitely. You never know, Seward could be our next senator. The Senate approves appointments to the federal bench, so she's being *very* deferential."

"She's always got an angle, that one," he said.

They fell silent again. Looking at him was like staring into the sun, so she looked away. Her gaze settled on the elevator call button.

"You didn't press?" she asked.

"I'm waitin' on this Mulqueen chick. She's in the ladies' room."

"Oh." She felt a violent stab of jealousy. Dan had volunteered to team up with Bridget to go interview Brianna Meyers's family. Who knew? Maybe he was attracted to the young detective. The thought made her ill, which in turn reminded her she was supposed to stay away from this guy. She should just decide she hated him. There was no excuse for how he'd cut her off. A normal person would not have done that.

"Here," he said, and pressed the button for her.

"Thanks." Her stomach sank. He didn't want to talk to her. Then again, she didn't want to talk to him either. She did and she didn't. She looked down at the floor again. Why didn't he just walk away if he didn't want to be here?

"So what was that about Whitney Seward's bedroom windows?" she asked, zeroing in on work. Work always made her feel better.

"Maybe nothing," he said. "But I had a case a few years back. Some jerk-offs hijacked a tractor-trailer loaded with Colombian cocaine. Thought they got away clean, but the Colombians hunted 'em down and killed 'em, one by one, like dogs. Anyways, one of the hijackers met his maker in some godforsaken little tract house on the edge of the Everglades. Middle of August, no trees anywhere around. Hundred and ten at high noon. But the body wasn't discovered until a week after the murder. You know why?"

"Air-conditioning?" she guessed.

He smiled. "Very good. You haven't lost your touch. Brand-new, heavy-duty A/C unit. Killer cranked it up to maximum capacity. It was so cold inside the house it was like the body was refrigerated. Nobody smelled anything. Not only was the killer long gone by the time the body was found, but the coroner couldn't even determine the date of death. We caught the guy and took him to trial, but he walked. Whitney's open windows reminded me of that."

"It was probably just the Crime Scene team airing the place out because it reeked, don't you think? That's not as suspicious to me as cranking the A/C. Besides, we have no reason to think the Holbrooke girls were murdered." She paused for a beat, eyes searching his handsome face. "Do we?"

He shrugged in a way that said there was enough to make him wonder. Dan was third-generation cop. He had flawless instincts, almost like something in the blood. He was generally right about stuff like this. On top of which, she had suspicions of her own.

"You have a weird feeling about this, too?" she asked.

"The windows bother me," he said.

"*Seward* bothers me," she confessed. "He took his time about calling the police. Says it's because he was worried about the press. I don't know, maybe I'm overreacting. But the building super was vague about the timing, too. It struck me as odd."

"Did Seward have any reason you know of to want his stepdaughter dead?"

"She was obviously a wild girl. Maybe she was a campaign liability?" Melanie ventured.

"Not as much alive as she is OD'd. Think how bad *that* looks."

"True."

"I'm with you, though. I'm raised up, too. I noticed another thing looking at the pictures of the bedroom just now," Dan said.

"What's that?"

"Kinda strange. Whitney's computer was set up with the mouse on the left side, so I'm guessing she was a southpaw. But the empty glassine was next to her right hand."

Melanie flashed on those dead girls' faces, and the hair on the back of her neck stood on end. Could someone have done that to them on purpose?

"You think the crime scene was staged," she said.

"I'm not saying definitely. There could be another explanation. Like Whitney rolled over the Baggie when she was dying or something."

"She was found in a sitting position, so I don't think that could account for it. But there was something else about the positions of the glassines that bothered me." She explained her concerns about Brianna Meyers's clothes being found in the bathroom, away from her naked body.

"If the ODs were faked . . ." Dan began.

"Then the girls were most likely murdered," Melanie finished. "And what would that say about Carmen Reyes's disappearance? I have my doubts she ran away. She just doesn't seem the type."

"If she didn't run away on her own steam . . ." Dan began, and Melanie knew just where he was going. Man, it was great how they *got* each other.

"Exactly," she said. "Carmen could be kidnapped or dead somewhere, Dan. We better figure this out ASAP."

"Your boss ain't gonna be too happy if we start looking into apparent ODs like they're something else," he pointed out.

"Oh, great. Justice should be sure and swift, unless it damages Bernadette's career? That's not what I signed up for when I took this job," she said, shaking her head in disgust.

"I always liked the way you talked." He grinned, his eyes lingering on her.

"We're going to investigate these deaths right, Dan. You and me. We'll just, *you* know . . ."

"Keep it on the down low?"

"You read my mind," she said.

"I'll follow up on the crime-scene stuff right away, see if there's anything else off," he said.

"I'll see what I can get out of this Salvadoran kid Carmen was hanging out with. We should follow up every last angle with Whitney and Brianna. Did they have secrets, enemies, anything?"

"Be careful, okay?" he said.

"I'm not worried. Look, if we find something, Bernadette will do the right thing. She always does in the end, if only to make herself look good."

"She's a pain in the ass, but she's not stupid," Dan agreed.

"And Albano seems like a decent guy."

"Salt of the earth. He'll keep her in line." Dan nodded. He was about to say something, but then the elevator doors opened. Neither of them made a move to get in. Their eyes held. The doors began to slide shut, and Dan stopped them with his hand, still looking at her.

"It's good to see you again," he said.

"I'd better go," Melanie said, her heart racing. "Ray-Ray's downstairs waiting for me."

"Oh, him. Right. I know that guy." He shook his head.

"What? He seems fine."

"If you like frickin' SWAThead gun nuts."

Melanie didn't respond. FBI and DEA always hated each other, but Dan's tone carried a whiff of more personal jealousy. He sighed and let go of the elevator doors, and she stepped inside.

"Catch you later," Dan said.

Bridget Mulqueen came barreling down the hall. "Hey, wait! Don't forget me!"

She plunged into the elevator, panting. Dan stepped in after her.

"So," Bridget said to Dan as the doors closed, "long time no see." She'd slathered on some hot pink lipstick, which stood out vividly on her pale tomboy's face.

"Since you were in the bathroom?" Dan asked.

"No, I ran into you like two years ago at the Lion's Den, that Super Bowl party? You remember? I told you I was Mary Alice Mulqueen's sister? She went to Our Lady?"

"Mary Alice? Doesn't ring a bell."

"Yeah, you went out with her one time."

"I never went out with any Mary Alice. You must have me mixed up with someone else," he said, shaking his head.

"No way could I mix you up, Dan. She used to drag me to watch you play ball through the fence at St. Ignatius when I was, like, ten. Mary Alice Mulqueen? She was the same year as you, with the sisters when you were with the brothers? You're probably confused because I'm younger and I don't really look like her. Wait'll I tell her I'm working with you! She's married now, to an Italian guy who does masonry. Makes a nice living. They're doing real good, four kids and all."

Dan flushed. "Couldn't've been me. I had the same girlfriend all through high school."

"Yeah, yeah, I know," Bridget said, nodding exuberantly. "Diane Fields. Nobody could believe the way you let her walk on you. Sure, she was so beautiful she was famous in all the other schools, but still! You could've had any girl you wanted, and they woulda treated you a lot better than she did."

They reached the lobby, and it wasn't until the doors opened that Melanie realized she'd forgotten to push the button for her floor, so riveted had she been by the conversation. She got off the elevator with them, still listening. Back when they first met, Dan had told her that he'd been married once and that his first wife had left him. Diane, he'd said her name was. It had to be the same girl. That was the sum total of everything Melanie knew about Dan O'Reilly's personal life. It bothered her to no end that Bridget seemed to know more about Dan than she did, and she found herself feeling irrationally angry at the girl. Melanie wondered what Dan had looked like, all those years ago when

Bridget was watching him play ball through the fence. Considering how he looked now, probably pretty damn good.

Dan grabbed Melanie's elbow. "Come interview Brianna Meyers's mother," he said.

"I can't. I'm supposed to be debriefing Peralta, remember? I just forgot to push my floor."

"Yeah, you're coming with me, Dan," Bridget said. "I'm parked a couple blocks over. I'm low man on the totem pole, so I'll drive. Let me go get my car."

Bridget strode off and pushed open the glass door, letting a gust of bitter wind into the lobby.

"Jesus," Dan said, watching her receding back. "What a wack job. I have no idea who she is, or her sister either."

"She's some bigwig's daughter," Melanie said.

"Oh, Jimmy Mulqueen? That makes sense. Explains how she got her detective's shield anyway."

"Don't say that. Maybe she earned it legitimately." Melanie felt compelled to defend Bridget, if only to reassure herself that she wasn't succumbing to irrational jealousy.

"You don't know the PD," Dan said.

"*We* don't know Bridget. People hold this family connection against her. Shouldn't we give her the benefit of the doubt?"

"You're very open-minded, Melanie Vargas. That's a nice quality in a person." He gave her a smile like the sun coming out on the first day of spring. It reminded her of old times, and she could hardly bear it.

"It's freezing down here. I'd better go," she said, and ran back into the elevator, moving too quickly to catch the hungry look in Dan's eyes.

12

E VERYTHING OKAY?" Ray-Ray asked, turning with a start as Melanie slammed the door.

"Fine. Sorry."

She'd better calm down and focus. This was an important interview. Juan Carlos Peralta might admit to providing the heroin, which would lay to rest any speculation about foul play in the girls' deaths. He might even be able to tell them where to find Carmen Reyes. Whatever information he had, Melanie wouldn't get it if she didn't control her emotions. Seeing Dan again had left her even more shaken than she'd anticipated, but she needed to put those feelings aside now.

She walked slowly and deliberately around the small conference table and sat down across from Ray-Ray and Peralta. Ray-Ray introduced her to a second DEA agent who was acting as a sentry, leaning against the wall near the door.

Juan Carlos's right hand was cuffed to the arm of the chair in which he sat. He leaned forward, holding a massive cheeseburger in his left. It dripped gobs of mayonnaise and ketchup onto the congealed fries in the round foil container below. The overpowering smell of grease so early in the morning turned Melanie's stomach.

A short, beefy kid with a crew cut, maybe in his early twenties, Juan Carlos wore baggy but perfectly creased khaki pants. The sleeves had been cut off his spotless gray sweatshirt, though you might not notice, since his buff arms were sheathed in elaborate tattoos from shoulder to wrist, mimicking the look of a garment. That much tattooing must cost a pretty penny, Melanie reflected. Juan Carlos obviously had a steady source of income.

"Where do we stand?" Melanie asked Ray-Ray.

"Juan Carlos here was just giving me some intelligence on MS-13. The big Salvadoran gang out in Corona?" Ray-Ray said.

"Sure. Is that why you're wearing that do-rag?" she asked, nodding toward the blue-and-white bandanna arranged just so around Juan Carlos's thick neck. These *cholo* kids were very precise with their fashion.

"Yeah, this they colors," he said, through a mouthful of burger. "I be initiated and shit. Know all about *la vida loca.* I got names, dates of meetin's, anything you want. I ain't never participate in nothin' illegal, of course. I jus' join for social purposes."

Juan Carlos talked like any other gangbanger from the projects. You'd never guess he wasn't born stateside. Luis Reyes had been right on the money about this kid.

"Intelligence on MS-13 is worth something, Juan Carlos," she said, "but not enough to get you a plea deal. We need to hear about the heroin Agent Wong found on you, and we need to hear about Carmen Reyes."

"Like I told your boy here, ma'am, those drugs ain't mine. I be holding for a friend. I ain't never sell. *Mi abuela,* she smoke me if she catch me scammin' dope."

"Yeah? What's your friend's name whose dope it is?"

"I ain't know his name. I just met him yesterday."

"What does he look like?"

"I don't really remember. He real average-lookin'."

"Funny, I've heard of this guy before. That nameless, faceless guy who the drugs *really* belong to. You know about him, right, Ray-Ray?"

"Seems like he's in on every bust I make," Ray-Ray said, chuckling.

"So you're really telling us with a straight face you don't sell drugs?" Melanie asked Juan Carlos.

"Yes, ma'am."

"They let you in MS-13 just because you're a nice guy?" she asked, raising her eyebrows.

"They're relaxing their standards," Ray-Ray said, laughing.

"Word. That's the truth." Juan Carlos nodded vigorously.

"Are you enjoying that burger?" Melanie asked him.

"Yes, ma'am."

"Good. Because the food in the MDC sucks. Even with only twelve glassines, you'll do time. After jail it's immigration lockup, where the food makes the MDC look like Le Cirque."

Juan Carlos put the burger down in the foil container. "Aww, shit! Come on, dawg, help me out here," he said to Ray-Ray.

"Much as it pains me, Juan Carlos, I can't help you if you won't help yourself," Ray-Ray said.

"What if I aks for a lawyer?"

"Then we'll stop talking and get you one," Melanie said. "You're entitled to due process before getting locked up and deported."

"Deported. Fuck! I step up and do my time, fine, but this my country. I live here since I'm five. God, apple pie, and the flag and shit."

"Not much we can do about it if you don't have papers, Juan Carlos. I hope you've kept in touch with your people in El Salvador so at least they give you a big hug when you get back," Melanie said.

"Okay, okay!" he said. "I cop to the drugs. They *was* mine. But it's the first time I ever sell. I ain't even know it was heroin. Thought it was *co*caine. That's less time, right?"

Melanie sighed. She'd been through the same song and dance a thousand times. This kid had probably been pitching dope since he was eight years old, but he'd never fess up. No defendant ever admitted anything unless you had it on video, and even then they'd do their damnedest to convince you they were somewhere else at the time and the guy on the tape was their evil twin.

"Look," she said, "we're very busy. If you don't want to talk, fine. I'll get Legal Aid on the phone, we'll arraign you and go about our day."

"But then I get deported!"

"You get deported anyway, unless we get you an S-visa," she said.

"What's that?"

"It's for witnesses who are needed for important cases. Since you're not talking, you don't qualify."

"I'll talk. I'll talk about anything you want."

"It's not a simple quid pro quo."

"Not a what?"

"It's not a given. It takes a lot to earn it."

"I'll earn it. You'll see. Go on, aks me something."

"Okay, tell us about Carmen Reyes."

"Carmen? What about her? She's my reading coach. My church got a program for kids who ain't read. Carmen be teaching me letters and shit."

"You can't read?"

He shrugged. "What of it?"

"Ray-Ray, did you read him those waivers out loud?"

"No, ma'am. He never said anything. He sat there and acted like he was reading them."

"Very funny, Juan Carlos," Melanie said, shaking her head. This kid knew what he was doing. The whole interview would've been thrown out in court. Melanie reached across the table and picked up the waiver of speedy arraignment and waiver of Miranda-rights forms and read them to Juan Carlos in both English and Spanish. "Still want to talk?" she asked when she'd finished.

"Whatever," the kid said.

"I need a yes or no, please."

"Yeah, all right."

"Make your mark, please."

She passed him the forms, and he signed them again. Next to his signature, she noted the time and the fact that they'd been read aloud.

"Okay, so Carmen is your literacy coach. And what else?" Melanie asked.

Juan Carlos looked back and forth from Ray-Ray to Melanie, his forehead wrinkled, like he was struggling to understand.

"Well, seems to me Carmen ain't popped her cherry yet, and I'm thinking about gettin' in her pants. I like virtuous girls. More of a challenge, you feel me? But we ain't never do nothin' much about it. I try to kiss her once, and she get scared and run away. But she sixteen, so why you care? That ain't statutory rape, is it?"

"I don't do those cases, but I think the age of consent is seventeen in New York," Melanie said.

"I don't think so," Juan Carlos said, shaking his head. "My shorty Bathead got locked up for statutory-raping some bitch who fourteen. I remember he say two more years and he wouldna had no trouble."

"Bathead, you said?" Ray-Ray asked, looking up from his note taking.

"Yeah. Call him that because his head got, like, a dent from where somebody smash him with a bat. He talk real slow from it, too."

"Can we focus, please?" Melanie said. "We don't have all day. Tell us about giving the drugs to Carmen."

"What drugs?"

"The heroin."

"Carmen told you I give her heroin? Why she say that?" He looked very confused.

Melanie turned to Ray-Ray. "What was the stamp again on the decks we found in his sock?"

"WMD," Ray-Ray said.

"We're not interested in WMD. Tell us about Golpe," she said to Juan Carlos.

"I don't know Golpe," he replied. "*¿Es una marca de drogas?*"

"I can't feed you the answers, Juan Carlos. *You* tell *me* what Golpe is."

"You talking about a stamp? Ain't nobody use Spanish stamps in

New York. Jersey neither. Only place I heard of Spanish stamps is Puerto Rico, the DR, some shit like that."

"Tell us about the two girls who OD'd. Whitney and Brianna. Did you ever meet them?" Melanie asked.

"The girls who OD'd last night, you mean?"

She and Ray-Ray exchanged glances. Now they were getting somewhere. "Yes," she said.

"Yeah, I heard about it on TV." As Juan Carlos looked at Melanie, his eyes suddenly went wide. Sweat began to collect on the dark fuzz of his upper lip. "The shit that OD'd 'em, it was WMD?"

"What?" Melanie asked.

"You sayin' those girls OD'd on WMD? You know, weapon a' mass destruction, the stamp I be moving?"

"Did you sell drugs to them, Juan Carlos?" she asked, avoiding his question.

His breathing got heavier, and he looked ready to cry. "I don't know what Carmen tell you, but that ain't me. They put WMD in every spot from here to Jersey City, okay? Hundreds of mu'fuckers movin' that shit. Coulda been anyone who sold it to them girls. It ain't me. I swear."

"Did Carmen ever introduce you to Whitney Seward or Brianna Meyers?" she asked, slowly and clearly.

"Why she tell you that? Why she say something that ain't true?" he asked, an edge of hysteria in his voice.

"I'm not asking you about what Carmen said. I'm asking you about what happened. Did you ever meet Whitney Seward or Brianna Meyers?"

Tears stood out in Juan Carlos's eyes. "No more questions. I want a lawyer," he said.

13

M ISS HOLBROOKE'S SCHOOL occupied several adjoining town houses on the south side of an expensive block in the East Seventies. Ray-Ray Wong double-parked in front of the main doors and slapped a police placard into the window of the G-car. Melanie climbed out, picking her way carefully through the slush to the curb. Their government sedan looked incongruous among the glamorous vehicles jockeying for position there. Navy and black Mercedeses and enormous, sparkling SUVs, driven by dark-skinned chauffeurs, all wearing blazers and cell-phone earpieces. Even if Melanie could've afforded to buy a brand-new Range Rover and garage it in the city—which, needless to say, she couldn't—it would never have occurred to her to hire a driver and ride around town in the back.

It was the last day of classes before holiday recess, and a few girls trickled in late. They varied in age from kindergartners to highschoolers, but all sported an identical look. Long hair, long limbs, beautiful faces with bored, careless expressions. Melanie and Ray-Ray followed the gazellelike creatures up the ice-slicked steps and into the lobby.

The space was dominated by a tall Christmas tree decorated with ornaments of scarlet and gold, which, judging from various banners hung around the room, were also the school colors. A plump, middle-aged woman in a dark dress sat behind the reception desk.

"Good morning," the receptionist said in a British accent, looking them up and down. "Are you here for an admissions tour?"

"No, we have an appointment with Patricia Andover, the headmistress, regarding a legal matter," Melanie said.

"Ah, very good." The woman appeared relieved, and judging by the crew of skinny blond moms parading through the reception area with furs tossed casually over their gym clothes, Melanie understood why. She and Ray-Ray hardly fit the profile for membership in the Holbrooke parent body.

"So Mrs. Andover is expecting you?" the receptionist asked.

"Yes. Assistant U.S. Attorney Melanie Vargas and DEA Special Agent Raymond Wong." Melanie flashed her creds and nodded at Ray-Ray, who did the same.

"Very well, then. Have a seat, why don't you, and I'll let her know you've arrived. She should be back from chapel by now."

"Chapel?"

"Every morning she leads the girls in prayer and announcements in the old chapel. It's a Holbrooke tradition, but perhaps a bit more solemn than usual this morning."

"Of course. Thank you."

Melanie and Ray-Ray took seats on a chintz-upholstered bench across from the reception desk. Portraits of former Holbrooke headmistresses lined the walls, the ladies' attire varying by decade. As a rule they were severe-looking but attractive, with steely expressions, of middle age. Above the portraits, beneath a heavy crown molding, the school motto repeated around the room in gold script intertwined with green vines: PULCHRITUDO VERITAS EST.

"Huh," Melanie said.

"What?" Ray-Ray asked.

"Holbrooke's motto. 'Beauty is truth.' I think it's from Keats."

"Oh." He nodded, obviously uninterested.

"You know what we should do?"

"What?"

"Get a list of the faculty and staff and run criminal-history checks. Just to cover our bases. Who knows? Maybe somebody has a narcotics record."

"Sure thing. No problem."

The receptionist put down her phone and looked at Melanie. "Mrs. Andover will see you now."

THE HEADMISTRESS OF HOLBROOKE was a petite, handsome woman in her forties, meticulously groomed, with a helmet of highlighted honey blond hair. Clad in a trim skirt that showcased her excellent legs, a cashmere twinset, Hermès scarf, and pearls, she radiated a cold, almost Stepford-like perfection. She also received them with the school's lawyer standing beside her, which struck Melanie as more than a little defensive. Was Holbrooke worried about something?

"This is a delicate situation, so I wanted my adviser present," Patricia Andover explained. She took a seat behind a dainty inlaid-wood desk and indicated that Melanie and Ray-Ray should sit opposite her. A tiny Yorkshire terrier that had been resting on a plaid dog bed leaped up and settled into her lap.

The headmistress put her nose right up to the dog's and spoke to it as if it were a baby. "We have guests, Vuitton. Mommy needs impeccable behavior, yes, yes I do," she said. Then she turned to Melanie with a studied smile, her glance seeming to note every imperfection, every hair out of place, and calculate the value of Melanie's clothing and jewelry in the process.

"Can I offer you something to drink? Coffee, tea, Pellegrino?" she asked.

"Thank you, but no. This shouldn't take long. We need some basic information and assistance in conducting searches, and then we'll be out of your way," Melanie replied.

"This is a shocking tragedy for our community. And right before Christmas, too. So terribly sad. Whatever you need, just ask. What can I tell you?"

"Anything you know about Whitney Seward or Brianna Meyers that might help us track down the drug dealer who sold them the heroin," Melanie said. "We're also interested in Carmen Reyes, who was at the scene last night and hasn't returned home. I assume she didn't come to school this morning?"

"No. She's absent today," the headmistress replied.

"Do you have any idea where she might be?"

"No, I don't. She wasn't one of our more . . . uh, visible girls, and I'm afraid I don't really know her well on a personal level. Was she doing drugs also?"

"There may be some link between the overdoses and Carmen's disappearance. We're not sure yet, but locating her is a top priority. We need to search all three girls' lockers and review their records. We also need to talk to other students who knew them," Melanie said.

"Of course," said Mrs. Andover. "I don't see any problem with any of that. Do you, Ted?"

Ted Siebert was Holbrooke's general counsel. A heavyset man in a rumpled suit, he shifted uncomfortably on the small chair beside Patricia's desk.

"Well, just a minute, Patricia," Siebert said. "I do. Holbrooke needs to think about its liability, with school districts getting sued left and right these days for letting the police search lockers. This is private property. The government should follow procedures before asking us to get involved in searches."

"Exactly what procedures are you referring to?" Melanie asked Siebert.

"We want to make sure everything is done by the book. Don't you need a warrant to do this?"

"Not for the victims' lockers. The girls are dead, so they don't have Fourth Amendment rights. There's plenty of case law supporting our right to search."

"I don't practice criminal law, but as general counsel I can't advise Mrs. Andover to risk this kind of liability without a warrant," Siebert said.

"I'm telling you, no warrant is required," Melanie insisted.

"Oh, dear," said Mrs. Andover. "We don't want to be difficult, Ted. I am a firm believer in cooperating with the authorities."

"Patricia, James Seward is on the board of trustees. He could raise quite a stink. We both know he loves to make trouble."

"I'm certain Mr. Seward would want us to assist the investigation in any way possible," Mrs. Andover said.

"Well, if you're so certain, why not call him?" Siebert suggested. "If we get the parents' consent, there won't be any chance of an issue later."

"Fine. If that's what it takes to make you comfortable," Melanie said with a sigh. She hated having to jump through unnecessary hoops because this guy wanted to make a show of earning his paycheck. But it turned out not to be a big deal. She spent the next ten minutes on her cell phone and quickly obtained consent from James Seward, Luis Reyes, and Buffy Meyers—who was in the middle of being interviewed by Dan and Bridget—for searches of their daughters' lockers.

"Thank you so much for indulging Ted by making those calls," the headmistress said when Melanie was done. "I never would've put you through it, but he's just trying to look out for us."

Ted Siebert gave the headmistress an angry glare. Melanie wondered what the subtext was here.

"No problem, Mrs. Andover," she said. "We'd like to search now, if you don't mind."

"Of course."

"Wait just a second. I don't think we've covered all the issues," Siebert interjected again. The headmistress's brow furrowed.

"Before we go ahead, Patricia, you should stop and consider the media implications of this. What if more drugs are found on school property? At the very least, I think we need assurances that nobody's gonna blab to the press."

"I won't be speaking to the press personally. I can promise you that. I can't make any representations about what others in my office might do," Melanie said, thinking about her boss.

"This is absolutely the wrong time for a scandal," Siebert insisted.

This guy was really starting to annoy Melanie. "The cat's out of the bag, Mr. Siebert. The scandal's already happened. And if there are drugs on school property, I'd think you would want them removed as promptly as possible."

"A few wild girls experimenting with drugs, and suddenly Holbrooke is labeled a druggie school," Siebert said. "We don't need negative press right now. It's a sensitive time, funding-wise."

"Ted's referring to the fact that we're in the middle of a major endowment campaign," added the headmistress. "It concludes this Friday with a black-tie holiday gala where we expect to announce a major contribution. Naturally we'd like this unfortunate event to get the minimum public attention possible, so as to have the least impact on our campaign. It's very important to the future of Holbrooke."

Two, maybe three, girls die, and they were worried about the effect on their fund-raiser? The headmistress seemed cooperative enough, but Melanie was running out of patience for her attack dog here. She didn't have time for this. Carmen Reyes was missing, and the morning was slipping away.

"Mrs. Andover . . ." Melanie began impatiently.

But the headmistress was nodding encouragingly. "Yes, I understand, Miss Vargas. Don't worry, I'm going to overrule Ted on this one."

"What?" sputtered Siebert. "Patricia, I must insist—"

"Ted, at a time like this, we have to pull together and help the authorities. Selfish concerns can't stand in the way."

THE HEADMISTRESS PERSONALLY escorted Ray-Ray to search the girls' lockers. Meanwhile, the school psychologist was pulled out of a grief-intervention session and assigned to help Melanie locate and review the girls' files, which contained transcripts, disciplinary records, and other possible items of interest.

"This is a small school, so faculty wear many hats," Dr. Harrison Hogan explained as they headed toward his office. "I'm head shrinker, science teacher, and director of college counseling all rolled into one. These girls were juniors, so I should have their files in my office for college-application purposes, although with my so-called filing system, you never can tell."

Hogan was lanky and good-looking, with longish dark hair and a sculpted face. He wore a tweed jacket over frayed blue jeans and projected an air of nonchalant cool. She followed him down a narrow hallway teeming with Holbrooke girls changing classes, many of whom checked her out, even eyed her with hostility. *Don't worry, I'm not his girlfriend,* she felt like saying. Hogan was obviously the object of his share of schoolgirl crushes.

Holbrooke girls hadn't changed much since Melanie's college days. They still had that slutty-preppy thing going on. Little plaid kilts barely grazing the tops of their thighs, exposing miles of lithe leg even in the dead of winter. Itsy-bitsy T-shirts and skintight cardigans with the buttons provocatively undone. Long, straight hair and smudgy eyeliner. Melanie's sister, Linda, the Puerto Rican diva, had dressed like a hooker in high school, but come on, they grew up in a rough neighborhood. These were rich girls—you'd expect better, right? The fact that these kids dabbled in heroin wouldn't shock anybody looking at them.

"You see why we're doing this endowment campaign," Hogan was saying. "We're really squeezed for space. Patricia wants a new building."

He was right. Holbrooke's square footage was clearly insufficient for its needs. Several town houses had been awkwardly combined into a cramped, confusing layout. The interiors were surprisingly musty and run-down, in need of a good sprucing, although you could imagine there would be fondness among the alumnae for the school's dear old WASPy worn-out look.

"How much money is the school trying to raise?" Melanie asked.

"The campaign was for fifty mil over two years. It concludes at the gala Friday night."

"Fifty *million*? Wow. Did they reach their target?"

"From what I understand, yes, or at least they will have by Friday. Holbrooke alumnae come from the wealthiest families in America. Besides, Patricia is a clever businesswoman. She gets what she wants."

Hogan opened a door with a frosted-glass window and beckoned her in.

"My humble abode," he said. "Sorry, I'm not much of a housekeeper."

The office was claustrophobically tiny, littered with files and papers, and had an absentminded-professor air about it. To say Hogan couldn't keep house was an understatement. Even the books in the shelves lay askew, as if they'd been shoved in any which way.

"Please," he said, indicating a chair shoved into a corner next to the door.

Melanie had to move a stack of books off the chair in order to sit down. She picked last year's Holbrooke yearbook from the top of the pile, flipping through it as Hogan searched through file cabinets looking for the girls' transcripts. Whitney Seward's photograph leaped out at her. Whitney had one of those perfect faces that made everyone else in the world look like a badly drawn cartoon. Absolutely symmetrical features, straight blond hair, and blindingly white teeth. Carmen Reyes was on the facing page, looking serious and shy, with big dark eyes and braces. Melanie had to search for Brianna Meyers. Despite being quite pretty, with long, curly dark hair, light-colored eyes, and a nose so pert that it smacked of the surgeon's knife, there was something nondescript about Brianna, something nervous and self-effacing. Melanie felt a ripple at the tip of her consciousness, like if only she could understand these girls, she'd solve the puzzle.

"While you're looking for those files, Dr. Hogan, may I ask you a few questions?" Melanie said.

"You can try. Anything sensitive, though, I'm gonna have to refer you back to Ted Siebert, the school lawyer."

"Why is that?"

"Patricia runs a tight ship. We don't give out personal information on students without the okay from our attorney."

"Mrs. Andover was extremely cooperative, I assure you. She sent me here specifically to get this information from you."

Hogan grimaced meaningfully. "She might've acted that way in front of *you,* but I know what side my bread is buttered on."

"Did Mrs. Andover instruct you not to answer my questions?" Melanie asked.

"She's too clever to come right out and say that. But I know better than to air dirty laundry about the daughter of a major contributor like James Seward."

"Was the faculty aware that Whitney Seward was doing drugs, Doctor? Is that what you're getting at?"

"I'm not gonna say Whitney was pure as the driven snow. That would be a lie."

"Can you be more specific? I'm looking for anything that would help explain what happened last night."

Hogan seemed to be avoiding Melanie's eyes. "Her grades were mediocre, and she was in danger of failing English, but college wasn't an issue. She was a legacy many times over at Harvard. Buildings named for her family, that sort of thing. She was getting in, no matter what. . . ." He trailed off, occupying himself once again with the file cabinet. Melanie nodded. She knew all about those Holbrooke girls who got into Harvard. But there was more here.

"I'm getting the sense you want to tell me something, Doctor. I understand you're concerned about the repercussions. You have my word I'll keep everything in strictest confidence."

Hogan looked up and sighed. "You didn't hear it here."

"Of course not. I never reveal a source."

"Whitney was big into the club scene. Mixed up with a bad element. You should check it out."

"Just the club scene generally? Do you know any names or locations?"

"She was hanging out at a club called Screen, with a guy named Esposito who's really sleazy."

Melanie noted the names on her legal pad. Come to think of it, they sounded familiar. "Thank you, Doctor. Anything else about Whitney?"

"I heard she had a blog where she was doing some wild stuff. Not sure, though."

"A Weblog? You mean like a personal Web page?"

"Yeah, I've heard some of the other girls talking about it." Hogan glanced nervously at the door, then at his watch. "Patricia is going to wonder what's taking us so long," he said.

"Two more questions, Doctor. What can you tell me about Brianna Meyers?"

"Okay, now, *Brianna* was troubled."

"Troubled? In what way?"

"Terrible home life. Parents divorced, father out of the picture, mother a big socialite who had no time for her. So Brianna acted out."

"Acted out how?"

"She was dating this creepy kid, kind of a goth type. He used to come around the school a lot. Had a really scary affect. Like, made you think of Columbine. I wondered about his mental stability."

"What was his name?" Melanie asked.

"Trevor Leonard. He goes to Manhattan Learning. It's a high-end school for kids with behavioral issues who are mainstream academically."

She noted the information on her legal pad. "Any reason to think he was into drugs?"

"That's possible, sure." Hogan nodded. "In fact, I'd bet on it."

"Okay. Last question," Melanie said. Hogan glanced nervously at the door again. Man, this guy was scared of Patricia Andover. Interesting, really, when you thought about it. "We're very concerned about Carmen Reyes. Apparently Carmen went to Whitney's apartment last night right around the time the girls were doing the drugs, and she hasn't been heard from since. Is there anything you can tell us about Carmen, her friends, her connections, her habits? Anything that might help us locate her?"

"Carmen was relatively new to the school, and I didn't know her well," Hogan said. "I could give you my gut reaction. But I'd rather not."

"Why not? What do you mean?"

"Well, it isn't based on much, frankly, and I hate to speak ill of a kid."

"What? Please tell me, Doctor. This is too important to stand on good manners."

Hogan sighed. "Okay," he said with obvious reluctance, "but you have to take this for what it's worth, which isn't much. As head of counseling, I knew that Carmen had real money problems. She was very concerned about paying for college, not only for herself but for her little sister, Lourdes, who goes to school here also."

"What's your point?"

"I don't know a faster way for a kid to make money than selling drugs. And Carmen struck me as *that* desperate." Hogan stopped talking and looked up at the ceiling, scratching his head. "Seems I'll have to get back to you on the girls' files. They're not here."

"Are you serious?" Melanie said.

"Yeah, I've gone through every pile. Somebody must've taken 'em.

Unless they're lost, which is always a possibility. As you see, organization is not my forte."

"Who would take them?"

"You could try Ted Siebert, for starters. He's been known to just walk into people's offices and remove records when there's some kind of legal issue."

There was a sharp rapping on the frosted glass of the office door.

"Yeah!" Hogan called.

The door opened inward, slamming into the back of Melanie's chair.

"Sorry, ma'am," Ray-Ray Wong said.

"We're just finishing up here, Ray-Ray," Melanie said. "Any luck searching the lockers?"

"*Oh,* yeah. We hit the jackpot big time with Carmen Reyes's locker. We found heroin. And it's the right stamp."

14

CARMEN REYES DRIFTED in and out of consciousness. She wanted desperately to stay asleep. Being awake was too horrible. But the physical agony of her confinement prevented her from escaping awareness for more than a few minutes at a time. She was in too much pain. Her limbs tingled with fiery numbness. She was parched and hungry. She needed to go to the bathroom. And breathing required actual thought, if she wanted to avoid swallowing the rag stuffed in her taped mouth.

In moments of lucidity, Carmen relived the events of the night before, seeing them again in the darkness with nightmarish clarity. Last night had felt like a bad dream even while it was happening. From the moment Carmen heard Whitney's voice, she'd had a strange sense of foreboding. She just *knew* something was off. If only she'd listened to that instinct.

"Aw, c'mon, Carm, we'll study for a while, then you can party with us," Whitney had said, in a wheedling tone Carmen had never heard her use before. It was bizarre, in fact, for Whitney to want *anything* from Carmen, let alone her company.

"Gee, thanks. But I shouldn't."

"No, seriously. I want you to come up. It's me and Brianna and a special friend of mine who really wants to hang with you."

"Who's that?"

Whitney gave an evil giggle. "It's a surprise."

Carmen felt sick with anxiety at the thought of what might be going on up there. Drugs? Orgies? She knew the gossip. Who didn't? Whitney was all anybody talked about.

"I really can't," Carmen replied. "Maybe you're ahead of where I am for the quiz. I really need to just, like, study all night."

"I need your notes, girl," Whitney insisted.

"Okay, well, I guess I could bring them upstairs. Do you have a way to copy them?"

"Duh, yeah, it's called like a fucking Xerox machine. What do you think?"

Carmen didn't exactly have a Xerox machine in her own apartment. "Okay. I'll bring them up, but I can't stay long."

"Fine, be that way. But come up now, okay? I mean, *right* now."

"Okay."

She'd told Papi she was going upstairs to the Sewards'. His whole face brightened, like he was proud his daughter had such fancy friends, and it made Carmen pity him and want to protect him at the same time. How could she explain that it wasn't like that?

She took the service elevator up to the penthouse floor. Inside the building, Carmen was help, not a tenant. Even if Whitney invited her, she wouldn't presume to ride in the front elevator. The service elevator let her out in the back foyer, where the Sewards kept their trash cans. It smelled of garbage and brass polish. All day, every day, Papi polished the building's brass fixtures. It gave him a rash that he had to treat with a special ointment.

Just as Carmen reached out to press the buzzer, the dead bolt opened from inside.

"Smile, you're on *Candid Camera*!" Whitney exclaimed, holding a tiny pink phone up to her eye and pressing a button.

"Did you just take my picture?"

"Mmm-hmm. God, I'm starving. Fucking major munchies. Want some smoked salmon or something?" Whitney asked, backing into the kitchen. Her eyes were funny, the pupils nearly invisible pinpricks in the light blue irises. Carmen knew enough to realize that Whitney was high on something.

"No thanks."

Whitney opened the door of an enormous stainless-steel built-in refrigerator and peered inside. She was dressed exactly as she had been in school earlier that day, in an abbreviated navy sweater, white thigh-highs, and electric blue Pumas, but she'd taken her kilt off and was walking around in teeny-tiny thong panties. She had a small flower tattooed on her lower back. Whitney turned, shoving a piece of orangey pink smoked salmon, sliced so thin it was nearly translucent, into her mouth with her fingers. The panties were sheer enough that Carmen saw Whitney had one of those Brazilian bikini waxes, everything gone except a small triangle, like a stripper. Carmen had read about that in a *Cosmo* magazine she kept hidden under her bed but had never seen it in real life. Whitney had a long, perfect torso and legs, tanned a dusky gold. Carmen tried not to stare, but it was almost impossible to look away from Whitney's unreal beauty, so recklessly displayed. In Carmen's house they didn't prance around half naked.

"Mmm, yum. Salty." Whitney licked her oily fingers.

"I brought the notes," Carmen said, holding out her calculus notebook.

"We'll get to that. Come on. Back in my room."

Carmen followed Whitney down the hallway leading to the rear bedroom, marveling as she had the previous few times she'd visited at the enormous, empty rooms they passed. A darkened dining room with a glittering chandelier and elaborate murals of New York in the time of the Algonquins. A library whose floor-to-ceiling mahogany bookshelves were filled with perfectly aligned hand-tooled leather books. A "music room" that held no musical instruments but boasted numerous settees, ottomans, and window treatments in candy-hued silk. It went on and on, all of it looking as if no people ever set foot in it. A neutron bomb might've hit and killed all the humans, so undisturbed were the spaces. Strange to be fabulously rich and yet leave no impression on your own home.

Whitney turned and walked backward down the hall in front of Carmen. She lifted her phone to her eye again and began snapping Carmen's picture repeatedly.

"Why are you doing that?" Carmen asked.

Whitney didn't reply.

They got to Whitney's bedroom. Whitney whisked in ahead of Carmen, heading straight through to the bathroom door across the room, and disappeared.

The second Carmen stepped over the threshold, she knew something was terribly wrong. Her nose told her. The whole room reeked of shit. There were piles of it in spots on the otherwise pristine white-and-gold carpet. At first Carmen thought dog and racked her brain trying to remember if Whitney had a pet. But no. The turds were human, no doubt about it, and here and there had these strange, bright orange *things* in them, like plastic pellets.

"Whitney?" Carmen called, her voice shaking. She felt cold and dizzy, practically welded to her spot near the door. But events were unfolding exactly like a nightmare, because Carmen simultaneously had a powerful compulsion to see what was in that bathroom. She knew it was bad. She knew she should turn and run screaming right out of that apartment and down fifteen flights of stairs. Yet instead her leaden feet advanced step by step across the floor until she stood right in front of the bathroom door, which Whitney had left slightly ajar.

A wheezing sound emanated from inside. Like ragged breathing. Of its own accord, Carmen's hand reached out and pushed the bathroom door inward.

Brianna Meyers sat naked on the toilet, reclining backward, almost sliding off, her arms and legs slack. Her eyes, which had been staring into space unseeingly, seemed to flicker in response to Carmen's appearance. Carmen remembered that Brianna hadn't been in school today, wondered how long she'd been in Whitney's bathroom.

"Jesus," Carmen whispered in shock, stepping all the way into the bathroom. "What is it, Brianna? Are you sick?"

Brianna's mouth opened and tried to form words, but no sound emerged. Her entire body dripped with sweat. It ran in rivulets down her belly. Her long, dark hair was wet, plastered to her forehead. Carmen looked down and saw streaks of shit on Brianna's legs and feet. Meanwhile, Whitney sat on the edge of the bathtub idly examining the label on an Ex-Lax package.

"Whitney, Brianna needs a doctor. We should call 911," Carmen said accusingly.

"It's something she ate. Right, Bree?" Whitney giggled, but this time Carmen saw real fear in her eyes.

"Listen to the way she's breathing. Something is really wrong," Carmen insisted. She still thought there was a possibility of salvaging this situation, of making things normal again. Little did she know.

Whitney's head jerked up. She was looking past Carmen, at the open doorway behind Carmen's back.

"Okay," Whitney said sulkily to whoever was standing behind Carmen. "Here she is. Happy now?"

The split second it took Carmen to whip her head around and see who was behind her was the most nightmarish of all. Because she instinctively knew who she'd see standing in the doorway, and the knowledge was terrible. With Whitney's words a lot of small events from the previous days snapped into a pattern for Carmen, with the precision of a mathematical sequence. It all made sense. Now she understood perfectly why she'd been lured to Whitney's apartment. She'd walked right into a trap. A trap she probably wouldn't get out of alive.

15

AFTER THE DEA AGENT found the dope in Carmen Reyes's locker, Patricia Andover excused herself politely, walked back to her office, and, nerves jangling, dialed James at home. It crossed her mind to worry about the trail of telephone records. Two calls this morning so far. But the next few days leading up to the gala were critical and dicey, and she had to make sure the ODs didn't disturb their carefully laid plans. Neither of them could put a foot wrong if they wanted to pull this off. The calls were necessary and could be explained if it came down to it. They were simply evidence of the headmistress's offering comfort to a bereaved family.

Charlotte must've been at least semiconscious—how unusual!—because when James answered, he pretended Patricia was someone from his campaign. He made her wait for what felt like ages while he went to his library, locked the door, and called back from his cell phone. Patricia sat there with palms sweating and heart pounding. Why put her through this? Screw Charlotte anyway, that drug-addled whore. Patricia could walk around that apartment buck naked, and Charlotte wouldn't notice. Goddamn junkie, just like her daughter. Patricia hated them both with a passion. Correction—*had* hated them, before Whitney got what she so richly deserved.

The phone on her desk finally rang. She snatched it up.

"Hello?" she said breathlessly.

"How'd it go?"

"Fine. It was her, the one you told me about. Melanie Vargas. She was with some DEA agent."

"Chinese guy, right?"

"Yes. I'm their best friend now."

He chuckled. "Good. That's the way to handle it, I'm telling you. Look at Martha Stewart. She didn't go to jail for anything she *did*. Just for lying to them. They hate it when you don't cooperate. Offends their little egos."

"Well, I cooperated, all right. I even had Ted Siebert go through this song and dance about a search warrant so I could pretend to overrule him. You know, good cop, bad cop."

"Oh, yeah. I was going to ask you about that, because that prosecutor called me for permission—"

"I know! I was sitting right there. Ted took me way too seriously. He wouldn't let it drop, so she had to mollify him. I swear, it was almost like he *wanted* them to think we had something to hide."

They were both silent for a moment.

"Do you think he did it on purpose?" James asked.

"What, over that old thing?" But Patricia considered the possibility. "You know he hates me."

"Honestly, with what I have on him, I don't think he'd dare. He has a position to protect. Not just his family either, but you know he's very big in the Bar Association now."

"What a thought." James laughed sharply, then stopped short, his tone turning ominous. "I'm glad it went well, but still . . . We need to talk. There's a problem, you know, Patricia."

"Yes, I know, dearest," she said. "You're angry about Whitney. I want you to understand, I *tried* to keep a lid on things. It wasn't my fault—"

"Whitney's the least of our problems. This is serious. It's about the second set of books."

"The . . . books?" Patricia's heart began to beat erratically.

"You told somebody, didn't you?"

"About our plan? Of . . . of course not, darling."

"You're lying."

"James, what's this about? Why are you talking this way?"

"Somebody's been tampering. Accessing the computer files behind our backs. Or at least behind *mine*."

Patricia felt suddenly ill. The fact was, she *had* told somebody. She'd been forced to. Did James really think she could handle the accounting all by herself? Or even the computer? She was not a math-science type. He knew that, and yet he'd refused to help her himself because he didn't want to take the risk. Naturally she'd had to turn elsewhere. She'd been so careful about whom she'd trusted. What could possibly have gone wrong? But she couldn't admit this to James now. He'd be furious at her.

"There are two possibilities," he said. "Either you told someone and *they* invaded the account—or you're fucking around with things behind my back. I'm giving you the benefit of the doubt and assuming the former."

"I swear, I didn't breathe a word to anybody, James. Why would I? How could it even *benefit* me to get somebody else involved?"

"I don't believe you, Patricia. Who was it? Was it Ted? Didn't it ever occur to you he'd double-cross us?"

"I would never trust *Ted*. Are you crazy? James, please tell me, is the money missing? Is that what you're suggesting?"

He paused, then said, "You're a talented actress, but you don't fool me."

"You think I would steal from our future? If money was what I wanted, don't you think I could've gotten it from you by now?"

"How, by blackmailing me? *Please.* How much could you really hope to gain from that? You know my situation."

She hated the way he was talking. James had promised to marry Patricia after the campaign was over, and she planned to make him keep his word. She'd worked so hard to overcome the obstacles. There was the small matter of finances. The real so-called Seward money belonged to Charlotte, and James had told her from the beginning there was an airtight prenup. He wouldn't get a red cent if he left. The endowment money would solve that little problem. Then there was the question of bloodline. Patricia had been born Andrewski, the daughter of a maid and a garage mechanic, Polacks from Paterson, New Jersey. The Andover, like the Mrs., had been her own invention. But she was confident James would overlook her origins once the financial end was taken care of. After all, Patricia was polished to a fine sheen, truly deserving of becoming Mrs. Senator Seward, whereas Charlotte spent her days so stoned she could hardly hold her head up.

Patricia couldn't take this. She'd call his bluff.

"If you don't believe me, James, I'll prove it! The Van Allen money doesn't get wired in until Friday night. I'll rejigger the accounts, put everything back the way it was, and we'll pretend this whole thing never happened. We can still be together. We don't need that money."

He said nothing.

"James?"

"*I* need it, Patricia," he said with quiet urgency. "Of course it's not about the money for me either, but campaigns are expensive. The new headquarters, those sixty-second spots in prime time, that smart Jew I hired away from Bell's staff."

"Get it from Charlotte, then!"

She waited to hear what he'd say to this. She had her suspicions. The rumors about what Whitney was doing for money, about the status of their finances. James would never admit he was broke, even if it were true. He'd never let her see that he was desperate.

"Charlotte would give it to me, but she's not happy about my running for office," he said nonchalantly. She suspected he was lying, that he'd bled Charlotte dry already, that there was nothing left. But she had no way of knowing for certain.

"I'm only in this because of you," she said heavily. That was actually true. Okay, Patricia was wearing a current-season Badgley Mischka to the gala, which naturally she couldn't've afforded on the pittance Holbrooke paid her, but how much was that, really? Six thousand? Maybe a couple of thousand more when you threw in shoes, bag, hair, makeup. Nothing in the scheme of things. She could scrounge up that much in gifts by giving some rich parent the evil eye. She didn't need to expose herself to hard time for a few baubles.

James drew an aggrieved breath, but she could feel him calculating on the other end of the line. Once all was said and done, she had the power to make him keep his word. If nothing else, she'd threaten to turn state's evidence, the last best refuge of the woman scorned.

"Of course, darling," he said finally. "We're in this together. You know that."

She felt faint with relief.

"What were you doing looking at the books anyway, silly? You could end up leaving an electronic trail if you're not careful. And I need to hear about this problem you found. You probably just misread the numbers," she said.

"I certainly hope you're right. But I don't want to talk about the details over the telephone."

"So let's meet. It's been too long. I miss you."

"This mess with Whitney is screwing everything up. I can't leave the house. The police could be watching me. The press *definitely* are."

"Why the police? You're the grieving stepfather. They should be bringing you a cup of hot tea."

"Are you kidding? They'd love to see me trip up. Melanie Vargas was all over me about the timing last night. Where was I, when did I call the police . . . ?"

Patricia caught an undercurrent of something in his tone. "I thought you were at that Guggenheim thing," she said suspiciously.

"Yes. Yes, I was."

"So why was she asking you, then?"

"Who knows? You know how these people are. I'm surprised she didn't ask *you*."

"Let her. I was home with the doggies." Patricia glanced over at Vuitton, who was napping. Coco was at the doggy shrink. Poor thing's eating disorder was acting up again, the way it did every year as January 1 approached. They lived in a building that barred dogs weighing more than twelve pounds because they took up too much space in the elevators. The annual weigh-ins were disastrous for Coco's body image, even though Patricia constantly reassured her there was no chance she'd hit the limit. Coco was tiny—barely eight pounds!

"So they searched?" James asked.

Patricia was distracted, her mind wandering to the bothersome question of where he'd been last night. "Hmm? What?"

"What did they search? They didn't ask about the school's computers, did they?"

"No. And I don't see why they would. It was just the girls' lockers they were interested in."

"But you'd gone through Whitney's—"

"Yes, of course!" she exclaimed irritably. "I came in at five to be sure nobody would see me. I went through everything, like you told me, all right? I left the innocuous stuff where they would find it so it wouldn't look too obvious."

"What do you mean? Was there anything you removed? Anything that *wasn't* innocuous?"

Did he really have so little idea what his stepdaughter had been up to? He was surely playing dumb. After all, if he didn't already know what was in there, why have her search? But she wouldn't tell him what she'd found. She didn't trust him these days; she needed something up her sleeve.

"No," Patricia lied. "Just the usual teenager crap."

"What about the other lockers? Did they find anything?"

"Yes indeed. As a matter of fact, they found heroin in Carmen Reyes's locker."

"Really?"

"Mmm-hmm."

"Well." He chuckled. "That's fabulous. Why didn't you tell me?"

"I just did."

"It makes so much sense. The little wetback with drugs in her locker. Just like I told them it would be. Now we can force them to stop investigating. Every second they're out there poking around, you know, we're at risk. And we don't need any problems before Friday."

"Believe me, I know."

"I'm so glad we're a team, darling."

THEY AGREED THAT James would try to slip away and meet Patricia at her place later. The hours until then would be difficult ones. Normally she enjoyed the anticipation of waiting for a rendezvous with James. But not today; this security breach he was hinting about had her worried. She couldn't make heads or tails of it. Had somebody *really* tampered with the second set of books? Was that possible, or was James lying? Testing her, maybe even screwing around with things behind *her* back and screaming bloody murder to cover his own tracks? Much as she adored him, she wouldn't put anything past him. James was treacherous. She loved that about him; it was exhilarating. He really kept her on her toes. Patricia tapped her impeccably manicured fingernails on the desktop, thinking. She'd better damn well get to the bottom of the problem and figure out her next move. Here in the rarefied air at the tippy-top, it was play or get played.

And damn that Carmen Reyes, too, disappearing at just the wrong moment.

16

THE DRIVE BACK to Melanie's office was slow because of holiday traffic, but not slow enough to come to terms with the evidence she held in her hand. A glassine bag, stamped GOLPE in red ink, sealed inside a clear plastic evidence envelope. Unlike the empty glassines recovered from Whitney Seward's bedroom, this one still held its stash of grainy white powder. On the outside of the evidence envelope, Ray-Ray Wong had neatly printed his initials, the date, and the place of discovery: "Miss Holbrooke's School. Locker of Carmen Reyes."

Why was Melanie so disappointed? So what if Carmen was the one who'd corrupted her friends, who'd provided the heroin that killed them? What did Melanie care? She hadn't even known the girl. Too often in life, the ugly, cynical explanation was the right one. She should just grow up and get used to that.

Ray-Ray dropped Melanie in front of her building and headed off to the DEA lab to get the heroin tested. She ran for the door, the bitter wind cutting right through her coat. The sky was an ugly grayish white, and she felt exhausted, cold to the bone, depressed. This case was pretty much over, and she didn't like the way it was turning out, but there wasn't much she could do about it. Juan Carlos Peralta had been remanded to custody and was refusing to talk any further. They'd seized heroin from him and from Carmen's locker. The only missing link—literally—was Carmen herself, who presumably would be found and arrested in short order. Juvie charges, but still enough to wreck her life and break her father's heart. Melanie told herself she should just accept the evidence the way it was coming in. Yet something didn't feel right.

There was a yellow Post-it stuck to her office door with a virtually illegible message scrawled on it. Melanie picked it off and squinted at it. Her best guess was: "Made arrest, 6th Floor, Dan." Man, he had terrible handwriting. And, *mierda,* she was infatuated. Because learning that new fact about Dan made her feel all warm and gooey inside. His handwriting sucks, how cute! *Barf.* Melanie hung her coat on the rack, slapped herself lightly on both cheeks, and muttered, "Snap out of it," under her breath. Only then did she go looking for him in the interview rooms on the sixth floor.

Dan and Bridget Mulqueen were debriefing a strange-looking kid Melanie didn't recognize. Pale and pimply, with long brown dreadlocks, his face riddled with eyebrow and lip piercings, an angry line of Chinese characters tattooed down his left cheek. The second Melanie stuck her head in the room, Dan leaped to his feet and came outside to speak with her.

"Who's *that*?" she asked. Dan pulled the door shut behind him and came to stand beside her—way too close to her, in fact. As if she didn't already have enough trouble ignoring his looks, his height, the clean way he smelled. She took a step backward.

"Name's Trevor Leonard," Dan said. "We picked him up about an hour ago on a failure to appear. Kid had an outstanding warrant for wire fraud from some Internet hacking scam. Heard about it from Brianna Meyers's mother."

She nodded. "Oh, right, Trevor Leonard. The school psychologist at Holbrooke says he was Brianna's boyfriend."

"I'll tell ya, he's a fucking treasure trove of information about these girls."

"So he's talking?"

"Yup. I grabbed him on the warrant, and come to find out he had twenty tabs of ecstasy in his jacket pocket. With the drug charge piled on, he rolled in a heartbeat."

"Great. I'll sit in with you so we can lock him into a statement."

"Yeah, sure, but one thing you should know first." Dan moved even closer. He was leaning down, practically whispering in her ear. There was no call for it. Yes, they were standing right outside the interview room where Bridget held the prisoner. But the door was closed. Dan couldn't reasonably think they would be overheard. Melanie took another step back, heart beating way too fast.

"What?"

"Bridget got Whitney Seward's phone records already," was all he said. "That wack job actually has good phone-company contacts, I'll say that for her. Anyway, you'll never guess who's all over Whitney's phones—cell *and* landline."

"Who?" Melanie asked.

"Jay Esposito. That nightclub guy."

"Right, the school psychologist mentioned him, too. Who *is* he?"

"Remember a few years back it was all over the papers? Wiseguy wannabe, owned a string of nightclubs, investigated for moving product?"

"Club drugs?"

"Nah, serious shit. Heroin, cocaine. I just talked to a guy I know on the squad that did the investigation. They were looking at Esposito for running a string of heroin mules. Moving Colombian product from Puerto Rico to New York."

"But they never arrested him?"

"They were just about to go up on a wire on his phone when their main snitch got fished out of the East River. Minus his head, which they never found."

"Wow."

"Yeah. Esposito doesn't fuck around. Since then, as you can imagine, nobody's been willing to flip on the guy. You never hear about him, unless he's in 'Page Six' with some model."

"And you say he shows up in Whitney's phone records?"

"Yeah, big time. We got numerous calls, including—get this—a call placed last night at nine-fourteen from the Sewards' home telephone to Esposito's cell phone, meaning Whitney called Esposito during the incident."

"Or someone else called Esposito from her telephone," Melanie pointed out.

"Excellent point, Counselor. You're very smart, you know that?" He gazed at her, grinning. Was he flirting with her?

"Puerto Rico is an important transshipment point for Colombian narcotics, because it's a domestic flight. No customs inspections," she said hurriedly, blurting the first thing that popped into her head to quiet her fluttering heart. She was beginning to think she should've refused to work with Dan. Not that Bernadette had given her any option.

"Mmm-hmm." He was still looking at her.

"You're thinking maybe Esposito supplied the heroin that killed the girls?" Melanie asked.

"There's another angle I'm just getting into with this kid, and it's even beyond that. It's gonna surprise you."

BACK IN THE INTERVIEW ROOM, Bridget and Trevor Leonard sat next to each other on one side of the conference table, Bridget cradling her head on folded arms. She jerked up when Melanie and Dan walked in.

"Finally! I was getting tired of shooting the shit with Beavis here all by myself."

"That's not too secure a posture, Bridget," Dan chided as he took a seat on the other side of the table.

"What? Kid's a pussycat. Plus, he's cuffed to the chair, right, Trev?"

Trevor didn't say anything. Underneath his fearsome looks, he seemed vulnerable and young.

"How old are you, Trevor?" Melanie asked, sliding into the seat next to Dan. If Trevor was a juvenile, they shouldn't be interviewing him without counsel and a parent present.

"Nineteen." His eyes were an unusual yellowy green, like a cat's, but wide and frightened.

"Oh, okay, good. You're legally an adult under federal law. Have you been advised of your rights?"

"He signed a waiver," Dan said, sliding a piece of paper toward her. Melanie glanced at it and nodded.

"I understand you were taken into custody on an outstanding warrant for fraud?" she asked.

"I was hacking. I sent out a game. If you were stupid enough to play it, it would invade your PC and steal some personal data. I didn't ever *do* anything with the information. I was just, like, punking on people. Like, for kicks."

"Unfortunately, it turns out that's a federal crime, Trevor. You skipped out on your warrant, which makes it worse. Plus, when these agents arrested you, you had a distribution quantity of ecstasy in your possession," Melanie said.

"Yeah, okay. A small amount, but enough to sell."

"Twenty pills. Not nothing. So you're facing some serious charges. Which gives you an incentive to talk to us, to get a more favorable plea offer. Now, have the agents explained what we're interested in?" she asked.

"Yeah, they just told me Whitney Seward hot-loaded last night."

"You hadn't heard?"

"No. I'm not much for reading the papers. I told these guys what I know about Whitney. She was hooking up with this total psycho club-owner dude, like, old enough to be her father. Now, *he* moves product. That's where you should be looking."

"Jay Esposito?" Melanie asked.

"Expo. Yeah. He owns nightclubs and sells heavy-duty drugs. My thing is strictly like X or K—"

"Meaning ecstasy and ketamine?" Melanie asked.

"Right. Club drugs, you know? Go down easy, don't fuck with your head too much. But Expo moves the real McCoy. We're talking H. Not that Whitney Seward messing with hayron surprises me in the least. That girl was constantly pushing the envelope, looking for the next jones."

"Brianna Meyers, too?"

"What about Brianna?" Trevor looked blank. Melanie glanced over at Dan, who shook his head almost imperceptibly. He hadn't broken the bad news to Trevor yet.

Melanie looked Trevor in the eye. "I'm sorry to inform you that Brianna Meyers OD'd last night also."

Trevor swallowed hard. His strange eyes welled up. "Did she . . . did she *die*?"

"I'm afraid so."

"Jesus. I didn't know that." He fell silent, his face reddening. Tears began to slide down his cheeks.

"Uncuff him," she instructed Bridget. Melanie stood up, got a box of Kleenex from a side table, and handed it to Trevor. Shoulders heaving, Trevor rubbed his wrist, then pulled out some tissues and pressed them to his eyes with both hands.

"Are you okay to talk, Trevor?" she asked, resting her hand on his shoulder for a moment.

"Yeah, okay. I had no idea." He took the tissues away and shook his head like he couldn't believe what he'd just heard.

"Did you know Brianna was using heroin?" Melanie asked gently, settling back into her seat.

"No. She wasn't. I mean, you can tell me that, but I don't buy it."

"You were dating Brianna?" Melanie asked.

"I've known her since nursery school, but dated, no. We're like BFFs."

"BFF?"

"Best friends forever. It's only since she started hanging with Whitney that things got weird with me and Bree. Whitney had Brianna pretty brainwashed. She only let me hang with them if I paid for shit, and it was at the point where Brianna was going along with her on that."

Melanie waited as Trevor blew his nose and wiped his eyes some more.

"What kind of stuff did they want you to pay for? Like, drugs?" she asked.

"No. I mean yes, but not only. Just *everything*, you know? Whenever we went out. My parents are divorced, and my dad's a dentist, which doesn't rate shit on the Upper East Side. So I start saying no, because I really couldn't afford it, and Whitney goes, 'Oh, Trevor, I used to like you when you gave me money, but now you bore me,'" he said, adopting a high falsetto. "The fucking bitch, I'm glad she's dead," he added, wadding the Kleenex into a ball in his fist, though his tears were still flowing. Melanie fed him a few more from the box, until he got himself somewhat under control.

"We're trying to figure out where they got the drugs that killed them, Trevor. Tell us anything you know. About Carmen Reyes, too," she said.

"Carmen? The custodian's daughter? What's she got to do with it?" Trevor asked, sniffling, his eyes and nose still streaming.

"She was there last night when they did the drugs, and now she's missing. We're wondering if she's involved somehow," Melanie said.

"You're messing with me!" He sat up straighter.

"No. Why?" she asked.

"Carmen's this, like, uptight priss. They just use her to cheat on tests and shit because she's a nerd, but they weren't *friends*. If Whitney scored some hayron, she would never share it with Carmen. She didn't owe Carmen favors like that, you? Carmen owed *her*, 'cause Carmen was a nobody and Whitney was the man."

"So you didn't know Carmen Reyes to be involved with drugs?"

"No way. That surprises me. But then again, I barely knew the girl. She wasn't part of the scene, you know?"

"What about Brianna and drugs?" Melanie asked.

Trevor smiled fondly through wet eyes. "Aw, y'know, me and Bree'd smoke weed and shit. I mean, we been doing that since we were ten years old. But it was all pretty mellow. Get high, watch old movies, and order takeout from this Szechuan place on First Avenue. That was our thing."

"Just marijuana? Brianna wasn't doing any other drugs, as far as you knew?" Melanie asked.

"Once in a while, I'd get her to do a hit of X so, you know, maybe she'd blow me or something." Trevor shrugged, blushing and looking down at the table.

"I thought you said you weren't dating."

"Oral sex isn't dating. It's just a way to pass the time."

Melanie raised her eyebrows. Kids today. She was gonna lock Maya in her room until the *chiquita* turned twenty-one. Make that forty.

"Seriously," Trevor said, noticing her reaction. "Holbrooke girls are pretty fast that way. They'll blow the delivery guy instead of giving him a dollar for the tip, but since most of 'em don't, like, actually fuck anybody, they pretend to be all virginal. It's kinda bogus, when you think about it. You heard of rainbow parties?"

"No."

"It's where every girl wears a different-color lipstick, and they all suck off some, like, football player or—"

"Trevor, we really need to focus in on what you know about these three girls and heroin, okay?" Melanie said.

"Right. Okay." He nodded, wiping his nose.

"Tell me what you know about Whitney's relationship with Jay Esposito," Melanie prompted.

"Like I said, Whitney was hooking up with him."

"Hooking up. You mean sex?"

"Yeah. Now, *Whitney* was no virgin. And, like, recently she made a buncha trips to Puerto Rico with Expo. She started getting Brianna into it, too. I got weird vibes about what they were up to, but Brianna was holding back on the details."

Dan shot her a glance, and Melanie instantly caught his meaning. Trips to Puerto Rico. Supposedly Esposito was moving heroin from Puerto Rico to New York. Could there be a connection?

"Whitney Seward went to Puerto Rico with Jay Esposito?" she repeated.

"Yeah. A few times. More than a few."

"Did she tell you anything about the trips? Why they went, where they stayed, what they did there? Anything?"

"I mostly heard about it from Brianna. She was jealous because Whitney always had a great tan and a lot of money. See, money was a problem for all of us."

"Well, Whitney was rich, right? I mean, did the money come from the trips, or was it just Whitney's own money?" Melanie was careful to keep the excitement out of her voice. Sometimes, when witnesses were eager to cooperate, they'd say whatever they thought you wanted to hear. Best not to clue them in as to what that was, or you'd get unreliable information.

"Oh, Expo was giving Whitney money," Trevor said definitively.

"How do you know?" Melanie asked, exchanging glances with Dan again.

"Brianna told me. She said every time Whitney went to Puerto Rico with Expo, she'd come back with, like, a lot of Benjamins and buy some amazing shit. Like, one time it was a Christian Dior bag with crystal charms on it, another time this kinda fetishy, like, Gucci dress. All stuff that cost thousands. And I saw it, really."

"Brianna said Benjamins? Meaning cash?"

"Yes."

"That was the exact term she used?"

"Yeah."

"But isn't it possible that Whitney was just spending her own money? That it didn't have anything to do with Esposito?" Melanie asked.

"No. That stuff about the Sewards being so rich? Done! They're burnt. The money's *gone*—at least that's what everybody says. It's tied up in the apartment and the houses or something, and there's not much else. That's why Whitney was always hitting me up to pay for shit. Either that or she was really cheap, which I guess is possible." He gave a harsh laugh, like a bark.

"Why would Esposito give Whitney such large amounts of money?" Melanie asked.

"Well, she *was* a hot blonde with a slammin' bod, and Expo was definitely doin' 'er."

"You're saying he was paying her for sex?" Melanie asked.

"Maybe, maybe not," Trevor replied, shrugging.

"What else could it be?" Melanie asked.

"Well, okay, something weird happened this weekend," Trevor said, kneading his eyes and sighing. "On Saturday I was supposed to hang with Brianna, right? But she texted me that morning and said she was on a plane to San Juan with Whitney."

"She texted you from the plane?"

"Yeah. Both ways, going and coming."

"It was just Brianna and Whitney? Did Esposito go also?"

"I think so. Because Brianna texted me Sunday, from the plane coming back. And she seemed scared."

"Wait a minute, let me get this straight. Brianna, Whitney, and possibly Esposito traveled *to* San Juan on Saturday morning and *returned* Sunday at what time?"

"Really late. I think they missed school yesterday, actually."

"I'll pull the manifests of all possible flights and see if we can corroborate that," Dan said.

"Do you happen to know which hotel they stayed in?" Melanie asked.

"Brianna said the El San Juan."

"Okay. Now, explain to me what made you think Expo went with them," she said.

"If you give me my phone, I can find the message."

Melanie nodded to Dan. He pulled a small silver phone from an evidence envelope and handed it to Trevor. Trevor fiddled with the buttons and handed the phone to Melanie.

"Here," Trevor said.

The message read: "Hey Tinks miss u DB is creeping me out with her fucked up shit her friend too you wouldn't believe who's here anyway she's coming back to the seat in a minute if I ever see you again give me a brain transplant don't let me do this again Friday for a fucking FB totally not worth it what was I thinking wanna smoke weed when I get home really really miss u luv bree."

Melanie looked at Trevor. "Translate this for me. I don't understand all the abbreviations."

Trevor took the phone back. Tears began rolling down his cheeks again as he scrolled through the message. He wiped them away with the back of his hand, sniffling violently, as he read.

"DB is Whitney. Short for Diva Bitch. And FB is Fendi bag. Brianna's saying, like, the bling isn't worth it, because whatever Whitney has her into is so fucked up that it's scaring her. Like, she realizes she made a mistake. And see, here it says 'her friend too you wouldn't believe who's here.' So somebody else was with 'em. I'm just guessing it was Expo."

Melanie took the phone back. "What does she mean, 'if I ever see you again'?" she asked Trevor.

"Beats the hell out of me. But it sounds like she's scared, doesn't it? Like she agreed to something thinking it was gonna be a big party, and now she's in over her head."

"What about 'don't let me do this again Friday'?"

"They must've wanted her to go back at the end of the week," Trevor said.

"Where were these girls' parents? I can't believe they just let their teenage daughters go off with a thug like Esposito," Melanie said, shaking her head.

Trevor shrugged cynically. "All Brianna had to do was say Whitney's name, and her mom would be, like, How fast can I pay for your plane ticket? Buffy was pumped her daughter was hanging with a Seward. The Meyerses were Jewish, like me, and Holbrooke is WASP Central. Brianna didn't fit in. Whitney taking her up changed everything for her socially."

"What about Whitney's parents? Were they totally out to lunch? I mean, these girls were only sixteen years old."

"Yeah, Whitney's parents *were* out to lunch. Out to something anyway. I was at her house a bunch, and I never once saw her parents. Her dad was always gone. Her mom stayed in her bedroom with the door locked, mainlining like OxyContin and vodka or some shit. If Whitney wanted to talk to her, she'd call her on the intercom, and most of the time her mom wouldn't even answer."

That certainly added up with the picture the tabloids painted of Charlotte Seward. Melanie briefly considered the implications of Whitney's mother's drug problem. Was it possible Charlotte had, knowingly or not, supplied the heroin that killed the girls? Perhaps she had a private stash and they swiped some? That would explain a thing or two—like why James Seward delayed calling the police.

"Dan, can you please make a note that we should interview Charlotte Seward right away?"

"Yes, ma'am."

"Now, Trevor, did Esposito ever give any money to Brianna? Not Whitney. I'm talking about Brianna."

A vein began to throb in Trevor's temple. "I really wouldn't know," he said.

He avoided her eyes, and a light sheen of sweat appeared on his forehead. Suspects held out on Melanie on a daily basis, but few were this obvious about it.

"I don't believe you, Trevor," she said matter-of-factly.

"Well, that's rude," he sputtered, flushing bright red. "Fine, then. Believe whatever you want. How should I know if Expo gave Brianna cash? I wouldn't know that. Jeez."

Melanie looked at him steadily. Trevor became even more uncomfortable and shifted in his seat.

Bridget Mulqueen had been shredding the label off a bottle of Poland Spring water, seemingly miles away mentally, but now she looked up. "Hey, Melanie, toss me that phone."

"What?"

"Trevor's phone. Chuck it over here."

Melanie hesitated but then did as requested. Bridget began scrolling through the text messages.

"What are you doing, Bridget?" she asked nervously. All Melanie needed was Bridget erasing her evidence by mistake.

"I looked through these before. Hold on a second. Here it is. What's this, Trev?"

Bridget held up the phone so Trevor could read the display. Without so much as a glance at it, Trevor thrust his chin out and said, "I don't have a fucking clue what you're talking about."

"Let me read it to you, then, jog your memory. 'That lechuga is in locker 4703 now the Delta counter but only get it if something really happens to me then blow it all on something nice in my memory wuv u Bree,'" Bridget read.

Lechuga—"lettuce" in Spanish—was common parlance for cash among drug dealers, rap artists, and the teenagers who loved to imitate them. Melanie, Dan, and Trevor all stared at Bridget in astonishment.

"How much money is in the locker, Trevor?" Melanie demanded.

"Brianna wanted me to have it," he whined.

"You're in a lot of trouble already. Don't make it worse for yourself. How much is in there?" Melanie said.

"Ten thousand," he replied in a small voice, averting his eyes. Debriefing this kid was like taking candy from a baby, after the hardened characters Melanie was used to.

"Cash?" she asked.

"Yes."

"Why did Jay Esposito pay Brianna Meyers ten thousand dollars cash, Trevor?"

"Well, I can't be a hundred percent sure, because she never came right out and said. But I have a pretty good idea Bree and Whitney were muling heroin for him."

17

B UD HAD KEPT his phone off all day, because he knew Jay would be going ballistic trying to call him, and he just didn't feel like listening to his bullshit. But when he turned the damn thing on and there were seven voice mails, every one of 'em a hang-up, he decided he'd better call back. Jay Esposito had been the same since their schoolyard days. If he smelled a rat, he'd move right in for the kill. Shoot first, ask questions later.

Despite the inconvenience, Bud knew he should call from a pay phone. He'd been thinking a lot about phone records these days, what would show up and what wouldn't if someone were checking into things. At the end of the day, he wanted to get away clean. That was his main concern. So he'd been taking precautions for a while now. Not only to deflect attention away from himself but also to focus it on Jay. Like, he'd purposely called Jay last night from the phone on Whitney's desk while Brianna lay dying. Jay said he wanted a report. Well, he got a fucking report, and it was like a big red arrow pointing the cops right to him, the prick. Bud had scores to settle with Jay going back to when they were five years old. Some big, some small, but the most recent one was a whopper. And he planned to get his revenge.

He knew of a phone in the back of a Korean grocery about ten blocks from his apartment, so he walked uptown for a ways, his scarf pulled up over his face, actually enjoying the sleet that the wind drove into his eyes. Soon enough he'd be in a warm, sunny place, all of this behind him

He bought three packs of Dunhills from the skinny old Korean man behind the counter.

"Got a telephone?" he asked, as if he'd never been in the place before.

"Yuh. Back. Near beer."

He headed toward the back of the small store. Bins of pungent-smelling root vegetables lined the shelves on either side of the narrow aisle, their strange odors assaulting him as he trod the uneven floorboards. He got to the phone, checked to make sure he was alone, then dropped the quarter into the slot.

"Yeah?" Esposito answered. He had a whiny voice, high-pitched for a guy his substantial size.

"It's me."

"What the fuck, Bud! You said everything was all right! Then I wake up to Whitney in a fuckin' body bag on the front page of the *Post*."

Bud had already decided how he would handle this. The lies flowed like honey from his mouth.

"Everything *was* all right when I called you, but things went south. Shit happens sometimes in this line of work. You know that."

"I'm gonna fuckin' kill you, pal! Those girls were prime merchandise. Seven trips I used Whitney, and every time she sailed through security like nobody's business. You want somebody looks like a rich girl on vacation, hire a rich girl and send her on vacation. Where am I gonna get another one of those, huh? Answer me that!"

"Take it easy, Jay—"

"Don't tell me to fuckin' take it easy! You realize what you've fuckin' done here, Bud? Young girl, fancy family. Not a lot of those willin' to smuggle heroin in their bellies. And not only is she hard to replace, but with her dead now, the cops are gonna be fuckin' all over us. *Fuck*."

Fuck, fuck, fuck. Every other word out of his mouth, the lowlife. Learn another *fuckin'* word, you *fuckin'* prick. Bud could barely stand to be associated with him. He had to take a deep breath to calm himself before speaking.

"Look, you wanna blame someone, blame the Colombians, Jay," Bud said, keeping his voice neutral with great effort. "They use cheap latex. You knew that since Mirta."

Mirta Jimenez had dropped dead a while back in the bathroom at Marín Airport before she even got on the plane to New York. Jay was always careful to sit several rows behind the mules when he rode shotgun, so he wasn't questioned in her death. He just got on the plane and flew to New York like nothing had happened, then took the opportunity to upgrade the quality of his employees by hiring Whitney Seward.

Esposito sighed. "Yeah, well, even so, the Colombians are gonna come after me for the product. So where the fuck is it?"

"I have most of it, and it wasn't pretty getting it, lemme tell you. We went through three boxes of Ex-Lax," Bud said.

"*Most* of it, you got? Where's the rest?"

Bud glanced around, lowered his voice. "I went out for cigarettes before the girls passed all the balloons. When I came back, they were dead. What was I supposed to do?"

"Fuckin' cut 'em open, for Chrissakes!"

"Jesus Christ."

"That's what I woulda done. Money's money."

He *would* have, the scumbag. Worrying about the mules' health was not Jay Esposito's style. When baggage screening tightened up post-9/11, Jay had immediately switched the girls over from suitcase carries to internal smuggling, and his biggest concern had been the fact that they demanded more money. Jay was a parasite. Bud would be doing the world a big favor by putting him out of his misery.

"Can I ask you something?" Jay said.

"What?"

"I thought Whitney was done swallowing. She wanted to be more like an escort, a coyote? Isn't that why she brought the new girl into the picture?"

Bud had wondered if Jay would notice that inconsistency. He was so fucking thick, you never knew. But now that he'd noticed, Whitney's death was difficult to explain. Luckily, Bud had prepared a response.

"Yeah, well, the new girl got cold feet. After like ten balloons, she freaked out and refused to swallow any more. So Whitney did the rest."

"Whitney always *was* good at opening her mouth."

"Yeah," Bud said, chuckling, "don't I know it."

"Give her a coupla tabs of X and she'd hump a fucking parking meter, too. Shit, that reminds me, though. I better destroy the videos we got of her. And erase that stuff on her blog."

Too late, you prick, Bud thought gleefully.

"Excellent idea, Jay," he said aloud. "Oh, hold on a second. The phone just beeped for me to put in more money."

Bud fed another quarter into the slot, checking all around to satisfy himself that he was still alone. No worries. With the lousy weather, the store was empty.

Esposito sighed again. "Jesus, I'm getting fucking teary-eyed, here. I should look on the bright side. Whitney *was* an unreliable cunt."

"She was a wild girl. You couldn't control her. Who knows what she was into that we weren't even aware of? That's why I think this OD explanation is gonna fly."

"Yeah, that was quick thinking. But wait a minute, you said you didn't get all the balloons. Won't they find the ones that didn't pass still inside 'em when they do the autopsies?"

Bud had thought of that himself, but only in the middle of the night last night, only after the whole thing was over and it was too late to do anything about it. Crime was always perfect in the movies. But in real life, in the heat of the moment, you improvised, and sometimes you missed things. Short of leaving town, Bud still hadn't come up with a solution to this one. And, of course, leaving town before Friday was not an option. No, he'd decided his best bet was to get Jay to slow down the investigation. All he needed was a few days, and Jay definitely had the will and the resources to take care of business, even if that meant going after federal agents. All Bud had to do now was convince Jay it was necessary and point him in the right direction.

"Yeah, I thought of that. We probably have a day or two before the feds get the autopsy results. When's that next shipment?" Bud asked, feigning ignorance.

"Friday, and it's a big one. How the fuck we gonna get another girl by then? We may even need more than one, with the weight we're movin'."

"I'll take care of that part, Jay. That's the least of our problems anyway. We need to think more defensively than that."

"Talk English, for Chrissakes."

"Friday is a big score, right?"

"That's what I just fuckin' said."

"We need to make sure it happens, so we have a nice cushion and we can lay low for a while, right?"

"Yeah. So?"

"*So.* We need to keep the feds off us until then."

"I'm with you on that. In fact, I sent Pavel and Lamar over to the courthouse to check shit out, look into who's investigating this," Jay said.

"Those idiots'll never come through. All they know is how to kill people. But lucky for you, I already got that information."

"That was quick. How'd you manage it? Your *day job?*"

"I do what I have to do to look out for you, Jay."

"You always did," Esposito said. "And I always show my appreciation in return, right, Buddy boy?"

"Yeah, right. But you catch my drift? I'm giving you this information to help you take appropriate steps."

"You don't need to spell it out. I'm making sweet money right now. I got an investment to protect."

"Good. I knew we'd see things the same way. What I have so far is the name of the lead investigator. She's a woman named Melanie Vargas, about five-six or -seven, shoulder-length dark hair, maybe late twenties, early thirties, attractive. . . ."

18

MELANIE STRODE PURPOSEFULLY down the center aisle of the cavernous ceremonial courtroom. With its twenty-foot ceilings and row upon row of spectator benches, the place was big enough to host a three-ring circus, and nearly every seat was filled at four in the afternoon. Judge Warner was on duty. Even though arraignments had been piling up since early that morning, he refused to assume the bench until every single case was ready to be called. And since he loved nothing better than sanctioning any lawyer unlucky enough to step out to the bathroom at the wrong moment, they all spent hours glued to their seats, twiddling their thumbs, waiting for the fearsome jurist to make his appearance.

Melanie slid into an empty chair at the government's table, setting down her armload of files and shrugging out of her heavy winter coat. She'd changed into the spare skirt and hose she kept in her office. It was well known that any female Assistant U.S. Attorney who dared to appear before Judge Warner in pants would lose her bail hearing as punishment. Some pretty serious offenders had made it out onto the street that way.

Brad Monahan, the clean-cut, square-jawed prosecutor in the next seat, leaned over to speak to Melanie.

"So, Vargas, is it true you caught this Holbrooke junkies case?" Brad asked wistfully.

"Holbrooke junkies? What a way to put it!"

"Not my words. Take a look,"

Glancing anxiously at the empty bench first, since Judge Warner had been known to sanction lawyers caught reading the paper in his courtroom, Brad pulled a *Daily News* from beneath his folded overcoat. A huge black headline proclaimed SCHOOL FOR SCANDAL. A smaller headline beneath it read, "Beautiful Holbrooke Junkies Include Candidate Seward's Daughter." Superimposed on a grainy shot of body bags being loaded into the medical examiner's van in front of Seward's building were the same wholesome, smiling yearbook photos of Whitney, Brianna, and Carmen that Melanie had seen in Dr. Hogan's office that morning. Under Whitney and Brianna's photos, boldface type screamed DEAD, whereas under Carmen's it said simply SUSPECT.

"Jesus, who leaked *that*?" Melanie whispered, feeling sick to her stomach. She sincerely hoped Luis Reyes and his daughter Lulu hadn't seen the papers.

"Face it, Vargas. You're a hotshot. First the Benson case, now this. How *do* you do it? You and Witchie-poo sorority sisters or something?" he asked, referring to Bernadette by the epithet favored among junior prosecutors.

"She was paging around last night, and I was stupid enough to answer my beeper."

"I sleep with mine under my freakin' pillow, and I don't get assignments this good."

"What's the big deal, Brad? This is just a low-quantity heroin-distribution case. Hardly the Cali cartel."

"Are you kidding, with these victims? I'd kill for a shot at this kind of media coverage."

She'd forgotten what a press hound Brad was. Melanie firmly believed that a good prosecutor did not seek press attention. The only appropriate moment to be quoted in the paper was after a big conviction, even then limiting your commentary to, "Justice was served." Anything more was grandstanding. The job was about the cases, not the prosecutors.

"I have to get my paperwork stamped," she said, pushing back her chair, relieved for the excuse to stop talking to him. Brad was a decent guy, but his relentless ambition gave her a headache.

Melanie approached the well of the judge's bench, where a tall, flashily dressed guy in his late twenties with slicked dark hair sat behind a desk talking quietly on the telephone. He held up an index finger to let her know he wouldn't be long. Within a minute he hung up and shot her a big smile.

"*Hola, mami. ¿Cómo estás?* Whaddaya got for me?" asked Gabriel Colón, Judge Warner's young deputy clerk.

Known among the prosecutors as "Gaby Baby" or "Gabriel Cologne," in honor of his fragrant hair product, Gabriel was the courthouse's resident Casanova. He'd hit on Melanie for a while after learning of her separation, but she'd turned him down politely. Charming and good-looking as he was, and despite their similar backgrounds, Gabriel didn't do a thing for her. Maybe she'd actually learned something from her failed marriage to Steve, because players turned her off now, *por supuesto*. Luckily, Gabriel had taken no for an answer and backed off graciously. And it *was* lucky, because Judge Warner's deputy wielded real power and could've made her life miserable if he'd chosen to.

"Okay, Gabe, I've got search warrants for computers, a camera phone, and a locker at JFK airport, all based on the same affidavit," Melanie said, lining up multiple documents for him to stamp. "And one new arrest. Trevor Leonard. I spoke to his dad, who's on his way and asks that we go ahead and assign counsel. It's a return on an outstanding wire-fraud warrant, with a new ecstasy-distribution charge added, and I'm prepared to agree to bail under the right circumstances."

"Related to the Holbrooke junkies case?" Gabriel asked, rotating the digits on his stamper to a new docket number and beginning to mark her papers.

"You know about that, too?"

"It's all over the courthouse that you caught that one, *mami*. And some curious eyes been watching you since you walked in. Normally I'd think it's just your pretty legs they're interested in, but I've had some inquiries."

"Who from? The press?" Melanie asked, resisting a powerful urge to turn and look over her shoulder. The whole thing about knowing when you were being watched was a complete myth. Whenever she'd been watched—and it *had* happened in other cases—she'd never had a clue until way too late.

"Mostly press," he was saying. "But a couple of guys I didn't like the looks of, too. Came in claiming to be friends of the victims. Looked like bad news to me. I pointed 'em out to the marshals just in case. Anyways, I don't see 'em now," he said, eyes scanning the spectator benches.

"Can you describe them?" Melanie asked.

"Real bruiser types. One black, the other white with a scar from a bullet *aquí en la cara*," he said, touching his finger to his cheek. "They asked if we had anything come in on the schoolgirls case. I didn't tell 'em a thing."

Melanie felt a prickling sensation run down the back of her neck. She tried to tell herself it was because the courtroom was drafty, but she didn't believe herself. Why would two thugs be looking into this? Esposito, maybe?

"They sound familiar?" Gabriel asked, eyeing her with concern.

"Not really, no. But let me know if you see them again, okay?"

"Sure. Meanwhile, be careful. Watch out if you go to the little girls' room."

"Don't worry about me, Gabe. I can take care of myself."

Nooo problem. She could take on a couple of huge, hulking bruisers. Melanie wiped her suddenly sweaty palms against her skirt, feeling slightly ill. She gathered up her papers, now stamped with docket numbers, and turned away. But after collecting her thoughts for a second, she turned back. If these goons were still here somewhere watching, they would see Trevor Leonard get arraigned. *Think about someone other than yourself,* she told herself. Melanie had plans for Trevor. He'd make a great informant in an investigation against Esposito. Arraigning him in open court would blow that possibility sky high. Not to mention that he seemed like a decent kid, and she would never want any harm to come to him.

"Any chance the judge would entertain a motion to close the courtroom?" Melanie asked, already knowing the answer.

"From the *government*? Get over yourself, *mami*! There's gotta be a hundred people in here we'd have to clear. Besides, you know how the judge feels about Big Brother stomping on the public's right to know."

She knew how the left-wing Judge Warner felt about the government, was what she knew. Deny the prosecution's every request, even if it meant getting a witness killed.

"At least take the arraignment in chambers instead of in open court?" Melanie wheedled.

"Not a chance." Gabriel shook his head firmly but then stopped after seeing the stricken expression on Melanie's face. "Why? You got a cooperator?" he asked.

"Possibly."

"He been threatened?" Gabriel asked.

"Not yet, but he probably will be. And he's young. I'm not sure he can handle himself."

"The judge likes to see evidence of actual threat on the defendant's life before he takes anything in camera," Gabriel said.

"That's not required by the statute."

"The statute is interpreted differently in this courtroom. The judge has his own rules. You know that."

"You can't always produce evidence of a threat, Gabe, even when it's real and the witness is at risk. *You* know *that,*" she said.

Gabriel was Dominican, from the Bronx. He knew how the streets worked. "Yeah, okay I know," He drummed his fingers on the desk, thinking. "It might be different if the motion came from the defense."

"Who's on duty from Legal Aid today?" she asked.

"Ah, what am I saying? No good. It's Stewart Steinberg."

"Shit. That totally sucks."

Stewart Steinberg was a short, stocky defense lawyer–slash–ideologue–slash–prima donna, a sixties throwback, intimate of Kunstler and Kuby, who hated prosecutors on principle. He argued every point to his last wheezing breath no matter how counterproductive for his client. People he represented refused to cooperate and turned down sweet plea bargains, mesmerized by his angry rhetoric, never realizing what a disservice their lawyer had done them. It was said that Stewart Steinberg got more people locked up for longer time than the FBI and NYPD put together.

"Not your day, huh, *mami*?" Gabriel said.

"Well, with Stewart representing him, at least I don't need to worry about death threats. The kid'll never cooperate," she said bitterly.

"You know, it pains me to see a beautiful woman look so unhappy. You're gonna give yourself wrinkles, and that would be a tragedy. So *papi*'s gonna take care of you."

Gabriel picked up his phone and dialed Legal Aid.

"Yeah, Sandra? . . . Gabriel from Judge Warner's chambers. How you doing, *mami*? . . . Sure, I'd be into that, especially the part about the cute chicks. You send me the invitation in the interoffice, okay? . . . Listen, I got a little problem. A new case came in. Stewart Steinberg's up, but he's nowhere to be found. Is he there? . . . Yeah, I'll hold." He covered the receiver with his hand, smiling at Melanie with sparkly white teeth. "Don't worry. Fat Stewie went over to the mob diner for his afternoon snack fifteen minutes ago," he said, referring to a diner across the plaza frequented by organized-crime figures. "He won't be back anytime soon."

Gabriel held up his hand for silence. "Yeah, Sandra? *What?* What you mean, woman? The case is getting ready to be called. The judge ain't gonna be happy, and he's in a worse mood than usual today. I hate to see him take it out on the entire Legal Aid Society . . . Okay, okay, tell you what I'm gonna do. I'm gonna cover for you. I'll appoint other counsel under the Criminal Justice Act. How's that? . . . Yeah, you owe me one, baby. Tell Mr. Disappearing Steinberg that, too. Fat Stewie owes me big time. Bye, now."

Gabriel hung up and grinned broadly at Melanie, then pulled a typed list of names from a folder on his desk. "As if *papi* ain't do you mad favors already." He dialed a pager, punched in a callback number, and hung up. "I'm gonna give you Patty Atkins to represent your cooperator. Just don't forget who's your candy man, babe," he said, winking at her.

19

IN JUDGE WARNER'S private chambers, everything went according to plan.

They stood before the judge's imposing walnut desk. Gabriel Colón turned on the tape recorder, called the case, and placed Dan O'Reilly under oath. Dan raised his right hand and attested to the truth of the information in the search and arrest warrants. Judge Warner signed the warrants with a flourish and handed them to Melanie. Trevor Leonard, who stood shackled between Patty Atkins and two burly deputy marshals, looked young and remorseful and spoke in a tiny voice. He'd been ferried up in the back service elevator just in case those thugs were still lurking around somewhere. And Melanie made her carefully rehearsed pitch, seconded enthusiastically by prosecutor–turned–defense lawyer Patty Atkins, who knew a good deal when she saw one.

"I hereby find that the defendant poses neither a risk of flight nor a danger to the community," Judge Warner intoned into the tape recorder, peering severely over his half-glasses. "This finding is made on the joint motion of the government and the defense, and takes into account that the defendant has agreed to cooperate with agents of the Elite Narcotics Task Force as requested. Mr. Leonard is ordered released on a twenty-thousand-dollar personal-recognizance bond, secured by his own signature. He will remain within the five boroughs unless permission to travel is sought and granted by this court. Anything further, Ms. Vargas?" Judge Warner asked, glaring at Melanie.

"Nothing from the government, Your Honor," Melanie said.

"Ms. Atkins?" Another glare.

"No, Judge."

"Very well. All records of this proceeding, including this audiotape, shall be sealed for Mr. Leonard's protection. So ordered."

And he smacked his gavel resoundingly on its base, suppressing a slight smile when they all jumped.

MELANIE, Dan, and Bridget were waiting outside Melanie's office door. Trevor Leonard was inside conferring with his lawyer and his father, trying to decide whether to go forward with the debriefing. The risks of cooperating in this case were obvious, given Jay Esposito's suspected history of witness killing.

"I have some real doubts about whether we should use this kid even if he wants to cooperate," Melanie admitted, tapping her foot nervously.

"You mean because he didn't come clean about the money in the airport locker?" Dan asked. His eyes were lingering on her face in a way that only made her more antsy.

"No, it's not that. Trevor actually strikes me as a good kid. But he's so young, so green. I'm not sure he can handle himself out there."

"That's our job," Bridget piped up in a squeaky voice. "If we do a drug buy or something, we'll supervise Trev real closely, keep him out of trouble."

Melanie and Dan exchanged glances. As usual, she knew just what he was thinking: Fine, but who would supervise Bridget?

"Let's take it one step at a time, okay?" Dan suggested. "The kid obviously has good information. Let's debrief him and see where it goes. As we talk more, we'll get a better sense of what his capabilities are."

Melanie nodded. "I agree about the debriefing. It's only the undercover I'm worried about."

"I'd take a wait-and-see on that, too," Dan said. "Kid could be valuable infiltrating Esposito's organization. And I'm starting to think Expo's a good target. Did I tell you there's information linking him to that Golpe stamp found with the dead girls?"

"No. What kind of information?"

"A reference in the NADDIS database from an old DEA report. I'm trying to track it down."

"That's excellent. If there's something solid linking Expo to the stamp . . ."

"Yeah, I know. It would make our case."

Just then Patty Atkins opened the door. She was a no-nonsense, no-frills woman in her forties, with pleasant brown eyes and short, graying hair, wearing a navy suit.

"Could you come in, Melanie? We have a couple of questions."

"Sure."

Melanie walked in and sat down behind her desk. Trevor had been bailed out, so they were meeting in Melanie's office rather than the gloomy prisoner-interview rooms on the sixth floor. Trevor and his father, who was thin and tired-looking with an aggrieved air, sat in her guest chairs. Patty took a seat beside them as Dan and Bridget filed in and stood in the back of the room.

"I have one major concern," Patty began.

"Your client's safety?" Melanie guessed.

"You got it."

"That's what I'd be thinking about if I were you. I have to admit, I'm worried about it, too."

"I calculated the sentence. Four to ten months, max. Not enough, in my opinion, to justify taking many risks."

"You're basing your calculation on the weight Trevor was carrying at the time of arrest," Melanie said. "But he's already admitted to a steady gig selling ecstasy and ketamine. He's looking at a lot higher, maybe up to three years."

"You're not going to make him plead to all that?"

"Come on, Patty, you know I don't have a lot of leeway when it comes to making plea offers. There are rules."

"Times have changed. The Sentencing Guidelines are only advisory now."

"A lot of the judges still follow them. Trevor needs to understand what his exposure is so he can make an informed decision."

"An informed decision requires more than numbers, Melanie. Don't I recall something in the papers a couple of years back about a decapitated corpse washing up on Roosevelt Island, linked to Esposito?" Patty asked.

"Oh, now, wait one minute! I don't like the sound of this," Trevor's father exclaimed. Trevor said nothing but went even paler under his tattoos and piercings.

"Nobody's hiding the ball here," Melanie said. "Trevor is facing two felony convictions and real jail time. Enough to derail him at this point in his young life. On the other hand, the target we need his cooperation against is undeniably dangerous."

"Exactly what kind of cooperation are you looking for?" Patty asked.

"At a minimum we want to debrief him and have him testify to any relevant information. Beyond that there's a possibility we'll want to use him as an undercover. If we were to do that, we'd make sure all proper precautions were taken. We care very deeply about Trevor's safety. But still, it's never possible to eliminate every risk," Melanie said.

"You bet. You know that firsthand, don't you, Melanie?" Patty turned to Trevor. "She had a witness killed on another case."

"That's a low blow!" Dan exclaimed. "Typical sleazy defense-lawyer tactic. That other case has nothing to do with this one."

Trevor stared at Melanie, who sat in stunned silence behind her desk, seeing Rosario Sangradur's face. Rosario's murder haunted Melanie. Rosario had been the very definition of innocent bystander, a middle-aged housekeeper who'd witnessed her wealthy employer brutally tortured and murdered at the hands of a sadistic killer. Melanie had gone to great lengths to persuade Rosario to cooperate and testify, on the assurances of the FBI and the PD that she would receive round-the-clock protection. The killer's ability to infiltrate their ranks and find out where Rosario was sequestered could not have been predicted by Melanie or anybody else. But that didn't make Rosario's death excusable. It wasn't okay and never would be.

"Patty's right," Melanie said, meeting Trevor's eyes, speaking with quiet intensity. "A witness was murdered on a case I did a while back. Agent O'Reilly's upset because he knows how much her death affected me. All I can say is, that experience made me understand in a very personal way how much is at stake when somebody cooperates." She shook her head slowly. "You know, we can probably make this case without you, Trevor. Maybe you *should* just eat the jail time and not take the risk."

The room exploded, everybody talking at once.

"But you said he's facing three years! He can't do that. What about college?" Trevor's father exclaimed.

"You and me should talk outside, Melanie," Dan said.

Patty Atkins blurted, "But I never said my client wasn't interested——"

Trevor waved his hand in the air. "Whoa, you guys, calm down. I'm not freaking out here. Nobody else should either, okay?"

"If he does this undercover stuff, does that mean he won't have to go to jail?" Trevor's father asked.

Melanie turned to Patty. "I assume you're looking for a probationary sentence?"

"Naturally. I mean, look at him, he's a baby. He'd get eaten alive inside," Patty said.

"I don't want to see him do hard time either, Patty. But the fact is, to get to zero jail time from where he is, he needs to produce something. And I'm not talking about just giving a statement. Without any arrests to his credit, he'll never make probation. So that's a reality you all need to consider."

"Maybe Trevor *should* go to jail," his father said. "It might teach him a lesson. God knows, I can't control him. It would be better than exposing him to something dangerous anyway."

"Jail *is* dangerous," Melanie observed. "Trevor's charged with a drug offense, so he'd get designated to a maximum-security facility. He'd be in with some hardened types."

"You happy now? See where you ended up? What did I tell you?" Trevor's father demanded, looking at his son in disgust.

Melanie sighed and got to her feet. "Look, why don't we stop for today. I'm beginning to feel like this isn't going anywhere."

"Not necessary," Trevor said. "I've made up my mind. You're missing the point. All of you, but especially you, Dad."

"Trevor," Patty said, "please don't say anything further until—"

"No, really! It's my life. Let me talk."

Melanie sat back down behind her desk. "Okay. We're listening."

Trevor drew a deep, sighing breath. Tears began to roll slowly down his cheeks.

"Brianna Meyers was my best friend. Dad, I'm not saying this to hurt you or anything, but you *know* me and her both came from some fucked-up family situations. Some of that stuff that went on before Mom left? That was some mad shit! And then after, when Mom wouldn't see us for two years? Brianna got me through all that. She was a great person. She was smart and kind. She played the cello. She had a pretty voice and a nice body. It's a fucking *waste* that she died, and that prick Expo is responsible. Bottom line," he said, turning to Melanie, "show me where to fucking sign, because I'm in."

"I respect your feelings for Brianna, Trevor," Melanie said gently. "We all do. But we need to make sure—"

"I'm *sure*," Trevor said firmly. "I'm definitely sure. And it's my decision. So let's do it."

Melanie considered telling him no. The final call on whether to allow a witness to cooperate lay in the prosecutor's discretion. If something happened to Trevor, it would be on Melanie's conscience, and she wasn't sure she wanted that burden. On the other hand, Carmen Reyes was still missing. Didn't Melanie also need to consider *Carmen's* future, *Carmen's* safety? Rosario Sangrador's death weighed so heavily on Melanie that she needed to watch herself lest she become a less aggressive prosecutor than she ought to be.

"All right," Melanie said finally. "If you're sure that's what you want."

A FTER HIS FATHER LEFT, Trevor Leonard gave them a full and complete proffer of information.

"I went to Screen just once with Brianna and Whitney, maybe two, three weeks ago," Trevor explained, sitting in a guest chair in Melanie's office, his lawyer still beside him. Melanie sat behind her desk. Dan and Bridget leaned against her filing cabinets, listening and taking occasional notes.

"No question," Trevor continued, "Whitney was hooking up with the dude. He comes up to us, like, the minute we walk in the door, says everything's on the house. And at first I thought he was into Brianna, right, because he's majorly checking her out. I remember he asked her how old she was, which I thought was weird. But then him and Whitney disappeared for, like, an hour. Whitney came back high off her ass and all skanky, like she just got finished doing the wild thing. Her hair a mess, her makeup smeared all over her face. She flaunted it, too, like she wanted everyone to know what a porn star she was. I was, like, go take a shower, skank, you disgust me."

"Did you see Esposito again that night?"

"No. Well, yes, but only from a distance. I never talked to him again."

"When you met him, was anyone else with him? Anyone who might've worked for him?"

"Yeah, actually. Two bodyguards. From what Whitney was saying, they drive Expo around in a big black Escalade and hurt people for him. She seemed to get off on that. Chick was a major thrill seeker, I'm telling you."

"Can you give us physical descriptions of Esposito and the bodyguards?" Melanie asked.

"Expo's, like, a fly-looking dude with a shaved head and this huge diamond earring. Thirties, forties, I'm not sure. Old anyway. The bodyguards are both as big as houses. One's black, one's white, and the white one's got a nasty-looking scar in his cheek, like from a bullet hole."

Melanie caught Dan's eye; he nodded at her solemnly. She'd already filled him in on the goons' descriptions as reported earlier by Gabriel Colón. Expo was watching the feds before *they* started watching *him*.

"Did you happen to catch the bodyguards' names?" she asked Trevor.

"The white guy with the scarface was Pavel. Russian dude, I think. The black guy, no. Oh, and there's another guy who works for Expo, named Bud. I never met him, but Whitney mentioned him, and Expo talked to him on the phone when I was at Screen that night."

"Did Whitney say anything in particular about Bud? Any details?"

"He was a go-between. The one who'd call her when Expo wanted her to do something."

"Trevor, let me ask you something," Dan said. "Just hypothetical, now. Think you could get into Screen, maybe take Detective Mulqueen with you, introduce her around so she can make a controlled buy of heroin from Esposito or one of his employees?"

Hey, wait a minute—" Patty Atkins began, but Trevor cut her off.

"Hey, it's cool. Really, Patty, I'm not afraid of any of this. I'm pretty into it."

"Trevor, Patty's right to be concerned," Melanie said. "I want to make sure myself that if you go to Screen, we have all the bases covered as far as your safety's concerned."

"Quite honestly, the last time I was there, I bought some X. The Russian bodyguard steered me to a house dealer who was operating out of the men's room. So it's cool, I've done it before. I'd recognize Expo's people, and they'd do business with me."

"And just so everybody's extra comfortable," Dan said, "Detective Mulqueen can do the actual buy. I'll go, too, blend into the crowd, observe and jump in if anything starts looking hinky. We'll be right on top of Trevor the whole time."

"There's just one problem," Trevor said.

"What's that?" Melanie asked.

"Screen moves around."

"You mean, like, the floor moves?"

Trevor giggled. "The floor? What, like *Saturday Night Fever*? What century are *you* from? No, see, Expo's regular clubs are strictly for the bridge-and-tunnel crew. Celebs and 'it girls' like Whitney Seward and their posses, they turn up their noses at those places. They only go to underground clubs, see?"

"Underground?"

"*Secret.* Not only do you have to know someone to get in, you have to know someone just to *find* the place. Screen changes locations every week, and people follow it around. It's always in some totally bizarre place. The time I went, it was in this secret bunker beneath the Waldorf that was built for some, like, railroad tycoon or something," Trevor said.

"So where is it now?" Dan asked.

"That, I wouldn't know. You can't just dial Information to find it, and I'm not hooked up. So like I said, there's a problem."

"No sweat," Melanie said. "I'll take care of getting that information. When it comes to New York City nightlife, I have the greatest source in the world."

20

B Y THE TIME Melanie finished debriefing Trevor Leonard, it was after six o'clock. She needed to get on the stick if she wanted to sneak her team into Screen that night to do a heroin buy from Esposito's people.

Melanie whipped out her cell phone, where she had her sister on the speed dial.

"Dígame," Linda answered.

"Hey, *chica,* where are you?"

"Getting a pedicure and a wax. I have a date later."

"You and Josh sure are getting hot and heavy. When am I gonna meet him?"

"Josh who? We broke up."

"You're kidding! When?"

"Mmm, yesterday."

"And you're onto somebody new already?"

"Why sit home?"

"Fast work, even for you. I'm impressed."

"Get with the program, *bebé.* You should take a page from my book."

"Yeah, right, I'll give it some thought. So, listen, what time are you going out?"

"Uh-oh. I feel a request to baby-sit coming on."

"If you're volunteering, I accept, but that's not why I called."

"So you're not working late tonight?"

"Well, actually I am, but—"

"*Again?* Your bodacious ass should quit that job, *chica.*"

"Right. As long as Maya and I can live with you, because then we'll be destitute."

"I'm serious. That boss of yours is a rhymes-with-witch."

"You're not the only one who thinks so, but this isn't on her."

"For God's sake, it's almost Christmas, Mel."

"Tell it to the bad guys. They're the ones making me work late. Anyway, I need a favor, and it's not baby-sitting. It's more in your skill set, sis."

J UST AS MELANIE was grabbing her coat to run home and steal some precious moments with Maya, the phone on her desk rang. The caller ID displayed Bernadette's extension. Melanie did the calculation in her head—how fast she could sprint to the elevator versus how long it would take Bernadette to get out to the hall and catch her. *Drat!*

She reached for the receiver. "Yes, Bern."

"Hey, girlfriend, I need an update on the Holbrooke ODs case."

"Okay, sure, no problem. We—"

"Not *now.* I'm on a conference call. Six-thirty, my office."

And Bernadette hung up. Melanie kicked her desk in frustration. *Why the helldja call me if you were already on the phone?* Now she was stuck waiting around, using up what was likely to be her only personal time for days to come. She tried not to feel sorry for herself, but really, she missed her daughter. Linda was right—it *was* holiday season, December 18 at 6:10 P.M., to be exact. Not many shopping days left till Christmas. Shouldn't she be home? Everyone else in the world was partying or decorating the tree or spending time with family. Wait a minute, though, not *everyone.* Not Carmen Reyes. Or Brianna Meyers or Whitney Seward. Melanie reminded herself why she did this job.

The thought of Christmas shopping made her crazy, though. Between work and Maya's being sick, she hadn't had time to get anything for her poor little daughter. She looked at her watch. Twenty minutes until Bernadette wanted to see her. Hmm, the miracle of the Internet. She knew she wasn't supposed to, but . . .

Melanie went online, searching for toys for Maya. She wanted a doll with dark hair and pudgy cheeks, one that looked like Maya. The selection on Amazon was vast, but nothing seemed to fit the bill. Dolls with bottles. Dolls that wet and cried real tears. Dolls that smelled like baby powder. Dolls with removable clothes to teach zipping and buttoning skills. None of them had the right look. Finally, time running out, Melanie started looking at storybooks instead. She didn't spend enough time reading with Maya. Heck, she didn't spend enough time doing *anything* with Maya.

"Melanie Vargas, *what* do you think you're up to?"

Melanie nearly fell out of her chair.

"Bernadette, I—"

"Your office Internet connection is reserved for official government business!" Bernadette snapped, looming over Melanie's desk.

"Yes, I know. I—"

"Yeah, since when is Dora the Explorer official business?"

"I'm sorry. I had a few extra minutes while I waited for you to—"

"I never hold this single-motherhood thing against you, Melanie. I even assign you a high-profile case. In exchange, I expect to see some discipline."

"Look, Bernadette, I apologize. It won't happen again. And you don't need to worry. Everything is under control on the Holbrooke case. We have a promising new angle, a cooperator—"

Melanie's phone rang. Saved by the bell! It was her boss's secretary, Shekeya Jenkins, calling to say Vito Albano was on the line for Bernadette.

"I'll take it in my office," Bernadette said. "*You,* come with me. I swear, I have to watch you every second."

Melanie's face went hot with indignation, but she held her tongue and followed Bernadette down the hall to her corner suite, which sat at the intersection of the two corridors housing the Major Crimes Unit. BERNADETTE DEFELICE, CHIEF, screamed the brass nameplate, all in caps. Why did it seem like every time she walked into her boss's office, Melanie's stomach was upset for one reason or another? She wasn't alone in this: Everyone else's relationship with Bernadette was the same way. Yet as much as she resented her boss, she admired her, too. Bernadette was exciting, dynamic, and good at her job. She got things done. She had the best Rolodex in the business and therefore brought in the best cases. She recruited talented prosecutors and demanded the best work from them. Too bad she accomplished all that by wielding a stick instead of a carrot, but still, Melanie wouldn't trade the experience for anything less dramatic or interesting.

"Wait here!" Bernadette commanded as they entered the anteroom.

Shekeya Jenkins looked up from her computer screen, contemplating Melanie sympathetically. Shekeya had been Bernadette's secretary for years, the only one who'd ever lasted in the position. A big woman with elaborate braids bleached orangey red, long, gem-studded fingernails, and a sharp tongue, Shekeya was one of the few people in the office who could do battle with Bernadette on equal terms.

"What she on you about now?" Shekeya asked, blowing a bubble with Day-Glo pink bubble gum.

"She caught me doing my Christmas shopping online while I was waiting to meet with her."

"Girl, don't listen to that bullshit. I shop online all the time and e-mail my psychic, too. The boss don't so much as look cross-eyed at me."

"She's probably afraid to, Shekeya."

Shekeya laughed and slapped her knee. "You got that right! Get back in her face is all is takes. And I *know* you know how if you want to."

"So what are you still doing here at this hour?" Melanie asked. Shekeya was normally gone by 4:55 at the latest.

"I can't do a little overtime if I feel like it?" she asked, working the bubble gum with her tongue.

"Oh, I get it. Christmas and all. I could use some extra cash myself." Unfortunately, attorneys didn't get paid overtime for putting in additional hours the way support staff did. Melanie's base salary was significantly higher, but she was expected to work as hard as it took to get the job done without additional compensation.

"No, it ain't even about that," Shekeya was saying. "You'll be seein' me around here all hours from now on. Khadija just got accepted in private school starting next semester. Public schools in my neighborhood suck. I want to give her the best possible chance in life, you know?"

"I'm with you there. I feel exactly the same way."

"Got to pay for it somehow. So I went in to see the boss, told her I was picking up a night job cleaning, and she say to me, why not do the extra hours here? There's always some filing or some shit needs doin'."

Since all the lawyers on the unit pretty much did their own word processing, Shekeya's job was limited to answering Bernadette's telephone, filling out the occasional requisition form, doing her nails—and, apparently, online shopping and psychic consulting. Obviously Bernadette had just been trying to help Shekeya out. That was the thing about Bernadette. Just when you were most disgusted with her, she'd do something truly humane, and you'd say, Oh, if only she'd act like that all the time, how much better would life be?

Speak of the devil. Bernadette poked her head out into the anteroom. "Come on in, girlfriend," she called. "I've got Lieutenant Albano on the line."

Melanie walked in and sank into a guest chair, feeling utterly drained. The sky beyond Bernadette's window was already ink dark. Melanie felt about a million years old, and like the day would never end.

"Vito?" Bernadette said.

"Still here, hon," Albano's voice squawked from the speakerphone.

"Melanie's with me now. Melanie, can you please explain what the hell the deal is with this new cooperator?"

Melanie sat up straighter. "You mean Trevor Leonard?"

"That freaky kid I saw leaving your office an hour ago."

"Yup, that's Trevor. He was a close friend of Brianna Meyers. Trevor says Brianna and Whitney Seward were working as drug couriers for Jay Esposito, the nightclub owner. Esposito's been investigated—"

"Jesus," Bernadette exclaimed, dropping her head into her hands, "you were right, Vito."

"I don't see what the big tragedy is," Albano said. "Sounds like a promising lead. We know about this Expo character from way back. Wouldn't surprise me at all if he's the supplier."

"Supplier, fine. But did you hear what Melanie just said? The last thing I need is an allegation from some slacker freak that James Seward's daughter was muling heroin."

Albano was silent.

"Vito?" Bernadette said.

"Yeah, okay, I see what you mean. It's a little sensitive."

"Sensitive, my ass. It's a lawsuit waiting to happen. Am I the only one who worries about the big picture around here? *Think,* people. What if the tabloids get ahold of it and then it doesn't pan out?"

"So don't tell 'em," Albano suggested.

Melanie plucked a copy of that morning's *Daily News* off Bernadette's desk. It was the same one Brad Monahan had in court earlier, with the word "Suspect" emblazoned beneath Carmen Reyes's photo on the front page.

"It *would* be better if nobody talked to the press," Melanie said. "About anything."

"Oh, what's that supposed to mean?" Bernadette snapped.

"Leaking this thing about Carmen Reyes being a suspect—"

"*Leak?* Watch your language. 'Leak' means you disclosed confidential information without proper authority. I'm authorized to tell the press anything I damn well please, so by definition I *can't* leak. I apprised the taxpayers of how we're spending their money. They're entitled to know. They pay our salary."

"Fine, whatever you want to call it, but the point is—"

"And you seem to forget that Ray Wong found heroin with the Golpe stamp in Carmen Reyes's locker. *That's* why she's on the lam, not because her picture's in the paper. But instead of trying to locate a girl who's obviously involved, you're spending your time debriefing this highly problematic witness about potentially libelous allegations."

"I *am* trying to locate Carmen, Bern. Believe me, I'm very concerned about her. And Trevor's not problematic. Young, yes, but he's quite credible when you talk to him. Like *you* always say, nuns and schoolteachers aren't the ones with inside information about drug trafficking."

"One look at this Leonard kid and anybody can see he's gonna *tank* in front of a jury. He was probably on drugs when you debriefed him, for crying out loud."

"He was *not*. Pretrial Services screens all defendants before arraignment and reports dirty urines. Trevor was completely clean. Besides, we're not taking his word for anything. We're doing a full investigation to corroborate him, including a buy tonight at Esposito's club."

"Yes, okay. That's what we wanted to speak to you about. Vito, are you still there?" Silence from the speakerphone. *"Vito?"* Again silence. "Christ, so much for *him*," Bernadette said irritably, and punched the button to hang up the line.

"Don't worry, Bernadette," Melanie began.

"What do they pay me for if not to worry about you hotheads screwing up? I can't believe you're actually sending this Leonard kid out to do a buy."

"Bridget Mulqueen is doing the buy. Trevor's just making the introduction to Esposito's people."

"That's hardly better. I want you in there personally supervising, Melanie Vargas. Do you understand me?"

"Well, I *was* planning to meet the agents later to give them instructions on getting into Esposito's club. But going in myself? Isn't that *their* job? I thought you said no cops-and-robbers stuff this time."

"*Don't* quote me to myself! I said that in a completely different context. I'm not suggesting you personally make a drug buy. Just keep an eye on things and make sure they don't fuck it all up, excuse my French. I don't trust Mulqueen, and I *don't* trust your cooperator."

Melanie shrugged. "Okay."

"I'm giving you some rope here by letting you explore this angle. Don't hang yourself with it."

"I won't. Really, Bern, I appreciate your confidence in me."

Shekeya buzzed Bernadette with a phone call. "If it's Vito, he better have a damn good explanation for why he hung up on me," Bernadette muttered, picking up the receiver. "*Who?* . . . Well, did you tell them she's in a meeting? . . . Oh, *all right,* put it through." Bernadette's top line flashed red. She pressed the button and picked up the receiver, holding it out to Melanie with the tips of her fingers as if it were radioactive. "It's for you."

Melanie stood up and grasped the receiver, pulling the cord taut across Bernadette's desk. "Hello?" she said tentatively.

"Melanie? Shavonne Washington from the Chief Medical Examiner's Office. Sorry to interrupt your meeting, but I thought you'd like to know that we just completed the autopsies on Whitney Seward and Brianna Meyers. You should get down here right away."

21

THE HULKING OCME BUILDING, at First Avenue and Thirtieth Street, loomed over the neighborhood like a haunted castle. By the time Melanie entered its depressing, institutional-looking lobby, Ray-Ray Wong was already seated in the reception area waiting for her. She needed an agent present to take chain of custody on the girls' personal effects, and Dan and Bridget were busy setting up the heroin buy for later that night.

"Evening, ma'am," Ray-Ray said, rising to his feet, nodding crisply.

They crossed a span of muddy brown carpet and signed in with the good-looking black guy behind the reception desk, who directed them to a freight elevator that would take them down to the morgue in the basement.

"So what were the autopsy results, ma'am?" Ray-Ray asked as he pressed the call button.

"Shavonne didn't want to go into it over the phone, but apparently the deputy M.E. is waiting to give us a report."

"Okay."

"Any developments on your end?"

"Yes. Well, this might be nothing, but . . ."

"What?"

"I had Gidget run rap sheets on the faculty and staff at Holbrooke, like you said?"

"Yeah?"

"Not much. An English teacher with a couple of DWIs. The guidance counselor had a disorderly from fifteen years back, but no details in the record."

"Probably some kind of political protest, knowing him."

"Yeah, okay, but here's the sort of creepy one. That lawyer?"

"Siebert?"

"Yeah. He's in a sex-offender database."

"Jesus, really?"

"Not because of an actual arrest. His name came up in an investigation. I contacted the NYPD guy whose case it is. He says Siebert was going on this Web site where a lot of teenage boys post profiles. It's like a known site for older men looking to hook up with underage prostitutes."

"You're kidding."

"No. I'm telling ya, this Siebert's a fucking perv. He actually messaged a fifteen-year-old kid who'd posted a picture of himself wearing jeans and no shirt."

"So why hasn't Siebert been arrested?"

"Because. Apparently he never asked to meet the kid or anything. He just messaged him about baseball."

"*Baseball?* You mean, like, how 'bout those Mets?"

"Right."

"I'm not sure that's a crime. How do we know he was even after sex?"

Ray looked at her like she was stupid. "It's a known site. People don't just wander into these things. Maybe he's working up his nerve."

"Huh. Well, but we have girls in this case. And so far there's no known sex angle."

"I know."

"Ours looks like a drug thing."

"Yes, I'm aware of that."

The elevator came, and they got in.

"That's weird," Melanie said. "We should interview Siebert, find out what he's up to. Who knows? Maybe there's some connection, although it doesn't leap out at me."

"We can't. I promised this detective I wouldn't burn his investigation."

"So we don't specifically ask Siebert about the Web site."

"Okay."

"Anything else?"

"I examined the dead girls' telephones with a guy from Tech."

"And?"

"Brianna's wasn't very interesting, but Whitney's phone was strange. First of all, you've got numerous saved photos of Carmen Reyes in Whitney's apartment last night. It's as if somebody decided to document Carmen's presence there," Ray-Ray said.

"Do we know when the pictures were taken?"

"Based on the time stamps, between seven-thirty and seven forty-eight P.M."

"What's Carmen doing?"

"Nothing really. Just standing around. But what really raised me up is, other than the photos and a couple of calls to a cell phone associated with Jay Esposito, the phone's entire memory's been erased. Including all records of calls dialed and received, phone numbers in the address book, everything. Some of that can be reconstructed using telephone records. But some of it can't."

"So somebody erased the memory purposely but left the photos of Carmen for us to find?" Melanie asked, thinking aloud.

"Looks that way."

Melanie felt a tiny tingle of fear—not for herself but for Carmen. Somebody had been in Whitney Seward's apartment last night, tampering with evidence, presumably at the same time Carmen was there. Whoever it was seemed to be trying to point the finger at Carmen. Why? Where was that person now? Wherever they were, Melanie had a bad feeling that Carmen was with them.

"Hey," Melanie said. "Why would they leave the calls to Esposito?"

"I don't know. Oversight?"

"Pretty stupid oversight. Do you think someone wanted us to find those calls? Like they're setting Esposito up?"

"Is it called a setup when the victim is actually guilty?" Ray-Ray asked.

They reached the basement and got out. Brightly lit, spick-and-span, with cheerful green and white tiles, it nevertheless reeked of death.

"Yuck!" Melanie exclaimed, clapping her hand over her nose.

"Breathe through your mouth and you won't smell it as much," Ray-Ray suggested.

She tried it; it worked. "Huh. Thanks, I'll remember that."

"Learned that in the Gulf."

They met up with Shavonne Washington at a booth near the back entrance. Shavonne stood guard over two white body bags that had been stacked on metal trays fixed to a wheeled gurney. Nodding hello to Melanie and Ray-Ray, she checked the bar codes on each body bag against a log, then wheeled the gurney carefully over to a narrow elevator. The elevator doors opened, and an orderly stepped out. Shavonne helped him maneuver the gurney carefully into the elevator.

"There go your girls," Shavonne said, coming over to Melanie and nodding toward the closing doors. "They're getting released to the families for burial now. Dr. Drucker's in the autopsy room scrubbing up, waiting to explain his findings to you."

Melanie and Ray-Ray followed Shavonne down the hall. All around them high-tech refrigerators gave off an eerily soothing hum. Shavonne pushed open a wide swinging door, and they trailed her into the large room, which held eight stainless-steel autopsy slabs, each with its own sink, scale, and array of scary-looking cutting shears and electric saws. A short, slight doctor wearing surgical greens, face mask, and shoe covers was just finishing drying his hands at one of the sinks. Shavonne made the introductions.

"As we expected, preliminary tox on both bodies was positive for the presence of heroin in the bloodstream," Dr. Drucker explained. "I'm prepared to certify acute heroin poisoning as cause of death on both victims."

"You refer to preliminary tox. Meaning . . ."

"We just do a preliminary screen that tests for the presence of particular substances of interest. In this case we tested for the presence of heroin and got a positive result," Dr. Drucker replied.

"So if the girls had something else in their bloodstreams . . . ?"

"Unless we expose the blood sample to the specific reagent for that particular substance, we won't detect it. So you'd have to notify us exactly what you want us to test for. Is there some other substance you have reason to believe they might have ingested?"

"No, not really," Melanie said, shaking her head. "You can't just do a generalized sort of test for narcotics and poisons?"

"No, it doesn't work that way. A full tox would test for a wider range of narcotic and nonnarcotic controlled substances, but still, it's limited. I *can* order up a test for common poisons, but we like to have some basis before we do that, so we're not wasting our time," Dr. Drucker said.

"There's a basis here. Their deaths might've been plain old-fashioned ODs, but they might've been something else. We believe that these girls were transporting drugs, not just using."

"Yes, exactly, that's why we called you in. You believe right, and now we can prove it."

"What? You found evidence?"

"Yes. The Meyers girl had heroin balloons in her stomach."

Melanie's insides did a horrible somersault. "Is . . . is that what killed her?" Melanie asked, her mouth suddenly dry. That poor, wrong-headed kid. Doing this to herself so she'd fit in with Whitney, so she could afford a Fendi bag.

"You bet. The balloons ruptured and just *poured* heroin into her bloodstream. Much more than what could be ingested nasally or even intravenously through intentional use. I'm afraid it's a very painful way to die. Here, come look," Dr. Drucker said, leading them over to one of the autopsy slabs.

An array of sample containers holding gruesome collections of organs and fluids was spread out on a small stainless-steel table at the end of the slab. Dr. Drucker picked up a clear plastic vial bearing a small label with Brianna's name and a bar code. Melanie took it and held it up to her eye. Inside were three small, round, orange pellets, coated in a fine slime of tissue and blood. She held up the vial for Ray-Ray, who examined it also.

"What you see are typical balloons of heroin used by drug couriers for internal smuggling," Dr. Drucker explained. "These were recovered from Brianna's stomach. Literally, they're *balloons*, like you could purchase in any toy store. We know that from the orange color. The other product commonly used by smugglers to wrap drugs for internal smuggling, as I'm sure you're aware, is the latex condom, which tends to be flesh-colored. Those are actually even more likely to leak, especially the . . . uh, ultrathin varieties."

"How do you know these balloons leaked?" Melanie asked.

"Under the microscope we saw small lesions on two of the balloons. The lesions occur when stomach acids compromise the latex. Extremely unfortunate for the victim," he said, shaking his head.

Melanie was silent for a moment, staring at the tiny orange pellets that had ended a young girl's life. There was no question in her mind that Jay Esposito was behind this. But she still had to prove it.

"What about Whitney?" she asked. "Did you find balloons in her stomach, too?"

"No. But that doesn't necessarily mean anything. She could've excreted them all prior to her death."

"Is there any other way to tell whether she OD'd from leaking balloons as opposed to snorting the heroin voluntarily?" Melanie asked.

"Not based on the toxicology results, no," Dr. Drucker said. "But we can look to other indicators. In this case Whitney had fresh track marks between her toes, so I'd say she probably ingested voluntarily. But not by snorting, by shooting up."

Melanie and Ray-Ray looked at each other in confusion. "That's weird," Melanie said. "We found empty glassines but no works. And the glassines were right beside the bodies. To shoot up they'd have to cook the stuff first, right? There was no indication of that at all."

Dr. Drucker shrugged. "I can only tell you what I observed in the autopsy."

"Is it possible Whitney died from leaking balloons, and that the track marks are unrelated?"

"Anything's *possible*, Ms. Vargas," the doctor said. "But how likely is it?"

"Still, I'd like to run those other toxicology tests. Who knows what Whitney was taking? I need the complete picture."

"Seems unnecessary, frankly, but I won't say no. I'll order up a generalized toxicology for common poisons and controlled substances. Given that it's Christmastime and we're understaffed, though, I have to warn you, it could take up to a month."

"A *month*? Isn't there some way to get it done faster?" Melanie asked.

"I can put a rush on it and see what we get."

"Thank you, I would appreciate that. The sooner the better."

Melanie and Ray-Ray took their leave and made their way to the elevator.

"Very fucking weird," Ray-Ray commented as they waited. "Girls like that swallowing."

"I agree, but it's a relief to finally have some solid evidence. It's looking pretty clear that Jay Esposito is responsible for these girls' deaths. And he probably knows where Carmen Reyes is, too."

22

THOUGH IT WAS WELL past rush hour, the number-six train was packed to the gills with commuters. Everybody was weighted down with parcels, having come straight from the Christmas shopping Melanie still hadn't found time for. She fought her way into the subway car just as the doors closed, ending up pressed against the glass with the sharp corner of someone's lavender Bergdorf's bag poking into her. Mmmm, Bergdorf's. Last year for Christmas, Steve had gone there and bought her an assortment of the *most* lavish Jo Malone perfumes and lotions. They came in gorgeous cream-colored boxes tied together with black ribbons and cost a pretty penny. Too bad she'd used them all, because Santa would *not* be visiting Melanie Vargas this year. At least until the settlement was finalized and she got a handle on her finances, her dollars were going to buy goodies for Maya. And she doubted anybody planned to buy Christmas presents for *her*.

The steep stairs of the Eighty-sixth Street station were slick with black water, the trampled remains of last night's snow. Melanie picked her way carefully up and emerged into a blast of cold air. Crossing Park Avenue, she looked at the row of Christmas trees stretching downtown as far as the eye could see, their white lights glittering like diamonds, and tried to muster some Christmas spirit. But she felt too alone on the elegant boulevard, watching her fellow New Yorkers bustle by laden with their expensive haul. Here she was, almost divorced, half crazy for some gorgeous, moody guy she barely knew and had to work with, who might or might not feel the same. Trying to be a mother to her daughter while working this insane case. Hardly a recipe for Christmas cheer.

The sight of Hector, her portly, balding doorman, cheered her. His Puerto Rican accent always reminded her of her father. What *didn't* was that he actually behaved in a fatherly manner.

"Hey, *mi'ja,* how you doing tonight?" he asked as he opened the door for her.

She sighed, not even trying to hide her feelings. "All right, I guess."

"Why so down? And don't deny it. I can tell."

Melanie glanced around the small lobby, dominated by an artificial Christmas tree and a partly lit electric Hanukkah menorah. Hector she trusted, but she didn't need the whole building knowing her business. Her first baby-sitter had quit after learning that Melanie and Steve were splitting up, and she'd been nervous ever since that the co-op board would have a cow, too, and get all nervous about Melanie's ability to make monthly maintenance payments. Luckily, none of her fellow tenants were around to eavesdrop at the moment.

"Just the usual, I guess. It's lonely facing the holidays being separated. I'm a little worried about money. That sort of thing."

"*No te preocupes, mi'ja.* I got the answer for your problems."

"You do?"

"Heck, yeah. You bring the little one over to my house on Christmas Day. My Manny's gonna be there. He's doing real good with his accounting business. Time he settled down. Nice girl like you, so pretty, who knows?"

Melanie had met Hector's Manny, and he wasn't for her. He might be making money as an accountant, but the boy's heart was still in the block. Which in his case meant he was a little too into girls with fake boobs and tattoos, who'd cook and clean for him. No thanks.

"Aw, Hector, that's sweet, but you know I'm not ready. Besides, Manny wouldn't be interested in somebody with a kid."

"Naw, he's fine with that."

"Well, listen, I'll think about it. Maybe after some more time goes by," she said, giving him a peck on the cheek.

She got her mail and leafed through it on the elevator. A pile of bills and a couple of Christmas cards. One of the cards had a San Juan postmark. Melanie ignored her father's handwriting, and opened the other one instead. It was from Amy Robards, a law-school classmate whom she hadn't seen in years. Amy had worked briefly at the same law firm as Melanie after graduation. Around the time Melanie went to the U.S. Attorney's Office, Amy married a senior partner, had three kids in rapid succession, put on forty pounds, and retired to Bedford to chair bake sales. Looking at Amy smiling out from the glossy photo card, ensconced among towheaded toddlers and a dull but steady-looking husband, Melanie was overwhelmed by a bitter wave of jealousy. Not that she wanted to turn back the clock in her own life. She hadn't liked being married to a two-timer, and Steve was in the process of proving he'd never change. But she couldn't help envying what this woman had. The contrast was just too stark: Amy so happily settled and Melanie without a clue where her own life was going.

A N HOUR LATER Melanie struggled out of a cab, juggling Maya and a shopping bag in one arm and a briefcase and folded stroller in the other. She pressed the buzzer to her sister's building with her elbow. It was nine-thirty, ten degrees, with a bitter wind blowing. The door buzzed, and she pushed it, stumbling toward the enormous, graffiti-covered freight elevator. Lofts! Linda was nuts to live down here. Melanie would take uptown any day.

"Gaaa, Mama," Maya said with a huge, wet smile, all gums and tiny front teeth. as they waited for the elevator. Her pudgy cheeks sparkled pink with cold. Melanie nibbled her daughter's ear where it poked out from a fleecy hat, eliciting giggles.

"You keep me going, you know that?" she whispered.

Upstairs, Linda opened the door, telephone pressed to her head, and motioned them inside. The bracelets on her manicured hand jingled like chimes. The foyer smelled of sandalwood perfume and scented candles.

"I know, but you *owe* me, Fab D," Linda was whining into the phone. "Okay, okay, fine."

Melanie studied her sister's outfit with dismay as she struggled after her. Linda had eventually agreed to baby-sit while Melanie went to Screen to supervise the buy. Granted, Linda was a fashion and entertainment reporter on a local cable channel. Given her position, she hardly stinted on the Puerto Rican glam. But even *she* wouldn't wear skintight gold lamé pants, a one-shouldered white top, and gold stilettos for dinner with baby. Would she?

"Lin, why are you dressed like that? You said you'd give me the location and then baby-sit!"

Linda waved her hand in annoyance.

"Fab D? I lost you for a minute, hon. . . . *What, again?* You attention ho! How many times can I plug your damn demo? All *right,* but only because I love your swishy black patootie to death. Okay, baby. Ciao."

Linda put down the phone.

"Would you take Maya before I drop her, please?" Melanie said.

"Is she clean?"

"Of course she's clean! You think I don't wash my daughter?"

Linda took Maya from Melanie's arms gingerly. "Don't get so offended. She got strawberry jam all over my white Michael Kors sweater last week, you know. Thank God I suck up to the guy at the dry cleaners."

"What were you doing wearing white to baby-sit anyway? And why are you so dressed up now? You said you'd watch her so I could check out this nightclub. I told you, it's *work.*"

Melanie stuck the stroller in a corner and dropped her shopping bag on the dramatic chaise longue that was the only place to sit in Linda's apartment. Linda's loft had once been separated into living and sleeping spaces, but she'd recently converted the sleeping area to a huge closet. The living area was now dominated by a canopy bed draped with fringed mosquito netting courtesy of one of Linda's decorator friends. The walls were painted in exotic stripes of lipstick red and gold. The once sleeping alcove, now closet, was divided off with elaborate gold draperies tied back with silk cords, continuing what Melanie thought of privately as the bordello theme.

"My friend Fabulous Deon, he deejays for Expo sometimes. I know he can get us into Screen, but he won't go unless I go," Linda said.

"This is law-enforcement business. You can't just tag along, and neither can he. All I need is the location of the club and the password."

"Are you arresting somebody?"

"No, nothing like that. Just poking around. But still, I'd rather keep you and your friend out of it. You never know. It could get dangerous."

"They know us at Screen. Nobody's gonna bother us there. Besides, there *is* no password. It's a velvet-rope-type thing, and you won't get in without me and Fab D by your side to say you're fly."

"So what am I supposed to do with Maya? It's way past her bedtime, and I can't take a one-year-old to a nightclub."

"Relax, *chica,* I took care of it. Mom's on her way over here right now. She'll take Maya back to your place and sit with her as long as we need," Linda said.

"How'd you arrange that?" Melanie's mother was even less interested in baby-sitting than her sister was.

"I'm telling you, ever since she started dating that widowed minister, she's very *familia*-oriented. She's trying to convince him she's marriage material. Unlike the rest of us."

"Speak for yourself. I was good at being married. It was my husband who fell down on the job," Melanie said wistfully.

"Oh, my God, that reminds me! I saw Steve in a club this weekend. I can't believe I forgot to tell you. He was with—"

"I don't want to hear it," Melanie said, shaking her head decisively.

"No, really, it was definitely him. You know, back when you first kicked him out, I was like, Hey c'mon, one little lapse, Mel, give the guy a break. I mean, people cheat, right? It's not the end of the world. But he's been on a rampage in the clubs since you two split. I told you about that time my friend Teresa saw him—"

"Lin, stop! Enough already. I don't need to hear every time he picks up some bimbo in a bar."

Melanie grabbed Maya from Linda's arms. She hugged her daughter close for a moment, then put her down and peeled off her pink snowsuit and fleecy hat. A stubby little ponytail on top of Maya's head sprang straight up. Melanie tweaked it playfully. Maya squealed and waddled away, toddling a few bowlegged steps before plopping down on the floor.

"Why not?" Linda asked.

"*Because.* It's not healthy. I'm trying not to feel sorry for myself, okay? Steve and I are legally separated, which was *my* choice. He's entitled to see other women, but still, I can deal with him better if it's not shoved in my face constantly."

"Deal with him? You mean, over the settlement negotiations?"

"That. Everything. He wants to spend Christmas with me and *la chiquita* here."

"You're not going to let him, are you?"

"He's her father. I couldn't stand it if he just disappeared out of her life, the way Papi did with us," Melanie said, a catch in her voice.

"You still obsessing about *that* ancient history? You know, ever since I wrote Papi and told him he was a rat bastard and I never wanted to hear from him again, I feel so much better. You should try it. It's very liberating."

"It's kind of an empty gesture to kick someone out of my life who's not even in it, don't you think? I just got a Christmas card from him from a totally new address. He signs it *'Feliz Navidad, Papi y familia.'*

That's it. No note saying he moved, no pictures of his kids, nothing. You believe that?"

"So tell him not to write to you. Then you won't feel bad when he sends you that impersonal bullshit."

Melanie thrust the shopping bag at her sister. "Here, help me figure out what to wear. I don't want to talk about this stuff anymore. Too depressing."

Linda rummaged through the shopping bag, her dark brows knitting into a frown. "You're kidding me, right?"

"I told you, mostly I own suits for work, and jeans. What about that red sweater? It's pretty sexy on. Or the black dress from when Steve and I were dating? It had a little tear, but I sewed it."

"Not if you plan to be seen in public with *me*! Get your butt in here," Linda said, flouncing through the gold curtains into her closet. Melanie picked up Maya and followed.

Inside the closet, mirrors covered one wall, reflecting hundreds of specialized shoe cubbies Linda had installed opposite. Four massive department-store-style metal clothing racks bearing extravagant garments in every color of the rainbow filled the rest of the space.

"*Quítate la ropa,*" Linda ordered, and disappeared into the racks.

Melanie stripped off the jeans and turtleneck she'd worn over to her sister's. She'd showered and blow-dried her hair when she went home to get Maya, and for reasons she couldn't explain—or didn't want to admit—donned her sexiest lingerie, a lacy black push-up bra and thong set trimmed in candy pink ribbon. Steve had given them to her for Valentine's Day last year, right around the time she began to suspect he was fooling around with that executive assistant. *You wish,* she'd thought, and stuck them in the back of a drawer. But tonight she'd pulled them out, and now she twirled around, checking herself in the mirror, fantasizing about how Dan's face would look if he saw her in them. How he'd come up to her, whisper to her in that incredible voice, back her up against the wall, put his hands all over her body—

¡Qué estúpida! Like she could afford to get obsessed with Dan O'Reilly again, with how lonely and vulnerable *she* was these days. She even did it with Steve a few weeks back when he came by to drop off Maya, that's how desperate she was for companionship—or, let's be honest, *sex.* She would never tell Linda. And yes, she regretted it, but it'd just *happened.* She'd been sitting on the sofa in the dark flipping channels and feeling depressed while Steve put Maya down in her crib. She'd looked up to find him standing in the doorway bathed in the blue light of the TV, staring at her with this incredibly potent combination of lust and nostalgia. Next thing she knew, he was on top of her and they were going at it like wild animals.

Not that there was any real danger they would slip into a reconciliation. Steve kept her on track. Lying naked on the couch afterward, half dozing, she'd heard a noise like the clicking of insects and looked over to find him tapping madly away on his BlackBerry. He'd been evasive when she asked him who he was texting. If she started thinking even for a second about getting back together, she could count on Steve to remind her why she'd left.

"Uh, what?" Melanie said, realizing Linda had been speaking to her.

"I *said,* I'm glad to see you finally took my advice and got yourself some cute knickers," Linda said, walking over and pinching Melanie's hips. "And you're looking real good, too. You were kinda porky there for a while, sis. What are you, on Zone or South Beach or something?"

"No, I just don't have time to eat."

Linda laughed.

"I'm serious," Melanie said.

"Hey, whatever it is, it's working. And I take it from your choice of undergarments you're planning to get lucky tonight?"

"*No!*" Melanie said, but she could feel herself blushing.

"Oh, wait one minute! I haven't seen that expression on your face since you were all crazy for that FBI hunk. Is there a new guy in the picture?"

"A new guy? Definitely not."

Linda scrutinized her. "You're not wearing that slutty underwear for my benefit, *chica*. Come on, give it up."

"It's not slutty."

"Hel*lo*, good girl. Slutty is a compliment."

"There's no new guy," Melanie insisted, still blushing.

"The *same* guy? He's back?"

"Dan? No. Well, I mean, he's assigned to my new case, but—"

"Assigned to your case!" Linda yelped and began hopping up and down, clutching herself. "Mel's got a boyfriend, Mel's got a boyfriend!" Maya, sitting on the floor playing with some plastic rings, looked at Linda and gave a hoot of hilarity. Melanie couldn't help laughing, too.

"Lin, I swear, sometimes I think you're still eight years old."

"That would make you ten, and, *chica,* with those curves you do *not* look ten."

Melanie watched in the mirror as her flamboyant sister waltzed around, holding on to a sparkly beige dress as if it were her dance partner. She was startled to see how alike she and Linda looked, with their shiny dark hair, almond eyes, and full lips. She thought of Linda as so much more beautiful than herself, but it wasn't true. Linda just acted the part, whereas Melanie was afraid to.

"Come on, spill it," Linda demanded. "What happened so far? And I want every gory detail. What he likes, the size of his—"

"Will you *stop*? Nothing's happened, and nothing's going to. Dan scares me too much."

"Don't be ridiculous. You're not afraid of anything."

"*This* guy, I am! When I get back into dating again, I'm taking it slow. He'd mess up my head, and I have Maya to think of after all."

"Huh. Well, okay, if that's how you feel. But I must say, I never saw a woman wear black lace panties for a guy she was planning to cold-shoulder."

"I'm not wearing them for *him*. I'm just wearing them."

"Yeah, right, Miss Jockey for Her. Like I believe that."

Linda held the beige dress up against Melanie, studying the effect in the mirror.

"Hmm, no. *Muy de modo* but too neutral. We need you in some bright, sexy colors, *chica*. Something that screams, Hello, FBI hunk, nail my *boricua* ass so I can go home and tell my sister all about it."

"Did you *hear* what I just said?"

"Oh, shut up and stop being so boring. Try this on, and we'll just see where your night ends up." Linda thrust a filmy scrap of tomato red fabric at Melanie.

"What is it?"

"It's a top, silly. D&G. Label whore that I am, you should thank your lucky stars I'm even *thinking* of lending it to you."

Melanie took the thing. There was barely enough to it to keep it on the hanger. She slipped it from its moorings and looked at it suspiciously.

"It won't bite you. Take off your bra, and I'll help you get into it," Linda said.

"Are you crazy? I *need* a bra."

"Oh, come on, it's a halter. It'll hold you up. I'm not on the itty-bitty-titty committee either, you know. Besides, the FBI hunk'll be on the edge of his seat, wondering if something's gonna pop out."

Melanie shook her head in disbelief.

"I'll fix it so it works, promise," Linda said, slipping the fabric over Melanie's head and carefully adjusting the ties behind her neck. Melanie looked at herself in the mirror.

"Wow," she said.

"Yeah. It's amazing what the right outfit can do. It makes you beautiful, keeps you young. It's almost like it cheats death."

"Right. I'll remember that the next time somebody shoots at me."

"Very funny, smart-ass. Oh, wait, I have the perfect pants! I scored 'em at a fashion show after I talked up the designer on air."

Linda disappeared back into the racks, emerging a second later with gauzy black chiffon pajama pants. Melanie stepped into them and zipped them up the side. They made her look thin and glamorous.

"Here, try these, too," Linda said, pulling sexy satin pumps from a white box with MANOLO BLAHNIK stamped in black letters across the cover.

Maya put down the plastic ring she'd been chewing on and leaned forward on her diapered bottom. "Shoes!" she cried, pointing.

"She's *your* niece, all right. That's only her fourth word," Melanie said with a laugh as she slipped on the stiletto-heeled pumps and studied herself in the mirror. Amazing what clothes could do. All of a sudden, she felt like a million bucks and life seemed full of possibilities.

Linda looked Melanie up and down approvingly. "You may or may not catch the bad guy, but I'll tell you one thing, *chica:* This FBI agent better watch the fuck out."

23

PATRICIA CHECKED HER WATCH for the fourth time. It was after hours. Holbrooke was deserted, and James—she hoped—was waiting for her at her apartment with a decent bottle of Bordeaux. The old building creaked and gasped all around her, steam radiators hissing, wind rattling the wavy glass in the ancient windows. Screw *charm*, this heating system was a goddamn joke. Patricia felt chilled to the bone. Who the hell did Hogan think he *was*, keeping her waiting?

Patricia was unpleasantly nervous. Her mind had been working overtime since this morning, when James had mentioned the so-called breach in their security. She hadn't believed him at first. Now, having investigated further, she knew he was right. She'd pulled up the endowment ledgers on the computer, both sets of them—the real and the doctored. A clever plan, if she did say so herself. Nobody but Patricia knew the *total* sum of the contribution pledges. Her private ledger reflected *all* the pledge money, but the doctored books, the ones for public consumption, reflected only *most* of it. A little missing here, a little missing there. No individual donor could know that the total amount was wrong. And so the public ledger held, thus far, about four million less than had actually been contributed. Not such a shortfall that anybody would notice, mind you. Even after her skimming, there was still a substantial amount of money going to the school—more than enough to hire architects and structural engineers and get that new building going.

And when the Van Allen pledge got wired in Friday night, all ten million of it . . . well, quite a lot of that was going to find its way into Patricia's private ledger. The new building would still be called the Van Allen Upper School. It would just be a bit smaller in terms of square footage. That's all. And Patricia would be *Mrs.* Senator Seward.

The problem was, the ledgers *had* been accessed—twice, earlier this morning, without her authorization. Try as she might, she couldn't figure out how that had happened. Both sets of books were on the Holbrooke computer system, but both were carefully disguised and password-protected. Patricia had fired the school's development director several months ago, for the very purpose of preventing anyone from discovering her scheme. Since then only one person other than Patricia herself had had access to the password. That person could not possibly have pulled up the books without her knowledge. So who had, then? James? But how had he managed? Someone else? Then who?

She checked her watch again, more anxiously this time. Patricia was in over her head, and she knew it. How had things gotten so crazy? She'd only intended to better herself, like any red-blooded American girl. Had she aimed too high? Twenty-five years ago, when her credentials weren't strong enough to land a job in the public-school system, Holbrooke had hired her happily. All they cared about was her look— young, pretty, blond, and fashionably dressed, appropriate for teaching the daughters of the rich. She'd had no idea what she'd be exposing herself to. The money was unthinkable, overwhelming. It took years of watchful coveting before Patricia even comprehended the full scope of it. The most important clues were also the subtlest. The quiet Hermès handbag that only a connoisseur knew cost fifteen thousand dollars. The fact that all the mothers had the same perfectly sculpted arms, courtesy of a few pricey society trainers who wouldn't work with outsiders even if they had the cash. The offhand mentions of staff, private jets, third and fourth homes that slipped out in casual conversation, things one toted up in full only after years of knowing a family. But over time she saw how it was, and the crush of jealousy just shriveled her.

Patricia's own attempts to marry money had failed. Once she hit her late thirties and had pretty much stopped meeting eligible men, she'd had no choice but to admit that to herself. The game was up. Then the only thing that slaked her bitter disappointment was exercising power over the families at school. Fortunately, her power was limitless. She held their daughters' futures in the palm of her hand. The mothers endlessly sucked up to her. It was not uncommon for families to let Patricia use their vacation homes, to give her a lift on their private jets and host her in Aspen or Bermuda, to take her out to lavish dinners or even give her expensive gifts at Christmas. They tripped over one another to do it, in fact, and nobody ever objected. Who'd make a fuss when Patricia had the final say on college recommendations? Everybody acted like it was completely normal. She'd even perfected the art—when college of choice hung in the balance—of wrenching nice, fat contribution checks out of the wealthier families. She'd simply drop a hint that a deficiency in the girl's record could be counterbalanced by the family's becoming more significant benefactors of the school. Colleges paid attention to the bottom line, Patricia would remind the parents, and were more likely to take on a middling student if the family were reliable donors. Patricia handled the whole process so deftly that families viewed it as realpolitik rather than extortion and even—pathetically—thanked her for her candor. When she skimmed money off those contributions, she was extremely careful. Nobody had ever so much as raised an eyebrow.

But ultimately her machinations were poor consolation. Patricia suspected that the mothers knew this as well as she did herself. When James came along and held out the hope of an eleventh-hour victory, was it any surprise that she leaped at the chance? That she fell hard? Did what he asked? And now, after she'd compromised herself, was it all to come to naught, because her plan had been discovered?

Patricia had no way of determining who had accessed the endowment account. If the Holbrooke computer system had some method of keeping track, she wasn't versed enough in its complexities to know. Asking somebody else to explore the issue for her would just rouse suspicion. So she'd considered her options and decided there was only one way. She'd called all the suspects in one by one and reminded them to toe the line. Reminded them of the consequences if they didn't. She had a little something on everyone. Teachers were human beings, after all, and human beings had their weaknesses. Holbrooke wasn't any worse than the outside world in that respect, but neither was it any better.

She'd dealt with Ted Siebert first, right after speaking with James this morning. She was certain Ted coveted the endowment money for himself. He also hated James with a passion—some feud stretching back years, having to do with James's embarrassing Ted at a board of trustees meeting. Ted watched Patricia's interactions with James with an eagle eye, suspecting something, looking for any evidence. But she'd been careful enough. There was nothing solid to go on. More to the point, Patricia knew things about Ted that his own wife surely didn't—for example, he regularly used the school's computer system to access gay-porn Web sites. It disgusted her, and yet it gave her power over him.

Likewise, the director of admissions had a gambling problem, and the head of the English department had three DWIs in the last ten years. She suspected each of them of being closet rebels, carrying chips on their shoulders, conspiring against her. And she'd now reminded each of them that she had the upper hand, simply by letting it slip that she *knew* but that she wasn't doing anything with the information. Not yet anyway.

That left one more candidate to deal with. Here he was now, rapping so self-effacingly on her office door.

"Come in!" she called.

"Hey, Patricia," Hogan said, strolling in like he hadn't just kept her waiting for an hour. He sat down in the chair in front of her desk. "I got the message you wanted to see me. What's up?"

"Where *were* you, Harrison? I've been looking for you for quite some time."

"Down in the lower gym, schmoozing with some of the junior class. These girls are going to need a lot of attention in the coming weeks, Patricia. We haven't even *talked* about the fact that this happened right before the holidays, when kids are already stressed to the max."

His earnestness bugged the hell out of her. She'd wipe that self-righteous smirk clean off his face.

"Students crying on your shoulder, hmm? It doesn't do to get too close to the girls, Harrison. I thought you were smart enough to understand that," she said.

Hogan positively blanched. Hah! This was going to be fun.

"What are you talking about?" he asked quietly.

"This is rather delicate. But it's my duty to speak up. It's come to my attention that you were engaged in an inappropriate relationship with Whitney Seward."

He sat up straight for once. "*What?* Who told you that? It's a complete lie!"

"Be silent, Harrison, and hear me out. This is a deeply serious matter, for Holbrooke and for your own future. I have solid evidence. I think you know what it is. You weren't particularly careful, were you?"

"Whitney was my student and my advisee," Hogan protested. "If we spent time together, it was only—"

"Please." She held up her hand. "I need to caution you not to speak further without representation."

"Are you kidding me?"

"Do I look like I'm joking?" Patricia's tone was quiet, menacing.

"What is this really about? You have an agenda here, Patricia, I know it."

"Don't try to weasel out of it. You were naughty, and you've been caught with your hand in the honeypot. Normally I would suspend you immediately, but I don't think the Holbrooke community could handle that right now, on top of these overdose deaths and with only a few days until the endowment campaign closes. But I felt it only fair to let you know, I have the evidence, and I could use it at any time. Do I make myself clear?"

.24

CARMEN DRIFTED IN and out of consciousness. When she was awake, sometimes she was lucid, sometimes she wasn't. When she knew what was happening, damn, it hurt so bad! She couldn't stand it. But not for herself. She thought only of Papi, wherever he was—home, somewhere, looking for her, waiting, going crazy. He must be tearing at his hair, pounding himself with his fists. Every second she felt Papi's agony. She imagined her captor, saw his cold eyes, remembered the gun he'd brandished at her. But in her mind she wasn't herself; she was her father, consumed by these terrible worries about his daughter. She saw her own death, bullets piercing her flesh. But she was Papi, visualizing her murder while sobbing over her dead body. It was his pain she experienced, not her own.

Eventually time stretched out and lost its meaning. Carmen began hallucinating. She knew she was hallucinating, but that didn't matter. The visions were blindingly real. A woman started visiting her in the closet, a woman who looked strangely like her dead mother. But she didn't talk like Mami had. This woman talked fancy, whereas Mami's English had barely been passable. And this woman was mean, whereas Mami had been very loving.

"Life is a nanosecond," the woman said. "Death is what lasts. Don't fight it."

"I can't die. Papi would be too sad. You already left him. He needs me." Carmen said this, even though she knew this woman was not her mother but rather a stranger masquerading as her mother.

"We don't choose when to die, Carmen. Death finds us, just like this man found you. When he comes back, he's going to kill you."

"No. I don't think so. Not right away anyway. He needs me to do something for him first."

"You're not going to do it, are you?"

"I have to. Otherwise he'll kill Lulu. He told me."

"And you believe him?"

"Of course I believe him. He killed Whitney and Brianna. He has the devil inside him, I know."

"Then you're making a deal with the devil. That's not smart, Carmen. You'll burn in hell. Resist him, say no. Let him kill you. It's not so bad where I live. Come, and we'll spend time together."

"Please, don't tell me to do that!" Carmen cried. "I need to save Lulu! I need to see Papi again! What the man's asking is wrong, but it's not so terrible. Who will it hurt if I do what he asks? Then maybe I could even escape—"

"*Escape?* You're a foolish girl if you think that's possible. Look at the way he tied you up. You'll never get out of this closet," the woman said.

"He *has* to take me out eventually, if I'm going to do what he's asking. Maybe I could escape then."

"No you can't. He has a gun."

"So maybe he won't use it."

The woman just laughed, an ugly cackle, nothing like Mami's.

"What's so funny?"

"*You* are, the way you fool yourself. How much time do you think you have left, Carmen? A day? A few hours? You don't even know how long ago it was that Whitney and Brianna died, do you? You have no clue."

"It can't be *that* long, because I'm still alive. If I'd gone a week without food and water, I'd be dead. I mean, I *am* still alive, right? . . . Right!" Carmen asked nervously.

"I'm not going to tell you the answer to that one."

"Someone will find me!" Carmen cried, in tears. "Someone will come rescue me, I know!"

"What are you talking about? Stupid girl! What makes you think anybody's even looking for you?"

25

THE TEAM HAD AGREED to stage out of a pub a block from the Worth Street subway stop. When Melanie and Linda arrived, the place was overflowing with drunken Wall Streeters who'd begun their Christmas revels early. Melanie stood near the door and scanned the crowd. After the bracing wind outside, the sudden heat and noise made her dizzy. No sleep and very little food— she was running on fumes. She shrugged out of her coat, taking a deep breath.

"You see your friends?" Linda shouted over the din.

"Not yet. Looking."

"Hey," Linda called after a moment. She leaned closer to Melanie. "There's a major hottie in the corner checking you out like you're a thick, juicy steak and he's a starving man."

"Where?"

"Over there, but— No, don't look, you no-brain!"

"That's Dan."

"What?"

"C'mon," Melanie said, grabbing Linda by the arm.

Dan *was* staring at her. And somehow, in these clothes, in this place, she could handle it. As she walked toward him, their eyes locked, and everything else fell away. Blood pounded in her veins. She forgot about their almost love affair, their sort of breakup, the nights she'd spent alone obsessing over the way things had ended. She looked right back at him and let herself remember how he kissed.

"That's *him*? His body is *sick*," Linda said.

"Shut up now, or I'm gonna smack you," Melanie said.

Bridget Mulqueen and Trevor Leonard, sitting on bar stools beyond Dan, popped into view as they drew near. She waved to them, not even trying to make herself heard over the racket. Dan stood up.

"Look at *you*," was all he said, but there was a soft light in his eyes that she wanted to memorize.

"My sister dressed me up so I could pass muster. This is Linda. She's gonna get us into Screen."

Dan shook Linda's hand. "Pleased to meet you."

"Likewise," Linda said. "Mel mentioned you once or twice."

"Oh, yeah?" He glanced at Melanie, looking gratified.

"Enough small talk," Melanie said. "We need to go over our plan."

"Was she always so serious like this?" Dan asked Linda.

"Yeah, since she was a kid. That's how she got into those fancy schools."

"I admire that about her," he said.

"Will you guys stop?" Melanie said, though she was eating it up. "Let's talk business."

She had told Linda that they were investigating heroin dealing at area nightclubs but given no indication that Esposito himself was their target or that the case was relating to the Holbrooke girls' deaths. She'd disclosed enough to warn Linda of the risks of the operation, without giving her details that could compromise their plan or put Linda in additional danger.

"So how do you know where Screen is?" he asked Linda.

"A friend of mine deejays for Expo sometimes, and he gets me in. Tonight they're set up in this abandoned subway station a few blocks from here. They bribed some guys from the MTA. You get on a certain train, and if you're on the list, they let you stay on when they go out of service. When they turn around at the end of the line, they open the doors for you—and presto, you're in Screen."

"It must be the old City Hall station," Dan said, nodding. "It was the jewel of the IRT before they shut it. The tile work on the arches is some of the most beautiful you're ever gonna see."

"Have you been in there?" Melanie asked.

"Yeah. Buddy of mine in the transit police took me on a tour once." He leaned closer to Melanie. "I know you think I'm about as sharp as a marble, but I'm really interested in stuff like that. I'll even go to an arty movie now and then."

"I don't think that," Melanie said, looking up into his crystal blue eyes.

"You don't?"

"No." She shook her head.

"So listen," Linda shouted. "My buddy Fabulous Deon can get a few of us in, but I'm not sure how many. And everybody has to look the part." She studied Dan, frowning.

"I don't fit the bill, huh?" he asked.

"To me you're a little too big and clean-looking. Honestly, you look like a cop," Linda replied.

Dan looked handsome and respectable in khaki pants and a navy V-necked sweater with a T-shirt under it. Melanie felt offended on his behalf.

"I don't know what you're *talking* about," she protested to Linda. "He looks like every one of these traders in here. I bet they could get into Screen, so why can't he?"

"I'm just saying—"

"Hey, it's okay," Dan said. "No need to have family strife over this. I know the layout. I'll figure out how to get myself in on the tracks. But those two over there"—he nodded toward Bridget and Trevor—"should go in the front door to make it believable."

"And me," Melanie said.

"Who said you were going in?" Dan asked.

"Bernadette. She wants me to vet the ops plans, make sure nothing gets screwed up. It's sensitive stuff, and she doesn't trust Bridget or Trevor."

Dan took her by the elbow and pulled her aside, out of Linda's earshot.

"You got to be fucking kidding me," he said. "Even if the Bureau let prosecutors review our ops plans, which we don't, and even if we let prosecutors ride along on buys, which we *totally* don't, *I* wouldn't let *you* put yourself in harm's way."

"Well, thank you. I appreciate your concern. But this is not your call. Bernadette wants it done this way. This is an ENTF case, not a Bureau case, and Albano's in agreement with her. So you're outvoted."

He shook his head in disbelief. "Craziest thing I ever heard. And don't pretend you don't agree."

"Hey, what's the big deal? I'll keep out of the way. With you there I'm not so worried about things going wrong, but still, I'm the one who looked Trevor in the eye and promised he'd be safe. Remember what happened to Rosario Sangrador," Melanie said, and at the very mention of Rosario's name, her eyes welled up. She'd never forgive herself for that.

Dan's face softened. "It means that much to you?"

"Of course it does."

"Okay, I'll go along with you, but listen up, sweetheart. You step out of line and get crazy on me, I'm pulling the plug on the drug buy. We clear on that?"

"Dan—"

"Just say yes. That's the only answer I'll accept."

"I'm not *planning* to do anything risky. I promise."

He looked at her quizzically, then broke into a grin. "Don't think you're getting over on me here. I see what you're doing. Jeez, you lawyers, always with the sneaky language."

"If you're done scolding me, can we go over the plan?"

"What do you want to know?"

"First off, is Trevor wired?" she whispered, glancing around to make sure nobody was eavesdropping. With the noise level in here, not much danger of that.

"Not until we get the lay of the land," Dan said. "Who knows, they could be doing pat-downs at the door. Besides, with the club underground in the subway tunnel, it'd be tough to pick up a signal anyway."

"Has Trevor been searched?"

"Yes, ma'am. I go by the book, every time."

Before making a controlled buy, a careful agent searched the cooperating witness to prevent him from sneaking in his own drugs and claiming he'd bought them from the target. For the price of a few Baggies and a little perjured testimony, many a drug dealer had bought himself a nice sentencing reduction without doing the heavy lifting of actually infiltrating the target's organization. Dan was too thorough to let an informant scam him like that.

"What's the ops plan once everybody's inside?" Melanie asked.

"Bridget sticks with Trevor every step of the way. He makes the contact with Expo's people, but she does the hand-to-hand. She tries to buy dime bags. We recorded the serial numbers on the buy money in advance 'cause that's procedure, but prob'ly we let the money walk this time. Don't make any arrests, try to build to something bigger. Ideally get a cell number or something, see if we can work up a wiretap."

Melanie had been listening with great attentiveness. Now she looked over at Bridget and Trevor, who were laughing together conspiratorially. Bridget was wearing tight jeans, a black T-shirt, and boots, and she'd made up her eyes. She actually looked cute in a butch sort of way, but very young.

"You really think she's up to this?" Melanie asked.

"Only one way to find out."

"Seriously, Dan."

"Look, she was on the mark with that text message before. I think we're underestimating her. Weren't you the one who said to give her the benefit of the doubt?"

Melanie sighed. If something got screwed up here . . . man, she couldn't even stand to think about it. Still, there wasn't much more she could do. In fairness to Dan, ops were really his baby.

"Okay," she said, nodding.

He signaled to the rest of their group. "We ready?"

Linda looked at her watch. "Yeah. Fab D should be at the station by now."

"Let's go," Melanie said.

FABULOUS DEON KNEW how to command a room. Resplendent in a calf-length mink coat, orange trousers, and patent-leather spats, he sported short, bleached-blond braids that stuck up all over his head like horns. His brown face was plump and sweetly feminine, his eyes sparkling with silver glitter eye shadow, so that the wispy little soul patch on his chin came as a surprise. His dubious gender and wild attire drew amused looks from some passersby in the subway station, while most others simply ignored him. This was New York, after all. Still, Melanie thought, they weren't sneaking in under the radar with *this* dude as their escort.

Deon waved excitedly to Linda, who rushed up to him.

"Hello, gorgeous!" Deon cried, double-air-kissing Linda while looking past her at Melanie. "Don't *tell* me this is your gorgeous sister! So much fabulousness in one family is just too much to *bear*!"

"Don't worry, D," Linda said. "She's not really fabulous. I just dressed her up tonight."

"She *has* to make a comment," Melanie said, smiling broadly. This guy was a trip. No wonder Linda liked him.

"Really, *mee*-ow. Don't listen to her, sweet sister! You're absolutely bey*ond.* The problem won't be getting you into Screen, it'll be fighting them *off.*"

"Thank you! This is my new best friend," she said to Linda, as Fabulous Deon air-kissed her, too.

"Those are her buds over there. What do you think?" Linda asked Deon, pointing to where Bridget and Trevor stood, beside a grimy pillar, going over some last-minute instructions.

"Rest easy," Deon said. "The pierced boy with dreadlocks will fit right in. Blondie's no problem either. If she were a bit scrawnier, she'd even look heroin *chic.*"

Heroin—he doesn't know how right he is, Melanie thought. "So, Deon, did Linda fill you in on what I do? I want you to have your eyes open. Because there's some risk—"

"Oh, pshaw! I bring people to clubs all the time without the teensiest clue who they are. That is par for the course. Nobody would ever dream of holding it against me if somebody turns out to be a narc."

"Still, a drug bust in Expo's club would reflect badly on him, and he's no pussycat."

"Funny you should mention that. The fact is, I have a bone to pick with Jay Esposito. The man owes me over three thousand dollars for work I've done for him and never been paid for. And when I tried to collect, he blackballed me at several other clubs. You have no idea how helpless I felt until La Linda called me up tonight. You're doing me a big favor by putting me in a position to exact some payback."

"If you're sure," Melanie said.

"I'm sure."

"Oh, and it's okay to use Linda's real name. They'll probably recognize her from TV anyway. But you and Linda only just met me and these others guys at a club earlier tonight, okay, and you don't know us very well."

Deon nodded. "Smart idea, precious. Do you have a favorite *alias?*"

They worked out fake names for everybody on Melanie's team.

"Ah, here's our train, my chickens!" Deon exclaimed, as a south-bound six rumbled into the station.

They all got on.

"Come, children. We have to go to the first car," said Fabulous Deon.

They'd gotten on about five cars from the front, so they slowly made their way forward through the moving train. Heavy sliding metal doors at both ends of the cars opened onto narrow platforms. Melanie stepped carefully across the couplings as the train bucked ahead, wary of trip-ping in the borrowed stiletto heels, holding her breath against the acrid fumes and ricocheting sparks in the open tunnels. When they reached the first car, it was relatively empty, and they all found seats on a bench across from the conductor's booth. Within minutes the train pulled into the Brooklyn Bridge station, opening its doors and turning off its lights to indicate it was going out of service. An announcement came on, telling everybody to exit.

"Stay here," Deon said, and went to knock on the conductor's booth.

The door slid open. Deon conversed briefly with the heavyset man inside, who consulted a list and nodded. Cash changed hands. Deon re-turned to his seat and flashed them an "okay" sign. A few minutes later, its lights still off, the train lurched forward. Looking out the window, Melanie saw blackness. A moment later the tracks curved, the train reached its southernmost point and just began to turn sharply uptown. A tumultuous scene came into view. Spotlights bounced off the soaring, tiled arches of a dimly lit, turn-of-the-previous-century subway station. The platform was mobbed with hundreds of writhing bodies dancing to earsplitting techno-pop music.

Melanie leaned forward and made eye contact with Bridget. "Are you all set?" she asked in a low tone, so Linda and Deon wouldn't hear.

Bridget took a deep breath. "No prob. If Esposito sells it, we'll find it."

The subway stopped; its doors opened.

"This is us," Fabulous Deon said, standing up.

They followed him off the train into the hot press of the crowd. Within minutes Bridget and Trevor had disappeared. Melanie would just have to trust the young detective to do her job properly and keep a watchful eye on Trevor. In the meantime she'd do some snooping around herself.

"What's the plan?" Melanie shouted into Fabulous Deon's ear.

"Let's hit the bar. This way."

Melanie and Linda followed as Fabulous Deon snaked his way through the densely packed crowd. The revelers were all young and gorgeous, the cream of New York City's clubgoers in all their finery. Pants were tight, tops revealing, and heels high, yet everybody managed to look sleek and sophisticated rather than cheesy. Melanie felt relieved Linda had dressed her up; she wouldn't have had a clue what to wear otherwise, and she would've stuck out like a sore thumb. Although the place was so jammed that most likely nobody would've noticed. The noise level hovered at a roar, swelling to a deafening clamor every few minutes as a train screeched into the station to discharge new revelers.

After waiting in line to check their coats, Melanie, Linda, and Fabulous Deon fought their way up to a mahogany bar set against a wall under an elaborate tile mosaic that spelled out "City Hall." The three curvaceous blond bartenders wore identical low-slung jeans and tiny halter tops that revealed pierced navels. After several attempts Linda got a bartender's attention and ordered them apple martinis. When the drinks came, Melanie took a sip of hers and gasped.

"Powerful," she choked out, eyes tearing up.

"They have a heavy hand here," Linda said. "It's one of the reasons Expo does well. He doesn't stint on the liquor. Speak of the devil— that's *him*. Told you he always puts in an appearance."

Linda nudged her and gestured toward a tall, muscular guy with a shaved head who stood between two lithe models at the far end of the bar. Jay Esposito looked every inch the mobbed-up nightclub mogul.

He was maybe forty, with handsome, Mediterranean features and dark eyebrows. In the middle of a New York winter, his attire was pure South Beach—a white linen suit and a black silk T-shirt setting off a deep tan, an enormous diamond stud glittering in one ear. As she watched, he threw his head back and guffawed, revealing a flash of white teeth. Melanie could see why a messed-up wild child like Whitney Seward would be attracted to this guy. He gave off criminal charisma like musk.

The target was right there in front of her. *Down, girl, down.* She should stay where she was. Sit back and allow events to take their course without injecting herself. Let the agents do their job. She scanned the jam-packed club, looking for Bridget and Trevor. Wherever they were, they weren't anywhere near Expo. Still, it wasn't her place. Even if this opportunity slipped through their fingers, surely somehow another would come along. She'd find Carmen Reyes anyway. Right?

Melanie turned to her sister abruptly. "Introduce me," she snapped, gesturing toward Esposito.

"I don't know him. But Fab D can hook us up."

Fabulous Deon was busy hitting on the bodybuilder type standing next to him at the bar. Linda tapped Deon on the shoulder. He leaned over, lips pursed in an annoyed moue.

"Honeychild, I am otherwise engaged."

"Fab D, are you blind?" Linda said. "That guy's straight."

"You think so?"

"Mos' def. Come introduce us to Expo before you get the shit kicked out of you."

"Oh, yes. I'm going to en*joy* this. Come along."

Deon sashayed ahead, beckoning to them to follow. As they approached, Esposito caught sight of Deon and waved at him with a fat cigar held between thumb and forefinger.

"Deon," Esposito said in a whiny voice, "why aren't you working tonight?"

"Funny you should ask, sire. Perhaps because you didn't *book* me and haven't paid me for the last six times you *did*?"

"Yeah, well, whaddaya want, things've been slow. Maybe if you'd stop whining like a little bitch, I'd tell my booker to call you." Esposito looked at Melanie and Linda appraisingly. "So introduce me to your friends."

"This is Linda Vargas, from Channel Sixteen, and her friend . . . uh . . . what did you say your name was, precious?" Deon asked.

"Marilyn Corona," Melanie said to Expo. "I just met these guys at another club, and they dragged me over here. They said Screen was way cool, and they're right."

As Esposito's eyes raked over her body, Melanie imagined she saw a flicker of suspicion. "Yeah? What club were you just at?" he asked.

"Railroad Forty-seven," Deon answered quickly, thank God, because Melanie couldn't've come up with a club name to save her life.

"Yeah, that place is a fucking pit," Esposito said, seeming mollified. "What're you girls drinking?"

"Appletinis," Linda replied.

"Cindy, apple martinis over here for my friends," he called to one of the blond bartenders, who slapped fresh drinks on the bar for them instantly. At Esposito's merest gesture, several patrons vacated their bar stools so Melanie and Linda could sit down.

"Thank you," Melanie said.

"Don't mention it." He leaned across her and mashed out his cigar in the remnants of somebody's drink. She caught a whiff of spicy cologne.

"Good crowd tonight, Expo," Linda said loudly, arching her back so her chest stuck out. It worked, because Esposito started talking to her cleavage.

"Yeah, we're busy this week. People still in town, but they're celebratin'," he said.

"You really come up with some hot locales. I'm crazy for this subway thing. In fact, I'd love to feature it in my nightlife segment." Linda was looking up at Esposito from under perfectly mascaraed eyelashes. Melanie nearly laughed out loud at her sister's blatantness. The girl *loved* to work the celebs.

"Nah, you know, I like press on my big clubs, but Screen I keep on the DL or else it loses its cachet."

"Oh, sure, I get it."

"You wanna cover the bash I'm doing down in Palm Beach on New Year's Eve, though, I'll get you on the list." Something behind them seemed to catch his eye. "Hold on a second," he said, and walked away.

Linda leaned over. "You think he likes me? He could really help my career, you know."

"You're not serious!" Melanie wrinkled her nose.

"*Chica,* that's why God invented dimmer switches."

"His looks aren't bad, Lin. It's the fact that he's a major criminal that bothers me."

"That's just PR! He cultivates that image to promote his clubs."

"Yeah, why do you think *I'm* here?" she said under her breath.

Melanie restrained herself from regaling Linda with tales of the evidence against Expo. Doing that while sitting in his bar was not a smart idea. She glanced around and spotted him, standing out like a beacon in his white suit. He was talking to an enormous guy with an angry, dime-size scar on his left cheek—presumably the bodyguard who'd been asking about the case in Judge Warner's courtroom earlier today. As she watched, they both turned and looked directly at her. The little hairs on Melanie's arms stood on end.

Calm down, she told herself. Gabriel Colón had said nothing when those thugs visited the courthouse looking for information, and Melanie was using a false name. Esposito couldn't possibly have a clue who she was. Granted, Linda had given her real name, and the two of them *did* look alike. But still . . .

The bodyguard seemed to melt away into the crowd. Esposito

walked casually back to the bar and threw his arm around Melanie's shoulder. Claustrophobia overwhelmed her instantly, but she steeled herself to accept his touch. A young girl was missing, and this might be a significant opportunity to find out more.

Copying Linda, Melanie smiled up at Esposito through flirtatious lashes.

"You're back," she said, in her most seductive voice, like she'd been waiting with bated breath.

"You're set, the botha youse. I put your names on all my lists. Anything you want in my clubs, just ask."

That must've been what he'd been talking to the bodyguard about. She breathed a small sigh of relief.

"Cool," Linda said, nodding but looking at Melanie with obvious confusion.

Esposito's thick fingers caressed Melanie's exposed back. She forced herself not to pull away. She'd make conversation, see where it went. If he liked her, maybe he'd give her some private cell number they weren't aware of or tell her some unknown address.

"It must be a lot of pressure, being a celebrity and all," she said, looking up at him seductively.

"Fuckin' A. But I love every second of it. You wanna know what my secret is?"

"You bet I do."

"Work hard, play hard. Do business all day, party all night. Blows off the steam."

"I'll drink to that," Melanie said, and took a swig of the appletini. It was going down easier with every minute that passed.

"Hey, if you like to have a good time, I can hook you up," Expo said, his fingers inching down her back toward her derriere.

"Yeah? What've you got in mind?"

"What's your pleasure? I have a little office in the back where I transact my private business. I can arrange whatever goodies you like. You name it, we got it."

Esposito's office, which was full of *drugs*? How tempting was *that*? But no, really, she'd promised Dan—no heroics. Well, maybe "promised" was too strong a word. Hadn't it been more like a statement of intention? And here circumstances had changed and all. . . .

"You interested or not?" Esposito demanded. "Because if not, plenty of others are."

"I'm game," Melanie said. She *had* to do this. Carmen was still missing.

"What about you?" Expo asked Linda, and then he winked, saying, "I can handle two girls at once."

Nervous as Melanie was about being alone with this guy, no way was she exposing Linda to danger.

"I'm not into that," Melanie said firmly. "She's here with someone anyway, right?"

Linda's eyes widened. Melanie couldn't tell if her sister understood what was going on or not. "Ri-ight," Linda said, hesitantly at first, then, "yeah, I'm with somebody."

"What the hell, it was worth a shot. Catch you later, then. Come on, you," Esposito said, yanking Melanie to her feet. The room swam. She'd been stupid to guzzle that drink, but it tasted so good going down. Man, she was pathetic at holding her liquor.

"Hey, Linda," Melanie said, putting all the significance she could manage into her facial expression, "find my friends and tell them I'm hanging out with Expo, okay? Will you do that for me, so they know where I am?"

"Okay."

Esposito took Melanie firmly by the arm and began to steer her toward the far end of the subway platform, where the tiled walls curved away into the blackness of the tunnel. Melanie threw a final, imploring glance over her shoulder to Linda, who had already turned away and was heading toward the dance floor. Melanie *thought* that Linda had understood, that she'd go find Bridget and give her a heads-up. God, she hoped so.

Esposito's powerful fingers bit painfully into her wrist as he pulled her through the crowd. He leaned over, his lips grazing her ear. "I love to party with Spanish girls, you know."

Oh, great, score one for *la raza*.

"Really?"

"Yeah. What's your name again?"

"Marilyn."

"You remind me of this old girlfriend of mine, Mirta. She was hot. Unbelievable blow jobs, this girl could give. She had no gag reflex. She died, though. Very sad."

"How'd that happen?" Melanie asked, her antennae up. No gag reflex. Could come in handy for more than just blow jobs. But Esposito acted like he hadn't heard her.

They had reached the far end of the platform. Esposito pulled a small flashlight from his pocket and shone it into the tunnel beyond. Melanie heard scurrying noises as the beam of light bounced off grimy walls, illuminating nothing. God, it was dark in there. As if from nowhere, the bodyguard with the bullet-hole scar materialized, nodded to Esposito, and took up a position at the edge of the tunnel. Even if somebody came looking for her now, Melanie had the sneaking suspicion Bulletface wouldn't let them pass. Whether Esposito wanted sex or had something more sinister in mind, Melanie was forced to admit that this was shaping up into a pretty bad idea. She needed to get away from this guy. Now.

"I think I heard rats," she said, stopping dead at the edge of the tunnel and beginning to backpedal. "I'm not going in there."

Had Linda found Bridget or Dan? Where the hell were they? She turned frantically, her eyes searching the turbulent crowd to no avail. Melanie was running out of time. Esposito tightened his grip on her wrist just as another number-six train roared onto the curving tracks.

"Fuck the rats, hon," Esposito said, yanking her practically off her feet. "I'll take care a' ya. Let's go."

26

CHELSEA PIERS WAS not a place he would normally choose to visit on a night like this, with a frigid wind blowing off the Hudson. Hell, there were icebergs bobbing in the river; he could see them from here. Fucking winters. Whatever happened to global warming? Urban renewal had turned the piers into a city kid's sports paradise—bowling alleys, climbing walls, and the like housed in brightly painted buildings. The transvestites and drug dealers of years past were long gone, but it was still a no-man's-land down here. Dimly lit, desolate. The perfect place to corner a vulnerable young girl. Which was exactly why he'd come.

There was so much information on the Internet if you had the first clue where to look. Like Lulu Reyes's ice-skating schedule, for example. There for all to see, with minimal digging. The evening hours were cheapest, it turned out, and the girl ranked competitively in her age group. She came here all by herself. People were so careless, so arrogant. They assumed that nobody would ever want to hurt them or their children. They almost deserved it, when you thought about it.

To get to the Sky Rink, you had to pass through a cavernous, deserted parking garage. His shoes had soft soles; they didn't make a sound on the concrete. Even if they did, the wind howling through the open rafters would mask the noise. Lulu would come this way when her ice time was over, huddled in her parka against the bitter night, and go wait alone at the bus stop. Nobody was around. It was very dark. Lulu was exhausted, grief-stricken, distracted. She wouldn't notice anything until it was too late, and then the river was right there to dump the body. Not that he planned to do that tonight. He needed her alive, to ensure her sister's cooperation. It was tempting, though. He had to admit, he was beginning to enjoy killing people, even though murder wasn't in the original game plan.

The big metal elevator heaved and shimmied its way up to the Sky Rink. He came out into a large seating area that reeked of what he first thought was vomit and then realized was the soggy cheese on the pizzas at the concession stand. A bunch of janitors sat around watching the Islanders game on a wide-screen TV mounted high on the far wall. None of them gave him so much as a glance, which was lucky, because the place was lit up like the Fourth of July. Anybody looking would have no problem identifying him later. But he wasn't worried. Like he always said, people were oblivious.

There were two rinks, one on either side of the seating area. He chose the one on the left. Got it on the first try. Lulu was immediately recognizable, nearly alone on the ice at this hour. She had the stringy limbs of a colt and an adolescent awkwardness, but you could tell she'd be really good with the proper coaching. A lot of the elements were already in place: impressive technical skill for her age, a ferocious energy in the way she attacked the moves. But she lacked artistry. He should really stop, though, shouldn't he? It wouldn't do to start thinking of Lulu as too much of a person. Better to keep his emotional distance and be free to take whatever action proved most . . . advantageous.

He climbed the aluminum bleachers and took a seat front and center. All she'd have to do was look up once and she'd see him. He had no doubt that Lulu would immediately understand why he was there. She wasn't stupid, and she knew enough about what had happened to the other girls. She *must*, or else she would have told the cops by now how to find her sister. Because she'd definitely seen him the other night.

He sat there for a while, the cold seeping into his bones as Lulu skated and skated. Jumps and spins and arabesques. Eventually she turned and began gliding smoothly toward the half door that led off the ice. That was when she looked up and saw him—and instantly tripped over her skates, tumbling facefirst to the hard, gleaming surface.

27

ESPOSITO PULLED MELANIE along a narrow ledge above the tracks. Light poured into the tunnel, courtesy of the headlamp of the number-six train that sat spitting and heaving in the station like some prehistoric beast. She'd better be damned careful of her footing: In a second the train would roar by, ready to eviscerate anything—any*body*—in its path. The thought that Esposito knew who she was, that he might decide to push her onto the tracks, was far-fetched. She tried to tell herself this but still couldn't seem to shake the terrible image from her mind. Esposito just gave off that vibe. And besides, she was doing something completely reckless.

Like most New Yorkers, Melanie knew by heart the sounds of a subway train gearing for takeoff. She listened to the familiar sequence now with intense focus. The singsong warning bells that accompanied the closing doors. The hissing as the brakes released. And finally—as her chest heaved with panic, as Esposito grabbed her arms with power-ful hands—the thunderous rumble of the train moving into the tunnel, heading smack for her. She screamed, throwing her body weight toward the wall, away from the tracks. Esposito laughed and, holding tight to her bare arms, let her pull him along, using gravity and his bulk to trap her against the slick tiles. In an instant, the train was gone, and she was twisting away to avoid his sloppy tongue kiss. It seemed he hadn't in-tended anything beyond a grope.

"You're a crazy one," he said. "I like that in a woman. Let's see what other tricks you got up your sleeve. My office is right here."

He pushed open a metal door set into the tile wall to reveal a small, brightly lit storeroom. It was meagerly furnished, with a couple of low foam sofas, a card table strewn with papers, and, leaning incongruously against the wall, a sleek leather bag holding a full set of titanium golf clubs. Her heart was still pounding with adrenaline as she quickly scanned the room. She didn't see any drugs—or anyplace to hide drugs either. Esposito pulled the door closed behind them and advanced toward her.

"Hey," Melanie said, backing away, "where's the candy store you promised me?"

"Just using me to get hooked up? That's not very nice, is it?"

"You *offered.*"

"I need a little showing of good faith first. Like one of them special Spanish-girl blow jobs."

He reached for his fly. She started to gag. So much for her resemblance to good old Mirta.

Just then the metal door flew open with a crash.

"What the fuck are you doing?" Dan O'Reilly demanded from the threshold.

"Who are you?" Esposito asked.

"That's my girlfriend, asshole!" He turned to Melanie. "Answer me, you slut. What are you doing in here with this scumbag?"

"Nothing," she said, shrinking away like she was afraid of Dan. "I swear, baby."

Dan stepped into the room and grabbed her by the arm. "You think I don't know what you're up to? I can't turn my back on you for ten seconds without you spreading your legs for some lowlife. You're coming with me."

"Yo, calm down, pal, nothing happened," Esposito said, making no move to stop them as Dan pretended to drag Melanie toward the door.

"Stay the fuck away from her, or I promise you you'll regret it," Dan warned.

Esposito just waved his hand nonchalantly. He let them go without a fuss, like it was nothing to him. But as she and Dan passed through the metal door, Melanie cast Esposito a final, curious glance and found him looking at her with cunning eyes.

28

AFTER A QUICK SEARCH failed to turn up anybody else from their team, Melanie and Dan decided to hop the next six out. She left a message on her sister's cell saying she was safe and another for Bridget telling her to come back to the pub where they'd met earlier once she'd completed the buy.

"We had a deal," Dan said as they settled into a booth at the pub twenty minutes later. He glared at her, so angry his breathing was rapid. "That was way out of line, what you did back there. You put yourself in danger, and other people, too. Prosecutors shouldn't work undercover. They don't know what the fuck they're doing, so they don't take basic precautions. Like a wire and a backup team and a prearranged signal for when things go south."

He paused for breath.

"You done?" she asked.

"*No,* I'm just getting started."

"Oh, come on, Dan, I wasn't looking to work undercover, and you know it. Bernadette *ordered* me to go to the club to monitor Trevor. It was just chance that I met Esposito. Once he told me he had drugs in that room, what was I supposed to do? Ignore the lead? This is an urgent matter. Am I the only one who remembers that Carmen Reyes is still missing?"

"Esposito lied. There were no drugs in that room. I checked it out before you ever went in there."

"Fine, he lied. How was I supposed to know?"

"Any idiot could see the guy was just trying to get into your pants. You're not taking any more risks like that. I won't allow it."

"What are you talking about? *You* take risks every day."

"That's my fucking *job*. It's what I'm trained for. You're a lawyer, not a cop."

"Hey, I can handle myself, all right? You have no business telling me what to do."

"Yeah? Whose fault is that?" he snapped back, eyes blazing.

A young waitress dressed in black pants and a white shirt came over and swiped at their table desultorily with a damp rag. "Menus or just drinkin'?" she asked.

Melanie stared at Dan, taken aback by his last comment, but he deliberately avoided her gaze. After a moment she gave up.

"I missed dinner," she said, sighing. "I could eat something."

"Yeah, okay. Me, too."

The waitress left them menus. Melanie studied hers for a second, then peeked over the top of it, watching him as he perused his. Whose fault *was* it that they weren't together? He seemed to be implying it was hers. A pang of longing swelled her chest, making it hard to breathe. Even when they argued, being around him felt so right. This thing between them didn't want to die, and maybe she shouldn't let it. Life was too short. Weren't they wasting time, being apart?

He looked up and caught her staring. "What?"

"Shouldn't we talk?"

"About what?"

"You know. You and me. Us. Before."

"What's there to say?" he demanded angrily.

"I don't know. Never mind."

Her heart sank. It must've showed on her face, because Dan's expression softened noticeably.

The waitress came back. Dan ordered a cheeseburger and a beer,

Melanie a club sandwich and a diet Coke, though she'd completely lost her appetite. Her stomach hurt, in fact.

"Hey, look," Dan said after the waitress left, "I'm sorry I snapped at you."

She didn't say anything.

"All right, you wanna talk about *us*? Fine. The way I see it, I laid my cards on the table from day one. I told you how I felt. And you said you didn't have room for me in your life. So I took you at your word and walked away. End of story."

"I never said that," she protested.

"You're right. You actually said something much worse. You said you didn't have room to fall in love, which told me you weren't. In love with me, I mean. August twenty-seventh of this year. See, I even remember the date. Not too often a person gets kicked in the chest like that."

Their eyes held, and so much meaning passed between them that Melanie could've sworn her whole life flashed before her eyes. The past and the future all wrapped up in one glance. She imagined herself much older, married to Dan, with grown sons who looked like him. Without fully intending to, she slid closer to him until their knees touched under the table. Dan's legs were as solid and powerful as tree trunks.

"You still with your husband?" he asked quietly, holding her gaze.

"No. That's over."

As they stared at each other, Bridget Mulqueen suddenly materialized at the end of their table. Her squeaky voice shattered the moment as effectively as a car alarm on a moonlit night.

"Hey, you guys! You'll never guess what happened. We almost did a controlled buy of fricking aspirin!"

Bridget smacked herself on the forehead comically with her open hand as she slid into the booth next to Dan. Trevor Leonard appeared and just stood there looking awkward. Melanie patted the seat beside her, and he sat down.

"Didja lose the buy money!" Dan asked, frowning.

"Naw, dude, I know what X looks like," Trevor said proudly. "I put a stop to it before Detective Mulqueen handed over the dough. Can't scam a scammer."

"I knew it was fake, too!" Bridget protested.

The waitress set down their drinks. Bridget picked up Dan's beer and took a big gulp, then realized what she'd done. "Oh, jeez, I'm sorry," she said.

"It's okay," Dan said.

"I was just really parched. I didn't think. I'm sorry." Bridget seemed on the verge of tears.

"Hey, kiddo, no big deal," Dan said, patting Bridget's leg. "Keep it. There's more where that came from. Want something to eat? You look like you could use it."

"Okay, sure."

Bridget gazed at Dan a bit too adoringly for Melanie's comfort. Though she knew Dan was simply acting like a decent human being, Melanie felt a sharp twinge of jealousy. This was getting out of hand. She'd better calm herself down and chill out about this guy. They had a case to do. A missing girl to find. She couldn't afford to get all distracted with emotions. Emotions were bad for your concentration.

"Yeah, you guys should both order something," Melanie made herself say. "But no alcohol, Trevor. Since you're underage, drinking is a violation of your bail conditions."

"Fill us in on what happened," Dan said. "What were you doing negotiating for ecstasy anyway? You were supposed to buy heroin so we could test it against the decks from Whitney's apartment."

"Well, we were trying to get to Expo's people," Bridget said. "Looking for the two bodyguards. Trevor recognized the big black guy, see, so we approached him. We told him we wanted to score heroin, but he steered us to the Russian guy, who said he only had ecstasy. So we said okay, figuring we start with ecstasy and work our way up, right? The guy asks for the money up front, but I didn't give it." She hesitated, struggling over what to say next, but honesty won out. "I mean, okay, I might've given it to'm, but Trevor, like, shakes his head not to. Then the guy brings back some blue tablets, and Trevor scrapes at 'em and goes, 'This shit is counterfeit.'"

"Oldest trick in the book," Trevor said. "They take fucking Excedrin, put a coating on it, and mark it like X. I tried pulling that once myself to make some extra cash, but for all the work you gotta do to pull the scam, it's not even worth it."

"But still, I think we made some headway, right, Trev?" Bridget said.

"Yeah, 'cause afterward we catch up with the black dude, and I go, 'Yo, your boy tried to rip me.' And he goes, '*Hakuna matata,* it's a little hot in here right now, son, but I'll catch you on the rebound.'"

"What did he mean by that?" Melanie asked.

"You know, no worries, like he'd do me solid next time. Make it right. Hook me up with some mad H," Trevor said.

"No, what I'm asking is, what did he mean by 'it's hot'?"

It was a question Melanie already knew the answer to. Anybody in law enforcement or with even a passing knowledge of the street knew what "hot" meant.

"That just means there's cops around," Trevor replied, his tone implying she was slow.

"Exactly," Melanie said.

"What are you saying? That Esposito's guys knew we were there working undercover?" Bridget asked.

"Well . . ." Melanie raised her eyebrows meaningfully and looked around the table at each of them. "They knew *something*."

29

FABULOUS DEON SPOTTED Linda at the bar. "Well, hello again, honeychild. Thought I'd lost you," he shouted over the music.

"I was hanging for a while with that guy Aidan who has that radio show, remember him?" Linda shouted back. She took a sip of her cocktail, pinkie extended.

"No, but you have so many men, how can one keep track?"

"Look who's talking, D!"

"Are you joking? I am in such a dry spell, I swear I'm thinking about paying for it!"

"Never say that! You take too many risks," she scolded.

"Ah, well, dearest, thank you for caring. But a person does need love."

"Sex is what *you're* talking about."

"Semantics."

"I'm gonna set you up with that lawyer I mentioned. The one who does work for the station? He's nice, and he's looking for a real relationship."

"I'll take a pass on that one. He sounds stu*pen*dously boring."

"You could use a little boring, and fewer party boys. Besides, this guy has a house in Amagansett."

"What good does that do me in December? Remind me next August, and maybe I'll be interested."

"Oh, look, D, Bettina Lloyd is over there! She just signed a major deal with Def Jam. I'm gonna see if I can score an interview. Catch you later."

Linda pecked Deon on the cheek and floated off into the crowd. Deon sighed and ordered a double Macallan straight up. He tossed back the booze when it came, glancing around restlessly, thinking maybe he should just go home. What would hanging around Screen get him, except a few hours older and a few more ego-bruising rejections? If recent experience was any guide anyway. Maybe he should take Linda up on her offer and meet Mr. Stable-and-Boring. He was turning thirty-five next week, and the party scene, which still held sway over him with its high-voltage thrills, was not welcoming him with quite the same open arms it once had. The writing was on the wall, the bloom off the rose. People had grown tired of him. Pretty soon even dull old sugar daddies like Linda's friend would look at him with indifferent eyes, so maybe he should set himself up while he still had the goods.

A completely hot young man wearing tight pants and a filmy wifebeater pushed his way up to the bar beside Deon and stood so close that their thighs touched in the tightly packed crowd. The boy had that look Deon went for every time—dusky-skinned, pouty-lipped, built. He ordered an expensive single-malt, then glanced back over his shoulder at Deon enticingly. Deon recognized the move. He'd used it to good effect himself, back in the day.

"Here, darling, let me get that for you," Deon said, reaching for his wallet.

"Yeah, awright." The kid had the sound of the projects in his voice. Which to Deon indicated that he might be more available than his dazzling looks would otherwise suggest.

"I haven't seen you around here before. What's your name?"

"Who askin'?"

"They call me Fabulous Deon. I'm well known in these parts. If you're looking for an in, I could be just your ticket."

"Maybe I'm lookin'. But why you gotta ask my name?"

The young man finished off his drink in a quick gulp, head tipped back, Adam's apple bobbing in his well-muscled neck. Then he wiped his lovely mouth with the back of his hand.

"You like your privacy. Not a problem. I'll just call you darling," Deon said, practically salivating.

"I know a place. C'mon, I ain't got all night."

The boy took Deon by the hand and pulled him through the crowd toward the edge of the platform. Deon wondered what the kid charged. He looked expensive, and Deon only had forty left in his wallet.

They reached the far end of the subway platform, and the kid pulled Deon into the darkness of the tunnel. "Where are we going? Wouldn't the men's room be more convenient?" Deon asked.

"Dis way," the kid said, gripping his wrist tighter.

Deon realized he was about to be robbed. He dug his heels in, but the kid was strong and had him in an iron grip. He yanked Deon a few feet forward, then pounded on a metal door barely visible in the half-light. It swung open to reveal one of Expo's bodyguards.

"Lamar, help! I'm being robbed!" Deon yelled. But Lamar grasped Deon by his shirtfront, threw him to the hard tile floor, and kicked him repeatedly in the gut with heavy work boots. Deon screamed at the top of his lungs, the sound masking the crunch of breaking ribs.

"It ain't feel too good being a rat now, huh?" Lamar said. He rifled through Deon's pockets and pulled out his wallet.

Through a haze of pain, Deon saw Jay Esposito talking to a tall, slender white man he didn't recognize. Jay nodded at Lamar, who gave Deon's wallet to the pouty kid. Jay peeled five hundreds off a money clip he took from his breast pocket, counting them carefully, and put those in the kid's hands, too.

"Remember, I know where you live," Expo said.

"Yo, we cool. You ain't got no problems wit' me," the kid said, stuffing the money and the wallet in his pants and heading for the door, which Lamar shut and bolted behind him.

Expo drew a large club from his leather golf bag and looked down at Deon, who lay moaning, tears leaking from his eyes.

"Did I mention, D, I been working on my golf swing?"

30

DAN OFFERED MELANIE a ride home.

"Tonight was a waste," he observed as they headed north on the FDR.

"No. I disagree."

"What did we learn? Other than the fact that Jay Esposito is hot for you, which I could've predicted."

"I wouldn't be so sure of that," Melanie said. "I got the distinct sense Esposito knew who I was and that's why he was interested in me. The bodyguards hinting around there was law enforcement in the club convinced me of it."

Dan's jaw tensed.

"You're gonna have to chill out about what I did tonight, you know," she said, studying him.

Illuminated by the headlights of a passing car, he smiled. "You don't miss a trick, do you?"

"I'm starting to be able to read you, despite the fact that you don't say much. So watch out."

"Oh, don't worry. I'm plenty scared of you already," he said.

It's mutual, she thought.

"You want to hear what *I* think we got out of tonight? Other than the fact that Bridget Mulqueen is hot for *you,* which I could have predicted," Melanie said.

"Mulqueen's all right. She reminds me of my dog when he was a puppy. All paws but a lot of heart. She might even make a decent cop someday."

"Mmm-*hmm,* I thought so," Melanie said, smiling.

"No way, you got me all wrong, sweetheart. I'm not egotistical like that," he said, smiling back.

"Oh, right. There isn't a man alive who doesn't love some girl looking at him like he's God's gift."

"If *you* looked at me that way, that'd be another story. *That,* I would like. But you need taming. I'd be doing the world a favor, getting Melanie Vargas into line. In fact, *you* better watch out, because I just might decide to try it."

"*Taming?* You're gonna pay for that remark, pal."

"Yeah, says who? I'm bigger than you, in case you haven't noticed."

She'd noticed, all right. His reminding her of that fact set her pulse to racing.

"Will you please stop distracting me from work?" she said, a warm, tingly feeling spreading through her body.

"Aw, c'mon, give it a rest with the work stuff. I'm having a lot more fun joking around with you."

"Resting is for dead people, baby."

"Lucky you look so good, because you can be a royal pain in the backside," Dan said, grinning, as he changed lanes smoothly and headed for the Sixty-first Street exit.

"Seriously, though. I think there's a connection between Carmen Reyes going missing and the internal carries," Melanie said.

"Yeah, that reminds me, I had an idea. What do you think of this? Maybe it wasn't that Carmen witnessed something or nothing. Maybe she's just scheduled to move the new shipment on Friday. The one Brianna Meyers mentioned in her e-mail. So they're keeping her on ice till then."

"Hmm. That's very interesting. But do you really think Expo

would use her as a courier now that her name's been in the paper?"

"Good point. Although the guy's pretty brazen. And stupid," Dan said.

"He could always have her travel with false papers."

"We should cover our bases, don't you think? We know the route. We know the likely dates of travel. Get her picture out to the guys at the airport, and Carmen shouldn't be too tough to spot."

"Yeah, fine, but I'm not prepared to wait till Friday. I think she's in danger, and I think we need to do more to find her *now*."

"Like what? Her description and photo are on every database. We checked out her known contacts, took a hard look at her routine, but we came up empty so far. This is a big town. Where else do we look?"

"I have an idea," Melanie said.

"Okay. Shoot."

"We have a cell number for Expo, right? Why not write for his phone?"

"You mean do a wiretap?"

"Yes."

"Wouldn't it take a while to develop probable cause?" Dan asked.

"We don't *have* a while. We use whatever we've got now and see if we can sneak it past a judge."

"What do we even have to put in an affidavit?" Dan asked.

"Well, Whitney Seward calling Expo's cell phone, including the night the girls died. Brianna Meyers texting Trevor that they were escorted to Puerto Rico. The flight manifest confirming that it was Esposito riding shotgun, when you get it."

"Whoa, hold your horses, princess. I *did* get it. Negative on that."

"Are you serious?"

"Yeah, sorry I forgot to mention it. I tracked down the manifests from the flights Whitney and Brianna took to and from Puerto Rico. No Esposito."

"Shit!"

"Yeah."

"Shit!"

"I know."

"Maybe he flew under a false name?" she offered.

"How we gonna prove that? You pointed out before, Puerto Rico's a domestic flight. No immigration checks, so no fingerprint scans."

"Well, all right, let's think what else we can use. We still have all the background from your friend's old case on Esposito, that he was previously investigated for heroin trafficking. We have the suggestion in Brianna's text that there's a new shipment scheduled for Friday."

"Isn't it all shot down by the fact that we tried making a buy tonight and came up with squat? So we don't got any drugs to put on the table to show a judge there's an ongoing operation here."

"Yes, we do! The balloons of heroin from Brianna's stomach. When you put that together with Expo's past history, it's something anyway. Right?"

He grinned. "You got guts, I'll say that for you. Not too many prosecutors I know would go to a judge with such crappy evidence. They'd be too worried about their precious reputations."

"I'm more worried about this missing girl."

"I know. That's good. Refreshing."

"Oh, and one more thing. Esposito let something slip. I think he lost a swallower before. A female, probably Puerto Rican, by the name of Mirta. If we could corroborate that, we'd have a slam dunk."

Dan pulled into an empty parking space on Melanie's block.

"See? I remembered where you live," he said, holding her gaze as he shut down the engine. With the heat off, the car's interior instantly cooled to frigid, but Melanie was in no hurry to get out. It was months ago now that they'd kissed, but she hadn't forgotten what Dan tasted like or the feel of his powerful arms around her.

"You remember my address from that one time?" she said, seeing her breath in the frosty air.

"It was twice. Besides, I've been stalking you."

"I don't think so," she said, her voice low and flirtatious. "I'd've noticed you."

"That's where you're wrong. I'm good at what I do. Nobody makes my surveillance unless I want 'em to."

He reached out and twined his fingers into her hair where it lay against her neck. Her heart started hammering wildly inside her chest.

"I *knew* you were crazy," she said, her eyes fixing on his strong, sensual mouth.

"When it comes to you, I'm a total fucking lunatic."

He slid his hands down the sides of her heavy winter coat and grabbed her by the hips, hauling her over the gearshift so she sat in his lap, facing him, her back pressed against the steering wheel. For a small eternity, they stared into each other's eyes, not even touching, their breathing growing heavier. She felt the muscles of his thighs under her and arched her back to press herself more firmly down against him. *Oh, yes.* They hadn't even kissed yet, but she was burning up with desire. Not just because she was starved for sex either; it was *Dan,* the effect he had on her.

He reached out, took her by the hair, and pulled her face toward him. His hands were trembling. Their mouths met greedily. His was hot and rough and demanding, tasting of the beer he'd drunk in the bar, yet, miraculously, soft and sweet, too. Jesus, she thought, I could lose myself in this man.

She pulled away, momentarily shaken by the intensity of the kiss. "Dan—"

"Don't," he said, looking up at her, his eyes vacant, heavy-lidded.

"It's just my mother I think is up there sitting with Maya, and—"

He put his hand over her mouth. "Don't say anything. I don't want to know about the limits you're putting on this or what you don't feel or why you can't be with me. This can be anything you want. It can be just sex. If I'm setting myself up for a fall, that's my problem. I'll take my chances. But I'm coming upstairs with you now."

S HE WAS GLAD it was late enough that Hector had gone off duty. The night-shift guy Melanie barely knew, and she scarcely acknowledged him as she and Dan hurried to the elevator.

They stepped in, the doors closing behind them. Dan glanced up at the ceiling.

"No camera in this elevator?" he asked, grasping her by both arms.

"No."

"Good. Because I can't keep my hands off you."

He pinned her against the side of the elevator and kissed her hard. Her insides melted all over again. She wrapped her arms around his massive shoulders, savoring the feel of his back muscles straining against his leather jacket. Dan's body was insane. He pulled away to work the buttons of her coat, but his fingers were shaking so much that he made little progress. Impatient, she undid them for him, and he stripped the coat roughly from her shoulders, revealing her chest in the red halter top.

"Jesus. You're so goddamn beautiful I can hardly stand to look at you," he said.

Slowly, breathing hard, he ran his hands over her face and throat and down her bare arms. His touch spread fire through her. He cupped her breasts, kneading them through the filmy fabric of the halter top as they stared at each other. She moaned, her head falling limply back, her hips thrusting forward to meet his. He pressed her hard into the wall, lifting her off her feet with one powerful thigh wedged between her legs.

"Ah, yeah, don't stop, keep going," Melanie said, the words ripped from her mouth almost involuntarily. Panting, she pulled up his shirt to get at his warm skin, her fingers brushing against his holstered gun. She drank in his tongue, forgetting everything else in the world. They'd better reach her floor soon, because in a second they'd be doing it standing up in the elevator.

"You are *so* hot," he whispered, his mouth against her hair. "I don't know if I can handle you."

She smiled dizzily, her eyes closing. "Oh, yes, you can."

The doors opened on her floor. Her knees were weak as she led Dan by the hand down the hall to her apartment. She shrugged her coat back into place and tried to get her breathing under control as she fumbled in her bag for her keys. She was a grown woman. Maya would be sleeping, and her mother would just have to deal with getting unceremoniously kicked out. Because Melanie *had* to have this man. *Now.* Her fingers found the keys, but then Dan, pressing against her from behind, started kissing her neck, and she dropped them on the floor.

"Let me open the door," she said. "You'll get me evicted from this building."

"Then you'll have to come live with me."

She had trouble getting the key into the lock. The noise must've roused her mother, because the door started to swing inward.

"Hands off now," she whispered to Dan, pulling away, trying to compose herself enough to introduce him.

But it wasn't her mother standing there. It was Steve, and he was holding two glasses of champagne.

31

LULU LET HERSELF into the darkened basement apartment with her key, relieved that the lights were out. Thank God that Papi was sleeping. She was nervous that if she saw Papi, she'd break down. She'd *tell*. She couldn't let herself. She had to keep her mouth shut, for Carmen's sake. Like *he* said tonight, when he came and found her at the skating rink. He'd scared the shit out of her just by showing up and sitting there. And as if that weren't enough, he'd explained exactly what he'd do if she told anybody.

Lulu reached into her coat pocket and fingered that lady's business card. She'd been thinking about calling the number and telling everything she knew, but now she definitely wouldn't. In fact, *he* told her she'd better call up that lady and lie. Throw suspicion onto somebody else. He'd even carefully given Lulu the name. She didn't want to do it, but what choice did she have? That man would kill Carmen without a second thought.

Lulu was getting choked up thinking about how much she wanted to call that lady. It would be such a relief to let an adult take this mess off her hands. But no, she was being weak. Babyish. For years now, Lulu had positively *longed* to have a grown-up take care of her. But she was determined to outgrow that nonsense. Grown-ups couldn't be trusted. Mami had gone and died on them. Papi was helpless and lost, like a child himself, needing *them* to take care of *him*. The teachers at school were evil, full of double talk, slaves to the rich girls. Carmen was the only one Lulu relied on, and now look at what *she'd* gone and done! Lulu *told* her to mind her own business. But no, Miss Smarty-Pants thought she knew everything. Had to be such a Goody-Two-Shoes and go tattle. So now *this* mess. He'd explained to Lulu very carefully tonight what she needed to do, what would happen to Carmen—and Lulu herself—if she didn't. Lulu had every intention of living a long, happy life, getting rich and famous and having tons of clothes and boyfriends, so she planned to follow instructions. But what if . . . what if she made the wrong choice? What if he killed Carmen anyway and she could've stopped it? How would Lulu live with that?

She ran to her room, snapped on the light, and fell to her knees beside her bed, still wearing her parka, staring at the picture of the Virgin hanging above the nightstand. Lulu folded her hands together and prayed with all her might.

"Hail Mary, Mother of God, *look*. I'm gonna cut to the chase. I know you're mad at me about the stuff with boys. But I wouldn't let Tyler Cole go to third base at the mixer Saturday night, like you told me, even though he'da let me wear his St. David's swim jacket if I did. And that jacket is fly, okay? So I don't think I deserve this. I know it was really bad about going to second with Jake Cooper, but I repented a lot, and besides, you already punished me when he forwarded my e-mails to all his friends. I'm trying. Really I am. I know this is your decision and all, and I'm not telling you what to do. But it seems to me you picked a punishment that hurts Carmencita worse than me. And we both know *she* didn't do nothing wrong. I mean, that girl, all she does is study and work and take care of this house. All she wants is to go to college. Okay, me, I'm boy crazy. I admit it, I'm bad. Definitely. But Carmen isn't like that! She's *good*. So why are you letting this happen to her? Why punish *her* for *my* sins? If you don't care about me, think about Papi! What's he supposed to do if shit gets messed up and Carmen dies? Who's gonna take care of him then, when you already took his wife? *Huh?* Our Lady? Are you listening?"

Lulu stared desperately at the picture, trying to discern any movement or change of expression in the Virgin's face. But the image was completely inert. Tears began falling in earnest from Lulu's eyes, and her shoulders heaved with suppressed sobs. *"Please! Please!"* she pleaded. "Dear Lady, I need an answer. Before it's too late."

Lulu buried her face in the stiff, scratchy bedspread, eyes and nose streaming. She remained on her knees for a long time, until she was so exhausted that she climbed on top of the bed and fell into a fitful sleep, still wrapped in her parka.

32

MELANIE WAS on her second Starbucks of the morning, but aside from bad caffeine shakes and a couple of trips to the bathroom, it was having zero effect. She was in a complete daze. As exhausted as she'd been last night, she'd barely slept. And she *needed* her brain to function today. The team would be here any minute to write the wiretap application for Jay Esposito's cell phone. The team, including Dan. *Concentrate, goddamn it. Stop thinking about him.* It was Wednesday morning, and between getting Main Justice approval and going before the judge, they were pushing it to be up on the cell phone in time for the Friday shipment as it was. She'd put all her credibility on the line with Bernadette and Lieutenant Albano, convincing them the wiretap was necessary, so she couldn't afford to fuck it up by obsessing over some *guy*.

But focusing her bleary eyes on the computer screen was more than Melanie could manage. She'd gotten only so far as typing the cell-phone and ESN numbers into the caption before she'd wandered off into her mental torture chamber, reliving the events of last night. The expression on Steve's face when he'd seen Dan. Worse, the expression on Dan's when he'd seen Steve.

UH-HUH," *Steve had said, nodding so knowingly you would've thought he caught her like this every night and twice on weekends.*

"I'm obviously interrupting something. Your mother said you were working, Mel. Did you misinform her, or was she covering for you?"

"Steve, this is my friend Dan O'Reilly from—"

"I know who he is." And he did. Steve had seen them kissing in a car once, months ago, right when he and Melanie had first separated.

Dan nodded at Steve grimly. "How you doing?"

"I was doing fine. Planning to have a little holiday celebration with my wife, if you don't mind," Steve said, gesturing with the two glasses of champagne in his hands.

"Your ex-wife. Almost," Melanie said hurriedly. "That's nice of you, Steve. And thanks for stepping in to watch Maya, but I have other plans right now."

"Apparently. You might want to fix your lipstick."

"Steve, come on, we're separated. As a matter of fact, Linda told me she saw you at a club Saturday night with some—"

"Hey," Dan interrupted, speaking to Melanie but eyes still on Steve, who stood there acting aggrieved in his expensive clothes and perfectly barbered hair. Melanie cringed inside. She knew Dan O'Reilly well enough to be pretty sure what was coming next.

"Dan . . ." she began, but he wouldn't look her in the face.

"It's late. Now that I got you home safe, I really gotta run, okay? Have a good night."

"Dan—"

"Gotta go."

"No, please, wait!"

But he'd already turned decisively on his heel and plunged through the fire door to the back stairwell, choosing to walk down eight flights rather than wait for the elevator.

RAY-RAY WONG strode in carrying a bunch of file folders. Melanie had been staring off into space, turning over in her mind what she'd say to Dan if he showed up first, alone. She had to admit she was kind of relieved to see Ray-Ray instead. Maybe Dan would just quit the case. But no, that would be awful. The fact was, she couldn't stop thinking about what had happened in the elevator last night. Oh, God, his mouth, his body, the way he was in such a hurry that he was kind of rough with her. *Muy erótico.* What she *really* wanted was to get past all the awkwardness about Steve and head straight back to that elevator. Any elevator. Get stuck between floors with Dan, for at least an hour. Mmmm.

"Did you hear what I just said?" Ray-Ray asked.

Stop, Melanie Vargas. Stop this instant.

"I'm sorry. I was worrying about this requirement in the Title III statute, whether we meet the criteria or not," she said.

"I've got something a whole lot more interesting, ma'am. Remember you told me what that guy Hogan said about Whitney Seward's blog?"

"Oh, right."

"Well, I located it last night, with some help from a friend of mine on the Tech Squad. It's pretty unbelievable. I have the Web address. May I?"

"Please." Melanie got up and came around the desk, and Ray-Ray went to sit in her swivel chair. "Just minimize my document. There's an icon for Internet access," she said.

Ray-Ray fiddled around with the computer. Melanie sat in a guest chair, trying not to think about Dan, which was only possible if she made her mind a complete blank.

After a few minutes, Ray-Ray frowned and said, "Huh."

"What is it?"

"It keeps telling me the page isn't available. Let me see if I can get my buddy from Tech on the line."

Ten minutes went by, during which Melanie leafed through the file folders Ray-Ray had brought while he consulted by telephone with the Tech guy. Work always made Melanie feel better. She busied herself marking the various subpoena responses with yellow Post-its. The details of telephone billing records and flight manifests between New York and Puerto Rico soothed her overwrought mind considerably. At the very least, by the time she'd finished, she felt like she could face Dan O'Reilly without either ripping off his clothes or bursting into tears and running away.

Finally Ray-Ray hung up. "You're not gonna believe this," he said.

"What?"

"The blog's gone. Vanished from the Web."

"You're kidding. Who did that?"

"Apparently somebody using Whitney's username and password. Happened at 2317 hours last night."

"Did you make a record of what was on it?"

"Naturally, ma'am. Copied everything to a disk in that folder there yesterday. That's not the issue."

"Yeah, I hear you. First, Whitney's cell-phone memory was selectively erased, now this. Somebody's out there impeding our investigation."

"And based on the content of the blog, I have a pretty good idea who it is."

Melanie handed the disk across her desk. "Okay, then, let me see what you downloaded."

She walked around to stand behind Ray-Ray as he pulled up the blog. The main page popped up, boasting a picture of Whitney sitting on her bed in her Holbrooke uniform, leaning back against her pillows with her legs spread, smiling broadly, wearing no panties.

"*Whoa!*" Melanie exclaimed, startled.

"It gets worse. Or better, depending on your point of view," Ray-Ray said, with a twinkle in his eye. "This girl was twisted, but you can't deny she's wicked hot."

"Ray-Ray! I'm surprised at you."

"My interest is purely professional, ma'am."

"Yeah, right. Hey, is that the Holbrooke crest at the top of the page?"

"You bet. Whitney's yearbook photo's in here, too, and even copies of her term papers and exams. It's partly the Holbrooke image that she was selling."

"*Selling?*"

"Yup, that was the whole point. She posted lists of items she wanted visitors to her site to buy for her, and whoever bought her the stuff first would get an e-mail back with their own private smutty picture. Whitney had a personal shopper at Barneys handling the orders for her, and the . . . uh, customers, I guess you could call 'em, would phone in their credit-card numbers to buy particular items. When the purchases went through, she'd send out a JPEG with the new picture as payment. We were able to track the correspondence, and it's pretty unbelievable. Men all over the U.S. and in other countries, too."

"Wow. This raises all sorts of new possibilities for the case."

"Like what?" Ray-Ray asked, frowning.

"First of all, this could be some weird kind of sex crime dressed up to *look* like a drug crime. To cover the bases, we should investigate every one of the men who visited the Web site."

Ray-Ray shook his head. "That's a shitload of names, ma'am."

"I realize that. But it needs to be done. And that's not all. If Whitney was running an Internet porn site trading on the Holbrooke name, I think we need to look more closely at *Holbrooke.*"

"I'm not following you."

"This may sound far-fetched, but think how crazed they are at Holbrooke right now over this endowment campaign. Not just the headmistress but the general counsel, too, who—remember—has some fetishes of his own. Think about the devastating impact Whitney's little business would've had on Holbrooke's fund-raising if it came to light before the campaign closed. The timing is exactly right. Their campaign ends Friday with some big gala."

"Let me see if I understand this," Ray-Ray said. "You're suggesting the headmistress or the general counsel of Holbrooke could've whacked

Whitney Seward in order to shut down her Web site so it wouldn't interfere with the Holbrooke fund-raising campaign? *And* made it look like an OD?"

"Yes. Well put."

"Due respect, ma'am, that's one of the craziest ideas I've ever heard."

"It's not crazy. It's thinking outside the box. It might even be the right answer."

"Right, and if my grandmother had wheels, she'd be a trolley car. Look, ma'am, I think I can tie Whitney's Web site right back into Jay Esposito and the drug angle. That theory makes sense to me. But yours? *Wicked* crazy."

"Fine. But I'm not dropping my Holbrooke idea." To make her point, and also since she didn't trust herself to remember *anything* this morning, Melanie carefully wrote, "Look at Holbrooke/Andover/Siebert involvement in deaths" on a yellow legal pad, circled it twice with black marker, and put a star next to it.

"Now, most of the pictures Whitney sent to her customers were pretty tame," Ray-Ray continued, glancing at her note with an exasperated smile. "They showed her alone, only partly undressed. A guy buys Whitney a pair of Jimmy Choos, he gets his own private JPEG of her in her Holbrooke uniform flashing some titty. That sort of thing. But bigger-ticket items got you more graphic pictures. One in particular I want you to see. In my humble opinion, ma'am, it explains the blog getting erased, and it figures a helluva lot more heavily in the girls' deaths than your so-called *Holbrooke* theory."

Ray-Ray brought up a copy of an e-mail that Whitney had sent to one "sugardaddy69" and clicked on the attachment.

"This user, we actually traced," Ray-Ray said. "He's fifty-four years old, a civil engineer in Kansas City, Mo, with a family and everything. No criminal record, no indication he was in New York at the relevant time. He did, however, buy Whitney a four-thousand-dollar alligator handbag from Barneys in exchange for this picture. The girl was commanding serious money. But it *is* a lot more graphic. The caption is 'See Whitney get . . . uh, expletive, from behind.' "

The digital photo appeared—crystal clear, in vivid color, leaving nothing to the imagination. Whitney was bent over a chair, looking back over her shoulder with a lascivious grin on her face. Her Holbrooke kilt was up around her waist, her panties around her ankles. The naked man doing the honors was muscular and deeply tanned, with a shaved head. His face was turned away from the camera, but the large diamond stud in his ear was clearly visible.

"I see what you mean about who erased the blog," Melanie said. "That's definitely Jay Esposito. *Not* that I've ever seen him naked."

Of course Dan O'Reilly had to pick exactly that moment to walk through her office door. And with *Bridget.* Melanie fumed with jealousy when she realized they must've ridden up in the elevator together. Boy, after last night, she'd never look at elevators the same way again.

"Yo, team," Bridget said. She carried a brown paper bag, which had split apart on the bottom. She set it down on Melanie's desk, where it instantly formed a puddle of sour-smelling coffee.

"I brought some joe for everybody, but I think it spilled. Do you have any paper towels?" Bridget asked Melanie.

"In the ladies' room down the hall." Melanie momentarily exulted at getting Bridget out of the room. But then she felt guilty, not to mention worried about her own mental health, and resolved yet again to calm down.

"Holy shit. Who's that doing Whitney, your boyfriend Expo?" Dan asked Melanie. His eyes were fixed on the computer, his handsome face clouded. She couldn't decide if he looked angry or just tired.

"He's not my boyfriend!" she protested. She'd meant to sound jokey, but it came out defensive.

"Too bad. If you could testify you recognized his naked butt, we could use the picture as evidence for the wiretap," Dan said.

"I can testify I recognize his naked head," Melanie offered, still searching Dan's face. But he wouldn't look at her. Hmm, he didn't seem mad, but he didn't seem *not* mad either.

"We're in pretty good shape to go up on Esposito's phone anyway," Dan said. "I spent last night at my computer following up on a few things. A woman by the name of Mirta Jimenez was found dead in a restroom at Marín Airport in San Juan ten months ago. Autopsy said cause of death was acute heroin poisoning, caused by leaking balloons in her stomach. She was booked on a flight to New York but never made it onto the plane. I already pulled the passenger manifest. One Jay Esposito was seated three rows behind her."

I N CERTAIN RESPECTS Melanie's fortunes had taken a turn for the better. Working swiftly, the team finished the wiretap affidavit and got Justice Department authorization by early afternoon. When they were ready to go to the judge for the final okay, the assignment wheel spit out the name of the Honorable Constance Stanchi, referred to fondly by prosecutors in Melanie's office as the Smiling Lady of the Bench, the one jurist who could be counted on to sign anything, anytime.

Melanie had had wiretaps before Judge Stanchi in the past, and the approval process was blessedly minimal. She brought Dan rather than Ray-Ray to swear out the affidavit, because Judge Stanchi was known to appreciate a good-looking cop. They were ushered in to the jurist's delightful chambers, which smelled of perfume and the large display of fresh roses on her desk. Judge Stanchi's snow white hair was, as always, beautifully arranged. Her impressive pearls, as usual, carefully peeked over the collar of her black robe. And her delicate, blue-veined, manicured hands cradled a copy of the affidavit, which, based on past experience, Melanie was fairly confident she hadn't read.

"Good afternoon, Miss Vargas," the judge said in her cultured voice, bestowing one of the beatific smiles that had earned her her nickname. "And who is this fascinating young man you've brought to visit me?"

"Judge, this is Special Agent Daniel K. O'Reilly from the FBI, who is prepared to swear to the truth of the allegations contained in the affidavit. We'd be happy to answer any questions Your Honor might have about the investigation."

"Questions. Hmmm. Yes."

Judge Stanchi opened the bound affidavit and began leafing through it. Before another judge this was the moment Melanie normally got major butterflies, worrying that he'd throw her some curveball she wouldn't be able to answer, deny the wiretap, and call up Bernadette screaming about Melanie's incompetence. Not like it had never happened before either. But with Stanchi you didn't sweat it. Not only was the Smiling Lady flipping through the affidavit from back to front, making it impossible to absorb its content in any event, but her delphinium blue eyes were busy ogling Dan rather than reading the document.

"Everything seems in order," Judge Stanchi said when she'd finished pretending to read. She smiled yet again. "Agent, please raise your right hand."

Minutes later they stood waiting for the elevator with the paperwork authorizing them to intercept Jay Esposito's telephone calls in hand. And that's when Melanie discovered that her fortunes hadn't actually improved, not when it came to *lo importante* anyway.

"Well, that was easy," she remarked.

"For *you,* maybe. I feel like I should take a shower."

The elevator came, and they got on. Dan pressed the button for the courthouse basement.

"Oh, c'mon," Melanie said, "Judge Stanchi's harmless. *Better* than harmless. In all the years I've appeared before her, she's never denied one application. Besides, she really looks the part, doesn't she?"

"And that really matters to you, doesn't it?" he snapped back, bitter and mocking.

Dan had been angry all along. He'd simply bided his time until they were alone so he could ambush her.

"What's that supposed to mean? Are you upset about last night?"

He didn't answer, his face closed and stony. They got out in the basement and headed for the tunnel back to Melanie's building so they wouldn't have to go outside, where it was snowing and sixteen degrees. Dan walked so fast she practically had to run to keep up, the three-inch heels of her boots clattering on the cheap linoleum floor.

"Hey, listen," Melanie said, "I know it was a buzz kill, Steve being there last night and all, but—"

He turned on her furiously. "*Buzz kill?* It was a fucking deal breaker, is what it was. I'm not your fool, lady! I don't give a *shit* if you're still messing around with your husband, but show a little more respect than using *me* as a fucking pawn. That was low." Dan marched ahead, disgust on his face. When he reached the elevator that served Melanie's office, he pounded the call button furiously, his back turned to her.

Breathing heavily, Melanie caught up with him. For a split second, she'd been speechless with shock, but now she was in such a rage that her entire body shook.

"You know, I'm tempted to just tell you to fuck off and never speak to you again," she began.

"Suits me fine!"

"In your dreams, pal. You're not getting off that easy! Normally I wouldn't even respond to your *disgusting* accusation. But I've been a prosecutor long enough to know that people take silence as an admission of guilt and I *refuse* to give you the satisfaction. So I'm going to say my piece first. Then we're *through*."

She glared at him fiercely, almost spitting the words, and Dan stared back at her wide-eyed. Melanie knew how to fight. She hadn't grown up on the block for nothing.

"If you really meant what you just said," she continued, her voice quivering with outrage, "then you are one vicious, cynical human being, Dan O'Reilly. You're *cold*. Something *damaged* you. Maybe it was your ex-wife, maybe something else. I don't know, since you never deign to talk about yourself. But don't go putting your ugly ideas on *me*. I'm not like that! I had no idea Steve would be there last night. I would never behave in the vile way you just suggested. Maybe your heart is too dead to understand." She shook her head in resignation. "And to think I thought you were the *one*. There's a sucker born every minute."

The elevator doors opened and Melanie hurried on. Dan made as if to follow.

"No you don't!" she commanded. "I'm not riding with you. We'll do this case, and that's *it*. I never want to speak to you again."

As she smacked the button for her floor, tears of fury stood out in Melanie's eyes. That didn't surprise her, since sometimes she cried when she was really angry. What surprised her was looking up at the very last moment before the doors closed and seeing Dan watch her disappear—unshed tears glittering in his.

33

MELANIE WAS way too busy and preoccupied to waste any more time thinking about Dan O'Reilly.

Shortly after she got back to her office, the telephone rang. It was Linda, sobbing so hysterically that Melanie could barely understand her.

"What is it? Is it Mom?" Melanie asked with her heart in her throat.

Linda wailed something incomprehensible.

"Please, Lin. I can't hear what you're saying. Are you okay?"

"It's Fab D. He's dead!" Linda cried.

Melanie went cold and quiet.

"How did it happen?" she asked Linda after a moment.

"I should've stayed with him, Mel. It's all my fault! He told me he was gonna do it."

"Do what? Slow down, okay? Did you see what happened? Was it Expo?"

"No. Expo? What are you talking about? D was looking for some action. He told me. I didn't take him seriously enough."

"What kind of action?"

"Sex! He said he was desperate, that he was planning to pay for it. I thought he was joking." Linda began sobbing again.

"I don't understand. Was he sick? How did he die?" Deon had looked perfectly healthy yesterday.

"He got beat to death. They found him in an alley this morning, frozen solid," Linda said.

"And you think—"

"I *know*. A friend of mine saw Fab D at the bar just *minutes* after he told me that, talking to some rent boy. I could've stopped him, Mel! I never should've left him alone in that crazy mood. I know how he gets."

"It's not your fault, sweetie. It may not even have been about that. I need to nail down what really happened, to make sure there's no connection to Expo. I want you to be careful. Stay in your apartment and don't open the door to anybody until I tell you it's cool, understand?"

"No way. I can't do that. I have tickets to Cabo with Teresa. We're going to that new resort. Fab D would never want me to cancel."

TO MELANIE'S SURPRISE, the story about the male prostitute checked out. Manhattan South Homicide had caught the case, and Melanie spoke directly to the lead detective. Several witnesses had indeed seen Fabulous Deon pick up a provocatively dressed young man at Screen the previous night and leave the bar with him. An individual matching the young man's description had been videotaped withdrawing cash with Deon's ATM card at a bank two blocks from Screen at eleven-thirty last night. That, combined with the fact that Deon's wallet was not found with his body, suggested that robbery was the likely motive. The detectives were now in the process of cross-checking the photo taken by the ATM machine against mug shots of male prostitutes arrested in the five boroughs in the past year. They expected to have a name shortly.

One fact troubled Melanie greatly, however. When Deon and the prostitute left the bar, they headed straight for the tunnel where Expo had taken Melanie. Nobody else seemed to think this was of much significance, but *she* did. The murder case wasn't under her jurisdiction, though, so the best she could do was fill the detective in on her own encounter with Esposito and make him promise to call her if he came up with any connections.

Melanie had an appointment at six o'clock at the Elite Narcotics Task Force to deliver a required lecture on wiretap regulations. She was attempting to review her lecture script, but she was so upset by Fabulous Deon's murder that she couldn't concentrate. She knew she should turn her mind to her work, build her case against Esposito brick by brick, get him off the street before he did any more harm. That was the way to vindicate Deon. But the words of the script blurred before her eyes. *You are entitled to intercept only criminal conversations. Shut down the recording device if the defendant is talking about something other than criminal activity. Shut it down if he's talking to his lawyer, doctor, or priest. If he's having phone sex with his girlfriend or asking his mother to fix him dinner. But you can listen if he's talking to his girlfriend or his mother about selling drugs.* Blah, blah, blah. And yet it *was* relevant. If they could intercept Expo talking on the telephone about Friday's heroin shipment and stake him out running some new drug mules back from Puerto Rico, they'd have enough to charge him in the Holbrooke girls' deaths. If they were lucky, maybe they'd come up with something tying him to Deon's death. If they were really, really lucky, maybe they'd even find Carmen Reyes in the process. They'd better, because Melanie couldn't handle another innocent person's dying on her watch. If it hadn't happened already—if Carmen was even still alive.

Melanie felt useless to the point of suffocation, sitting at her desk while Carmen was out there somewhere, needing her help. She had a couple of hours before the lecture, and even though the team had covered the bases according to the missing-persons protocol, she worried they weren't doing enough. There had to be something more, some lead not fully plumbed, some neglected rock that could be turned over, its teeming underside examined and reexamined.

She'd go back to square one and start over, on the principle that where a young girl's life was at stake, you could never do enough.

34

THE RECEPTIONIST with the British accent sat at her post in Holbrooke's lobby with perfect posture and a smile on her face, seemingly oblivious to the gathering darkness and snow outside. No doubt about it, Patricia Andover ran a tight ship.

"Ah, yes, Miss Vargas. How may I assist you today?"

There were plenty of people Melanie could talk to here, but she'd start with the one she knew had been overlooked.

"I want to see Ted Siebert."

A few minutes later, she was seated in a tiny back office across the desk from the general counsel, who was sweating despite the chill in the air.

"You probably expected grander quarters," he commented, mopping his forehead with a handkerchief as Melanie glanced around the sparsely furnished room. "I'm an independent contractor, not a Holbrooke employee. My firm has offices downtown. So Holbrooke lets me use this space as a courtesy when I'm working on school matters."

"I guess I'm lucky to catch you in, then."

"Between the drug scandal and the endowment campaign, it's a busy time, so I've been here a lot this week. Speaking of busy," he said, looking at his watch, "what can I do for you?"

"Yesterday I was so focused on searching the girls' lockers that I didn't take the time to interview you properly."

"Interview *me*? About what?" Siebert asked warily.

"Well, first I'm trying to get copies of the girls' records. Dr. Hogan thought you might have them."

"Shouldn't you be out arresting drug dealers instead of worrying how these girls were doing in calculus class?"

"I'm not just looking for transcripts, Mr. Siebert. I was told that each Holbrooke student has a file, akin to a personnel file. I need the files on Whitney, Brianna, and Carmen Reyes."

"I don't see why their files are relevant to your case."

"That's not your call," Melanie replied. Why was this guy so intent on stonewalling her? It was making her wonder about him, even more than she already did. "*I* think they're relevant. Disciplinary problems, medical and psychological issues, records of family strife, conflicts with other students. I need to look at all of that."

"Those are exactly the kinds of records we guard most closely. Your request raises major confidentiality issues. I'd like to help you out, but my hands are tied."

"That's just not true. There's no law against disclosing the files, and Mrs. Andover has given her permission."

"Well, she should have asked me first. I'm the general counsel, Ms. Vargas. It's *my* job to worry about breach of confidence."

"Breach of *whose* confidence? The girls' parents don't object. Enlighten me, because I don't see a problem here."

"The parents may *say* they don't object, but if the files make their kid look bad, I'll get hit with a lawsuit faster than you can say 'litigation.' Little Susie doesn't get into Princeton, your average Holbrooke parent's first instinct is to haul my ass into court over the recommendation letter, and I'm tired of it. They don't pay me enough to put up with that garbage, and I don't need any more problems over these dead girls, thank you very much."

The window behind Siebert's desk faced out onto a dismal back courtyard. In the halo from an outdoor light, the snow was coming down harder than ever.

Melanie looked Siebert in the eye. "Not to put too fine a point on it: Your ass is about to get hauled into court for obstructing my investigation. There's a young girl missing and two others dead. Give me those records now, or we've got a problem."

Siebert flushed purple. "I need a subpoena before I'd even consider it."

"I'll fax you one in the morning if you're so determined to cover yourself. But we both know you have no basis for objecting, so enough already."

They stared at each other. Looking at the guy, Melanie couldn't help thinking about his chat-room activities. A pervert, Ray-Ray had called him. Maybe, maybe not, based on the evidence, but he definitely *was* an obstructionist. It was on the tip of her tongue to confront him with what she knew, just out of sheer annoyance. But Siebert saved her from doing that by suddenly deciding to cave. He opened a desk drawer, pulled out three files, and, leaning forward so his large stomach spilled onto the desk, slapped them down in front of her.

"Thank you," Melanie said coldly, picking them up.

"You can review them now, in my presence. If you find materials that interest you, I'll arrange to have them copied."

"Fine."

For fifteen tense minutes, Melanie examined the files as Siebert pretended to work at his computer. But every time she looked up, he was watching her. She did her best to ignore him and concentrate on the task at hand.

The files told her little she didn't already know. Whitney Seward's grades had been average at best, Brianna Meyers's quite good, and Carmen Reyes's excellent. Brianna was being treated for an eating disorder on the recommendation of the school nurse. Whitney had been suspended for two days during her freshman year for appearing intoxicated at nighttime-volleyball practice. Melanie found details on Carmen's scholarship arrangements, including a letter of recommendation signed by James Seward. There were no names or addresses in Carmen's file that shed any light on her disappearance. The only truly interesting fact Melanie discovered—interesting in view of something Melanie had on her list to ask Harrison Hogan about—was that Whitney Seward's best grade sophomore year had been an A-minus in Hogan's biology class. That grade stood in sharp contrast to Whitney's other science and math grades over the years, which had never risen above a C-plus.

When Melanie was finished, she closed the files and laid them back on Siebert's desk. "I'll take copies of everything for my records. I'll send someone by to pick them up tomorrow."

He shrugged. "Be my guest. Are we done, then?"

"No. I need to ask you a few questions. Let's start with Carmen Reyes. How well did you know her?"

"Look, you're wasting your time. I'm the school lawyer. I don't interact with students, okay? I don't even deal with parents unless they're on the board or involved in school matters. I didn't know any of these girls personally. Now, can I get back to work, please?"

"James Seward is on the board of trustees. You know *him,* right?"

"Yeah, unfortunately. We're not fond of each other. So what? Does that make me the guy who sold drugs to his daughter?"

"Nobody's suggesting that. Why are you so hostile, Mr. Siebert? I'm doing my job here. Do you have a problem with that?"

"*My* problem is that you have a problem with *me* doing *my* job. I'm paid to give aggressive legal representation to this school. What is that, a federal crime now? The ego on you people."

Melanie held Siebert's gaze, disliking him intensely, dying to confront him. But there was nothing to be gained by that.

"We're done for now. But you'll hear from me again," Melanie said, picking up her briefcase and heading for the door.

"I can't wait," Siebert tossed after her.

Let him have the last word. If Ted Siebert had any involvement in the girls' deaths, she'd make it her business to find out. His turn would come.

35

TED SIEBERT wasn't the only reason Melanie had come to Holbrooke. She planned to pay a surprise visit to Dr. Harrison Hogan. She'd dug up some interesting stuff on the good doctor as well, and she was hoping he could explain it away. Hogan was her best source inside the school, and she hated to think he was keeping a dirty secret.

Melanie made her way to Hogan's office and rapped on the frosted-glass window of his closed door.

"Yeah!" Hogan called.

She poked her head in. "Hi."

"Oh, hey. What brings you here?" Hogan asked.

"I wanted to let you know, Ted Siebert found the girls' files."

He smiled good-naturedly. "Great. I'm glad they weren't lost, especially since it probably would've been my fault."

"Do you have a minute?"

"Sure, come on in," he said, leaning back and putting one Nike-clad foot on his messy desk. "What's up? Any leads on where the girls got the drugs?"

"We're working on it," she said, taking a seat. No reason to enlighten Hogan about Brianna Meyers's autopsy results and the drug-smuggling angle. Especially since she now suspected him of hanky-panky with one of the victims.

"Actually," she said, "I'm here because I have a few questions for you about Whitney Seward."

Did she detect a slight trace of alarm in his eyes, or was she imagining it? But Hogan didn't move from his relaxed position, just ran fine hands thoughtfully through his shaggy hair.

"Sure," he said casually.

"I was hoping you could tell me a bit more about *your* relationship with Whitney."

"Okay. No problem. Nothing much to report, you know? I think I mentioned yesterday, I was her college adviser. I also taught her tenth-grade biology, and I would've had her in chemistry next semester. Oh, and I was helping her out with English, too, which she was failing, but that wasn't entirely her fault. Mrs. Stein is an old battle-ax, and she couldn't get past the fact that she loathed Whitney on a personal level. By the way, Melanie, I'm brewing up some green tea with echinacea. You want some? Good herbal remedy in this weather." He gave her a concerned look, which she tried not to interpret as a diversionary tactic.

"No thanks. So, in your various roles, how much contact did you have with Whitney Seward?"

"Contact?"

"Phone calls, e-mails, visits, that sort of thing?"

"Can I ask, did Patricia say something to you?"

"What do you mean?"

"Just . . . don't believe everything you hear."

"Is there some bad feeling between you and Mrs. Andover, Doctor?"

"Call me Harrison."

"It's better for the investigation if we keep things on professional terms."

"Oh." He seemed somewhat taken aback. "Okay, if you're more comfortable that way. Well, how to put this? Patricia favors some . . . uh, *unorthodox* methods of maintaining control of staff members she sees as threats. Unfortunately, I fall into the threat category. Not only am I popular with the student body, but I question Patricia's authority too often for her taste. She hates that."

"You're suggesting Mrs. Andover would actually lie to the federal government about you?"

"Sounds crazy, right? But welcome to my world—that's Holbrooke for you. I guarantee, if Patricia said something about me and Whitney, she did it for some Machiavellian reason of her own."

"Mrs. Andover didn't say a word. I happened to subpoena Whitney's telephone and e-mail records. They show an awful lot of contact between the two of you."

Hogan shook his head from side to side slowly, as if he couldn't believe his ears. "You know, it's really sad to me how things get misinterpreted in this day and age. That's one of the worst by-products of the child-abuse scandals of the past decade, if you ask me. Because my friendship with Whitney Seward was totally aboveboard. The kid was messed up, and I tried to help. End of story."

"So the nature of the interaction—"

"Look," he interrupted, "I'm not saying Whitney never came on to me or even maybe sent me a suggestive e-mail now and then. But I'm trained in adolescent psychology. If a girl like Whitney behaves in an overtly sexual manner toward an older male authority figure, I see it for what it is. A normal developmental phase. I take it in stride, and I work with the student to overcome the transference issues, even transform the crush into something positive."

"Such as?"

"Well, did you see Whitney's grade in my biology class? The kid worked hard for me." Hogan looked at her carefully as he said this.

"But if Whitney was sending you suggestive e-mails, that's hardly 'nothing to report,' as you said a moment ago."

"Isn't it?"

"Not to my mind."

"Reality's in the eye of the beholder. Maybe you should stop and ask yourself what assumptions you bring to the table."

PATRICIA ANDOVER, it turned out, brought some pretty serious assumptions to the table.

"Harrison was sleeping with Whitney," the headmistress declared flatly when Melanie confronted her on the subject.

"How do you know that?"

"Because! Whitney was sending him naked pictures of herself. I don't suppose he mentioned that to you?"

"No. He said she'd sent him suggestive e-mails. He didn't say anything specific about naked pictures."

"Of course not."

Melanie had to admit, Hogan's nonchalance about the whole thing *was* suspicious. Had it been an act—or the calm of true innocence? Or was Patricia Andover lying about the pictures?

"Tell me more about these naked pictures. Have you actually seen them?" Melanie asked.

"With my own eyes. I make it my business to know what's being done with school computers, for liability reasons, you see. These were absolutely pornographic. Whitney in . . . *various poses.* With her genitalia exposed."

Melanie certainly believed that such pictures existed, since she'd seen similar ones on the blog. But that didn't necessarily mean they'd been sent to Hogan.

"I'd like to get copies of the pictures and the covering e-mails, Mrs. Andover. This may have some connection to what happened with—"

"*No.* I'm very sorry, but that won't be possible. I erased them all." Patricia looked suddenly flushed, with a faint dew of perspiration on her forehead. Melanie had serious doubts as to whether she was telling the truth.

"You *erased* them? That seems very strange to me. Weren't you planning to *do* anything about the fact that one of your teachers—at least as far as you believed—was having a sexual relationship with a student?"

"Oh, Jesus," Patricia dropped her head into her hands and kneaded her eyebrows. The Yorkie lying on a satin dog bed in the corner perked its head up, then jumped into Patricia's lap and began licking her face. "Yes, darling, Mommy's upset," Patricia said, stroking the dog, which settled into her lap.

"Frankly," Melanie continued, "that seems quite out of character for you, based on what I've observed about how carefully you run this school." *In other words, I don't believe you.*

"What can I say? I reacted emotionally, out of deep disgust. Everybody's human."

"What *are* you planning to do about this alleged sexual relationship?"

"I've already confronted Harrison. He knows he's going to be suspended as soon as the gala is over and the endowment campaign closes. But given the furor over the ODs, I couldn't do it before then without hurting the school. I promise you, Harrison won't be left alone with any of the girls between now and then."

"When you confronted him, did he admit to having a sexual relationship with Whitney?"

"No. He denied it."

"So what do you plan to use for proof if you deleted the e-mails?"

"Look, I made a mistake. I've admitted that. What do you want me to do?" Patricia said. This woman was a tough opponent; she had her story and she was sticking to it. But Melanie was pretty convinced she was lying. Maybe the e-mails had never existed at all, or maybe they'd existed but Patricia had never erased them. Either way, it looked like Melanie would have to get a search warrant and check through Holbrooke's entire computer system, which was going to be an annoyingly time-consuming process.

"You're not planning to go public with this, are you?" Patricia asked.

Melanie hesitated. She wasn't, but let the headmistress sweat it. "I haven't decided yet."

"If you ever did, I can tell you what Harrison's defense would be: that Whitney sent the e-mails unsolicited and that he didn't stop her, because he was playing therapist."

"You don't believe him?" Melanie asked.

"Psychobabble. Lies."

"Well, like I said, it seems to me you're going to have a difficult time making your case, since you destroyed the best evidence. Anyway, I'm not wasting any more time on Dr. Hogan right now. Let me ask you about another staff member. I've found Ted Siebert somewhat . . . difficult. Hostile."

The headmistress nodded, smiling. "That's Ted for you. He's a good lawyer."

"Is there anything about *him* that I should know about?"

Patricia flushed again. "No. Not that I'm aware of."

Melanie studied the headmistress's face. She had the feeling she just wasn't getting straight answers out of this woman. "Hmm. Okay. One more question, then, Mrs. Andover, and I'll let you get back to work. I'm sure you understand, we need to cover all bases. This is simply a matter of gathering information for the record."

"Fine. Fire away."

"Where were you on Monday night when the girls OD'd?"

The headmistress stroked her dog, considering for a moment. "May I ask why you're interested in *my* whereabouts, Miss Vargas?"

"As I said, only as a matter of routine. We're asking the same question of everyone we interview."

"Of course. I understand. I appreciate how thorough you're being. Well, I must confess to being rather dull. I was home alone on Monday night with the doggies. I took a bath, drank a glass of wine, and turned in early."

"Okay, thank you." Melanie made a note on her yellow legal pad, then looked coolly back at Patricia. "You wouldn't happen to know, would you, where James Seward was then?"

Patricia went bright red. Her mouth fell open a split second before she was able to get any sound out. "James Seward? I . . . uh, no, I don't," she said, then closed her mouth again, doing her best to act as if that were a perfectly normal question.

A FTER DELIVERING the wiretap lecture at ENTF head-quarters, Melanie searched out Ray-Ray Wong. She found him speed-typing reports in his pathologically neat cubicle.

"Holbrooke is apparently a hotbed of corruption and lies," she said cheerfully. "Let me ask you, from what you saw on the blog, did Whitney Seward send any of her dirty pictures to a Holbrooke e-mail address?"

"What's a Holbrooke e-mail address look like?"

"I think it's the person's first and last name, at Holbrooke dot e-d-u."

"Definitely not. I would have noticed something that obvious. Why?"

"Because Patricia Andover claims to have intercepted dirty pictures that Whitney sent to Hogan."

"Hogan, the school psychologist?"

"Yes."

"There weren't any. I'm sure of it. Could Andover be making that up for some reason?"

"*Hogan* says she is. But Whitney's cell-phone records say different. I went through them very carefully when we were working on the wiretap affidavit. It turns out Hogan is all over them, going back almost a year. Long calls, late at night, mostly between her cell and his home tele-phone, some to his cell and his office. The volume can't be explained by 'You're failing English' either, though that's what he claims."

Ray-Ray shrugged. "Doesn't surprise me if he was bangin' her. All those longhaired sixties throwbacks are morally corrupt."

"We need to subpoena Hogan's phone records to see what else comes up and get a warrant for the Holbrooke computer system as well, to track down the e-mails. *Someone* figured out how to access Whitney's blog and take it off the Web altogether. Maybe it was Hogan. Maybe he erased all the e-mails to himself, and that's why you didn't find them."

Ray-Ray looked at her like she was insane. "Not for nothing here, ma'am, but we're up on a drug wire on an extremely viable target, and so far it ain't going too well. Very few pertinent phone calls. We should be concentrating on that, instead of trying to find out if Hogan was in Whitney's pants. Let's just agree he was and move on, all right? I mean, it's a safe bet."

"We should definitely pursue the wire aggressively, but we can't just drop other leads. What if the drug smuggling isn't why the girls died? What if there was something strange going on at Holbrooke?"

"Brianna Meyers had balloons of heroin in her stomach! How can that not be why they died?"

Melanie frowned. He had a point there.

"Esposito and the drug-smuggling angle are what matters," Ray-Ray continued. "*Not* who was bangin' Whitney. Shoot me for thinking that—I'm a DEA agent."

Melanie sighed. "Oh, hell, maybe you're right. I'm just frustrated that we don't have more leads on Carmen Reyes."

"Yeah, about that?"

"What?"

"I hate to be a downer, but it occurred to me: If Carmen's not a drug dealer, if she's just a witness like you said, who stumbled across something at Whitney's house . . ." He hesitated, looking uncomfortable.

"Yeah? Spit it out," she said.

"Don't you think Esposito's killed her by now?"

36

RAY-RAY WONG'S SUGGESTION that Carmen might already be dead left Melanie feeling desperate. She decided it was time to get more aggressive. Trouble was, the only plan she could come up with to help Carmen Reyes would put Trevor Leonard in danger, and she had no intention of simply trading one young life for another.

Melanie got off the elevator, buzzed herself through the bullet-proof door, and walked toward her office, so lost in thought she almost didn't notice the note taped to her door. "SEE ME NOW—B. DeF," it read in black felt-tip marker.

"Great. Just what I need," Melanie muttered, tossing her coat and briefcase on her chair and heading down the hall.

It was nearly eight, but Shekeya was still at her desk in the ante-room. A large plastic plate sat before her, piled with vivid orange cheese cubes and rubbery shrimp cocktail. Despite the dubious look of the food, Melanie's stomach rumbled. Shekeya glanced up and caught the greedy expression on her face.

"Oh, no, you don't!" Shekeya said. "The Christmas party on for another hour. Go get you own."

"If I had time for that, I'd be in there partying with everyone else," Melanie said.

"That your own problem. Don't expect me to share. I ain't missin' no meals for nobody."

Melanie raised her hands in front of her, stuck out her tongue, and started begging like a dog.

"Don't *think* you cute, because you ain't!" Shekeya insisted, but Melanie kept on panting. "Girl, wasn't you on some diet anyway? . . . Oh, all right, take some. You lucky I lost my appetite watchin' you act like a fool."

"Really? Oh, thank you, thank you!" Melanie exclaimed.

"Yeah, you better hurry up before I change my mind."

Melanie plucked a napkin off the desk and loaded it with cheese and shrimp, which still left plenty on the groaning plate for Shekeya.

"You should check out the party anyway. Judge Warner runnin' around in a Santa suit. Quite a sight," Shekeya remarked.

"That's what they call ironic," Melanie said, sticking a shrimp in her mouth. It tasted unpleasantly of ammonia, but she was too starved to care. "I don't know why everyone thinks I'm on a diet. I'm not," she said, mouth full.

"The way you chowin' down, obviously not."

"I need to keep my strength up to talk to the boss. She in?"

"Yes, she is, but you don't *wanna* be goin' in there. She bustin' on poor Joe Williams for some shit he did when Susan be gone. I brang in some paperwork for her to sign, and he sittin' there with his head in his hands like he gonna faint. I love the boy to death, but I swear he the timidest black man on God's earth, let a woman treat him like that."

"Joe's not timid, he's sensitive. Besides, you know what *she's* like."

"Yes, I do, which is why one of these days y'all gonna be bailin' me out after I commit justifiable homicide."

"So how's the working late going?" Melanie asked, finishing the food and wiping her hands with the napkin. She had a bad taste in her mouth now.

"Sucks. I miss my kids."

Didn't she know it! Melanie looked at her watch again. The minutes were ticking away, and every one that passed made it less likely she'd see Maya tonight. Third night in a row she'd miss bedtime. Melanie visualized her daughter's chubby face and imagined sitting in the glider rocker swaying gently back and forth with Maya in her lap. God, she was about to make herself cry. And if this was how *she* felt, what must Maya feel? Maya couldn't even understand why her mommy was gone or when she'd be coming home. Melanie had a sudden powerful impulse to rush into Bernadette's office and resign. But then what would she do for money?

"Do you ever worry about what it does to your kids? This working-late stuff?" Melanie wondered aloud.

"I don't let myself go nowhere near that one. What the use? Less I hit Powerball, I gotta work."

"This OD case I'm working on now? Never would've happened if the parents were around more."

"Shut up, girl, you depressin' me."

"I know. I'm sorry, Shekeya. It's just, I'm really blue about it tonight."

"And now you goin' to Puerto Rico and all. *Girl,* I feel for you. Oh, that reminds me, I gotta get your seat assignment. You prefer window or aisle?"

"What?"

The door to Bernadette's inner sanctum flew open, and Joe Williams sprinted through the anteroom with his head down, looking extremely upset. Bernadette appeared in the doorway, her color high, a smug expression on her face.

"Oh, there you are, Melanie. Come on in," Bernadette said.

Melanie walked in and stood facing her boss. Between the shrimp cocktail and what Shekeya had just told her, she felt like throwing up. "Bernadette, what's this about me going to Puerto Rico?"

"Yes. I'm *so* pleased about this Esposito wiretap. I had a long talk with Vito Albano about what a unique investigative opportunity this is."

Melanie had spoken to Albano privately about convincing Bernadette to start supporting their investigation instead of interfering with it. Apparently he'd done his job too well. Now Bernadette was so enthusiastic that she was sending Melanie traveling with no notice.

"You know," Bernadette was saying, "Vito really changed my mind about some of the angles you're pursuing. And guess what?" Bernadette giggled girlishly. "He asked me out. We're having dinner at this cute little place he knows in Bensonhurst. Do you think he's attractive?"

"Uh . . ."

"*I* do! You know what they say. Power is the great aphrodisiac. Anyway, Vito and I decided to send you and some of the agents down to San Juan to monitor the drug shipment. Isn't that fabulous? It'll be great for the case. I want to take some time now to go over strategy. Then you can run home and pack a bag."

MELANIE THANKED her lucky stars that her current baby-sitter was flexible. Sandy was originally from Trinidad, tall, stately, and quiet, twenty-seven, recently married. She was trying to pull together a down payment for a two-bedroom in Crown Heights, so she didn't mind working overtime to earn some extra money. When Melanie got home on the nights Sandy stayed late, she always found Maya sleeping, the kitchen spotless, and Sandy sitting quietly reading her Bible. Overall an excellent situation, as good as Melanie could ever wish for. But it hardly made her feel better as she headed back to her office after a lengthy meeting with Bernadette. Melanie didn't know what upset her more—the fact that she was being told to fly to Puerto Rico with no notice or the fact that it was now almost nine o'clock, meaning Maya was fast asleep.

The stress was catching up with her. Melanie walked through her office door, swept her coat and briefcase to the floor and collapsed into her swivel chair in a total funk. The very next second, her phone rang. Just as well. She wasn't cut out to be a drama queen. Dwelling on your problems did nothing to solve them.

"Melanie Vargas," she answered, trying to sound composed.

The person on the other end of the line drew a sharp breath but said nothing.

"Who *is* this?" Melanie demanded. It was creepy enough around the office at night without some heavy breather harassing her.

"What's up?" Dan O'Reilly said sheepishly.

"Oh, it's you," she said, relieved. "Making obscene phone calls now?"

"You took me by surprise, is all."

"*I* took *you* by surprise? I tell you never to speak to me again, and you call the same night and start breathing into the telephone?"

"Jeez, I was just trying to leave a voice mail. I didn't think you'd be there this late."

"Some people work hard."

"I shoulda known. You're like the Energizer Bunny," he said, and she could almost hear him smile. He sounded so normal, so *himself,* with that deep, sexy voice, that she felt herself relaxing. Wanting to forgive him. But she'd fight that temptation to the death. Those terrible things he'd said about her! Who the hell did he think he was?

"For your information, I don't love being here this late, so get to the point."

"Whaddaya, there by yourself? Didn't I tell you to be more careful, with Expo's goons running around?"

"Please, spare me the phony concern for my safety."

He sighed. "Fine, I give up. Forget we ever had this conversation. I'll call back and talk to your machine."

"*Fine,*" she said, and hung up.

A moment later her phone rang. Melanie let it roll over to voice mail. But she couldn't help feeling curious: Dan was leaving a long message. An apology, perhaps? Maybe if he apologized profusely enough . . . But no way, José, she'd never forgive him. When the little red light finally came on, though, she grabbed the receiver and retrieved the message so eagerly that she felt embarrassed for herself.

"Ms. Vargas," Dan began coldly, *"Special Agent Dan O'Reilly from the FBI calling to fill you in on a development on the case. Listen, I checked out James Seward's whereabouts the night of the ODs. I'll tell you, for a royal pain in the ass, you got excellent instincts. His timing is fucked up, just like you thought. The people seated with them at that holiday benefit claim Seward and his wife left way earlier than what he told you. Shortly after nine o'clock, to be exact. Everybody noticed, because the missus was trashed out of her mind. Seward had to practically carry her out. So I go after the Sewards' doormen, like, What the fuck, you scumbags, you're holding out on me, and wouldn't you know, one of 'em miraculously gets his memory back. He tells me Seward brought the missus home, dumped her at the front door so hammered she could barely walk, slipped him a twenty to take 'er upstairs, and ran off. Chivalry's fucking dead, ain't it? Anyhow, the guy has a real clear recollection of what happened next, because—get this—he goes up in the elevator, holding Mrs. Seward so she doesn't collapse, and rings the bell. Whitney comes to the door in her panties, looking stoned off her ass, goes, 'Thanks, I'll take it from here,' and brings her mother inside. Three things this tells us: One, Whitney was still alive at around nine-fifteen or nine-thirty. Two, Mrs. Seward was home, prob'ly out cold, when the girls died. And three, Mr. Seward's whereabouts are unaccounted for between, say, nine-thirty and midnight. Uh, that's it. Have a nice life."*

Melanie mentally added a conclusion number four to Dan's list: Luis Reyes, in confirming that the Sewards arrived home *together* around midnight, had lied to her. And if he'd lied about that, what else might Reyes be lying about?

Man, people sucked sometimes. Witnesses lied to Melanie about matters of importance on a daily basis. Not just criminals either, but civilians. Some out of fear, some because they were covering for friends or family, some because they just enjoyed dicking around with the authorities. Whatever. Melanie expected it, she took it in stride. It was her job to zero in on the lie and blast away at it until she got to the truth. Once in a while, in egregious cases, she'd bring perjury or obstruction charges. But on a personal level, she was past caring, past disillusion. Or so she'd thought, until now. Strangely, Luis Reyes's dishonesty truly stung. She'd cared about this *papi,* seemingly so distraught over his missing daughter. Yes, she understood that people in Reyes's position often didn't trust the police. But come on, she was no uniform, she was on his side. She'd spoken Spanish to him, like one of his own. She felt betrayed. Her blood boiling, Melanie grabbed her coat from where she'd thrown it on the floor, ready to rush over to Reyes's basement apartment, barge in, and confront him.

But then her phone rang again. This time she saw from the caller ID that it was the phone outside the bulletproof door. She remembered she had an appointment, a plan. Even if Reyes had lied, she still had every intention of finding his daughter—hopefully, before much more time passed.

A few minutes later, Melanie was back at her desk, Bridget Mulqueen and Trevor Leonard seated across from her.

"I had an idea," Melanie said. "So far Jay Esposito hasn't said anything illegal over the cell-phone wiretap, am I right?"

"Nothing. Squat," Bridget replied. "Everybody at HQ is majorly disappointed."

"What if somebody were to approach the bodyguards tonight with something so huge that Esposito has no choice but to talk about it over his cell phone? I don't mean a drug buy, now. They get those at Screen every night of the week, and obviously Expo's cautious about talking drugs over the phone. I'm thinking of something much bigger."

"Like what?"

"Like Carmen Reyes. There's a good chance Esposito knows where she is. If we were to go to the club and start asking about Carmen, my guess is the bodyguards call their boss right away. Then, bingo, we've got 'em talking about criminal matters over the tapped phone. What do you think?"

Trevor nodded enthusiastically. "Righteous. I'll do it!"

"Not you, Trevor, *Bridget*," Melanie said. "If Expo really is responsible for Carmen's disappearance, you start asking about Carmen, you become a target. It's too dangerous."

"So? I don't give a shit."

"Well, you should. This is no joke. Something awful happened last night."

She filled them in on Fabulous Deon's murder.

"That bludgeon vic was Deon?" Bridget said. "Jeez, that sucks! For being light on his feet, I liked the guy. But Expo's not behind the murder. My cousin Frankie Leary from Manhattan South caught the case. He says it was a prostitute robbery gone bad."

"Detective Leary is your cousin?"

"Yeah. He's a hundred percent sure the killer was a pross. So Trevor can do the undercover."

"I'm not saying don't *do* it, but I refuse to use a civilian like Trevor. *You* go in there, Bridget. Claim to be a friend of Carmen Reyes's," Melanie said.

"Sure. I mean, if that's the way you want to go, I can do that."

"That doesn't make sense!" Trevor objected. "Expo's people know me. They know I hung with Whitney and Brianna. Coming from me, it looks real natural to ask about Carmen."

"Trevor, trust me, it's just not smart," Melanie said. "Danger is part of any undercover operation. But when you're nosing around about a missing girl who's possibly kidnapped or murdered, people like Expo don't play games. They kill you."

"I don't care. I'm not scared. I want to do it," Trevor said, a calm, resolute look on his pierced face.

"Did I tell you about this witness I had on another case? A really sweet woman named Rosario Sangrador—"

"Yeah, yeah, you told me all about her. Different time, different place."

"Don't be so blasé. This could happen to *you*. Do me a favor, talk to

Patty Atkins before you make a final decision. Please? She works late. I'll get her on the phone," Melanie said, reaching for the receiver.

"No!" Trevor insisted. "Hear me out, okay, Melanie? The way I see it, my whole life so far, all I did is get wasted and sell drugs. Maybe I got a decent grade now and then, but I never accomplished anything real, you know? Nailing Expo for what he did to Brianna, finding Carmen—those things matter. Your plan is sound, man. I want to do it for *myself,* like a self-respect thing. You couldn't talk me out of it if you tried."

You gotta love this kid, Melanie thought. She imagined he'd make a fine cop—if it weren't for the small matter of his criminal record.

"I'm responsible for your safety," she protested, but she knew she was fighting a losing battle. She could see in his eyes that he'd made up his mind.

"It's my life."

Melanie sighed. "Okay, then we need to work out our plan very carefully. Because I can't even *think* about what might happen if we screw up."

AFTER TREVOR AND BRIDGET LEFT, Melanie sifted through her in-box and pulled out a copy of Ray-Ray Wong's DEA-6 report detailing the interview with Luis Reyes. She wanted to give Reyes the benefit of the doubt, but damn, there it was in black and white: proof he'd lied. "REYES informed the undersigned that Mr. and Mrs. James Seward arrived back to the residence at approximately 2330 to 2400 hours and met up with REYES." No mistake about it either. Ray-Ray Wong was a careful note taker, and besides, the report only confirmed Melanie's own recollection of what Reyes had said. It was after ten, but this couldn't wait. She was leaving for Puerto Rico first thing in the morning. She'd confront Reyes tonight.

The snow had turned to heavy sleet. Melanie exited the glass lobby doors, heading across the plaza toward the empty street. Small icy pellets hit her face, stinging her, collecting on her hair and eyelashes. She pulled her coat tighter, looked up at the strangely backlit gray-white sky and wondered if her flight would be canceled tomorrow.

Making it uptown was starting to look like a chancier proposition than getting to Puerto Rico. Melanie stepped off the curb, squinting through the driving sleet at oncoming traffic, looking for a cab. But the wide avenue, which ran through a canyon of tall courthouses and office buildings, was virtually deserted given the hour and the weather. Several blocks down, a few vehicles sat at a red light. The light changed, and they struggled slowly toward her, fighting for traction. A beat-up white van fishtailed on the glassy blacktop, then righted itself. Melanie spotted a taxi with its off-duty light on and hailed it frantically, but the driver ignored her.

After a few more minutes, an enormous plow sped by, spitting foamy black slush from its blade, forcing her to jump up onto the curb to avoid getting splattered. Once it passed, she stepped into the street again and sank into a puddle up to her ankles. The frigid water soaked right through her good suede boots.

Melanie trudged out of the puddle, feeling like the last person left on earth. Nobody out on foot, no vehicles approaching as far as the eye could see, the clicking sound of pelting sleet muffling everything else. She was beginning to feel vulnerable out here all alone. Not to mention cold and wet. Two more minutes and she'd give up and take the subway. She hated the deserted platforms at this hour, but the street on a night like this was hardly better. Anyway, who knew how long it would be before the next taxi happened by?

Across the avenue and up several car lengths, the headlights of a parked SUV flashed on. Strange. Melanie couldn't recall seeing a person approach that car or hearing its engine start up either. Maybe she'd been distracted by her search for a cab? The enormous vehicle was covered in crusty snow, its outline softened and obscured. But as it maneuvered to pull out of the tight parking space, Melanie recognized it as an Escalade by its size and shape. It looked black, too—the same make and model Expo's bodyguards were known to drive. In less than a minute, judging from its angle, the massive thing would pull free and head toward her. It would be in perfect position to run her down, too, with nobody to stop it and no witnesses. Melanie couldn't see in through the tinted windshield. Granted, some soccer mom from Connecticut could be behind the wheel just as easily as Expo's thugs. But she was beginning to have a bad feeling about this. Best not to stick around to find out.

There was only one small problem: To get to the only subway entrance, Melanie had to cross the street, making her a sitting duck if the Escalade came after her. She glanced over her shoulder at her darkened office building, but it was even farther away than the subway. And at this hour, if the lobby security guard took a bathroom break, you could stand there for ten minutes pounding on the locked door to no avail.

She looked back at the Escalade. It was nearly out of the space now, its massive wheels swinging toward her ominously, as if in slow motion. Shit. *Run for it!*

Melanie bolted into the street and raced for the subway entrance with all her strength. At the same instant, the Escalade finally escaped its parking space, tires spinning and crunching the sleet as they gripped the road. Fricking thing had unbelievable traction! Melanie was halfway across the street in one shot, heart in her throat, cold air stinging her lungs. *Goddamn boots! You had to be vain and wear three-inch heels!* Her eyes were fixed on the subway entrance, but her ears couldn't ignore the roar of the Escalade close behind her. She hit the opposite sidewalk at a dead run, mere feet now from the subway stairs. Fumbling in her pocket for her MetroCard, panting with fear, she turned to look over her shoulder just as her boots hit a patch of ice. Melanie's legs flew out from under her, her tailbone connecting with the hard cement and sending a wave of pain shooting up her spine as she skidded forward. In her peripheral vision, she saw six thousand pounds of steel jump the curb, barreling straight for her, as the sound of her own screams filled her ears.

37

BUD HAD a new cell phone in a fake name, to take Jay's incoming calls. The way things had heated up lately, you couldn't be too careful. No point in getting caught now. He planned to make it to payday, and Friday was only forty-eight hours away.

The fucking thing was already ringing as he walked in the door to the apartment. He glanced at the caller ID. What a surprise—Jay's cell. Some wannabe kingpin this guy was! He couldn't do a goddamn thing on his own.

"Yeah?" Bud said.

"Look, I think we might got a situation. I'm not sure," Jay said, a roar of music and voices behind him. He must be at Screen.

"What?" Bud asked.

"Kid's in here asking around about one of Whitney's friends."

"By name?"

"He says Carmen."

Bud was silent for a moment.

"Well?" Jay demanded.

"I'm thinking, I'm thinking." He sighed. "What's the kid look like?"

"Real freak. Pierced up the wazoo, dreads, the whole nine yards."

Okay, him. Now Bud had a clearer picture of what was going on.

"Did he say anything else?" Bud asked.

"Yeah, actually. Wants to score some H."

"You should really be more careful what you say over the phone, you know, Jay."

"Far as I'm concerned, anybody listening can suck my dick."

"Ha, ha, very funny. You better hope nobody is." *We both better,* Bud thought. His mind was racing, thinking about what the kid's angle might be here. He had his suspicions, and if they were on target, action needed to be taken. Fast. "Listen, Jay. If the kid's into all that, you think maybe he wants to make a quick buck?"

"What, like Friday?"

"Why not?"

"I thought you had a girl lined up."

"It's always good to have a fallback. This is why I was a better Boy Scout than you. Be prepared."

"You were a fucking pansy, is what you were."

"It was a joke, for Chrissakes. But about this pierced kid, I think we should chill out. It doesn't mean anything, him asking around about shit. Whitney hung out at the club, maybe some of her friends did, too. So what?"

"That's *it*? I coulda thought of that myself."

"What do you want me to say? Ice the kid?"

"Nah, you're right. That would draw unnecessary attention."

"You bet your ass it would."

"Were you serious, though, about Friday?"

"Yes, as a matter of fact. I mean, why the fuck not?"

"It'd never work! You gotta see this kid. He's a walking advertisement for profiling."

"What if you cut his hair?"

"He's got a real crazy tattoo down the side of his face."

"So? If the feds are watching, they'll be looking for rich girls, not freaks with dreadlocks."

"Huh. Well, you got a point. Okay, maybe it's not such a bad idea after all. We can at least give it a shot. I'll have Lamar chat him up, see if he bites."

"Good. Now, what about that other thing we talked about before?"

"I sent Pavel to take care of it. He's out now. Haven't heard. It might not go because of the weather."

"Huh. *That's* not good."

"I don't know why you're so hot to take action on that front. Talk about drawing unnecessary attention."

"That one's worth worrying about."

"Like I said, I don't see it, and I don't get why the rush all of a sudden. But if it makes you happy, Buddy boy, I'll indulge ya for old times' sake."

"I appreciate it, Jay," Bud said calmly. *And it'll be one of the last things you ever do, you condescending prick. I fucking make you, with all the ideas I feed you, and this is how you talk to me? You'll get yours.*

38

CARMEN SAT at a perfectly ordinary kitchen table, slurping chicken noodle soup ravenously from a green plastic bowl. *He* sat next to her, guarding her as she ate. Normally she would've been too self-conscious to eat this way in front of anybody. But she was too hungry to care. She remembered something she'd read in English class last semester. A story about Jews getting shipped off to concentration camps, how the Nazis purposely fed them salty soup right before packing them into sweltering cattle cars with no water. She looked up at her captor, into his cold gray eyes, and understood that the Jews would've drunk the soup even if they'd known about the Nazis' diabolical plan. Hunger made you do things. So did fear.

He reached into his pocket unexpectedly, and Carmen dropped her spoon, cowering.

"Relax," he said with a chuckle. "You think I'm gonna shoot you *now*? How stupid would *that* be? I have something I need to show you, that's all."

He tossed a necklace onto the table with a clatter. A silver peace sign on a tan cowhide string. Carmen recognized it immediately and started to whimper.

"Calm down, for Chrissakes, or I'm putting you back in the cage," he said, irritated.

"You killed my sister!" Carmen shouted as her shoulders shook with small, coughing sobs.

"No, but I could have. You need to understand that. And I could kill you, too, if you make problems. But I'm sure you already know that."

Carmen's sobs grew to a keening wail.

"Shut up! You saw what happened to Whitney. You wanna be next?"

But that reminder only served to push her over the edge, and she began shrieking wildly. He leaned forward and clamped his hand over her mouth. Carmen bit hard, her teeth sinking into the soft flesh of his palm.

"Aagh! You little twat!" He stared at the blood seeping into the ugly red wells made by her teeth. Seeing the rage on his face, she drew a breath and started screaming again, hysterically, at the top of her lungs. He raised his fist and punched her in the face. He was stronger than he looked. The blow sent her crashing over backward. Carmen's head hit the sharp edge of the granite countertop with a sickening thud, and she collapsed motionless to the floor.

"I feed you, and this is how you fucking repay me?" he spit at her inert form. "You go and fuck everything up? What am I supposed to do on Friday if you're dead?"

39

MELANIE SCREAMED with terror as the giant SUV hurtled straight for the spot where she sat. She threw herself sideways, rolling over and over on the cold, hard pavement as fast as she could until she reached the subway entrance. The Escalade screeched to a stop mere inches from the stairs, its driver throwing it into reverse to get into position for a second go at her. Melanie leaped to her feet and bolted down the icy steps two at a time, gasping for breath and praying she wouldn't fall. The familiar, pungent odor of the New York City subway rose to greet her like an old friend.

She reached the turnstile and swiped her MetroCard with a shaking hand. As she sprinted for the ramp to the uptown express, the presence of the clerk in the glass token booth gave her little comfort. What could he do except call the cops to come collect her dead body?

Thank God! An uptown number-four train sat waiting on the platform. Melanie bounded aboard just as the doors closed, then turned around and leaned against the glass, catching her breath, looking back at the empty platform. Just as the train pulled away, she spotted him. Bulletface, running down the ramp she'd just come from, his head swinging back and forth as he scanned the station for her. Until that very moment, she'd been cherishing the illusion that this whole ordeal was nothing more than some paranoid overreaction on her part. Well, *qué lástima,* it wasn't. Jay Esposito had just tried to have her whacked.

I T WAS HARD TO SAY what made Melanie carry on with her plan to confront Luis Reyes about his false statement. Maybe she was in a state of shock. Maybe she was just plain stubborn. If somebody was trying to kill her for doing her job, then she'd damn well do it just to spite them. Nobody was going to stop *her*.

At the Sewards' Park Avenue building, Melanie flashed her creds at the doorman. A minute later she was leaning on the Reyeses' buzzer down in the basement. It was after eleven now, but a sliver of light under the door told her that she wouldn't be waking anybody up.

"Yeah, who's there?" Reyes called gruffly.

"Melanie Vargas, Mr. Reyes. May I come—"

He ripped the door open before she could finish her sentence, a wild look in his eyes. *"You find her?"* he asked desperately.

"No, no, nothing like that. Please, I need to speak to you."

"Come."

She followed him into the living room. Reyes turned to her as they sat down on the threadbare sofa, and she saw that he'd been crying.

"I can' stand it no more," he said. "I don't eat or sleep since she gone. At first I waiting for her to walk in the door, but now, a coupla days gone by, and I don' know, I got a very bad feeling." He put his head in his hands. "Please," he said through his fingers, "please tell me she okay. Because I don' know how I'm gonna go on if sonthing really happen to her."

Now, how was she supposed to confront a man in this condition? Only by reminding herself that getting the facts was key to finding Carmen.

"Mr. Reyes," Melanie said gently, patting his shoulder, "you have to be strong. I promise you, I'm doing everything in my power to locate your daughter. But I need your help."

"Yes, of course," he said, straightening and wiping his eyes. "Anything I can do, I do."

"What you can do is be completely truthful with me," Melanie said, giving him a hard look. "I'm concerned that when you gave your statement the other night, you lied."

Reyes didn't even try to deny it.

"Ma'am, I very, very sorry about that. Yes, I lie to you, but I swear it wasn't about nothing important. I wanna tell the truth, but I stuck, like they say, with a rock and a hard place."

"It's not *up* to you to decide what's important in this investigation, Mr. Reyes. For all you know, the things you lied about may have a direct bearing on what happened to Carmen."

"I never lie about sonthing with *mi hija*! Never. The only thing I do is cover for Mr. Seward, because he ask me to. What I supposed to do? I need my job!"

"Cover for him for what?"

"Please don' tell him I tell you this, but he got a little sonthing on the side. I'm not saying is okay, but a lotta guys do that. He don' want it in the newspapers, so he ask me be quiet about how he with his lady friend when I tell him about Whitney."

Wait a minute now. There was more to this than she'd originally thought.

"So when you first called Mr. Seward, you actually spoke to him?" she asked, keeping her voice calm, as if this were no surprise. But, man, she was pissed.

"Yes. Maybe ten-thirty I fin' the girls dead, then I call him and speak to him. So, okay, I lie about that part, when I say I only leave a message. I told him wha' happen, but he say he can' come right then, he *busy*. I know what he mean, because I seen him with his lady friend before."

"Did he actually say he couldn't come because he was with another woman?"

"No, he never say that. But what else, right?"

"So you're just guessing."

"Yeah, okay, but . . ." Reyes waved his hands and gave her a knowing glance, implying they were both worldly creatures who understood these things.

"How long was it before Seward showed up?"

"Like I say, maybe a coupla hours. A while."

"Doesn't that seem strange? You tell a man his stepdaughter and her friend are lying dead in his apartment, and he wastes two hours on some tryst?"

Reyes shrugged. *"Amor."*

Please. As a betrayed wife herself, Melanie felt like smacking Reyes.

"You say you'd seen him with this woman before?" she asked.

"One time she come here when Mrs. Seward away for treatment. See, I got a little sympathy, because Mrs. Seward, she drinkin' too much all the time. Is very difficult for a man to have a drunk for a wife."

Or maybe Charlotte Seward drank *because* James Seward cheated? Steve's infidelity would've driven Melanie to drink if she hadn't gotten her act together to leave. But Luis Reyes didn't see things that way. It was the woman's fault.

"By the way," Melanie asked, "where *was* Charlotte Seward while all this was happening?"

"Okay, I not tell the truth about that either, and I'n very sorry. Mrs. Seward was pass out in her bed. I go in there and find her. I wake her up, and she run in the bathroom to throw up. I come back later and fin' her pass out again on the bathroom floor."

To be so wasted that your daughter dies in the next room and you don't even know? Melanie couldn't begin to imagine the grief and humiliation. But the bottom line was, Charlotte Seward had been at home during the events in question. She needed to be interviewed—the sooner, the better.

"This other woman. What does she look like?" Melanie asked.

"Oh, very nice. A real lady. She older, too, maybe forty, forty-fibe, blond hair, dress real expensive."

"What's her name?" Melanie asked.

"Patricia."

Melanie's jaw literally dropped. "Are you sure?"

"Yes. I hear him say it to her."

"And you're sure they were . . . involved? *¿Amantes?*"

"Oh, yes. Because that time before, she was here, like, four o'clock in the morning. I working in the basement getting the recycling ready for the Sanitation, and he sneaking her out the back door. He wink at me, so on the way back, I give him high fibe. You know, like a guy thing. He give me an extra-big tip for Christmas this year, because he know he can trust me."

Barf. What a thing to be proud of.

"So, just to make sure I've got this all straight, you called James Seward around ten-thirty, right when you discovered the bodies. He said he was too busy to come home immediately, but he asked you not to call the police. Two hours went by before he showed up, at which point he called the police himself."

"Yes."

"Did Seward specifically ask you to lie about the missing two hours?"

Reyes avoided her eyes.

"Mr. Reyes, answer my question! *Truthfully.*"

"Yeah, okay. He never say to me, lie. He say he always appreciate how trustworthy I am. I got a lotta discretion. That kinda thing. But I know what he asking me to do."

So she had James Seward on obstruction. It was leverage, at least.

"You not gonna tell him I say that, are you?" Reyes asked nervously. "I lose my job."

"Mr. Reyes, has it ever occurred to you that since Mrs. Seward was at home when Carmen was abducted, she might have seen or heard something that could help find your daughter?"

Reyes opened his mouth and then closed it again. Confusion and grief chased each other across his face. He dropped his head into his hands again and rubbed his bloodshot eyes. When he finally looked back up at Melanie, though, he was resolute. "You right," he said. "Go tell Mrs. Seward what I say and get her to talk to you. God help me if she know sonthing and I coulda find Carmencita faster."

MELANIE WAS WAITING for the service elevator when she saw the Reyeses' door swing open again, silently this time. Lulu Reyes emerged, then turned and closed it so carefully that it didn't even click. Melanie would've spoken, but Lulu put a finger to her lips and beckoned Melanie to follow her down the dank gray hallway. Lulu led her to a basement laundry room painted an angry mustard yellow. Fluorescent lights buzzed overhead.

"What is it? What's the matter?" Melanie asked.

Lulu looked at her with huge, solemn eyes. "I did a very bad thing," she said softly.

"Does it have to do with Carmen?" Melanie asked.

Lulu nodded miserably. "I know something I didn't say. You won't tell Papi, will you?"

"No, of course not. Prosecutors are very good at keeping things confidential. What matters is that you tell me now so I can use the information to find your sister. She's in danger, and every second counts."

Lulu started to say something, then hesitated. Indecision and fear flickered in her eyes.

"Lulu, it's okay. You can tell me."

"I want you to know, I'm just doing this to help Carmen. That's the only reason."

"Of course, sweetie. I understand. I have a sister, too. In fact, you and Carmen remind me a little bit of my sister and me."

"Carmen's, like, a really good girl. But she doesn't have common sense. She got mixed up in stuff that was too big for her to handle."

"Nobody's blaming Carmen for anything, okay? All we want is to find her. I need to know what kind of stuff she got mixed up in."

Lulu paused again, then drew a deep breath and blurted, "Okay, this girl Whitney, right?"

"Yes?"

"She was really messed up. Like, totally."

"In what way?" Melanie asked, pretending ignorance in order to draw Lulu out.

"Heavy into drugs. Not just using either, but, like, maybe even selling or something. I'm not sure. Carmen found out, and she was really upset about it. I said she should mind her own business, but that one always has to be a good citizen."

"So did Carmen do anything with the information?"

"I don't know for sure. But she might've. I'm thinking maybe what happened to her has something to do with that. Oh, and one more thing."

"Yes?"

"You should check out a guy named Jay Esposito. They call him Expo."

"What's he got to do with all this?"

Lulu shrugged. "Carmen mentioned him, is all."

"Anything else?"

Lulu hesitated for another moment, studying Melanie's face as if looking for answers there. "No," she said finally. "That's everything."

"You did the right thing by coming forward, Lulu. I want you to know, we're already checking out Jay Esposito."

"Really?" Lulu seemed surprised.

"Yes. And the information you just gave me is very important. Because it helps us know we're on the right track with Esposito and that we should continue devoting resources there."

"Oh."

Lulu looked almost disappointed. Melanie couldn't tell exactly what was going on with the girl, but she had the sense it was more than met the eye.

Melanie gave Lulu a hard look. "You sure there's not something else you want to tell me."

"Why *would* there be?" Lulu said, her mouth settling into a stubborn pout.

Melanie sighed. "You have my phone numbers. If anything occurs to you, or even if you just want to talk, call me. It could mean the difference between life and death for your sister. Do you understand?"

"Yeah, whatever."

They walked back down the hall, and Melanie buzzed for the service elevator again. Lulu turned to go back inside.

"Hey, c'mere," Melanie said, determined to reach out one last time. She opened her arms. Lulu hesitated, then walked over and let Melanie hug her.

"You're a brave girl for coming forward, Lulu. You should be proud of yourself."

Lulu nodded and mumbled her thanks. The elevator arrived. As Melanie got on, she looked searchingly into the girl's face, but it was clouded and closed.

40

*M*ELANIE ROCKED—*back, forth, back, forth in the glider rocker—caressing Maya's dark head, lulling and soothing, singing softly. Maya's hair was like silk, her small body warm and heavy and delicious with drowsiness. The little girl sighed, her eyelids fluttering in wordless dreams.*

When Melanie was certain the child slept, she rose to her feet in a fluid motion, holding Maya gingerly, like a piece of fine porcelain. She stepped over to the crib and lowered the side rail with her knee, then gathered her daughter near. Sniffing Maya's neck, she drank deeply of the powdery scent. Love rose in her throat like tears.

Melanie placed Maya gently on the mattress. She raised the crib rail, turned, and walked to the center of the room, where she stood waiting silently. She wasn't sure for what, but in a moment she understood. A strange blue light shone down on the crib. A gurgling sound rose from within.

Melanie walked back over to the crib and looked down into it.

"Help me," Carmen Reyes begged, raising her arms as blood began to stream from her nose and mouth.

Melanie opened her eyes with a gasp, mouth dry, nightgown soaked with sweat. The clock read 4:20. The alarm was set to go off at four-thirty, so she'd have time to pack and catch an eight o'clock flight out of JFK.

She sat up. Then she heard it. A strange sound coming from the direction of Maya's room, and this time she wasn't dreaming. She leaped out of bed with a pounding heart and raced to the hallway. A sharp pain in her lower back reminded her vividly of the Escalade bearing down on her last night. Why the hell hadn't she done anything about that? She hadn't even reported it to other members of her team, let alone requested any protection. Just because some witness lied to you, to forget all about the fact that your main target tried to have you whacked? Jesus, how stupid could you be?

In the darkened hallway, she glanced nervously over her shoulder and listened. Nothing. Dead silence except for her own rapid breathing. Whatever she'd heard, she wasn't hearing it now. She snapped on the hall light, recoiling at the glare, then hurried to Maya's room.

When she saw what awaited her, Melanie almost *wished* it had been one of Expo's goons in her house. Maya sat upright in her crib, a dazed expression on her face. There was a sour smell in the room. In the glow from the night-light, Melanie saw something pale-colored standing out against her daughter's dark hair. Taking a step closer, she saw that it was an undigested piece of macaroni from last night's dinner. Maya was covered with vomit.

"Oh, no!" Melanie cried, lowering the crib rail and lifting Maya out. She rested her cheek against her daughter's forehead. Maya was burning up. "Poor baby, you can't catch a break. Sick *again,* when you're just getting over the last one? Don't worry. Mommy's gonna make you feel better."

She turned on the overhead light, dimming it so it wouldn't hurt Maya's eyes, and held her daughter away so she could get a better look at her. Maya stared back with a glazed, feverish look. She moaned softly, then spewed hot vomit all over the front of Melanie's nightgown.

"Oh, boy."

Melanie rushed to the bathroom, gently undressed Maya, sponged her with a warm washcloth, and changed her into fresh clothes. She stripped off her own nightgown and threw it in the wash along with

Maya's jammies and bedding. During the next half hour, Maya vomited twice more, including throwing up the fever reducer Melanie tried to give her. So, walking around her chilly apartment stark naked because she didn't even have time to get her bathrobe, Melanie mopped the floor, changed and washed Maya twice, and beeped the pediatrician, who was annoyed to be disturbed so early. There was a stomach bug going around, he said. Give the child lots of fluids and call the office in three days if it hadn't resolved.

Melanie didn't know what to do. She couldn't imagine going off to Puerto Rico and leaving Maya in this condition, with some patchwork combination of Steve, the baby-sitter, and Melanie's mother looking after her. She felt more panicked than she had last night with the car chasing her. The sky outside her windows was turning pink, and time was ticking away for her to pack and get to the airport.

She called and woke Steve. Fifteen minutes later, he showed up at her door and he was better than Melanie ever expected. He helped her get a fever reducer into Maya, then looked after her so Melanie could shower, dress, and pack. But the best thing he did was calm Melanie down.

"First of all, she's gonna be fine. It's just a stomach bug," Steve said, standing in the bathroom doorway holding the now sleeping Maya as Melanie, clad in bra and panties, applied her makeup.

"Hey, turn around," she said, waving the mascara wand at him.

"What, like I never saw you in your skivvies before?"

"Come on. Be nice."

He made a show of turning his body sideways, though he was clearly still watching her.

Melanie sighed profoundly. "I just can't *stand* not being with her while she's suffering like this. I mean, she doesn't understand why she feels so bad, you know?"

"I know, baby. It's just awful that you have to work. That's one thing that could be different if you and I got back together."

She remained conspicuously silent in response to that comment.

Like she would up and quit her job and go back to him when he'd been spotted out clubbing mere days earlier. Fat freaking chance. Still, she was grateful he was here.

"But, look, she'll be well cared for," Steve said, glossing over her silence without missing a beat. "We both think Sandy is good, right? And at night I'll stay over here and take care of her. I'm her daddy, after all. Just leave your mom's number in case I have a work crisis myself."

"Thank you. I appreciate it so much. Like I said, I'll be back Saturday morning at the latest."

"That's good. You know, I was thinking. My parents are in St. Barth's. I don't have any plans. Maybe I should just bring some things by, and the three of us could spend the weekend together. That way if she's still sick, I can pitch in and help, and if she's better, we can all enjoy the holiday time. It's almost Christmas, you know."

She paused with her lipstick in her hand and gazed over at him leaning against the doorframe. He looked so good that she was almost tempted. He was wearing old sweatpants and a soft cashmere sweater he'd had for ages—patrician and hunky at the same time. But Melanie knew there was more to marriage than sexual attraction. And she'd learned the hard way that the other ingredients were missing from *this* equation.

"Gee, thanks for the offer, but it's not a good idea," she said.

"We wouldn't have to sleep in the same bed."

"Oh, like that's an option!" she exclaimed with a laugh.

"Why not? That night I came by to drop Maya—"

"That was a *mistake,* Steve. Backsliding. It was late. We were lonely."

His face clouded over. "This is about Musclehead, isn't it?"

Finished with her makeup, Melanie walked into the bedroom. Steve followed her and laid Maya down carefully in the center of the big bed, placing pillows all around her.

"You mean Dan?" Melanie asked, opening the closet door.

"That guy from the other night."

"No, not at all. He has nothing to do with it."

"Wait a minute, is *he* going on this trip, too? Is this even a work trip?" Steve was asking.

"Of course it's a work trip! *Steve,* come on, do you think I would lie to you about that?" she said, turning to him.

He looked down at the floor and then back up at her. He actually looked upset. She felt bad, what with him being so nice about Maya and all.

"I hope not. You *wouldn't,* would you?" Steve said.

"Of course not. Listen, the fact of the matter is, I had a huge fight with Dan and we're not even speaking. It's going to be totally awkward dealing with him. *And* there'll be lots of other people from the team around."

"Okay. Good. I'm relieved to hear that."

Melanie found her summer stuff in the back of the closet and picked out a suit with a fairly short skirt. What the hell, she needed a lift. She'd wear it with heels and no hose, freeze on the plane, but show some leg stepping onto the jetway in her ancestral land.

Steve watched her as she got dressed.

"You sure you wanna wear that? If you make Musclehead come after you again, I might have to beat the crap out of him."

"Will you stop about him?"

"I know, but it's like I can't help thinking about it. Seeing him here the other night, I realized how much I hated the idea of you with another guy. Amazing what a little competition'll do for your perspective, huh?"

She shot him a disgusted look. One thing she could always count on with Steve: Whenever they started getting along, he was sure to go and ruin it.

41

ON THE PLANE Melanie sat alone while Dan and Bridget sat together several rows behind her, a result of the fact that two different government agencies had purchased their tickets. This was fine with Melanie, since she was still fuming at Dan. But she was desperate for an update on what had happened at Screen last night and whether her plan to get Esposito talking about Carmen Reyes had worked. When the Fasten Seat Belt sign was turned off, she'd swallow her pride and go ask them.

They beat her to the punch. Surprisingly, given that it was the beginning of holiday travel season, the seat next to Melanie was empty. The minute the sign went off, Bridget appeared and dropped down beside her.

"Hey," she said cheerfully.

"Hey," Melanie replied flatly. She wasn't in a terrific mood, and she found Bridget annoying at the best of times.

"Dan sent me to fill you in on developments in the case."

Gee, thanks a lot. Couldn't talk to me yourself? But, she should remember, she was the one who'd told him to shove off.

"Great. I really want to hear how it went at Screen last night, but speak quietly." Melanie leaned closer to Bridget, who was wearing perfume and an uncharacteristic amount of makeup. She looked alarmingly pretty, in fact.

"Trev had a major breakthrough," Bridget said.

"He found out about Carmen?" Melanie asked eagerly.

"No, even better. They asked him to mule tomorrow's shipment."

"Are you serious? In his stomach?"

"I mean, we won't let it get to that point, but yeah. Is that the *best*, or what? We never thought we'd get so lucky. Oh, and just so you feel okay about things, there was no sign of trouble from Expo *whatsoever*. They went for it hook, line, and sinker."

"I don't get it. Did Trevor even ask about Carmen? I mean, how did the idea of him muling come up?"

"There was an interception last night over Expo's phone that—"

"Shhh!" Melanie said, looking around.

"Oh, right." Bridget lowered her voice. "It's Expo talking to this guy Bud LNU."

"LNU" was cop talk for "Last Name Unknown," pronounced "La-NOO" when spoken aloud. Melanie's first week on the job, she'd been assigned several unrelated cases with subjects known only by first names, and she'd assumed the Lnus were some depraved Vietnamese crime family who, unbeknownst to her, had come to dominate New York City's underworld. The senior prosecutor who enlightened her had a good laugh at her expense.

"Trevor told us about this Bud guy. An associate of Expo's, right?" Melanie asked.

"Yeah. We thought he was a lieutenant, and maybe he is. But Expo seems to be taking a lot of cues from him. Who knows, maybe Bud's really the one pulling the strings."

"So what did they *say*?" *Get to the point!* she felt like screaming.

"Dan has the line sheet. You can read the call. Check out the part where Expo goes 'anybody listening can suck my dick.' I laughed so hard I almost peed my pants."

"No, what did they say about *Carmen*? That was the whole idea, remember? To see if we could get them talking about what happened to her?"

"Oh. Hmm. Well, they didn't say much about Carmen. I mean, it wasn't clear to me from this call that these guys had anything to do with her disappearance at all. Anyway, about the drug case, the plan is for Trev to fly down this afternoon with one of the bodyguards. We're gonna be all over it with surveillance. Ray-Ray and another guy on the flight. Tons of guys in the airports. You, me, and Dan and some backup from the locals at the El San Juan Hotel."

Melanie gave up on asking about Carmen. She'd read the call, and maybe that would tell her something. But Bridget was useless, so Melanie might as well focus on worrying about the *other* vulnerable young witness.

"Listen, Bridget, I'm not convinced this is a smart idea. No matter how much surveillance we do, how can we protect Trevor sufficiently? He'll still be out of our sight a lot of the time, in their custody."

"Lieutenant Albano already gave the green light. This is the biggest break in the case so far."

The flight attendant pulled a wheeled metal cart up to Melanie's row, braking it with her foot.

"Something to drink?" she asked Bridget.

"Oh, I'm seated a few rows back. I'll go back to my seat."

"Coffee, please," Melanie said.

"Hey, do you have, like, a mirror or a compact or something?" Bridget asked.

"Yes, but it's under my seat. I can't reach it now," said Melanie. The flight attendant was in the process of pouring hot coffee into a cup on Melanie's open tray table.

"How's my friend doing?" Bridget said, pointing to a big pimple on her chin. "My zit *had* to come to Puerto Rico, too. Doesn't that *always* happen just when you're trying to impress a guy? Is it really bad?"

"No, it's fine," Melanie lied. Actually, it *was* pretty bad, now that she mentioned it. The foundation makeup Bridget had caked onto it only made it more obvious. And then, because she couldn't resist, even though she knew the answer, Melanie asked, "So which guy are you trying to impress?"

"Dan!" Bridget practically squealed. "Isn't he *hot*? I have a total crush on him. I think he likes me, too. We went out for beers last night."

Melanie had to swallow very carefully to avoid choking on her coffee. "Really? Did you have fun?"

"*Oh,* yeah, big time! I mean, nothing sexual or anything. Not yet. I want him to look at me like a potential long-term relationship, so no hootchy-kootchy on the first date."

"It was a *date*?"

"Well, it was him, me, and Ray-Ray. But then Ray left and Dan stayed, so yeah, it turned into, like, a date."

"And he seemed interested?'

"I *think* so. I know he's definitely looking. See, me and Dan come from the same background. Families on the job and whatnot, so we know a lot of people in common. Dan's cousin Brian, who he's close to, is a fireman with my brother-in-law Nick, and our dads are, like, the same generation in the PD. Anyways, so I know Dan's been wanting to settle down for years, ever since Diane Fields dumped him, that evil bitch. In the whole time he had, like, one serious thing. It was pretty recent, actually, but it didn't work out."

"Oh. Why not?"

"I heard the woman was married, although it surprises me Dan would get involved in a situation like that."

"How do you know all this?"

"I'm interested in him, so I ask around."

Melanie knew she should stop, but she just couldn't. "So did Dan act interested in *you*?"

"He was playing it cool, but I'm pretty sure he *was*. And then I had my cards read by this old hippie chick who hangs out in the pub, and right in front of Dan she goes, my future husband is someone I'd been drinking with that night. Is that amazing or what? I think it's a *sign*."

"Maybe she meant Ray-Ray,"

"Ick! No way would I ever marry a Chinese guy."

"Why not?"

"Don't get me wrong, I'm not racist or anything. I mean, Bruce Lee was hot. Even Jackie Chan is hot. Well, sort of. I'm into the martial-arts thing. But Ray-Ray? He's way too short."

"He's taller than you."

"Nope, I'm sticking with my own kind and marrying a big Irish hunk. Dan's the one for me. Whether he knows it yet or not. But listen, I better get back to my seat and catch the stewardess before she passes me by. The coffee smells good."

"Okay."

After Bridget left, Melanie stared out the plastic window at the bright, empty sky. Mere minutes earlier she'd been fairly confident her relationship with Dan was over, and all for the best. So why did she feel this devastated at the thought of him with someone else?

Amazing what a little competition'll do for your perspective.

42

A WHILE LATER Melanie was still absorbed in staring out the airplane window when someone once again sat down in the empty seat. When she turned and saw Dan—looking spectacular, smelling clean and yummy, staring back at her with clear blue eyes—she felt such a wrenching sense of loss that for a moment she couldn't even speak.

Seeing her face, Dan held up his hand. "Don't get upset."

"I'm not upset," she said quickly.

"You *look* upset."

"Well, I'm not."

"You shouldn't be. I'm only bothering you because Bridget said you wanted to see the line sheet from that intercept last night. Otherwise I would never've come over here."

"Can't we put this fight behind us?"

"Sure, I get it. We're grown-ups. We keep our distance, keep it professional. When the case is done, we go our separate ways."

She hadn't meant it like that, and she was disappointed he'd taken it that way. Maybe Dan wasn't, as Melanie secretly hoped, waiting for an overture from her. Maybe he'd be better off with Bridget. The two of them had so much in common, after all, whereas Melanie and Dan might as well have grown up on different planets.

"Right. Professional," Melanie said, then drew a deep breath. "So show me that line sheet."

"Here."

He handed her a copy of a handwritten page taken from the wire-tap log. The federal wiretap statute required that a real live human being listen in on every tapped phone call as it was being recorded to make sure the bad guys were talking about crime; if they weren't, the tape recorder had to be shut off. To prove they were monitoring properly, the agents took contemporaneous handwritten notes summarizing the conversations. The piece of paper she held in her hand contained the monitor's notes of a phone call intercepted the previous night at 9:48 P.M., between subject Jay Esposito and subject Bud LNU, aka George Eliot.

"Where do you get this aka?" Melanie asked.

"It's the subscriber name on the cell number Expo placed the call to."

"It's a fake."

"Why do you say that?"

"Oh, come on, George Eliot? Wrote *Middlemarch*?"

"What, you spend all your time in the library in high school?" Dan grinned.

Man, he had a movie-star smile. Her chest hurt, thinking of him out last night with Bridget.

"Yes, as a matter of fact, I did. I like libraries. The quiet. The smell of old books. Very Zen."

"They give me the heebie-jeebies," Dan said. "Anyway, no low-life drug dealer is gonna know about George Eliot. I mean, *I* don't know about him."

"*Her.* Eliot was a woman."

"See? What'd I tell ya?"

She smiled. "Still, you make a good point. Maybe the name *is* real. Did you run it?"

"Yeah. We got nothin'. Too common. We managed to ID the black bodyguard, though."

"How'd you do that?" she asked.

"Had a coupla uniforms traffic-stop him last night and ask for ID. One Lamar Gates. He's got a pretty good rap sheet. Assaults, a few criminal sales, that sorta thing. Did a stretch in Rikers a few years back. This is who Expo has working security for him." He shook his head in disgust.

"What about the Russian?"

"Pavel LNU. We got shit on him."

"Hmm, okay. Let me read this." Melanie scanned the line sheet. "Jesus, and Bridget told me they didn't say anything about Carmen!"

"Are you kidding me? She's got her head up her butt, that kid."

"Yeah, it reads clear as a bell."

"With how nervous they sound, they gotta be behind it, don't you think?"

"Sounds like it," Melanie agreed.

"But nothing concrete. No locations," he pointed out.

"God, I'm getting nervous about Carmen, Dan. Especially now that they're recruiting Trevor to mule the shipment. Granted, that could just be because they're afraid we're on the lookout for her. But part of me worries it's because they don't have her in pocket anymore."

"Settle down, now, I got a theory about that. I think there might be two separate deals in the works, so maybe they still *are* planning to use her. Here, take a look at this, right here," he said, leaning across her and pointing, giving her a thrill that she had to work hard to ignore. "Expo sends Pavel to do something at Bud's request last night. It must be some kind of separate drug shipment."

"It's not," she said, shaking her head as she read the portion he'd indicated.

"Why not? Bud asks about 'that other thing we talked about before.' Expo says he sent Pavel to take care of it, then he says, 'It might not go because of the weather.' What's that, if not a drug deal?"

A crystal-clear vision of the Escalade barreling down on her flashed into Melanie's head, making her shiver.

"It was me Powel tried to run me down with the Escalade when I left work last night."

Dan stared at her in shocked silence. After a moment he said, very quietly, "You better be bullshittin' me, or I'm gonna be incredibly pissed at you."

"Why at *me*? I wasn't the one behind the wheel!"

"You think this is a joke? You don't call to tell me this happened, so I could watch out for you? What if they tried again?"

"They didn't."

"Not *yet*, maybe, but I guarantee you they *will*. Serves you goddamn right, missy, because now I'm gonna stick to you like glue, whether you hate me or not."

"Okay, I guess I'll just have to tolerate that," she said, her lips curving involuntarily into a smile.

"What's so funny?"

"Nothing."

"Whaddaya, busting my chops?"

"No. I appreciate your concern. Really."

"*Somebody* better watch your back, with the crazy risks you take. So why the hell didn't you call me last night when this happened?"

"Because I was in such a rush to follow up on that information you gave me about James Seward. And it was very interesting. Luis Reyes came clean right away. Seward leaned on him to hold back on us, not only about Charlotte Seward's being home when the girls died but about the fact that Reyes actually reached Seward on his cell at least two hours before anybody called the police. You know what that means? We have Seward on obstruction!"

"Why the hell would Seward do that and leave those poor girls lying there? It almost makes you think he was involved somehow, that he needed the time to pretty up the crime scene. Which reminds me, I talked to Butch Brennan from the Crime Scene Team, jeez, it's gotta be a couple days ago now. Things've been so crazy, I forgot to tell you."

"You mean, about whether it was staged?"

"Yeah. He tells me there was something very odd. No latent prints of value anywhere in Whitney Seward's bedroom or bathroom. Only smudges. Like the whole place'd been wiped clean."

"Hmm."

"You put that together with the open windows and the drugs planted near Whitney's right hand when she was a lefty, and I'd say it's pretty clear. Somebody else was there, knew there was monkey business, tried to delay discovery of the bodies, and tried to make the deaths look like voluntary ODs when they weren't. What I *don't* get is, why would *Seward* be the one doing that?"

"Covering up out of concern for his political career?" Melanie suggested.

"But he'd have to know there was something *to* cover up."

"I agree, it's very strange. Maybe there's some other explanation. Luis Reyes thinks Seward only delayed because he got caught with his pants down in the middle of an assignation with Patricia Andover."

"Isn't she . . . ?"

"The headmistress of Holbrooke, yes. Apparently Seward's having an affair with her. Reyes has seen Patricia in the Sewards' building at odd hours."

"I don't buy that. Why hang around the love nest a minute longer than you need to in the middle of a crisis like that? Only makes it more likely you'll get found out."

"I agree. Anyway, the bottom line is, we need to interview Charlotte Seward and confront her husband. I almost did it last night, but I figured they'd refuse to speak to me without a subpoena."

"With everybody working on Expo as the top priority, I don't see how we can talk to them right now. Don't get me wrong, I hate to back-burner it as much as you do. Seward raises me up big time. He reminds me of that guy, you know, that rich guy in that movie with Jeremy Irons."

"*Reversal of Fortune?* Where Claus von Bülow was tried for poisoning his wife?"

"Yeah, that's it. That's it exactly. Guy's guilty as sin, and he walks. Liberal fucking defense attorneys for ya."

"Great movie, though," she said.

"You know why I like you? You always get what I'm talking about."

She tried not to lose it, looking into his eyes. Work, work. Think about work. "Expo is definitely the top priority," Melanie repeated. "Lulu Reyes told me last night that Carmen even mentioned him. Carmen knew about the drug running and may have spilled the beans to someone. And if that's why Carmen is missing . . ."

"I know. You don't have to spell it out. This guy takes care of witnesses."

"Which makes me very worried," Melanie said. "For *Trevor.*"

43

BUD HAD the logistics worked out with split-second timing, but he was concerned the relevant players would refuse to go along with the plan. Turned out he was worrying for nothing. It was candy from a baby with these idiots.

First he convinced Jay that it would be stupid for him to show his face in San Juan with the feds watching. Piece a' cake. Jay was only too happy to delegate the shipment and get busy making the scene around town. Covering his own ass was the dickhead's primary concern. Little did he know that he was setting himself up to look like the perpetrator of a particularly gruesome crime that hadn't been committed yet. *Sweet.*

The next part was even easier, if that was possible. Once Jay told Pavel that Bud was temporarily running the show, it took no convincing whatsoever to get Pavel to follow his somewhat unexpected instructions. He should've known. Anything that required violence, the Russian was only too happy to do. With relish, no questions asked.

"Where you want I should take him?" was the only thing Pavel had inquired about when Bud called him that morning. Bud was relatively confident the communication was secure, since his own cell phone was brand spanking new and Pavel wasn't a big enough fish for the feds to bother wiretapping.

"Pick the kid up just like Jay told you," Bud instructed. "You drive, the kid sits in the front passenger seat, Lamar sits behind him. Take him to that warehouse Jay owns. You know where I mean?"

"Sure, sure. Williamsburg, right?"

"Right."

"What do I say when he notice we not going JFK?" Pavel asked.

"Tell him you need to take a leak. Or just hit him over the head. Who gives a shit?"

"Oh. Is okay, then, if he show up damage?"

"I'd like to get some information out of him first, is all," Bud said.

"So he need to be able to talk still."

"Yes."

"Wery good, I understand," Pavel said, and hung up.

44

I T WAS eighty-seven degrees with a beating sun, but Melanie rolled the taxi window all the way down as they sped through the Isla Verde section of San Juan. Screw air-conditioning. She'd drink in the hot, wet breeze. Brightly colored houses and palm trees flashed by in a blur. She was a New Yorker born and bred, had rarely been to Puerto Rico, but something in her blood remembered this island like she'd lived a lifetime here. She craned her neck and caught a flash of aqua sea glittering in the bright sunlight. Bridget sat beside her, Dan in the front seat next to the taxi driver. He turned, glancing over his shoulder, and gave her one of those million-dollar smiles as the wind ruffled his dark hair. In that moment Melanie felt so happy she could've died right then and there.

The hotel sat on a broad tropical boulevard lined with high-rise condos and hotels. When she walked into the lobby, her excitement only grew. An enormous tinkling chandelier hung from a blue dome as ornately frescoed as a Fabergé egg, and under it was a gorgeous mahogany bar shaped like an oval. Even at this early hour, people sat at the tiny tables scattered around the cool marble floor, sipping their cocktails and talking a mile a minute. With how grim her life had been lately, Melanie felt more like joining in than judging. Hey, it's five o'clock somewhere—why *not* have a rum punch? To her right the lobby opened onto a cheery casino full of slot machines and flashing lights.

Jay Esposito didn't stint; you could say *that* for him, and Melanie was thrilled to be along for the ride. The government would never have shelled out the bucks to put them up *here* if not for the need to keep Expo under surveillance. Okay, she was working a harrowing case; she was distraught at leaving her vomiting daughter; her personal life was in a shambles. She knew she shouldn't be so elated. But she couldn't help it. She felt like some Park Avenue femme fatale on a sexy tropical jaunt with the guy of her dreams.

Once they checked in and changed into casual clothes so as not to stand out in the touristy crowd, reality reared its ugly head. The flight carrying Trevor and the bodyguard wasn't scheduled to land until late that afternoon, and they had work to do in the meantime. Bridget set off for local DEA headquarters to pick up a G-car. Dan went to scout surveillance locations. And Melanie started canvassing hotel employees, looking for anyone who might have seen anything during last weekend's drug-smuggling trip, showing photos of Brianna Meyers, Whitney Seward, and Jay Esposito. But this was a risky proposition. Rich drug dealers had *mucho* friends. Someone like Expo, who oozed criminal cachet and threw tips around like nobody's business, was expert at wooing hotel employees. Anybody Melanie and Dan questioned might be a double agent who'd turn right around and snitch to Expo and his thugs that the feds were on the premises. So Melanie had her cover story ready, though she knew she was chasing the horse after it got out of the barn. After all, she held a special distinction: Expo's people already recognized her on sight.

Melanie talked to whoever would talk to her, but nearly two hours of canvassing left her coming up empty and getting discouraged. Either Expo had already paid everybody off or else the El San Juan was just too big and too jam-packed on weekends for its employees to notice particular guests. Nobody remembered anything about her subjects. Her thong sandals were giving her blisters; her bare arms, exposed to hotel air-conditioning in a skimpy sundress, were all goosefleshy. She was sorely tempted to call it quits, track down that Dan O'Reilly, and entice him into taking a dip in the glorious azure swimming pool beckoning through the hotel windows.

She decided to compromise with the devil, since he was whispering so insistently in her ear. She'd head out to the pool area, interview people there. At least then she'd get a little sun, *por supuesto*. No point in flying all the way to San Juan and coming home without a tan, right?

It was lunchtime. The casual poolside restaurant was overflowing with glamorous revelers nibbling tropical salads, the men as well as the women with buff bodies, skin oiled to luscious shades of bronze and cocoa, wearing the teeniest, trendiest bathing suits. Who gave a damn about sun damage when you were young, wealthy, and had your own pool cabana? Melanie put on her sunglasses and turned her face to the sky as she waited to be seated.

The waitress who eventually came to take her order was named Nelly, and by the looks of her she was a veteran. In her fifties probably, with thick ankles, leathery skin, and a plump, benevolent face, Nelly was working half the restaurant with efficiency and good cheer while two younger, hotter waitresses skulked in a corner gossiping and ignoring their tables. Melanie smiled and exchanged pleasantries with Nelly in Spanish, deciding to wait for a moment when the woman was less obviously burdened before asking any questions.

When Melanie had eaten about half of her Caesar salad, Nelly gave her the perfect opening.

"Are you with that fashion-industry convention?" Nelly asked, in Spanish, when she came over to check if Melanie needed anything else.

"No, but thank you for thinking I might be," Melanie replied with a laugh.

"Ah, you're pretty enough, but maybe not snotty enough," Nelly said, smiling in return, showing a gold tooth.

"I'm actually here trying to find someone. You look like a lady who pays attention to people. Maybe you could help me."

"Sure. Me, I never forget a face. Is important in this business. You need to remember who's a good tipper, who ditches their check. That kind of thing."

Melanie reached into the straw beach bag she'd brought along and pulled out several photographs. "My little cousin," she said, flashing Brianna Meyers's yearbook photo, "got herself into big trouble. Drugs."

"*Ay,* so terrible. My niece, same thing! Such a beautiful, religious girl, and now she's walking the streets!"

"It's a curse," Melanie said, and she meant it.

"But I'm so sorry, *hija.* I don't recognize her. And I promise you, if she'd eaten here on my shift, I *would.*"

"Okay, what about either of these people?" she asked, laying down photos of Whitney and Expo. "These are the ones who led her astray."

"This one, no, definitely not," Nelly said, pointing to Expo's photo, "but this one was in here last weekend. *Her,* I'll never forget." She tapped Whitney's picture disapprovingly.

"You saw her? Really?"

"Oh, yes. And I'm not surprised she corrupted a nice girl like your cousin. This one was a little whore."

"Why do you say that?"

"Okay, during lunch hour last Saturday, just as crowded as it is now, mind you, she comes in here with her boyfriend. A much older guy. Old enough to be her father. Disgusting, if you ask me. Anyway, she's wearing this little bitty bathing suit, and she decides to change. Not in the ladies' lounge or back in her room. Not even modestly behind a towel. No. This one has to stand up, make sure all the men are looking at her—which, of course they *were,* since she has long blond hair and a body like a goddess—and take off her top! She bares her chest for the whole world to see, nipples sticking out and everything. Then she puts on a T-shirt that says 'Boy Crazy' in Spanish. The man had just bought it for her." Nelly clucked her tongue in disgust.

"But the man she was with. It wasn't *him?*" Melanie asked, pointing to Expo's photo again.

"No."

"Are you *sure*?"

"Of course I'm sure. It wasn't nothing like this bald man in the picture. This guy was older, too, but he had hair. One hundred percent I'm sure."

"Can you describe him?"

"Maybe forties, handsome, but cold-looking. There was something scary about him."

Pavel?

"Was he a Russian, by any chance?" Melanie asked.

"No. Definitely gringo. I heard them talking, and they mentioned New York. I speak English very good, you know. He sounded rich. Educated."

Bud, then? Must be.

"Hair? Light, dark, long, short?"

"Dark, I think. Length, I'm not sure. He was wearing a baseball cap, and it stuck out enough that I could see it."

"Anything else about his appearance?"

"He had some of that colored sunblock on his nose. Pink, it was. Looked foolish. That's what I'm saying. The only reason this young girl would be with him was if he was buying her."

"Were they definitely together like *that*?"

"Oh, yes. He tongue-kissed her and put his hands on her chest, almost like he was showing off. Everyone was looking."

"Would there be any way to find out his name? A credit-card receipt? A reservation book?"

"No. This place doesn't take reservations. And I remember, he paid cash. He paid me with a hundred on a thirty-dollar tab, which is a pain in the ass. I have to get my manager to write on the bill with a special marker, they're so worried about counterfeiting around here. You don't have large bills, do you?" Nelly asked suspiciously.

"No. I promise."

"Listen, another customer is calling me."

"Thank you so much, Nelly. You've been very helpful."

"I hope it helps you find your little cousin. Such a waste, a nice girl like that."

45

DAN AND BRIDGET were nowhere to be found. With the canvassing done and a few hours still to spare before the real action started, Melanie went back to her room. She checked in with her baby-sitter, who told her Maya was still running a fever but hadn't vomited all day. Then Melanie opened her suitcase to dig out her white bikini.

But a small, square red envelope sitting on top of her clothes brought her up short. Papi's Christmas card. She'd placed it there purposely when she'd changed earlier so it would hit her in the face the second she opened the bag. Funny how the brain works. Until she saw it staring back at her, she'd forgotten all about it. Her subconscious, doing her a favor.

She picked it up and looked at it. The devil was back with that whispering campaign again. Why not let sleeping dogs lie? Wasn't her life difficult enough? Didn't she come by everything she had the hard way? Why waste these precious moments of luxury on something that was bound to leave her stomach in knots and her heart aching? Put that bathing suit on and lounge by the pool, *chica*. Order yourself a piña colada, forget your troubles for once.

But the pull exerted by her broken relationship with her father was too strong. She found herself moving to the telephone as if in a trance. Picking up the receiver. Calling Information. Before she knew it, her father's telephone number was written on the notepad on the bedside table. Not that there was anything magical about having it. She could get the same number from the same computer-generated voice by calling Information from her phone back home any day of the week. She could decide to contact her father anytime, even if she didn't happen to be in his neighborhood.

But she wouldn't. She knew that.

Melanie dialed the phone, playing mind games with herself. If *he* picked up, she would speak. If it was his wife, Gladys, who'd never been secure enough to be kind to Papi's children from his first marriage, she'd hang up and go about her day.

"Dime," a female voice said.

Melanie's heart sank. Somewhere inside she'd imagined a whole beautiful reunion scene. *Had* imagined it a thousand times, in fact.

"Dígame, por favor," said Gladys, more insistently this time.

Then in the background, very clearly, she heard her father speak.

"¿Quién es, mi amor?" he asked. And the tenderness in his voice as he spoke to his wife made Melanie choke with pure jealousy.

Melanie hung up swiftly. She tore off her dress and plucked that white bikini from her suitcase. In seconds flat she was ready for the pool. But when she went into the bathroom to reapply her lipstick, she couldn't escape her own eyes in the mirror. It might be years before she came back here again, or it might be never. Her father had shown no disposition to visit *her*. If she ever imagined doing anything to heal their bond, now was her chance. Don't blow it by being a coward.

She studied the return address on the Christmas card. She'd checked it out on a map when she'd first arrived. It wasn't more than ten or fifteen minutes' drive from the spot where she stood. She yanked a pink terry-cloth tube dress on over her swimsuit. Sometimes you just had to pull the trigger.

MELANIE PAID THE DRIVER and stepped from the taxi she'd caught at the hotel. The house was modest by the standards of the neighborhood, but cheerful and well tended. A single-story concrete bungalow painted cream with fanciful iron grillework over the windows and doors, it boasted a graceful, leaning coconut palm in the front yard. Her hands were sweaty at the thought of seeing her father after so many years. So intent was she on her goal that—just as she'd been back at the hotel—she was completely oblivious to her surroundings. She hadn't noticed the dingy old sedan idling in the El San Juan's porte cochere when she'd first hailed the cab. And she didn't notice it now when it slowed to a stop farther down the block as she approached her father's front door.

The door was decorated with a jaunty cardboard Santa whose red metallic suit glinted in the hot sun. Melanie walked up the shallow steps, their handrails bristling with unlit Christmas lights, and pressed the buzzer. A dog began barking furiously inside the house.

"*Cálmate, cálmate, chiquito,*" she heard Gladys say.

Gladys opened the door. Melanie hadn't seen her father's wife in twelve years, since their wedding. Gladys was extremely pretty then, and she'd aged well—the only obvious change wrought by time being the chunky blond highlights in her stylishly short dark hair. She was about fifteen years younger than Melanie's mother, with a cute figure. Same old story.

"Melanie?" Gladys asked, eyes widening.

"I was in the neighborhood so I thought I'd drop by."

"What a surprise," Gladys said in nearly accentless English, her tone implying that the surprise was not a pleasant one.

"Is Papi around? I brought you guys something," Melanie said, indicating her straw bag.

"Yes, of course. What am I thinking? Come in, come in."

Gladys pushed the still-yapping beagle away from the door and ushered Melanie into a small living room to the right of the entry hall. It was cool and dark, with a white tile floor and blinds drawn against the afternoon sun. A whirring air conditioner poured a continual stream of icy air into the room. Gladys opened one of the blinds, letting in some light.

"Stay here, and I'll get him. You're lucky, you know. Normally he'd be at work during the day, but they put him on night shifts because they're so busy over the holidays." Melanie's father had changed jobs a couple of years back and now worked as a banquet manager for one of the major hotel chains on the island.

Gladys strode off. The dog followed her, its nails clicking on the tile floor.

Melanie sat down on the edge of a Naugahyde recliner and swept up a photograph from the side table. It was a picture of her father's twins, two boys who must now be around ten. They were good-looking kids, but they favored Gladys. Melanie didn't recognize her father in them, let alone herself. She felt slightly sick, wondered why the hell she'd come.

At the sound of a footstep in the doorway, her head jerked up. Her father stood there, grayer and with more lines in his face but looking otherwise the same. He'd always been a handsome man, tall for a Puerto Rican, with aristocratic features and poet's hair that flopped into his eyes. But despite his relatively unchanged appearance, Melanie couldn't reconcile the person standing before her with her childhood memories. Maybe she'd just pored over those memories one too many times. Looked at all the old photographs—of her sitting in his lap or him holding up her birthday cake for her to blow out the candles—until they got so blurred with overuse that she couldn't truly see them. Because this man felt like a complete stranger.

Her father hesitated, momentarily catching her awkwardness, but then opened his arms wide and gave her a big smile. "What a nice Christmas present to see you, *hija*. Come give me a hug."

She went over and hugged him, feeling numb. When the hug was over, she wasn't sure what to do next.

"Let's sit down," he said, indicating the sofa. They took seats facing each other. "Alvaro Junior and Armando are still in school. They won't be home for another hour. So we have a little time to catch up."

Was she being paranoid, or was he subtly asking her to leave before his sons returned? She'd never actually met her half brothers. She wasn't even sure they knew she and Linda existed.

"So what brings you here?" he asked cheerfully, in the same tone he might've used for any acquaintance he'd run across unexpectedly after a number of years. There was something else different about him, but she couldn't put her finger on it.

"Business, actually. I'm here on a case, and I had a little downtime. I'm staying at the El San Juan, and it's close by, so I thought . . ." She trailed off.

"Oh, very nice place. You must be doing well for yourself. And that husband of yours? Still making a good living?" Papi asked.

"Yes," Melanie said. Then, after a moment, "Actually, we're getting divorced."

"Oh. I'm sorry to hear that. Didn't you just get married a couple of years ago?"

"Over six years ago now. Remember? You came to the wedding." That was the last time she'd seen him, in fact.

"Time flies. And how is your little one?"

"Maya," she said, wondering if he remembered his granddaughter's name. "She's great. She's the best, actually. So funny and cute. Here, I brought you a picture of her." Melanie pulled the gift from her bag. She'd put it in a nice frame and wrapped it in gold paper tied up with a red satin ribbon. She handed it to him, but he just took it and put it on his lap, unopened.

"Thank you. I'll save it for under the tree. I'm afraid I don't have anything for you."

"No, of course not. You didn't know I was coming."

Melanie suddenly realized what was different about her father. His English was astonishingly improved from what it had been years ago.

"Papi, you speak so well," she said, confused, almost for a moment wondering if she was in the right house. But of course she was.

"That Gladys. She makes me practice every night with a tape. But she's right, you know. It's helped me a lot to move up at work." He smiled. An awkward silence settled over them, which Melanie felt powerless to break.

"So," he said after a pause, "how is your mother? And Linda?"

"Both in fine form. You know, you can't stop *them*."

He forced a laugh. "Linda wrote me a very nasty letter a couple of years back. Made me feel bad."

"Well," Melanie said, then stopped. She had to side with Linda on this one, even if she herself preferred to handle things in a less confrontational way.

"Very nasty," Papi said again, but his words were belied by the mild look in his eyes. Melanie had the distinct sense he didn't really care that much about getting kicked out of Linda's life.

"I guess she never got over your leaving us like that," Melanie said.

"You'd think she'd understand now that she's older."

"You never really explained it to us. I guess I don't understand myself." Her words came out sounding more accusatory than she'd intended.

Papi shrugged. "Your mother and I, we fought like cats and dogs. You saw that. It was bad for us, bad for you. With the robbery, getting shot and all, I almost died. I realized I only had one life to live, and I wanted to spend it with Gladys. That simple."

"What about me and Linda?"

"Your mother's a tough customer. I knew she'd take care of you, that you'd be fine."

But we weren't, Melanie thought. *I wasn't.*

Papi must've sensed she wasn't buying it. "Look," he said, "it's different when you face death. Things get very clear. You can't bother with following the conventions."

Melanie had faced death herself a couple of times. With a gun in her hand, staring down a vicious killer on the Jed Benson murder case. And again just last night, with six thousand pounds of steel hurtling toward her. Funny, those experiences hadn't made her want to abandon Maya. Quite the opposite, in fact. But then Maya was more to her than a "convention" that she felt bound to observe.

"Whatever, Papi. I suppose it's ancient history now," Melanie said hollowly.

"That's right. And I'm very lucky, because God gave me a second chance with my boys. I'm a very good father to them. I feel like they're my *real* kids, you know?"

What was I? she thought. *Practice? A bad dream?* But there was no point in asking.

"Listen," she said, standing up, "I'd better be going."

"I should get back to what I was doing, too. Gladys has me out in the hot sun replacing the patio tile. The iguanas get in the yard and shit all over it. Takes the finish right off. My wife is a slave driver, but she keeps things nice, you know?" He smiled indulgently.

Melanie walked over to the door, and he followed her. She thought about asking for Maya's photograph back but then decided it wasn't worth it. He'd probably throw it away, but who cared, really? It was only a picture.

"Well, it was very nice of you to stop by," he said, leaning across her and pushing the door open. "You're looking very beautiful, very grown-up."

"Thank you." She studied his face for a final moment, wondering if she'd see him again in this life. She didn't think she'd try. She was virtually certain *he* wouldn't. He was so obviously relieved that the visit was ending quickly, without an upsetting emotional scene.

"I mean that. I said the same thing at your wedding. You turned out nice," he said.

"Thanks, Papi. You take care." She pecked him on the cheek and walked out the door, putting on her sunglasses, staring straight ahead.

It was around three o'clock now, and the afternoon had turned muggy and airless. Melanie started walking with no thought of where she was going, the heat of the sidewalk coming up through the thin plastic bottoms of her flip-flops. *How blind could she be?* Of all the answers Melanie had ever imagined to the urgent question of her father's abandonment, she'd missed the most obvious one: He didn't really care about her. It wasn't that he longed to call but had been prevented from doing so by Gladys. It wasn't that he blamed Melanie wrongly for some slight or some fault that she could correct or put right. There was no mystery, no magic solution. He just wasn't that interested in her. She'd spent her life fixated on her father, preoccupied with his betrayal, experiencing her own relationships through the prism of his absence. But *he* didn't spend *his* time thinking about *her*. And there wasn't anything she could do about that either, except get over it and move on.

A distant rumble of thunder finally roused Melanie from her chaotic thoughts. Skies were clear where she stood but black and threatening to the west. If she got caught in a terrible downpour, it would only be a fitting conclusion to her visit. Yet why put herself through that? Nobody else seemed to be suffering. Why should *she*?

She started paying attention to the street signs, annoyed at herself for leaving her map behind in the hotel. The neighborhood was residential, quiet. No taxis on the streets, not many cars, and certainly no people walking in this withering heat. A gray sedan started its engine and pulled out behind her, cruising along slowly. Melanie glanced back over her shoulder, waiting for it to pass her by. But it didn't. The glare on the windshield from this angle prevented her from seeing inside. She felt the tingle of déjà vu, and not in a good way either. Wasn't this sort of like last night? Okay, the weather and the setting couldn't be more different, but wasn't this just like the Escalade pulling out of that parking space? Could they possibly try to run her down twice in less than twenty-four hours? That would show a distinct lack of creativity in the MO department. But what else could it *be,* the way this car was acting? Her heart started beating rapidly.

Melanie walked faster. The car kept pace with her. She looked all around. Nobody to help her. She stopped dead, panting with fear. The car pulled up beside her. She turned to run, just as somebody shoved open the passenger-side door.

46

WHAT THE HELL are you doing? Get in. It's gonna rain," Dan said.

Melanie heaved a tremendous sigh and practically collapsed into the waiting passenger seat. "Jesus. You scared me."

"You *should* be scared. Fear is healthy for someone as reckless as you."

The inside of the car smelled musty, as if the windows had been left open during a rainstorm, but the air-conditioning still came as a relief. And Dan, in jeans and faded T-shirt that clung to his muscular body just so, one powerful forearm draped over the steering wheel, looked sexy as hell.

"Where'd you get *this* jalopy?" she asked, trying to sound nonchalant, like it didn't affect her to be around him.

"Bridget requisitioned it from the local DEA. Albano must have major juice, because they dropped this one off for me and she got one, too."

"I hope hers is better."

"Stop complaining, princess, or you can walk back to the hotel."

"You're bluffing. You wouldn't do that."

He glanced over at her. "Maybe not. You look pretty good in those shades." He looked out at the road, then did a double take, looking back at her again. "What's that, a bathing suit you're wearing under that thing?"

"Yeah." She'd been in such a rush that she'd engineered the whole profound encounter with her father—one she'd been imagining for years—while dressed for the beach! She slouched down against the mushy fabric seat, too drained to explain herself. They drove in silence for a few minutes.

Eventually she said, "Aren't you going to ask what I was doing?"

"I already know. Had headquarters run the address while you were inside. Your father?"

"Yes." Melanie had explained to Dan early on about her parents' divorce and her father's abandonment.

"How was it seeing him again?" he asked.

She started to speak, but the lump gathering in her throat stopped her.

"Aw, I'm sorry," Dan said. He reached out and patted her head like she was a dog. It was a silly gesture, one he probably resorted to out of fear that anything more would be unwelcome, but it made her feel infinitely better. She realized that, in a strange way, ever since she'd known Dan, she felt less alone. Whether they were together or not.

"You don't talk much about yourself. What are *your* parents like?" she asked, wanting to feel closer to him, to heal their breach for real.

He shrugged, studying the road. "They stuck around. I'll say that for 'em."

"That's not exactly a ringing endorsement."

"What am I, on the couch now? I thought we were talking about *you.*"

"Don't get me wrong, I love to talk about myself," she said, laughing. "But once in a while we have to talk about *you,* don't you think? It's only fair. I need some basic information."

Dan took his eyes off the road long enough to see she was waiting for his answer. He smiled. "You're not gonna let me off the hook, are you?"

"Not a chance."

"Well, okay, it was like this. They did the best they could."

"That's *it?* Please. Details."

He smiled again, shaking his head. "You're somethin', you know."

"Come on. Spill it."

"All right, all right." He took a deep breath and let it out slowly. "My dad's a hard man, but he's got his reasons. Retired as a lieutenant. He was good at his job, and 'cause of that he drew one shithole precinct after another. They'd send him into places other guys couldn't handle, and it took its toll. He worked so hard and had so much stress when I was growing up that he was a pain in the ass to be around. He's more relaxed now. Sometimes I'll go over there on a Sunday, watch the game or whatever. That's nice."

"And your mom?"

"Well, she had seven boys real close together. It wasn't easy."

"*Seven?* I had no idea. You have six brothers?"

"Four now. My second brother, P.J., died in a car crash when he was sixteen. Out with some buddies, and they were drinkin.' He was my mother's pet, so that was rough on her. And my youngest brother, Sean, was a probie in the fire department on 9/11."

"Dan! I had no idea. I'm *so* sorry."

"Yeah. That one was hard to take. But he was doing his job, right? If the next big thing happens on my watch, I'm going down with the ship, too."

"God, don't say that."

"Why not? You'd do the same. I know you step up when your name's called. I seem to recall not so long ago walking into a room and finding the bad guy dead on the floor and you with a gun in your hand."

"Exactly. The bad guy buys it, and you live to tell the tale. Like in the movies. The hero never dies."

"Nice work if you can get it."

"That's *my* plan. Or at least my hope anyway," she said.

"Don't count on that with me, missy. Life *without* a plan is what you're looking at here. I'm not too good at keeping my head down. But I'll tell you one thing I *do* believe in."

"What's that?"

He grinned. "The hero gets the girl."

"Oh, yeah?"

"You're not making any promises, huh?"

She smiled tantalizingly. "I don't want to give away the ending."

"Keeping me in suspense. I like that."

"*So* . . . back to business. Where were you in the birth order of all these brothers?"

"Birth order? Jeez, this *is* like the frickin' shrink!" Dan said, but his smile told her that, for all his protesting, he loved talking to her about himself. "I was fourth. Smack in the middle, guaranteed nobody would pay any attention to me. Suited me fine, though. I went about my business. Always did okay, never in trouble. People left me alone."

They stopped at a light, and Dan consulted a map. She was about to ask him another question, but when the light changed, he just started talking again. "You know, people think big families are always jolly. I love kids, and I want a bunch of 'em. But you gotta be careful. Too many, and you can't give 'em enough of your time. In my house you had to fight for everything you got. Like with laundry. We had a clean pile and a dirty pile. When you got up in the morning, you'd go dig around in the clean pile for something that fit. You never *owned* anything. If I found something I liked, guaranteed somebody bigger would steal it away. Same with food. You had to get to the table early, grab what you wanted, and eat fast, or you'd go hungry. Not that I'm complaining. That's just the way it was." He looked over at her. "How's that, Doc? Satisfied now?"

"You did good."

"How the heck you always get so much information out of me? Nobody else does."

She giggled. "Ve haff our vays."

Their eyes met, and for a long minute neither of them could look away. Suddenly a horn blared, and Dan swerved, narrowly missing another car.

"Jeez, we better stop talking like this, or we'll end up roadkill," he said.

"Okay, I guess you're off the couch for now."

They were silent for a moment. "So any developments on the case?" Melanie asked.

"Well, Albano asked me this morning if I'd join his task force," he said. "I mean, that's not exactly about the case, but—"

"Permanently?"

"I think the minimum commitment is a year."

"Did you accept?"

"I'm thinking about it. I'd like to work for the guy. My boss now is a real mutt."

"Narcotics is kind of a backwater these days," she pointed out.

"Yeah, but Albano's starting up a new narcoterrorism initiative. Bureau, DEA, and PD together. Joint task forces are big again now, with all the intelligence sharing. I'd be the lead guy. Albano's offering me primary relief supervisor, the whole nine yards. They'd probably team me with Bridget."

"*Bridget?*" Anger flashed through Melanie, so powerful that her head felt hot.

"Yeah." He glanced at her. "You don't think much of her, do you?"

"Oh, sure. She's fine if you want to be on the arm with Jimmy Mulqueen!"

"What?"

She shook her head. "Forget it. Never mind. Just go ahead, I'm sure it's a smart career move."

He grinned broadly. "You're jealous!"

"I am *not*. Why should I care who your partner is?"

"Ha, I can't believe it. Melanie Vargas, queen of cool, is jealous of little Bridget Mulqueen over *me*!"

"That's ridiculous."

"I'll say it is. I mean, come on. She's a kid. You're a woman. There's no comparison."

"I told you, I really don't care. It's not *about* that."

"Why can't you admit that you feel the same way I do? Huh? Tough guy?"

She folded her arms stubbornly. "Shut up and drive."

"Right? I caught you." He chuckled to himself as he looked out at the road.

They arrived at the hotel. Dan threw the keys to the young valet, who regarded the G-car with undisguised contempt.

"Just park it, for Chrissakes," Dan snapped as they headed for the lobby. "Kid's making minimum wage, but if it's not a Ferrari, it's beneath him to touch it," he said to Melanie. "Lemme stop and check messages."

He went over to the reception desk. Melanie watched him walk off. The powerful way he moved made her catch her breath. Why the hell was she fighting so hard against her feelings for him? It would be such a relief to just give in.

"Yeah, okay," Dan said, returning a minute later. He leaned toward her, speaking in low tones so as not to be overheard by people passing through the lobby. "Bridget went back to the airport with a couple local DEA guys to watch the incoming flights for when Trevor comes in. They're being real careful, just like you said. You and me're tasked with staying here, seeing if any of our subjects show up."

Melanie looked into Dan's eyes and promptly forgot what she was about to say. "Okay, good," she managed. "I mean, I'm pleased they're looking out for Trevor. With the surveillance and such."

"You all right?"

"Sure. Maybe a little cold." She rubbed her bare arms.

He moved in closer, leaning down so his mouth nearly brushed against her hair when he spoke. "I think we look less obvious if we stick together. You know, pretend to be a couple on vacation. Will you do that with me? For a little while? Please?"

"You mean, act like lovers?"

"*Lovers*? Now, who uses a word like that anymore? A smile crinkled the corners of his eyes.

"I do. I like that word."

"Well, I gotta admit, it sounds pretty good coming from *your* mouth. But then you have a beautiful mouth."

"You think so?"

"Mmm-hmm."

A powerful wave of lust washed over her, impossible to fight. She was conscious of the muscles of his chest inches away, intensely aware of the steady beating of her own heart. She felt tongue-tied, weak-kneed, helpless. All she could think about was rushing up to her fancy room and rolling around in the king-size bed with him. But they had work to do. She'd better pull herself together. He wasn't helping any, standing so close.

"So you probably need a sweater, right?" he asked, staring into her eyes.

"What?"

"Come on. Let's go up to your room and get you a sweater."

He took her by the elbow and propelled her toward the elevator bank. They stepped onto a crowded elevator. He pushed the button for her floor. She stared straight ahead, the mere touch of his hand on her arm enough to wipe all other thoughts from her mind.

"We should probably work," she attempted, but her pulse was racing.

"Not much going on right now. We have a window," he replied.

They got out of the elevator. She felt light-headed, thinking about what would happen next. She was getting in over her head with this guy, but she should just do it, *live* for a change, before it was too late.

The whole walk down the long, carpeted hallway, they didn't speak or look at each other. She stuck the card key into the lock, saw the green light, and turned the handle, acutely aware every second of Dan's presence behind her. He followed her in, taking the time to put out the Do

Not Disturb sign and lock the door. She walked to the center of the room and stood in front of the bed.

"So," she said breathlessly, turning around.

His eyes never leaving her face, Dan removed his gun from where it had been hidden under his shirt and placed it on the dresser. Then he walked over to Melanie and slid the terry-cloth dress down to her ankles. She stepped out of it and kicked it aside, watching his eyes as they took in her body in the bathing suit. Her senses felt almost unbearably heightened. Everything—Dan's face, the luxurious room with its tropical furniture and crisp smell of air-conditioning, the blackening sky beyond her balcony—stood out in sharp relief, as if it would be imprinted on her memory forever, as if she were already remembering it from some distant point in the future.

"You wanna stop, tell me now before it's too late," he whispered huskily, pulling her toward him.

"Why? What happens after that?"

"You'll see."

Dan backed her up until her bare thighs hit the silky white duvet covering the bed. The rock-solid feeling of his body against her was almost too much for her to take.

"Scared?" he asked.

"Should I be?" She raised her face to him, her lips parted.

"That all depends on what you're lookin' for."

"I think I'm looking for you," she said.

Then she was falling backward onto the bed, falling through time and space, like everything beautiful and everything sad in her life were all tangled up in Dan on top of her, his hot mouth on her neck, her breasts. She tore at his clothes, couldn't get to his skin fast enough. They went at each other tooth and nail until they were naked, panting, drenched with sweat, and then, just as he held himself poised over her, ready to enter her, they both slowed down and looked gravely into each other's eyes. She saw that all the sex she'd had in her life before this—

with any number of ex-boyfriends, even with her husband — had been casual, of little consequence. But not this; this was dead serious. He would own her now, to her bones. And she wasn't sure how well she would tolerate that.

"Go ahead," she said, playing her tongue around his mouth, which was swollen from their savage kissing. "Just do it. I can't stand it anymore."

So he grabbed her by the ass and plunged into her, leaving bruises shaped like his fingers that would last for days afterward. Just at that moment the storm finally hit, sending sheets of hard water sluicing against the glass doors to the balcony.

47

B UD GAVE the bodyguards an extra hour to work before heading out to Williamsburg himself to speak with Trevor Leonard. Softening-up time, he thought of it as. So it came as no surprise when he let himself in the back door of the warehouse and found the kid lying unconscious on the bare concrete floor, his face a pulpy mess.

Pavel was sitting against the wall eating a meatball hero.

"He's not dead?" Bud asked.

"No, you say not kill him yet," Pavel said, speaking through his food, sounding defensive.

Bud dropped the leather bag containing Jay's golf clubs next to the kid's inert body. He'd paid attention to which one Jay had used the other night. Bud had a well-thought-out plan for how he would use that same club again and where he would dump it afterward. He'd brought along rubber gloves for the main event. Until then he was careful not to touch anything so as not to leave prints anywhere.

"Everything go okay? Where's Lamar?" Bud asked.

"We have problems after we pick kid up. Cops is watching."

"Shit. Are you serious? Did they follow you here?"

"Not to worry. I have brain."

"So what happened?"

"We arrange to meet kid like you say, in front of subway stop near Hunter College."

"Yeah, because it s crowded there, but you re not too far from the bridge."

"Was good choice for location. But we get there, is like five sedans with dark windows."

"Shit."

"Cops."

"Yeah. So what'd you do?"

"We drive, not stop. We call kid on cell number you give us, tell him get on subway and go to Grand Central instead. We wait for him there, outside."

"Smart."

"But by the time he come out, we see sedans again."

"So he's definitely talking, the little prick."

Pavel's lips twitched into the semblance of a smile. "He pay for that already, believe me."

"Okay. So? How'd you lose 'em?"

"In Russia, man I work for, he teach me drive good. I know."

"You just . . ."

"Go around block here, cut in front of cars there. They trying to hide so we don't see them, but I know they are there, so I make move. Is not difficult."

"But where's Lamar?" Bud repeated.

"Even though we lose them, is not good use same car to go to airport. So we pull car into garage here. Lamar go to get another car."

"All good. But you know, if the feds were watching before, they'll be looking for you at the airport."

"Is no problem. They look for three men together. So Lamar and I go separately. Kid by then we are done with, he is not with us. They will be tricked."

Bud looked at his watch. "You should get going already."

He was sending them to San Juan as if everything were normal. He didn't want Jay suspecting anything too soon. Besides, the feds would find a way to follow the trail of the purported drug deal. They'd run off to Puerto Rico, too, leaving Bud free to take care of business here in New York.

"*You* handle this kid now?" Pavel asked dubiously. Pavel underestimated Bud. They all did. It didn't bother him; in fact, he preferred it that way. Put him at an advantage.

"I'm just waiting for Jay. He should be here any minute, and then I'm leaving. What happens next is his decision," Bud said.

"Of course."

"I'm serious, Pavel. Jay's gonna be fucking pissed if you miss that flight. We have a shipment to deal with."

"I finish one minute. They don't give you nothing eat on airplanes these days."

Bud looked down at Trevor. A shame, all these bright young lives getting snuffed out before their time. But that's what happened when you fucked around with people's livelihoods.

Pavel crumpled the soggy deli paper into a ball and tossed it aside. He stood up, rubbing his greasy hands on his jeans.

"Did the kid say anything?" Bud asked.

"Yeah, of course, right away he give up that he is working with prosecutor."

"I'll call you with further instructions once you're down there. You don't call me, understand? And whatever you do, don't call Jay. He's chilling on this one, and he doesn't want any paper trail."

"I know."

Pavel pulled on his bulky leather coat and headed for the exit. Only after he heard the door slam did Bud draw back his foot and kick Trevor in the head hard enough to wake him up.

"Aagh," Trevor grunted, coming to but having trouble opening his swollen eyes.

Bud looked down at him with interest. It was funny, how little he minded the violence. Or, more accurately, how much he enjoyed it.

With the neighborhood he was from, and hanging out with Jay all these years, he'd seen a lot of depraved, fucked-up things but had been careful to keep his hands clean. Recently, with his new goal, that had to change. He found he stepped comfortably into the role of brutalizer. Like that girl he had at home, who was still, fortunately, alive. He understood all the stories now, the ones where some local man in a desolate town kept a woman chained to the wall of his shed. He'd systematically torture her to death over a long period of time while keeping up his everyday routine. Bud saw how easily something like that could happen. Having Carmen tied up in his closet seemed natural to him now. Taking her out and terrorizing her had become simply something interesting to look forward to as he went about the rest of his day.

Trevor succeeded in opening his eyes, registering Bud's face with obvious surprise.

"You really fucked up, my friend," Bud said, smiling.

Trevor licked his split lip, trying to speak.

"Just a second," Bud said. He went to the bathroom, concealed behind a flimsy plywood door in the corner of the space. There were no cups. But rummaging in the trash, he found an empty plastic Coke bottle and filled it with water from the rusty tap, using a crumpled paper towel to handle everything. He came back and poured a small amount of water into Trevor's mouth. The kid looked pathetically grateful.

"I understand you're friendly with Melanie Vargas. That's a big problem for me and some friends of mine," Bud said.

"She forced me," Trevor managed, wincing with pain as he spoke. "She arrested me for selling X."

"We all have our reasons for what we do, Trevor. But we all have to suffer the consequences when we make poor choices."

The kid started to snivel, wet snot mixed with blood dripping from his broken nose. The sight only served to fill Bud with anticipation. He drew the rubber gloves from his jeans pocket and pulled them on with a snap. Then he took the nine-iron from the leather golf bag. Jay had danced away from the law so many times that he thought he was invincible. He never even bothered to clean his weapons, which gave Bud a golden opportunity now. This golf club was covered with Jay's prints and soaked with the blood—and DNA—of his last victim, that cross-dressing club rat. Bud could kill the Leonard kid with it now and hand Jay to the feds in a nice, neat package, looking good for both murders. So Bud could truly relax in his tropical paradise when the time came. Not too long now either.

Trevor was watching Bud's every move with eyes like saucers. Either the kid was scared shitless or he was completely incapacitated by the beating Pavel had given him, because he never even tried to get up. It continued to amaze Bud the way people let you take advantage of them. He'd massacre this kid without meeting a single flicker of resistance.

He walked over and stomped his left foot down square in the middle of Trevor's chest, eliciting a shocked grunt, then raised the nine-iron in a perfect arc, bringing it down fast and hard, stopping a millimeter shy of Trevor's skull. The kid was sobbing now, eyes fixed on the head of the golf club, which bore sticky clumps of blood and tissue from its last victim.

"I'm sorry, dude. I'm sorry, sorry, sorry. Ple-ease!"

"Remorse is bullshit, Trevor. Doesn't mean jack unless you deliver on it. Luckily, there's something you can do for me."

4 8

MELANIE SAT bolt upright on the edge of the bed.
"The message light's on."
"So?" Dan said.

"Was it on before?"

"Honestly, I wasn't paying attention."

"Did the phone ring while we were . . . ?"

"Not that I remember. But a bomb coulda gone off and I wouldna noticed." He grabbed her by the wrist. "I was just resting. You're not done."

"Sweetie, we'll never be done, but we still have a case to solve." She took her hand away and picked up the receiver, studying the complicated telephone with its profusion of buttons.

"*Sweetie.* I like that. You're not too free with the endearments, you know." He traced a finger down her back, down the curve of her behind.

"Hey, stop distracting me," she said, shooing his hand away. "I can never figure out how these things work. Do you push the red light? Oh, wait a minute, here it is." She pressed a small button.

"You have one *unheard message,"* an automated operator said.

The next voice she heard was Trevor Leonard's.

"It's Trevor! I *knew* it." Melanie put the call on speaker, stomach churning with anxiety. Goddamnit, she couldn't believe she'd missed this call!

"*. . . couldn't get away before to reach out to you,*" Trevor was saying.

Dan raised himself up on his elbow, and Melanie looked at him grimly. She knew the team was covering Trevor carefully. Surveillance at the pickup location, at JFK, on the flight, at Marín Airport here in San Juan. But she couldn't shake this sick feeling in the pit of her stomach every time she thought about Trevor. It was too easy to imagine how things could go wrong.

"*I'm with Expo, but he left the room. I can only talk for a second. They're, like, worried about surveillance, so they changed the flight. We're gonna be coming in later, okay? I don't have a time or a flight number or anything, but don't worry if you don't see me till tonight. So here's the important part. Expo said something about meeting the connect in the bathtub at El Yunque at eleven o'clock to get the product. That's all I know. Shit, gotta go.*" And he hung up.

"Meeting the connect in El what?" Dan asked.

"El Yunque. It's a rain forest, maybe forty-five minutes from here. But the bathtub? I don't know what that means."

"We'll find out. Holy shit. If we can surveil the hand-to-hand and then move in and pop 'em, how great would that be? I got to give you credit, sweetheart. This kid Trevor is coming through for us big time. You were really right about him."

"Yeah, but don't you think he sounded . . . I don't know."

"What?"

"Stressed?" she said.

"Absolutely. Anybody sneaking a phone call in the middle of an undercover who's *not* stressed is a fucking idiot."

"I guess you're right."

Dan pulled on his clothes and grabbed his gun from the dresser top. *Mira,* that body. She couldn't even let herself look. She was crazy for this man, but maybe it wasn't such a bad thing if work came between them for the moment and slowed down their mad rush. Because he scared her to death. Not to mention distracted her.

"I'm gonna want backup from the locals," Dan was saying.

"Of course. I want this surveilled every step of the way, too. We've got our witness on the line here. Let's get Albano on the phone and have him make the call. Time to pull rank. We need all the help we can get."

"Not 'we.' You're staying here," Dan said firmly.

"And get an herbal wrap at the spa while my witness is in danger? I don't *think* so. Plus, Carmen Reyes is still missing, and I promised her father I'd find her. We'll never do that if we don't nail Expo."

Melanie got up and searched through her suitcase, which sat open on a stand waiting to be unpacked. What did you wear to surveil a drug deal? She chose black pants and a black wrap shirt for their dark color. Fading into the underbrush would be key.

"Sweetheart, I'm serious," Dan said. "You're here for the legal end. We need you safe to draft charges and get the scumbags extradited after we arrest 'em. I'm not letting you walk into a hand-to-hand in a fucking *rain forest* late at night. I mean, these guys down here, they don't fuck around. They got AK-47s and *dogs,* as a matter of routine."

She knew that Dan was right. But the thought of sitting in the hotel with no control over what happened to Trevor Leonard was simply intolerable. Bernadette had told her no cops-and-robbers stuff. But Bernadette had *also* said not to let Trevor out of her sight, and Melanie had a selective memory.

"So I won't get right in the middle of the surveillance," she conceded. "But you're *not* leaving me here."

Somebody knocked loudly on the door. Melanie tied her shirt closed, then went to look through the peephole.

"It's Bridget," she reported over her shoulder in a low tone.

"Shit."

"What should I tell her?" Melanie whispered.

"I don't know, but don't let her in."

He was right. With the tangled sheets and Melanie's clothes still strewn across the floor, sex was in the air. Bridget would figure it out instantly.

Bridget knocked again. Leaving the chain on, Melanie opened the door a crack.

"Hey, Bridget," she said.

"Hey. I was about to give up. Were you in the shower?" Bridget asked.

"Yes, actually. I'm still getting dressed. What is it?"

"I just got an update from Ray-Ray, wanted to fill you in. They lost track of Trevor temporarily—"

"Oh, my God! You're kidding me!"

"No. I'm sorry."

"Jesus, Bridget, how could that *happen*?"

"It wasn't their fault, really. They were told to hang back so they wouldn't hink anybody up. They weren't planning on the fact that this Pavel LNU character is a talented countersurveillance driver. But not to worry. Pavel's vehicle was last observed bound for Brooklyn on the Williamsburg Bridge, so we're sure they're gonna get on the BQE and head to JFK. We got the airport swarming with guys. We'll pick up the scent there, I'm positive."

"I just got a voice mail from Trevor. I'm not sure when he left it, though. Could've been from earlier," Melanie said.

"Really? What's he say?"

"He gave me the time and location of a possible hand-to-hand later tonight."

"Great. That's excellent. So, worst-case scenario, we get him back in our sights then."

"I'll tell you all about it. Just let me finish getting dressed, and then I'll meet you down at the bar. Because we have to get on top of this. I'm very upset that Trevor's out of pocket. *Very* upset."

"Yeah, I understand. Hey, you haven't seen Dan, have you? I can't find him, and he's not answering his pager."

"No, but if I see him, I'll tell him to meet us there, too."

"Okay."

"I'll be down in two minutes," Melanie said, and closed the door.

She turned back to Dan. "Did you hear that? Can you believe it? We have to *do* something!"

He walked over to her and looked down at her indulgently. "It'll be okay, I promise."

"Don't talk to me like I'm a child," she said, looking up at him with blazing eyes. "It'll be okay if we make it okay."

He stepped back. "You're right. So let's move. You call New York and have the lieutenant get us some reinforcements to cover the hand-to-hand tonight. I'll take Bridget and go scout out the location. Now, this is just a *suggestion,* missy, so don't get all bent out of shape that I'm telling you what to do. But it would make sense for you to stay put and coordinate things. At least for now."

She sighed. "You're right. I agree."

"You *do*?"

They locked eyes. She couldn't help thinking about what they'd been doing a few minutes earlier. She could tell he was thinking about the same thing.

"Yeah," she said, with a smile and a toss of her head. "But don't get used to it."

49

PATRICIA MADE IT home through the falling snow just in time to receive Coco and Vuitton, who were being dropped off at six with the doorman by the dog groomer's limo. Patricia was bringing both doggies to the benefit tomorrow, so they'd had shampoos, blow-dries, pedicures. And their new leashes were ready— matching his and hers from Gucci. Her doggies were just as well groomed as anybody's, and they'd be even more so soon enough, because Patricia would be Mrs. Seward and *that* rich. At least she still held out hope, though she had to admit that things were not going according to plan.

The limo pulled up to the curb just as Patricia arrived, and the uniformed driver got out and demanded to see identification before turning the pooches over to her. Patricia appreciated the security. You couldn't be too careful. Coco and Vuitton were such perfect miniature Yorkies, so very petite and delicate, who *wouldn't* covet them? Satisfied, the driver released them to her care. Patricia scooped up her babies and kissed them passionately, which did little to relieve the anxiety rising in her throat.

It was not the benefit that worried her. All arrangements had been completed months earlier by a committee of mothers whose party-planning skills were beyond question. These women dominated every museum board in town, and for good reason. They had personal relationships with the best caterers, florists, auctioneers, bandleaders. The theme this year was Christmas in the Alps. Every facet of the evening had been meticulously crafted to fit, down to the authentic lederhosen on the gorgeous young waitstaff and truckloads of evergreen boughs lit with tiny electric candles that looked uncannily real.

The benefit would begin with a live auction held in Holbrooke's auditorium, where everything from the trendiest ski togs to time-shares in Gstaad would go on the block, called by a prominent auctioneer from Sotheby's. Then Patricia would get up and read the names of the donors in Miss Holbrooke's Inner Circle, which was reserved for those who'd given in excess of two hundred fifty thousand dollars to the endowment campaign. Then the main event—and this one Patricia would've resisted if she hadn't feared looking suspicious. Roger and Enid Van Allen would ascend to the stage at precisely seven-thirty, their bankers on standby. In a dramatic live-action PowerPoint presentation projected for the audience's entertainment, they would transfer ten million dollars into Holbrooke's account. Patricia would then unveil the architect's drawing of the new Van Allen Upper School Building.

After the show was over, guests would be ferried by a squadron of horse-drawn carriages hired for the occasion to the grand ballroom of a nearby hotel for a banquet featuring beluga caviar, squab, rack of lamb, and raspberries sabayon paired with appropriate wines and champagnes, followed by dancing and the distribution of lavish Burberry gift bags containing goodies worth hundreds of dollars, provided free of charge by merchants looking to score points with the Holbrooke parent body.

Her own preparations for the big event would take Patricia most of tomorrow. A final fitting of the dress with her tailor scheduled for first thing, followed by facial, manicure, pedicure, retouching of highlights, blow-dry, and makeup at Elizabeth Arden. She should be finished by four. All the financial details had been attended to. The Van Allens' bank had the requisite codes and account information, and Holbrooke's bankers stood ready as well. Patricia was not at all concerned about the money's getting wired *in*. No. That wasn't the problem.

What troubled her, what had her positively *beside* herself, was how in hell to get the money *out*. The whole scheme had been months, years even, in the planning, and now a key element had gone and failed on her. Had up and, actually, disappeared. Which made her desperately afraid that there was some unknown wrench in the works. The safeguard made so much sense at the time she put it in place. She didn't want her own fingerprints—literally speaking—on the account. Of course not, that would be foolish. She didn't expect that the skimming would ever be discovered, but if it were, she needed deniability. She needed a scapegoat, a fall guy. So naturally she chose somebody she believed she could easily manipulate. Carmen Reyes.

Patricia poured herself a scotch and sighed deeply, walking over to look out her window, thirty-three stories above street level. The evening sky was a luminous gray with black clouds like thumbprints scudding across it. Powdery flakes blew sideways in the wind, obscuring the midtown skyline in a cottony veil. She understood there was no way around this problem. If Carmen didn't turn up by tomorrow, Patricia would simply have to tell James the scheme was off. But not before she asked him where he'd been on Monday night when his daughter died. Because, despite what that prosecutor seemed to think, he hadn't been with *her*.

50

MELANIE WAS CLIMBING the walls. She'd been sitting on her butt in the hotel room, supposedly waiting to play switchboard operator, but since the rest of the team was incommunicado, they hadn't required her services. Dan and Bridget had driven off to El Yunque hours ago with five enormous local cops in mirrored shades and flashy uniforms. By now they should have taken up position around El Baño Grande, a decrepit and overgrown stone swimming pool in El Yunque park where the drug deal was supposed to go down in two hours. They were maintaining radio silence, so Melanie couldn't exactly call for an update. Nor could she reach Lieutenant Albano or Ray-Ray Wong, who presumably were on a plane to San Juan tailing Trevor Leonard. At least she *hoped* that's where they were. Trevor's safety was her greatest worry right now, and there'd been no news on him since she'd first learned he'd dropped from view.

She decided to check her office voice mail back home in order to have something productive to do.

"You have two new messages."

The first was left at 1:47 P.M.—Shavonne Washington from the Chief Medical Examiner's Office.

"Hey, Melanie, we just got the results on that comprehensive tox screen you requested, and they're pretty interesting. Brianna Meyers's came out like you'd expect, just heroin. But Whitney's tox had a little added bonus. Lethal levels of not only heroin but OxyContin—repeat, OxyContin. Oxy's a pow-

erful prescription painkiller. People do use it recreationally and overdose accidentally. But you should also know it's the drug of choice for murders made to look like ODs. Whitney had about twenty times the therapeutic dosage in her blood. To get levels that high, you'd have to cook the Oxy and heroin together and shoot up the cocktail, but still, you woulda had to make one huge wrongheaded mistake on the dosage. If you recall, the doc found fresh tracks between her toes, so that looks good for point of entry. But like you said, where's the syringe? This is all starting to smell kinda funky, you ask me."

Whitney Seward had been murdered, and somebody had gone to great lengths to make it look like an accidental overdose. Melanie and Dan had suspected this from day one; now there was official confirmation. The obvious explanation was that Esposito had done it, of course. Maybe Whitney had become a liability somehow. Maybe she'd threatened to go to the police, tried to blackmail him. A guy like Esposito hardly needed an excuse to order a hit. But, tempting as it might be to bow to the obvious, that theory just didn't sit right with Melanie. If Esposito *had* been responsible, he'd want to keep his name out of it. So why fake an OD using Golpe packets that would lead the cops right back to his operation? Why erase all the numbers but his own from Whitney's cell phone?

Melanie was already thinking "frame-up." Then she listened to the next message, and became a hundred percent convinced.

The message had been left on her office voice mail at 7:20 P.M., which, adjusting for the time difference, was less than an hour ago. *"Um, hi, it's Lulu. Look, I said I told you everything I know, but that wasn't true. Carmen was real upset about something going down in the school office at Holbrooke that didn't have nothing to do with Jay Esposito. The Esposito thing . . . well, somebody made me say that, okay? I can explain. Please call me, because I'm real scared and I need to talk to you."*

The school office at Holbrooke? Melanie didn't know what to make of that one. She listened to that message three times through to get a clearer understanding, and the major thing she came away with was that somebody was out to frame Jay Esposito. Lulu Reyes had been ordered by an unknown individual to implicate him in Carmen's disappearance. *Falsely.* That could mean Expo didn't have Carmen. Beyond that, it could mean he wasn't responsible for the deaths of Whitney Seward and Brianna Meyers either. So what did that say about the entire direction of their investigation? Or even about this drug deal tonight? Was the hand-to-hand in El Yunque for real but just unrelated to Whitney and Brianna's deaths? Or was the drug deal orchestrated by the true killer, an elaborate ploy intended to throw off the cops? A hoax, a diversion— God forbid, an *ambush*?

Melanie dialed the Reyeses' apartment with shaking hands, thinking of Dan out in the rain forest. Was he walking into a trap?

Luis Reyes answered. Melanie immediately told him she had no news about Carmen, in order not to get his hopes up, but said she needed to speak to Lulu right away.

"She not here right now. She got ice-skating practice in Chelsea Piers till ten o'clock tonight. I think it's good she keep up her routine, you know?"

He gave Melanie the number for the Chelsea Piers Sky Rink. She called there right away, but the woman who answered the phone refused to get Lulu off the ice, claiming she was too busy to leave her station. Melanie insisted it was an emergency. The woman grudgingly took a message, but Melanie had zero confidence Lulu would ever see it. *Damn.*

Melanie paced like a caged animal, agonizing over her next step. She *wanted* to go find Dan in the rain forest and warn him the drug deal might be some kind of hoax. That's what she *wanted* to do, but she kept telling herself it wasn't smart. She was a prosecutor, not a cop. She could screw things up, barging into the middle of a surveillance. Not to mention get hurt.

The phone shrieked, and Melanie jumped. She grabbed the receiver, hoping it was Lulu calling back.

"He-hello?"

"Yo, Ms. Vargas, Frank Leary, Manhattan South Homicide, calling to give youse a heads-up on developments with this Deon Green murder."

"Oh, sure, Detective," she said, struggling to focus her brain on something other than what was happening in El Yunque.

"We locked up the pross in question earlier today. One Samir Khan, aka Sammy. Guy rolled right away. Claims he was paid off to lure the vic into a beatin' by none other than your boy Jay Esposito."

"Huh. Really." Melanie fell silent. The thought that Fabulous Deon had thus in all likelihood been killed for snitching made her sick to her stomach. But another part of her experienced a guilty jolt of relief. If Expo were responsible after all, then Dan was just surveilling a normal drug deal. Nothing to worry about.

"Hello?" Leary asked after a moment.

"Yes, I'm still here," she said. "I hate to hear that. It means Fabulous Deon was probably murdered in retaliation for his work with us."

"Jeez, sorry about that."

"God, that's just awful. Deon was a good man."

"So let's move fast on this Esposito asshole, make him pay."

"Yes, definitely. Our team's set up right now at a location about forty-five minutes from here, where Expo's people are doing a hand-to-hand tonight. We're expecting him to show up there."

"Expo? In Puerto Rico? No way. He's in New York tonight. I got good intelligence says he's at one of his clubs."

"Are you sure? That's different from what we've been hearing."

"The snitch I'm working with is real reliable, so I'm pretty confident. My partner and I are gonna take a ride right now and bring 'im in."

"Detective, do me a favor and let me know as soon as you've got Esposito in custody? If he's not down here, we need to know."

"Sure thing."

Esposito at one of his clubs in New York? What could that mean, other than that she'd been right? Somebody was playing them. They were being set up. Jesus, she'd better warn Dan. But he had his phone and his radio turned off.

Melanie desperately started dialing team members, even though she assumed nobody would answer. She left messages on Dan's and Bridget's cells begging them to call her at the hotel because she had important new information. Then she called Ray-Ray Wong. Much to her shock, he picked up on the first ring.

"Ray, it's Melanie. I'm so glad I got you! Did you land yet?"

"Did I *what?*"

"Are you in San Juan? I couldn't reach you before, so I figured you guys and Trevor were already on the plane. I have some important new information."

"Whatever it is, it'll have to wait. We got a serious problem up here."

Melanie felt suddenly cold and light-headed, like she was sick with something. She knew what was coming. The thing she'd tried so hard to avoid. She closed her eyes and saw Trevor's face.

"Tell me," she demanded with quiet urgency.

"It's Trevor. He never arrived at the airport. The Escalade they had him in hasn't been seen in hours. We've lost them somehow."

51

MELANIE WAS BUSY negotiating with a cabdriver named Raúl in the hotel driveway when Lamar Gates and Pavel LNU walked right by her and got into a waiting convertible. What the hell were they doing in San Juan? Did they have Trevor stashed around here somewhere? She didn't have a clue what was going on, but one thing she *did* know: She couldn't afford to waste time. She quit arguing over a few bucks and jumped in the back of the taxi.

"Follow that car!"

"Lady, are you crazy? That's a Porsche," Raúl said, looking at her in the rearview mirror. He was middle-aged, with a bristly mustache.

"Do it! Hurry up! We're gonna lose them."

"You pay twice the meter and cover any damage to my cab."

"Deal."

Once his foot touched the pedal, Raúl did not disappoint. He ran red lights all the way to the highway. They got on, heading for El Yunque, and Raúl wove in and out of traffic, doing a minimum of eighty, keeping the Porsche in his sights yet somehow remaining far enough back so as not to blow their cover.

Another benefit of doing eighty was that it made El Yunque that much closer. Twenty minutes later they turned off the highway onto a smaller road that ran beside a diminutive river, more like a stream. In the distance black mountains massed, shrouded in mist.

"That's it," Raúl said, pointing out the front window.

Melanie shivered. "Are there snakes?" she asked.

"Probably, but I'm no expert. I don't like nature. Too dirty for me."

They'd seen the Porsche cross through El Yunque's gates some distance ahead of them and disappear into the blackness. Now Raúl drove up to the portal, marked by a National Park Service sign, and stopped the cab.

"Here you go," he said.

"This isn't my final destination. I'm going to El Baño Grande."

"Lady, the park is closed."

"I'll pay extra."

"I'm not going in *there* after hours."

"Raúl, this is important. Like I said, I'll pay."

"Twice the meter *y cincuenta pesos más.*"

"Fifty bucks extra? You're crazy."

"Fine, *chica,* there's the door."

"I don't even *have* that much. I'll pay you twice the meter plus twenty-five."

He shrugged. "Okay." He put the car in gear, then stopped, looking at her over his shoulder. "Your friends in the Porsche, they got guns?"

She hesitated, not wanting him to change his mind. But she wasn't the type to lie, not when another person's safety was at stake.

"I'm not sure, but probably," she said, expecting him to turn the cab around. Instead he turned off the headlights, and they entered the park in complete darkness.

"When we get farther in, I'm gonna have to put the lights back on or else we'll crash before your friends ever get us. But for a little while, I can drive by the light from the town."

Within minutes the air streaming through the windows became pungent with the smell of wet earth and alive with the sounds of peeper frogs and insects. Melanie smacked a mosquito on her arm, but not before it took a serious bite out of her.

They drove for a while longer. When the road became impossible to see, Raúl flipped on the headlights again. Melanie gasped at the wealth of insect life swarming their windows in the sudden illumination.

"If the bugs scare you from the car, what are you gonna do on that trail?" he said, glancing at her in the mirror.

"What trail? You said you'd drive me there!"

"I'll take you as far as the road goes, but you *can't* drive all the way to El Baño. Don't worry. It's not more than ten or fifteen minutes' walk from where the road stops. The moon is strong tonight. You'll be fine as long as you keep to the path."

"What happens if I don't?"

"*Then* . . . you'll be in trouble. People get lost in here, and they find the bones picked clean."

Melanie's stomach lurched with fear, and her hands clenched together in her lap, but what was she going to do? Turn around and go back to the hotel? Dan was in there somewhere; she needed to warn him. And she needed to find her witness.

A while later Raúl shut off the headlights and braked.

"What—" Melanie began.

"Shhh!"

The route continued upward, but a short distance ahead she made out the shape of a structure by the roadside. In the moonlight she saw the Porsche in the small parking area.

"The information center," Raúl whispered. "The trail leaves from here. Looks like your friends already started walking."

"Looks that way," she said, swallowing hard.

"You want, I just take you back to your hotel."

"No. Thanks, but I have to do this."

"Okay," he said.

He sat there silently, and she realized he was waiting to be paid. Melanie gave him everything that was in her wallet, then wrote him a check for some more.

"I got a flashlight if you like," he said as he counted the cash.

"How much do you want for it?"

"Twenty."

"You're kidding."

"You see a hardware store around here?"

"I'll have to write you a check."

"Okay."

"Where is it, though? I want to see it."

He took the flashlight from the glove box and handed it across the seat. It was a grimy old plastic one. She turned it on, and the bulb glowed a dull yellow.

"No way. I'm not paying twenty bucks for this thing," Melanie said.

"Ten then."

"No. With what I just paid you, you can throw it in."

Raúl frowned. "Okay. Normally I'm not such a pushover, but I'm worried about you, *chica*. Whatever you're up to, it's definitely not smart."

"I'll be fine. It's nice of you to worry, though."

"Hey, people saw me pick you up at the hotel. If you turn up dead, who do you think they'll come looking for?"

Melanie tried laughing off his comment, but the sound emerged high-pitched, almost panicked. She got out of the car, closing the rear door as quietly as she could.

"So do me a favor, be careful," Raúl said.

He backed up, waved jauntily, and headed down the road. As she watched the taxi disappear from view, the sounds of the night closed in around her, and Melanie felt as alone as she ever had in her life.

52

D AN'S CHEAP plastic watch had one thing going for it. The display lit up if you pressed a button, so he could see it was almost eleven, just about five minutes to showtime, and professional drug dealers tended to be prompt. He swatted another mosquito, looked up to see dozens of large bats swooping in and out of the tree he was crouching behind. The PR cops had a good laugh about that. He understood enough Spanish to hear them joking around before, when he took up position under the *níspero* tree, where the bats roosted at night. Like Dan could give a shit about a few bats. This was the best vantage point. From here he had a dead-on view of the eerie stone swimming hole and the patch of cleared path beyond that was the only possible place for a hand-to-hand. These Puerto Rican guys were just actors pretending to be cops, Dan thought, not the real deal, or they would've understood that he picked his spot for a reason. They should try working narcotics in New York, see the vermin you ran across there.

Dan was trying to figure out if this was a setup or not. It wasn't like he was so high on himself, but he did trust his own gut. And something about this deal didn't feel right. He hadn't said anything to Melanie because he didn't want to upset her, but Trevor's voice in that message before *did* sound stressed, in a bad way. He wondered if the kid was okay. Shit, Trevor could be dead by now, and they would never know. How many times had a government witness just up and disappeared off the face of the earth? Guys like Jay Esposito always had a favorite dumping ground, The Flatlands, The Gotti Graveyard. The city was full of 'em. Dan hated to think how Melanie would react if something happened to that kid. That was what really got him about her—unbelievably smart and beautiful, yeah, but she had a heart.

A beam of white moonlight was shining straight down on the water in that big stone pool. It was so hot and misty out here that Dan drifted into a momentary fantasy about swimming naked with her, what they would do in the warm water. The sex was intense. If he thought he couldn't stay away before, now he was *really* hooked. Everything in his life just felt like waiting to be with her again, to touch her, to taste her. When they were together again . . .

Who was he kidding? *If.* If, not when. Dan didn't scare easily, but being under Melanie's spell had him fucking petrified. She just might take it into her head to decide they weren't right for each other or she was too busy or had too many responsibilities. Some fucked up shit like that. And not because she didn't care about him either—he *knew* she did—but because that's just how she was. What would he do then? The thought of it made him want to punch the tree or pull out his nine-millimeter and shoot some bats. What *could* he do? He was sunk. Done.

He heard a rustling in the leaves and moved his hand to his gun.

"It's me," Bridget whispered. Her blond hair was hidden under a Mets cap.

"Jeez, you gotta be careful. I could shoot you in the dark like this."

"Better than Pedro feeling me up."

"Seemed to me you looked pretty happy over there," he teased.

"No thanks. Those guys have been around the block too much for my taste."

"Well, cops are dogs everywhere."

"Not you," Bridget said.

Her eyes in the dark stood out clear and blue, and she looked very young. Now why couldn't he go for a nice average girl like this, who'd say yes in a New York minute to what he was asking of Melanie? Bridget would never hurt him. She wouldn't want to, and he wouldn't care enough to let her. But his emotions were beyond his control; his body, too. He was obsessed, nothing he could do about it. And if his relationship with Melanie felt like heartbreak waiting to happen . . . well, he had a sneaking suspicion that was part of its allure. It had a dark magic he couldn't seem to fight. Plus, at some level he did set a high enough store by himself that he figured he'd win Melanie in the end. How sweet would *that* be?

"I'm trying to figure out if we're being played," Dan said to Bridget.

"Really? That never occurred to me. What should we do?" Bridget asked.

"Wait and see. If this is for real, it won't be long now."

She moved in closer to him, whipped out a pair of binoculars, and trained them on the swimming hole. Bridget was very petite. Dan wondered how a little girl like her would measure up as a partner. She'd probably be pretty fast, maybe even quick on the draw, but how would she ever manage to pull some two-hundred-pound animal off him in a dark alley? Not like a partner had never been called on to perform that service. It'd happened, all right, about five years back. Randall Walker had proved he was still one tough son of a bitch that night, with some spark left in him, and because of that, Dan was still walking around. Okay, Bridget smelled a damn sight better than Randall, but realizing that only made Dan long for Melanie, so it wasn't much reason to join forces.

"Hey," Bridget whispered.

"You got something?"

"Yeah, two guys about ten o'clock. Could be the Colombians."

"Lemme see," Dan said, holding out his hand for the binoculars, but Bridget wouldn't give them up.

"Definitely the Colombians. One has a duffel bag. Must be the product. And—Jeez. *Shit.*"

"What?"

"They got AK-47s. And dogs."

M ELANIE TOLD HERSELF this was just like any old nature trail. She was in a national park. There was a path. It led from Point A to Point B, it was slippery but only moderately steep, and it was marked. All she had to do was stay on it. Maybe it was dark, but she had a flashlight. Maybe a lot of *things* were flying through the air and crawling underfoot, but—

"Aaghh," she cried involuntarily, swatting at something that knocked into her face. Jesus, it was crunchy and sinewy. Some sort of whirring insect, but the size of a small bird.

She broke out in a cold sweat and thought about turning back. The problem was, where would she go? The park gates were so far away that she wouldn't make them by sunup. And she'd have to walk through a dark ocean of creepy-crawlies to get to them. Melanie was a city girl. A lot of things *didn't* scare her: police sirens, gunshots outside her window, the ominous beating of military helicopters during orange alert. But the forest at night—forget about it! Her legs were quivering like jelly.

She forced herself to continue on, shielding the flashlight beam with her hand and keeping it pointed at the ground. Her goal was to use the weak light to avoid stumbling off the path without alerting Expo's bodyguards to her presence. When she got closer to El Baño Grande, she'd do some reconnaissance and try to locate her team members. *How,* she wasn't exactly sure, but something would come to her. It'd better.

She walked on resolutely for about five minutes more, the path sloping steadily upward, challenging her thigh muscles. She'd feel this tomorrow. If Raúl had been correct that El Baño Grande was only ten or fifteen minutes' walk from the information center, she should be coming up to it soon. Her heart had stopped pounding; her breathing was steadier. Hell, this wasn't so bad.

Just as she finished congratulating herself on how well she was handling the thick sounds of the night echoing in her ears, the flashlight flickered and went out, plunging her into darkness. For a moment she stood completely still, not quite believing her bad luck. Then she flipped the switch back and forth several times to no avail. Hopeless. Fucking thing was a piece of crap. She threw it into the bushes and drew a deep breath, trying to figure out what to do next. There weren't many choices. She could stand rooted to this spot all night, till the sun came up, and hope Expo's goons didn't step on her on their way back down the path. She could sit on the ground and let bugs crawl all over her. Or she could wait for her eyes to adjust and keep walking. Not much of a choice—she'd keep walking.

The night was clear. Because the rain forest on either side of her was thick with vegetation, all she had to do was look at the thin corridor of starry sky overhead to keep to her route. And the moon was up, casting an unearthly white glow she could almost taste. After a moment she could see the path pretty clearly. She started walking, insides tight with anxiety, but then immediately stumbled over a tree root, tumbling to her knees, her hands lighting on disgusting, slick wetness. *Ugh!* Mud, wet leaves, bugs. Getting back up, she felt like bursting into tears. She hadn't appreciated how much that pathetic flashlight had comforted her. The darkness was full of hidden threats. Damn it, why wasn't she a smoker? Then at least she'd have a cigarette lighter in her bag. Or matches or . . . wait a minute. Frantically, Melanie grabbed the leather bag she'd been carrying over her shoulder and dug around its dark insides. Her fingers hit the hard metal of her cell phone. She pulled it out and turned it on. No reception, but it cast a warm, glowing light. She walked on, feeling calmer.

Five minutes later she turned off the phone. The path had ascended steeply, and now she stood on a shallow ledge overlooking a round, dark shimmer that had to be El Baño Grande reflecting the moonlight. She'd reached her destination, but now what? How would she find her people without alerting the enemy?

Directly ahead, all at once, lights flashed in the darkness. Loud pops registered in her ears, and a swarm of bats rose into the air from their perch on a nearby tree. Melanie threw herself down on the slimy path, stomach clenching with dread.

This was the place, all right. She'd wandered into the middle of a firefight.

53

THINGS WERE GOING like clockwork for Bud. This was no accident but rather the result of brilliant planning. Finally some payoff for being smarter than everyone else yet eating their shit so patiently for so long.

Jay called Bud's cell phone at eleven-thirty from the office at Noir, the club in the Flatiron District that was strictly for the bridge-and-tunnel crowd. Noir was always packed on a Thursday night. Bud had advised Jay to be seen out and about so that he had an alibi for what went down in Puerto Rico, and Jay had fallen for it easily. Every step was carefully mapped, down to the fact that Jay's office at Noir had a private back door that led out to the alley. Anybody watching would witness Jay enter his office from inside the club, alone. And plenty of people would be watching, because all eyes were *always* on Jay at his clubs. That was one of the perks of being a celebrity, and Bud was counting on it.

"Where the fuck *you* been?" Jay demanded, hearing the sirens in the background as Bud walked down the street. Bud was carrying the golf bag, annoyed that his feet were wet from the slush at the corners, that he didn't have the cash to take a cab on a miserable night like this. That was about to change, but not soon enough for his taste.

"I'm not too far from you. I'm gonna stop by. I don't want to get into details over the phone," Bud said.

"Fuck that pussy-ass shit."

"You'll thank me later, Jay."

"I want an update. *Now.*"

"Relax. I talked to Pavel. The deal happened already. Everything's cool," Bud lied smoothly. He was enjoying every second of this double-cross.

"If the transfer was made, why the fuck haven't I heard from the Colombians?"

"I'll be there in five minutes to explain. Leave the back door unlocked, okay? It's better for you if nobody sees me."

There was something very ultimate for Bud about this impending confrontation. It had become much more to him than just a settling of old scores. He felt like he'd finally be liberated from all the things in his past that smacked of failure, of defeat, of unfulfilled promise. He'd finally be free.

His mother and Jay's had been sisters, Italian girls from Bensonhurst. Both had married minor thugs, but Jay's father made a good living at it, whereas Bud's was an Irishman with the Irish curse. He drank himself to death, but not before beating the crap out of Bud for enough years to fuck him up good. Then Bud and his mother were charity cases, living off Jay's family, never allowed to forget that either. Everything Bud got his hands on—money, girls, drugs—Jay felt free to take away, and none of it was ever enough. Jay hadn't stopped, never would. The guy had an appetite. Bud got his education, he got his job, and Jay had to put his hairy paws all over that, too. Bud found this perfect young girl, taught her all about sex. It made him want to cry, thinking about Whitney's tits. Then Jay took her for his own purposes and ruined her, so she didn't want to be with Bud anymore except as a way to get to Jay. That was the straw that finally broke the camel's back.

Bud reached out with his gloved hand and pushed open the back door to Jay's office. The place had been done by some trendy designer, and it was butt ugly. Black rubber floors, concrete walls, and strange lighting made from silver tubing. Jay was sitting in his silver swivel chair with his back to the door, talking on the phone. Fricking chair was so weird. Looked like it was covered in duct tape, but Bud happened to know it cost four grand. For a goddamn chair. Any idiot should've realized that a few nightclubs could never support Jay's lavish lifestyle, yet somehow the guy had managed to skate along and avoid getting locked up. The feds were so incompetent it was hardly much of a challenge to beat the system.

Jay whipped around in the chair, phone in his hand. Bud could see from the expression on his face that the game was up. More than *up:* played out to the bitter fucking end.

"Jesus, Javier, I have no fucking clue how the cops found out about El Yunque," Jay was saying as he stared at Bud with savage rage.

I do, you prick. I arranged for that little snitch to tell them, right before I beat his brains out with your golf club. Now I waltz away and everybody else gets locked up. Everybody except you. I have other plans for you.

Bud had bought the gun a week earlier in a dingy stairwell in the East Harlem projects. It was untraceable, with a defaced serial number, but it fired like a dream. He knew, because he'd been practicing.

Jay covered the mouthpiece of the telephone with his hand. "You're a dead man," he said to Bud. Then his eyes followed the golf bag as Bud dropped it on the floor, and he looked confused.

Bud held the gun in his right hand, hidden in the folds of his long overcoat. He lifted it in one beautiful, fluid arc just as he stepped up to the swivel chair and grabbed Jay by the throat. Bud had the advantage of complete and utter surprise, or else Jay would've twisted away easily. Jay had always been the stronger of the two by far; Bud had scars to prove it. But this time, when Jay's mouth fell open in shock, Bud jammed the gun straight into it and squeezed the trigger, firing up and back. He blew Jay's brains all over the designer walls, then carefully folded his limp, dead fingers around the gun. It was the perfect suicide, perfectly timed, just as the feds were closing in.

"'Ello? 'Ello?" the receiver squawked. And Bud replaced it carefully in its cradle before slipping out the back door.

54

LUCKY THING Melanie was so enamored of Dan O'Reilly's voice. It had this killer rough-sweet quality, gravelly and totally sexy, with a noticeable New York accent. It was so distinctive to her ear that she even recognized its fingerprint in a brief grunt that emanated from a nearby *níspero* tree when the shooting started.

Melanie instantly plunged into the underbrush, heading for that tree. The air was thick with flapping bats and bright flashes of gunfire. Sharp branches tore at her clothes, but damn it, she was zeroing in on Dan.

"Shit, behind you!" she heard Bridget Mulqueen exclaim.

The next second something whizzed by Melanie's ear, and it wasn't a mosquito. The bullet knocked a branch off a tree behind her head. It fell with a crash, and she dropped to her knees into a tangle of thorny brush, her heart in her throat, the hair on the back of her neck standing up, every nerve quivering.

"Stop, stop! It's me, Melanie! Don't shoot!"

She knew she was yelling louder than safety counseled, but Dan was an excellent shot. If she didn't stop him, he'd kill her, and what kind of ending would that be to their love story?

Dan stopped firing. "Melanie?" he called, pitching his voice low.

"Yes. I'm getting up. Don't shoot."

She stood up slowly, shaking all over, her arms and legs stinging where thorns had pierced her skin. She made her way the remaining ten feet to where Dan and Bridget crouched behind the tree.

"How'd *you* get here?" Dan asked, rubbing his eyes like he thought he was hallucinating.

"I took a cab."

Bridget looked at her as if she were crazy, but Dan laughed. "That's you, all right," he said.

"I'm sorry, but I *had* to come," Melanie whispered urgently. "Trevor's missing. Esposito is still in New York. He never got on a plane to come here. I was thinking this deal was either a diversion or an ambush, and that I needed to warn you. But then I saw Lamar and Pavel coming here, so now I'm completely confused."

"Uh," Bridget said, mouth still hanging open in astonishment at Melanie's presence.

"The hand-to-hand's definitely going," Dan said under his breath. "Two guys came in from the right less than five minutes ago, prob'ly the Colombians, because they were carrying a duffel bag, which we gotta assume has the product. Armed with assault rifles. One of 'em has a pit bull. Right before the shooting starts, Pavel and Lamar show up from the direction you just came from. They're about to do the hand-to-hand when all hell breaks loose."

"We think the local cops jumped the gun, started shooting for no reason," Bridget explained.

"We can't be sure. I don't want to prejudge guys. You can barely see your hand in front of your face out here. But I gotta tell you, nobody was supposed to move until I gave the signal, and I did *not* give the fucking signal. It's quiet now, but we don't know if anybody's hit," Dan said.

"If *we* don't know that, chances are the bad guys don't know either, right?" Melanie said.

"What's your point?" Dan asked.

"If you could call the locals off, maybe after a while the bad guys would assume whoever was shooting at them took a hit?"

"It's possible."

"Then maybe they'd make their exchange and try to leave. If we could pick off Expo's guys and arrest them with the drugs, we'd have a prosecutable case. I know where they parked. We could set up on their car."

"Huh," Dan said, thinking.

"Well?" Bridget asked.

"Maybe. Not bad, actually. Our only other choice is to shoot it out, and obviously we're not gonna fire first," he said.

Somebody else made the decision for them. The moment the words left Dan's mouth, bullets began to fly again up ahead. Bursts of gunfire mixed with shouting and cursing in Spanish. Dan and Bridget raised their weapons, ready to advance.

Dan threw a final glance over his shoulder at Melanie.

"You move from this spot, I'll shoot you myself," he said. But he gave her his gorgeous smile, backlit by gunfire, before he turned and strode off toward the battle.

55

MELANIE SLURPED hot café con leche from a bowl, struggling to keep her eyes open under the buzzing fluorescent lights of the Luquillo police station at three o'clock in the morning. Just as she was about to lose the fight and nod off, Lieutenant Albano walked in and marched up to her borrowed desk.

"What the hell happened out there?" he asked. Gotta love New Yorkers. Not one second wasted on preliminaries.

"I came in late, but from what I understand, the hand-to hand was about to go down and the locals just . . . opened fire." She held up her hands in dismay.

"Ah, crap."

"The guy who shot first claims one of the Colombians was reaching for a weapon."

"Was he?"

"Well, the Colombians definitely had assault rifles, so maybe. But now we have to deal with an IAB investigation in the middle of our case. It screws everything up."

"Shit."

"I'm just amazed nobody was killed. One of the Colombians is in the hospital with a bullet in his leg. I arranged with the local U.S. Attorney's Office for a bedside arraignment later this morning. And we locked up Pavel Stepanov, Esposito's bodyguard."

"That's good."

"Yeah, except our case on him sucks. Once the shooting started, the hand-to-hand never happened, and the second Colombian ran off with the drugs. So we have no product to put on the table. It's just a circumstantial conspiracy case. I mean, we could charge an attempt, but . . ."

"Son of a gun. It just gets worse," Albano muttered.

Melanie paused, looking for a diplomatic way to bring up the subject that was foremost on her mind. But there was none. "So listen, Lieutenant."

"Yeah?"

"What went wrong with Trevor? I mean, how could you lose him like that?"

Albano looked at her like he was seeing her for the first time. "Yeah, sorry about that one, kid. What can I say? The good guys don't win every inning."

"That's it? I mean, Trevor's a solid human being. What are we doing to find him?"

"We *were* following up a tip that I *thought* came from you about the hand-to-hand tonight, thinking maybe the Leonard kid got by us somehow and that he'd show up here. But obviously things didn't play out that way."

"No, obviously they didn't."

"Well, I don't know what you want from me," Albano said irritably. "We got Dan and Bridget still out with the Puerto Ricans searching that area again, on the off chance anybody's around. But it's a long shot. Who knows, maybe this joker Pavel'll start talking and tell us where the kid is."

"He won't. He invoked. So he can't be questioned without a lawyer present."

"Jesus H. Christ."

"Yeah, and when counsel's appointed in the morning, it'll be for extradition purposes only. That lawyer'll just tell him not to talk until he gets transported to New York and gets his real lawyer, which could be *weeks* from now given how slow the Marshals' airlifts are."

"This is when I hate the fucking system. A kid's life is at stake. You'd think we'd be allowed to go in there and beat the crap out of that Russian prick till he gives it up."

"That's what separates us from the barbarians, I guess," Melanie said.

"Look around. Nothing separates us from the barbarians these days, so why stand on ceremony?" Albano popped one of his ever-present Rolaids. "Stay put for a few minutes, wouldja? I'm gonna see if I can raise the supervisor here and get an update."

"Okay." Melanie drew a shaggy breath.

Albano patted her arm. "Buck up, kid. The game ain't perfect, but we gotta keep playing it."

"You're right."

Exhausted, she put her head down on the desk.

Sometime later Ray-Ray Wong shook her shoulder. Melanie lifted her head blearily. A paper clip that had been stuck to her cheek fell to the desktop with a ping.

"Morning, ma'am. The lieutenant asked me to drive you back to the hotel."

"What? Why? What's happening?"

"Zero. *Nada*. Everybody in custody invoked, so they can't be questioned. I'm tasked with returning you to the hotel for some shut-eye and then heading on to assist in the search at El Yunque."

Melanie sighed and stood up. She had a headache so bad it felt like there was an ice pick stuck in her eye. Insect bites and thorn pricks on her arms and legs stung like hell. Trevor was missing. Carmen was *still* missing. Melanie was beginning to think they were probably both still in New York, dead or alive. And here *she* was in San Juan, at a big fat standstill.

56

MELANIE WASN'T one to stand still for long. After Ray-Ray dropped her off, she packed her suitcase, checked out, and took a cab to the airport. There was a seat available on a 7:00 A.M. Delta flight that got into JFK before lunch, so she handed over her credit card. Sitting in the airplane waiting to take off, she left a voice mail for Dan telling him where she was going, and why.

About five hours later, she stood in the harsh light of the baggage-claim area at JFK waiting to collect her suitcase. Supposedly a blizzard was on the way, and the woman next to her said the airport was closing in half an hour. So much for the prospect of reinforcements for whatever it was she hoped to accomplish here. The rest of the team would be stranded in San Juan. *Lucky them.* She shivered for fifteen minutes straight standing in the taxi line. On the ride in, New York City did its best impression of hell, with decaying highways, steam rising from enormous fissures in the roads, garbage and graffiti everywhere.

She checked her voice mail from the cab. A message from Detective Frank Leary prompted her to go straight to Noir, Jay Esposito's club in the Flatiron District. The taxi let her out in front of an industrial-looking brick building on a cramped side street. She hauled her suitcase into the dark nightclub, breathing in cigarettes and stale beer, and found Detective Leary at the bar finishing an interview. When he was done, he escorted her back through the club, past the coat check and restrooms, toward Jay Esposito's office.

"Apparent suicide. I'm all ready to slap cuffs on the asshole, and he goes and offs himself. Whaddaya gonna do? Leary shrugged. He was a burly Irishman in his thirties, with a pleasant face and a receding hairline.

"I hate that. You're just about to arrest somebody and they die. I always feel like I should do the case anyway," Melanie said.

"Good news is, we think we found the murder weapon from the Deon Green case. Prick used his golf club, you believe that? We got the nine-iron with hair and blood still on it. Sent it to the lab for testing, but it matches up perfect with the bludgeoning MO in the Green case."

"What makes you think Esposito killed himself?" Melanie asked as they entered the office, which was crowded with cops.

"I got maybe ten, fifteen witnesses saw Esposito come in here alone at eleven-thirty last night. Me and my partner show up around one, find him with a gun in his hand and his brains splattered all over that wall there. M.E. hauled off the body already, but you can see the debris."

A nauseating amount of chunky tissue and clotted blood adhered to the concrete wall behind Esposito's desk. Someone had drawn a large circle around it with red Magic Marker.

"I see," Melanie said, swallowing hard, turning away.

"Found him slumped in the chair. Looks from the trajectory like he put the gun in his mouth and pulled the trigger."

"I have to tell you, Detective, based on what I know about Jay Esposito, he'd never kill himself."

"Maybe he figured he was going down and he couldn't stomach the thought of the inside. Some guys can't," Leary said.

"Esposito would just hire a big-name lawyer in a two-thousand-dollar suit and try to beat the charges. He wouldn't go without a fight. I'm sure of it."

"What are you saying? You think he was murdered and the shooter faked a suicide?"

"Maybe. Who knows?" She paused, thinking about all the evidence that Esposito was being framed by somebody, then said more firmly, "Yes, I do."

"Got any suspects?"

"Esposito was running a string of heroin mules between San Juan and New York. The suppliers were Colombians. A deal scheduled for last night went south in a big way."

"That'll do it. Colombians'll whack ya as easy as they'll say hello, and if you fuck with their transactions, forget about it," Leary said.

"Or it could be somebody else we just haven't identified yet. Esposito had a lot of enemies. What I'm saying is, I wouldn't take anything for granted."

"Don't worry, we're not. Crime Scene guys've been here for hours already, processing the place just like it was a murder."

"Have they found anything?"

"They're still working. So far the only item of interest besides the gun is a key they found, like, hangin' out of Esposito's jacket pocket. It was just kind of in a funny position, you know? Half in, half out, not natural. Like maybe somebody went through his pockets looking for something and knocked it out by accident."

"Hmm. Do we know what the key is for?"

"Yeah, actually, that was weird, too. It had a tag with an address in Williamsburg. Not too often you find a key with the address actually written on it, right?"

"Maybe somebody wanted us to find it."

"Huh. Interesting thought," Leary said, looking at Melanie with enhanced respect. "Anyways, I dispatched a squad car a little while ago to check the place out. I'm waiting to hear."

"I'd like to talk to the Crime Scene detectives."

"Sure thing. Yo, Butch," Leary called.

Butch Brennan from the Crime Scene team came over to them.

"Hey, Melanie."

"Hey, Butch, what's up?"

"Ms. Vargas here thinks based on the case she's doing there's a chance our boy was whacked," Leary said. "You got anything points to that?"

Butch smiled. "Funny you should mention that. C'mon outside."

Butch opened a nearly invisible door faced in the same concrete as the wall. "We dusted the doorknob. Pretty interesting in itself. Nothing. Wiped clean," he said.

They stepped out into a narrow back alley that was covered in a pristine carpet of fresh snow. A horde of pigeons that had been eating from a Dumpster took off with a flapping of wings.

Butch pointed out several faint indentations in the snow in a small area cordoned off with blue police barricades.

"See here? We photographed three footprints around four o'clock this morning. Right, left, right, leading away from the door. Snow's picked up since then, so they got kinda blurry, but they were real clear when we shot 'em."

"Could you tell what kind of shoe made them?" Melanie asked.

"I'm gonna say a male. Looks like a sneaker. More specific than that, we need to consult our footprint guy."

"When were they made?"

"The snow wasn't crusted or nothing, so they looked pretty fresh. I'd say late last night. But this is the interesting part. Take a look at the left print here."

Butch knelt down, took a little handheld broom from his pocket, and began dusting at the middle impression. "Don't worry. We already photographed it and took samples and everything."

As Butch carefully removed the top layer of fluffy new snow, a small patch of dark purple appeared.

"Blood," Melanie said.

"Yup. I'm betting it was the victim's. Lab'll confirm that. We're photographing the black floor inside with the infrared to get a better look at any footprints in the blood spatters. There *should* be some. He had to pick the blood up someplace, right?"

"So the shooter stepped in Esposito's blood when he was leaving and tracked it outside into the alley?" Leary asked.

"That's what I'm thinking," Butch replied.

"He's not as smart as he thinks he is," Melanie said, nodding enthusiastically. "We'll get him."

DETECTIVE LEARY WAS a nice guy. When Melanie couldn't get a cab in the snow, he left his partner in charge at Noir and drove her back to her office so she wouldn't have to lug her suitcase on the subway. Melanie loved that about cops. They'd drive you anywhere, at the drop of a hat.

"So you got my little cousin on this case, I understand. Bridget Mulqueen," Leary said, maneuvering his unmarked sedan expertly down the slick avenue at top speed.

"Oh, right, Bridget's your cousin. I forgot."

"How's she doing?"

Melanie looked out at the falling snow. "You know. She's doing okay."

"Yeah, she's green," he said with a smile.

"She's all right. She has the makings of a decent cop," Melanie said, quoting Dan.

Leary glanced over at her quizzically, like he wondered if she was bullshitting him. "Well, just so you know, the job wasn't exactly her life-long dream."

"No?"

"She was a phenomenal soccer player, Bridget. Did everything you could do with it. You Google her, she still comes up as the top scorer in her division. She wanted to go semipro."

"So what happened?"

"Her old man was against it. My Uncle Jimmy's an A-plus guy, but he's a ballbreaker. I can say that, 'cause I love him to death. Larger than life, Jimmy Mulqueen. Definitely the type who needs somebody to follow in his footsteps. Aunt Beattie didn't give him no boys. Four girls, he has. Bridget's the youngest, and he wanted her on the job."

"Oh. I see."

"You know how it is with girls and their fathers sometimes."

"Yes," Melanie said. "I definitely know that."

"Bridget's crazy about her dad. So she came on when maybe it's not the ideal life for her."

"That's a shame."

They pulled up in front of Melanie's office building. Leary looked at her with mild, trusting eyes. "Listen, you'd be doing me a big favor if you could watch out for her. She's a good kid."

For a second, Melanie wished that she didn't want the one thing in life that Bridget so obviously wanted, too. But there was nothing she could do about it. With every day that passed, Melanie was more convinced that she and Dan O'Reilly were born for each other. Besides, didn't *she* need Dan more than Bridget did? Here was Bridget, part of a cozy NYPD family, with this and that relative looking out for her. Bridget could get along without Dan. Melanie wasn't so sure she could say the same for herself.

"I'll do my best. Thanks for the ride," Melanie said, feeling a sharp stab of guilt.

"Don't mention it. I'll call ya if we get anything interesting off this Williamsburg warehouse thing. And be careful, okay? Whoever got to Expo's still out there."

57

MELANIE PLOPPED DOWN at her desk with her coat still on and called home. Sandy told her Maya was fine. No fever, no vomiting, sleeping peacefully. So Melanie heaved a sigh of relief and dialed into her voice mail. She still hadn't bothered to remove her coat, which was a lucky thing, because otherwise she would've just had to put it right back on again.

The message was only twenty minutes old.

"Mel, Stew Steinberg. This is the type of call you know *I don't make lightly, but a young Latina woman's safety is at stake, so I'm considering co-operating a client. I'm sure that comes as a shock to you. Defendant's name is Juan Carlos Peralta, a hardworking kid from the projects, wrongly accused. He says you were trying to pin those rich-bitch ODs on him. Let me emphasize, Juan Carlos knows* nothing *about the OD case. But he* does *have some information about a girl named Carmen Reyes, who got herself mixed up in some type of embezzlement scheme that may have led to her abduction. He thinks he can help you find her, if you're willing to drop charges. Give a call so we can get over to the MCC and proffer him ASAP."*

Embezzlement? The more Melanie thought about that one, the more she scratched her head. But who was she to quibble at this point in her investigation? Carmen and Trevor were still missing. Every moment that passed left her feeling more hopeless and desperate about their fates. Jay Esposito, her most promising target, was lost to the silence of the grave. The circumstances of his death further convinced Melanie that somebody else was out there pulling the strings. In short, she was desperate for a fresh lead. Juan Carlos and embezzlement would have to do.

But it was a snowy Friday afternoon. Christmas was Tuesday, so nobody was around, and whoever was, wasn't doing any work. After several messages the receptionist at Legal Aid finally called back to tell her Stewart had last been sighted heading to the chief judge's Christmas party. Melanie paged Stewart five times to no avail, then decided to go out looking for him. She wandered around the near-deserted courthouse for a while and dropped in on a few Christmas parties that Stewart had been at but just left. Eventually she found him eating a late lunch at the mob diner. She had to wait for Stewart to finish his meal, walk over to the Metropolitan Correctional Center, wait for the CO on duty to decide to help them, and wait *endlessly* for the guards to bring Juan Carlos Peralta down to the claustrophobically tiny interview room. Hours had passed already. Finally Juan Carlos appeared on the other side of the wire-mesh screen, clad in a bright orange prison jumpsuit, looking none too happy.

"What the fuck, Stew, pullin' me outta general population at three o'clock on a Friday! Looks bad. All the MS-13 guys gonna think I'm telling," Juan Carlos complained.

"Talk to *her*," Stewart replied, waving at Melanie. "Believe me, I'd rather be home now myself. She'll dismiss your charges if you help locate this Carmen Reyes person, but she wasn't willing to wait."

"Yo, Ms. Vargas, you messing with my shit here."

"Tell them it's a defense-attorney visit, Juan Carlos," Melanie said. "No reason to think you're talking to the law."

"Right before Christmas? Who gonna believe that? Ain't no defense lawyer in this town working this afternoon."

"Stewart is Jewish. He doesn't celebrate Christmas. This is a convenient time for him."

Juan Carlos paused, then nodded. "Oh, okay. My shorties stupid enough to buy that one."

"Are you ready to proceed?" Melanie asked Stewart.

"One thing I need to clear up. My client believes you view him as a suspect in the Holbrooke ODs case," Stewart said.

"The investigation has progressed significantly since I last spoke to Juan Carlos. I can represent to you that he's no longer a suspect," Melanie replied.

"Okay, good. We're under standard proffer-agreement terms, I take it?" Stewart asked.

"Yes. I have the agreement right here."

Melanie removed a piece of paper from her briefcase, signed it, and handed it to Stewart, who signed as well.

"Very well. Juan Carlos, I'm recommending that you speak to Ms. Vargas."

"Yeah, awright. What you wanna know?" Juan Carlos said to Melanie.

"Your lawyer says you have information about Carmen Reyes being involved in an embezzlement scheme. Tell me about that."

"She ain't involved herself. Somebody trying to use her."

"Who's trying to use her?"

"Peoples at her school. Carmen work in the office there."

"How did *you* find out about this?"

"A few days before she go missing, me and Carmen meet at a Starbucks near her school for our regular tutoring. She real upset, so naturally I'm concerned. Carmen good peoples. I don't like to see her low."

"When exactly was this? Do you remember?"

"Last Thursday. We always meet on Thursday afternoons. That's why I tell Stewie here to call you yesterday, because I remember it Thursday. It make me think of her, and I'm gettin' real agitated for her safety, you feel me?"

"You did the right thing. So you're meeting with Carmen, she's upset, and what does she tell you?"

"Well, at first she ain't tell me nothing. She just say she got problems at school or whatever. But then *I* say, 'When it come to trouble, girl, I got life experience you *ain't* got, so maybe I be of assistance.' And that musta convince her, because she look over her shoulder and all around, then she tell me real quiet-like what be going down."

"Which was?"

"Okay, Carmen working in what she call the development office at the school, right, where they keeping track of all this money rich peoples be donating. Carmen original boss get fired by the head of the school, a real nasty bitch named . . . uh, Andrew, Landau, wait a minute—" He snapped his fingers.

"Andover?"

"Yeah, that it. Mrs. Andover. Anyway, this Andover bitch trains Carmen on some spreadsheet programs and shit so she can do the fired lady's job, right? But she think Carmen too stupid to get what going down, because little by little this Andover be telling Carmen skim off money and send it to funny accounts. At first Carmen think she imagining it, so she start making records and keeping real careful track. Pretty soon she convinced this Andover bitch be robbin' the school big time."

Melanie stared at Juan Carlos in utter astonishment. Whatever she'd thought Patricia Andover might be up to, she'd never imagined something like this.

"Are you *sure,* Juan Carlos? Because that's a serious accusation."

"Sure, I'm sure. I'm sure that what Carmen *say* anyway, and she ain't got no reason to lie to me."

"So what did Carmen do with this information?"

"Well, that what she trying to decide when she talk to me."

"Did you tell her to go to the police?"

Juan Carlos grinned. "Not exackly."

Melanie sighed. "What did you tell her, Juan Carlos?"

"Look, Carmen say they millions of dollars in those accounts, and ten million more due to come in. Come in sometime *today,* if I remember right. What normal person not gonna be tempted by some Benjamins like that?"

"Ten million today," Melanie said under her breath. She looked at her watch, saw again that *today* was rapidly waning.

"Natural response, you feel me?" Juan Carlos said.

"So you told Carmen to steal the money."

"I *suggest* it. It was already gonna get stolen anyway, right? I jus' point out she could win big, get a payday, and she maybe give me a commission to help her figure shit out."

"What did she say?"

"She say no. That's Carmen. She honest as a motherfuckin' nun."

"So then what?"

"Then I drink my chai latte and be on my way. I ain't pressure her or nothing."

"That's it? You just dropped the subject of the money?"

"Carmen say she got somebody she trust, that she gonna tell about it and ask for help."

"Who's that?"

"I don't know. She didn't give me no names. But somebody legit. Important, like."

"Did she say anything else about this person?"

"I know it a man because she call him a 'he.' But that it."

"Do you know whether she went through with it and confided in this guy?"

He shrugged. "After I left the Starbucks, I ain't heard from her no more."

Melanie fell silent, her mind reeling with all of this new information. As far as she could tell, none of it had anything to do with the deaths of Whitney Seward or Brianna Meyers, or the use of Holbrooke girls to mule heroin, or anything else they'd been spending law-enforcement resources on investigating for the past week.

"Let me ask you something, Juan Carlos," Melanie said. "Did Carmen ever mention any drug smuggling going on at Holbrooke, or a guy named Jay Esposito, or anything like that?"

"No, never."

"Huh." Melanie was totally confused.

"Are we done?" Stewart Steinberg asked, looking at his watch.

"Just a minute, I'm thinking," Melanie said. "Juan Carlos, what makes you think the embezzlement scheme is linked to Carmen's disappearance?"

"Whoever want this money need Carmen, or at least they need her fingers," Juan Carlos said definitively.

"Why do you say that?"

"Because. The accounts got what they call biometric protection. Ain't no money goin' nowhere without Carmen fingerprints to verify the transaction."

58

CARMEN SHOOK HER HANDS OUT, feeling the blood rush back into her tingling fingertips. She rubbed her wrists where they'd been tied together, then stood up so quickly that she saw stars and began to sway.

"Whoa, careful there," Bud said, steadying her.

Like he cared. He just needed her in one piece for a few more hours. Carmen knew that the biometric triggers didn't work if she was dead, or else he would surely have cut off her fingers and discarded the rest of her. She couldn't believe she'd once trusted this man. How stupid could you be? She touched the lump on the back of her head. The hair covering it was crusty with blood. She thought about asking for a doctor, but she knew he wouldn't listen. He was only letting her out now because it was *time*. She knew where he planned to take her. Her best bet was to act all cooperative and wait for the right moment to make her move. She *had* to find a way to escape. Because knowing what she knew about him, he'd kill her for sure after they finished their business tonight.

He read her mind.

"Just in case you get any bright ideas, remember this," he said, and pulled his big black gun from his coat pocket, displaying it for her.

Carmen stared at it with wide eyes.

"I'll use it, too. I already have," Bud bragged.

"On who?" Carmen's voice, untried for days, came out as a hoarse croak.

"None of your business," he said.

Carmen visualized her sister dead, and her eyes overflowed with tears.

"Shit! Stop blubbering. How the fuck am I supposed to take you out on the street like that?"

The tears rolled unchecked down Carmen's cheeks. She just couldn't help it. She was feeling so weak, physically and mentally. Really, she didn't see how she could beat him at this game. He held all the cards. And now she was convinced he'd killed Lulu.

"It wasn't anybody you know!" he exclaimed, exasperated. "But if you give me trouble, it *will* be. Remember, I can get to your sister whenever I feel like it."

"No-oo, ple-ease!" Carmen wailed.

"I don't know why you're so fucking broken up over her! Lulu hasn't done *shit* for you, Carmen. We both know she saw me at Whitney's the other night."

It was true. Lulu had seen him there earlier that night, had told Carmen about it. Ironically, his presence was part of what had made Carmen feel comfortable going upstairs in the first place when Whitney called her. Even at that late date, Carmen hadn't suspected a thing. It wasn't until the final, horrible moment in Whitney's bathroom when she turned around and found him standing behind her that everything fell into place. She realized how corrupt he was, realized she'd picked exactly the *wrong* person to tell about the money. But by then it was too late. She was already caught.

"Lulu doesn't know," Carmen protested. "Just because she saw you, that doesn't mean she understands."

"Oh, *she* understands. Lulu's a lot quicker than *you* are, Carmen. But she's smart enough to look out for herself, so don't expect her to come to your rescue."

He put the gun away, grabbed a loose black overcoat and knit cap off a nearby armchair, and shoved them at her.

"Put these on. It's time to go," he commanded.

Looking into his dead eyes, Carmen saw no other choice. She swallowed her tears and did as she was told.

59

EAVING THE JAIL after talking to Juan Carlos Peralta, Melanie was convinced of two things: First, Carmen Reyes was still alive. Second, she wouldn't be staying that way for long.

Melanie's suspicions of something sinister afoot at Holbrooke had been right on the money. Literally. Carmen had stumbled across a major embezzlement scheme, one that couldn't be completed without her fingerprints transferring the final ten million. Once the money moved—presumably shortly after seven-thirty tonight—Carmen became not only unnecessary but a huge liability, which meant Melanie had to find her ASAP. And while she'd love to march right into the Holbrooke benefit and haul Patricia Andover off for a haute couture perp walk, she didn't have enough hard evidence. She needed to let the scheme unfold and pounce at the right moment.

But there was something major that Melanie just didn't get. What did any of this Holbrooke stuff have to do with the heroin case she'd been assigned to investigate? Melanie couldn't ignore the significance of the drug angle. Just look at all the people who'd died because of it. Whitney Seward and Brianna Meyers. Fabulous Deon and—though she could barely stand to think of it—possibly Trevor Leonard as well, for informing on Esposito. And Esposito himself, killed overnight, his murder made to look like a suicide. She'd originally been convinced that the drug case held the key to finding Carmen, but now she wasn't so sure. Were the two schemes linked at all? The only point of intersection Melanie could even think of was the fact that Carmen Reyes had last been seen at the Sewards' apartment the night Whitney and Brianna died.

The hair stood up on the back of her neck.

For a while now, Melanie had a strange sense that somebody was out there, pulling the strings, doctoring the evidence, trying to throw her off. She hadn't listened to this instinct before, but now she felt certain of it. Call him the unseen hand. She didn't know who he was, or where to find him. But she knew where he'd *been*—at the Sewards' the night Whitney and Brianna died and Carmen disappeared. And if he'd been there, she could think of one person who just might have seen him.

FOR MELANIE the most difficult thing about paying a visit to Charlotte Seward was that it brought her closer to her own apartment than she'd been in two whole days. The temptation to rush home and cuddle with her little girl was overwhelming. But she reminded herself that Maya was safe, snug, and well cared for, whereas Carmen and Trevor were still out there somewhere, lost in the cold night.

And night it had become. The sun had set while Melanie was on the subway heading uptown. The wind blew furiously down Park Avenue, whipping a fine spray of crystallized snow into her face. She put her head down and rushed into the Sewards' lobby, where she stood stamping her feet while the doorman called upstairs. Melanie was almost surprised when he gave her the okay to proceed to the penthouse.

At the Sewards' a uniformed maid escorted her to an opulent sitting room. The maid took Melanie's coat and disappeared without a word, only to return a few minutes later with a harassed air.

"So sorry, ma'am. The missus change her mind. She's not feeling well enough to receive you after all." Her facial expression suggested that such whims were a regular occurrence.

"Look, tell Mrs. Seward this isn't a matter of choice. I'm investigating a crime. Either she talks to me or she talks to the grand jury."

"She won't care, ma'am. She don't listen."

"Where's *Mr.* Seward?" Melanie asked—not because she thought he'd be of assistance, quite the opposite. Melanie was half convinced James Seward *was* the unseen hand. Certainly he'd been in this apartment on the night in question, and his whereabouts during critical hours were still unaccounted for.

"He went to Whitney's school for a party."

He'd be at Holbrooke during the transfer of the ten million, then. It was more evidence pointing to Seward's involvement. But at least the fact that he was gone now meant he couldn't stop Melanie from wringing information out of his wife.

Melanie stood up. "Take me to Mrs. Seward," she demanded.

"If you insist, ma'am."

The maid turned, leading Melanie down a darkened hallway to a set of ornately carved double doors. Following her into the gloom of the bedroom, Melanie nearly gagged on the heat and the smell. It must've been ninety degrees in there, with a close odor consisting of equal parts unwashed flesh, musty sheets, and stale cigarette smoke. Charlotte Seward languished on a heap of pillows in the halo of a single lamp, wearing a satin bed jacket with a large wet stain down the front. The table next to her bed was littered with dozens of tiny prescription bottles—some open, some closed, some empty and lying on their sides.

"Excuse me, ma'am, this lady from the police, and she say she need to see you," the maid announced.

"What the *hell!*" Charlotte said, her eyes darting toward Melanie with alarm. She was rail thin, with a frozen face that spoke of too much Botox and plastic surgery.

"I tell her no, but she insist, ma'am," the maid said.

"Magdalena, you're on thin ice already, and you pull a stunt like this?" Charlotte fished around on the bedside table for a cigarette, which she lit with shaking hands.

"Melanie Vargas from the U.S. Attorney's Office. I'm investigating your daughter's death."

"Whoop-de-do. That doesn't give you the right to barge into my *bedroom*!" Charlotte said, dissolving into a fit of phlegmy coughing.

"I apologize for the intrusion, but we're at a critical point in the investigation, and I really need your help. I want the people responsible for your daughter's death caught and punished."

"Hooray for you. Now, get the hell out of here, or I'm calling the authorities."

"You miss the point, Mrs. Seward. I *am* the authorities. I need to ask you some questions. You can answer them here in the comfort of your home, and I'll go away and leave you alone. *Or* I can drag you before the grand jury."

Charlotte contemplated Melanie with eyes that were simultaneously sunken and much too bright. Judging from the massive pharmacy on her bedside table, it wasn't difficult to see why. After a moment she sighed, her shoulders drooping in resignation.

"Magdalena, leave us please. Close the door on your way out, and no listening at the keyhole. I know your sneaky ways."

The maid cast her employer a long-suffering glance and strode out of the room.

Charlotte waited until the door snapped shut, then turned to Melanie. "Honestly, you're wasting your time. Whitney got careless with drugs and OD'd. Locking up some dealer isn't going to bring her back. Besides, I don't know where she got her stash. She didn't get it from *me*, I assure you. Heroin was not my poison. I didn't think it was hers either."

"I'm not interested in your drug use, Mrs. Seward. I'm not even concerned with your daughter's. I'm here because I have new evidence suggesting Whitney was murdered."

Charlotte had been dragging on her cigarette, but Melanie's words sent her into another violent coughing fit. "Jesus, you're kidding," she said after a moment, her eyes watering.

"No. Unfortunately, I'm not."

"Sit down," Charlotte said, nodding toward a chair in the corner. Melanie pulled the chair over to the bed.

"You know, I loved my daughter," Charlotte continued. "Things between us were never easy. But I loved her a great deal."

"Of course. I'm a mother, too. I understand."

"To hell with that motherhood crap. This was different. Whitney was the only good thing I ever did, the one thing I accomplished in my life. So if somebody killed her, that would really *piss* me off."

"Well, I would hope so."

"I'd do anything in my power to hunt that person down."

"Of course."

Charlotte shook her head. "But, you know, I find what you're saying hard to believe. Whitney OD'ing makes so much more sense to me than somebody purposely killing her. You see, Whitney was like me. A thrill seeker. When you're born with everything, what else is there? Whatever you achieve, people think it was handed to you. What's left but to flame out spectacularly? When she died, I assumed that was what she was doing. Asserting her personality. You could almost say I applauded her choice."

No wonder the girl went so wrong, Melanie thought. Her mother set the perfect example of a wasted life.

"Our evidence is solid," Melanie said.

"But who would want Whitney dead?"

"What about your husband?"

"You're not here to investigate *him,* are you?"

"It depends. Carmen Reyes is missing. She was working on the Holbrooke endowment campaign, and somebody's trying to embezzle a lot of money from it. Your husband may be involved."

"Carmen," Charlotte said, startled, and looked away.

"Do you know something about Carmen?"

"I just— No, I'm not sure." She kneaded her forehead with her fingers.

"What about the Holbrooke endowment money?"

"Well . . ." Charlotte fell silent, looking absently at her cigarette, which was dripping ash onto the comforter.

"Mrs. Seward, you can't pick and choose what to talk to me about. Things may fit together in ways you can't understand."

"I don't want James arrested. I've spent too much time and money keeping him *out* of trouble to let that happen."

"I'm going to follow this trail wherever it leads. If it leads to him, I'll find out anyway. So you might as well tell me whatever you know about the endowment money now."

Charlotte looked gaunt and ill, and there was misery in her eyes. "Honestly, I don't know. He's sleeping with that headmistress, and she's an evil, scheming little *bitch*. James would do a lot for money. He's stayed with *me* all these years, hasn't he? All right? Satisfied, now that you've humiliated me?"

"I'm not trying to upset you, Mrs. Seward, but I have to ask these questions. Carmen Reyes disappeared from *this* apartment the same night your daughter and Brianna Meyers died. I know you were here then. Is it possible your husband—"

"Wait a minute! You say Carmen was here, in my house?"

"Yes. She came upstairs around seven-thirty. I know your husband brought you home around nine o'clock."

"Let me ask you something," Charlotte said, her mind behind her tortured eyes working furiously. "What exactly is the evidence you have that Whitney was murdered?"

"The toxicology screen found a suspicious mix of substances in her blood."

Charlotte clutched at her throat as if she couldn't breathe, "*What substances!*"

"Highly lethal doses of heroin and OxyContin—"

"Aaagh!" Her eyes popping, Charlotte hauled herself to the edge of the bed and began digging furiously among the bottles on the bedside table. Tears began to stream down her hollow cheeks.

"What is it? Are you okay?" Melanie asked, alarmed.

"Bud! I trusted him! I thought he was helping her. Yes, here it is!" she cried, holding up an empty bottle. "OxyContin. It was full, and now it's empty! He was here that night. I'm remembering."

"*You* know Bud?" Melanie asked, startled.

"Of course."

"The Bud who worked for Jay Esposito?"

"For *who?*"

"Jay Esposito, the nightclub owner."

"*Bud* worked for a nightclub owner?"

"Yes, the same one your daughter was dating. Esposito was murdered last night."

"Whitney was dating a nightclub owner who was murdered? I never heard *any* of this! Are you making it up?"

"No. Of course not! Listen, Mrs. Seward, please, this is *extremely* important. You say Bud was here that night. What can you tell me about him? Do you know his last name or where he lives? A telephone number, a physical description? Anything, anything at all that might help us locate him."

"Are we talking about the same man? Bud *Hogan!* He was Whitney's guidance counselor at Holbrooke! I remember now. I came home in bad shape. Whitney took me to my bed. I heard a voice calling, and it sounded like Carmen. I've known the child for years, you see. Then it just . . . *stopped,* like she'd been silenced. I asked Whitney about it, and she told me I was hallucinating. Which was entirely possible, given everything I'd ingested that night, so I believed her. I passed out. And then, sometime later, I woke up to find Bud standing over my bed, going through my pill bottles. He told me I was dreaming and to go back to sleep. So I did."

"Harrison Hogan is *Bud*?" Melanie said.

"Yes, that's what Whitney called him. And he killed my daughter!"

60

AS SHE LEFT the Sewards', Melanie reached Detective Leary on his cell phone and explained what she'd just learned. She needed a patrol car dispatched to Harrison Hogan's apartment right away. But there was a problem. Charlotte Seward hadn't known Hogan's home address, and it turned out his telephone number was unlisted. That meant that the fastest way to get the address—short of asking somebody at the school, which might tip Hogan off—was sending a rush subpoena to the telephone company. But by the time Melanie could get back to her office, type a subpoena, and fax it over, Hogan would be long gone with the money, and Carmen would probably be dead. No—their best bet was intercepting Hogan at the school before he could transfer the ten million.

Detective Leary agreed and said he would back her up as soon as he could get there.

"But I'm on the Williamsburg Bridge now, heading for that warehouse Esposito owned," he said. "Remember? The one we found the key to? I just got a call from the blue-and-white that checked the scene. Whole place is drenched with blood."

"Blood? From . . . from who?" *Trevor!*

"Don't know. It can't be from Deon Green, because he was killed in that subway station. But they didn't find no other body. *Somebody* got seriously hurt there, that much is clear, and not too long ago neither. So when you think this money transfer is gonna happen? Should I just come straight to you and leave this for later?"

"*No.* What you're doing is much more important. I have a witness missing. It could be related." She told him about Trevor.

"Okay, I'll be on the lookout for a body matching that description."

That was *not* what Melanie wanted to hear, though she couldn't ignore the terrible ring of truth to it. She wouldn't let herself think about Trevor dead. Not now. There was still work to be done, and she needed to hope in order to function.

"However you want to play it," Detective Leary was saying. "But if I'm not gonna back you up myself, let me find you some other guys."

"Yes, but here's the problem: If the school's suddenly crawling with cops, this scumbag will just disappear with the missing girl. We'll never find her, or my witness either, since he definitely knows where both of them are."

"I can ask for plainclothes instead of uniforms, if that helps."

"That would be better," she said.

"Let me see what I can do. With Christmas and all, not a lot of guys working overtime. Give me your cell number, and I'll call you soon as I know something. But do me a favor, okay? Hang back till you hear from me?"

"I'll try. But hurry, okay?"

Melanie needed every second between now and seven-thirty to prepare for what was coming next. The worst thing she could do would be to walk into an encounter with a known killer with no backup and no way to defend herself. She of all people knew how stupid that would be, because she'd done it once before, on the Jed Benson murder case. She'd survived, but she'd rather not make that same mistake twice.

Rushing toward her apartment, Melanie called Dan's cell phone but only got his voice mail. Even under these crazy circumstances, Dan's voice on the recording thrilled her. God, she was gone on this guy. It scared her how much. She took a deep breath and left him an all-business message detailing what she'd learned and what she planned to do. This call was just intended to keep the team in the loop, after all. But before she hung up, she couldn't resist adding something more private.

"Hey, listen, I hope you're not mad that I ran off. I had no choice. Like you said, I step up when my name's called. There's something I want you to know, though, something I want to tell you before—"

Her other line beeped.

"Oh. Hold on," she told Dan's voice mail, and picked it up. "Hello?"

"Melanie?" said a young girl's voice.

"*Lulu?* Where are you?"

"Listen, something bad is going down. Dr. Hogan is messed up."

"Do you know where he is? Or where Carmen is? You need to tell me!"

"I think he's gonna take her to Holbrooke to try to get some money. Then I'm afraid he's gonna kill her."

"Yes, I know. I'll be there to stop him, don't worry."

"Me, too! I'm going over now."

"*Don't,* okay? Let me handle it. I've got the police coming and everything. Just go home. I promise you, I'll protect Carmen."

"I know my way around the school. I can help."

"Lulu, *no.* It's not safe."

"Yeah, whatever," Lulu said, and hung up.

Damn. Lulu wasn't going to listen. Melanie clicked to the other line, but Dan's phone had cut off. She'd reached her apartment by now. She'd better go in, and fast. She needed something from her closet, and it wasn't an outfit.

Melanie unlocked the front door and walked into darkness.

"Hello?" she called, flipping on the light.

Silence echoed back at her. A note taped to the mirror above the front-hall table read, "Maya much better. Took her to my place for the night. Steve."

Her stomach hurt with how much she longed to see her daughter. But it was a quarter to seven. She didn't have a moment to spare if she wanted Carmen to live.

In her bedroom Melanie stripped off the pants and top she'd put on yesterday, in her room in the El San Juan after having sex with Dan. *Don't think about that now.* They wouldn't pass muster if she planned to crash the Holbrooke gala, especially not in their current bedraggled state. The invitation she'd borrowed from Charlotte Seward was un-equivocal: black tie required. She took a two-minute shower, as much to wake herself up as to get clean, and slicked her wet hair into the pre-tense of an elegant knot at her neck. She did her eyes in five seconds flat, stroked on some killer red lipstick, and headed for the closet. Linda's outfit from the other night was the best she could do. She pulled it on, then reached for the thing she'd *really* come home for.

It rested in a locked metal box hidden at the back of her closet—the nine-shot Beretta she'd bought in a fit of anxiety in the aftermath of the Benson case, when she was dealing with the emotional consequences of having killed a man, of almost getting killed herself. She'd never once fired it, and she didn't plan to now. By the time they got to the gunplay, the real cops would have arrived. But it made her feel cold and hard and equal to the task before her.

She opened the combination lock and lifted it out reverently. It was a sexy little gun, matte black and neat in her hand. It looked great with her outfit and fit perfectly in her beaded evening bag. She snapped out the clip and cocked the hammer, making sure there was a round in the chamber so it was ready to fire. Otherwise why bother to bring it? Nothing more useless than an unloaded gun.

B Y   T H E   T I M E Melanie reached Holbrooke, it was 7:10 and snowing heavily. The school's many windows were lit with graceful holiday tapers, its red double doors thrown open and decked with evergreen boughs. New York's elite poured from chauffeured Mercedeses and BMW sedans. The men looked distinguished and aloof in their tuxedos. The women wore expensive furs and couture dresses, diamonds twinkling at their ears as they held their tiny evening bags over their heads to keep the snow off their freshly styled hair. Down the block a row of horse-drawn carriages waited. They were all draped with banners in the Holbrooke colors of scarlet and gold.

Melanie blended into the line of guests waiting to present their engraved invitations at the door. Around her, people greeted one another effusively, air-kissing, chatting of this Caribbean island or that ski resort. She was alone, unknown, and, even in her best things, underdressed for the power crowd. Nobody questioned her. Nobody paid her the slightest bit of attention, in fact. She might have been invisible, which suited her purposes exactly.

The exquisite young man who checked her invitation was an actor or a model by the look of him. He gave her a blinding smile and directed her to the main auditorium.

"Ladies' room?" she asked.

"Down the stairs to your right. The live auction is under way, and champagne and hors d'oeuvres are now being served in the auditorium."

"Thank you."

When she reached the lower level, Melanie glanced around to make sure nobody was watching, then proceeded quickly to the deserted back staircase and up to the second floor. She walked the empty, shadowy corridors, stepping lightly so her borrowed Manolos wouldn't clatter on the linoleum and give her away. She was looking for the development office, which she remembered passing when she'd interviewed Patricia Andover. Hogan had no choice but to bring Carmen there in order to move the ten million. The Holbrooke account required biometric identification, which could happen only via a specialized fingerprint scanner connected to the development office's computer. Her best shot was to hide in the room, let Hogan access the account, and call in the raid before he could transfer the money. She glanced at her watch—7:20, and she still hadn't heard from Detective Leary. She took her cell phone from her bag and checked to make sure she hadn't missed any calls. Nothing. She dialed Leary's cell but got voice mail.

"Detective," she whispered into her phone, "it's Melanie Vargas from the U.S. Attorney's Office again. Please call and let me know what arrangements you've made to get me backup. Nothing's happened yet, but I'm expecting Hogan to show up any minute. In fact, I have to turn my phone to silent, so if I don't pick up, *please* leave a message. It's very urgent. I really need your help. Thanks."

She hung up nervously. Surely Leary would come through for her. She'd made the situation sufficiently clear, hadn't she? He had to understand that she was in danger, although she would've thought he'd have called back by now. There was nothing more she could do at the moment, however. She wouldn't call 911 to get a car dispatched unless the situation became truly desperate. If Hogan saw uniforms, he'd just cut and run.

Rounding the corner to the administrative wing, Melanie pulled back sharply, her heart skipping a beat. Goddamn it, he'd beaten her here! The entire hallway was dark, except for a single rectangle of light illuminating the floor in front of the development office. The door was closed, two distinct shadows visible in relief against its frosted-glass window. The muffled voices coming from within sounded low and urgent, as if they were arguing. That was bad. She'd better move, before Hogan did something to Carmen, before he harmed her.

Hugging the wall, Melanie advanced toward the brightly lit door, struggling to control her anxious breathing, to still even the rustling of her clothes. But when she got within a few feet, she realized that Hogan hadn't trumped her after all. The voices coming from the development office belonged to James Seward and Patricia Andover.

"I don't understand why you won't do this one thing for me," Seward whined.

"How many times do I have to explain? I *can't*. Changing the fingerprint access requires Carmen!" Patricia sounded on edge, almost hysterical. "Besides, I'm not doing *anything* until you answer my question. Where were you Monday night when Whitney died? Answer me, damn it!"

"You think I was *with* someone?"

"I just need to hear that you didn't kill your stepdaughter!"

"Are you serious? Wow, Patricia, that's crazy. Completely insane. Although I have to admit, I'm somewhat flattered."

"You didn't?" The audible relief in Patricia's voice confirmed for Melanie that the two were having an affair. The headmistress obviously cared for this man.

"Of course not. Whitney's death was extremely ill timed for me."

"Just tell me where you were, so I believe you."

"Take my word for it, it's better if you don't know the details."

"You *were* with another woman, weren't you?"

"*No!* Jesus, Patricia, you're like a broken record. Not that it's any of your goddamn business, but I was doing some fund-raising."

"So why the big mystery?"

"*Because.* It was with a gentleman who represents a consortium of interests that prefer to avoid government scrutiny. Do I make myself clear? Now, don't ask me anything else."

"If you have other sources of money, James, why the hell are you putting me at risk like this?"

He chuckled. "What's that line about too rich and too thin?"

"You have *enough*, James," she said flatly.

"Oh, come on, you know I need money, Patricia. You promised you'd help. I thought you had the guts to see this through," he said.

"I can't believe this! You don't give a rat's ass if I get caught, do you? I'm going downstairs right this instant, before the Van Allens end up at the podium without me. You can come or not. I don't give a shit anymore. And I'm not going through with it. I'm just *not.*"

The door flew open with a bang. Melanie shrank back into the darkness, heart pounding, as Patricia Andover flounced down the hall-way in her ball gown. Seward immediately followed, flipping off the light and pulling the door of the development office closed behind him. He didn't lock it, so unless the door locked automatically, she should be able to get in.

Melanie waited, holding her breath, until their footsteps had faded away and everything around her was deathly silent. Then she crept swiftly back toward the door, grasped the handle, and turned it. It *was* locked. What an idiot—why hadn't she thought of this? The office held not only confidential financial information but evidence of Patricia's crimes. The headmistress was a careful woman; she would never leave it open. Melanie should've thought about getting her hands on a master key somehow.

"*Goddamn it,*" she muttered, jiggling the handle, then sucked in a startled breath. Around the corner, behind her, she'd heard something. Like a footstep. A footstep that stopped when she made noise. Man, she was screwing this up big time. Get smarter, Melanie Vargas! She hurried on tiptoe to the next office: HEAD, LOWER SCHOOL. She turned the han-dle as silently as she could. It gave. *Yes!* Diving in and pulling the door closed behind her, she silently thanked the head of the Lower School for being so careless.

Melanie caught her breath and strained to listen. The footsteps started up again. Reverberating in the deserted hallway, they advanced toward her. She made out the sound of one person walking. Yes, *defi-nitely* one person. Could Hogan have killed Carmen already? Wait a minute! The footsteps passed the development office's door. They were moving closer. They were outside the door of *this* office. Melanie backed farther into the room, looking around frantically. In the dim light filter-ing through the blinds, she saw only one place to hide. Under the desk. She pulled the swivel chair out and crawled into the desk well, dragging the chair in behind her, heart hammering against her rib cage. Just then she heard the doorknob turn. Somebody was coming in after her.

61

THE FOOTSTEPS HAD STOPPED outside the office door. For a moment nothing happened, and chill silence prevailed. Melanie slipped her hand into her evening bag and grasped the Beretta, getting ready to defend herself. The door squeaked open on noisy hinges. She heard the sound of ragged breathing and thought it was her own, that it would give her away. But it came from her pursuer.

"Carmen? He-hello? Are you here?" a frightened voice called out.

Dizzy with relief, Melanie pushed the swivel chair out and rose to her feet. "It's me, Melanie."

Lulu was in the act of reaching for the light switch.

"Don't!" Melanie covered the distance to Lulu's side in two rapid steps, knocking the girl's hand away in the nick of time. "No lights," she whispered urgently. "Hogan could show up any minute. He could already be in the hall. You *have* to leave."

"Carmen's my sister. I'm staying."

"What you're doing *won't* help her. If I have to worry about you, too, I'll get distracted. Go. *Now.*"

"I want to help."

"Fine. There's something important you can do for me. I have a detective who's supposed to show up to make the arrest, but I haven't heard from him in the last half hour. I need you to call him. Take my phone, go outside, tell him where I am and to get here fast. Just hit re-dial. His number is the last one I called."

Lulu looked at her in confusion. "I . . . I don't know. I—"

"Do it!" Melanie commanded. "Trust me, it's the only way. Come on, I'll take you to the front staircase. Hogan will use the back, and I don't want you running into him by accident."

Grabbing Lulu firmly by the wrist, Melanie leaned out the office door and stole a furtive glance down the hallway. "It's clear. Let's go."

They hurried along the dark hall in the opposite direction from the way Melanie had come. When they reached the main staircase, Melanie gave Lulu her cell phone and physically turned the girl so she was point-ing downstairs. "Go. And don't you dare come back."

Lulu started down but then turned, throwing a pleading look over her shoulder. "You'll protect her? Promise?"

"*Yes.* Now, get out of here. And be quiet about it."

Melanie watched Lulu creep down the stairs until the girl's slender form disappeared from sight, and then she turned resolutely back. But what she saw froze her in her tracks. A flashlight beam, bouncing wildly off the walls, kicking up strange shadows. Two figures struggling. Melanie drew her gun and advanced stealthily. Clinging to the darkness along the walls, she moved forward until she could see them clearly. They were standing in front of the door to the development office.

"Want me to *fucking* kill you?" Hogan said. In the crazed violence of the sound, Melanie just barely recognized the psychologist's laid-back voice. He had Carmen by both arms.

"No."

"Then don't try that again, stupid bitch. Nobody can hear you with what's going on downstairs anyway."

Hogan pushed Carmen away roughly and fished in his coat pocket. Melanie tensed, thinking he might pull a gun, but he brought out a set of keys and inserted one into the lock. In a second they were inside. Melanie crept right up to the door, listening. Hogan didn't turn on the light. Instead the beeps and groans of a computer sounded, and a blue glow emanated from the frosted-glass window. Hogan had booted up the computer. Melanie looked at her watch—7:29. In just one minute, ten million dollars would flow into Holbrooke's account, Hogan would force Carmen to execute the commands transferring it out, and then he would have no further use for her.

"Hurry up," she heard Hogan tell Carmen. "Pull up the account. I need to be in it when the money comes."

Melanie realized that giving her phone to Lulu had been a big mistake. Now was the moment to call 911. But in the time it would take Melanie to search out another telephone, Carmen could die. She looked down at the gun in her hand and back up at the office door. At least she could stop *that* from happening, even if she had to do it by herself.

62

PATRICIA WATCHED from offstage, struggling to compose herself before walking out in front of the audience. The auctioneer brought down the final gavel, and she knew it was over. Not the auction, but everything. The scheme. Her relationship with James. Her hopes of wresting victory from the jaws of defeat. The taste of this long-awaited moment was like ash in her mouth.

She strode up to the podium in the glare of the spotlight and smiled. She was one of those people who always managed to function as long as she had a goal in mind. Her object now was clear: to avoid getting caught, to stay out of jail. The status quo, which an hour ago she despised as a humiliating second best, already seemed precious to her, lost and irretrievable.

"Members of the Holbrooke community," she began, and tears welled in her eyes at the thought that she might never utter those words again. She looked out over her audience—so rich, so beautiful, so lavishly attired. If they found out the truth, they would no longer defer to her, no longer count her as a power in their world.

Patricia stopped, overcome, and looked down at her hands twisting wretchedly before her. The audience held its collective breath, and in the long, pregnant pause that followed, Patricia resolved things in her own mind. She wouldn't give in. She refused to let this happen. She saw a way out. She would reveal the plot, pretend she'd stumbled across it, play the hero safeguarding the school's millions.

Patricia squared her shoulders and began again. "First let me say that your generosity overwhelms me. This has been a tragic week for our school. All of you—alumnae *and* parents—could have chosen to turn your backs on us in our hour of need, in the wake of these shocking events. But you didn't. Instead you embraced Holbrooke, with goodwill, with open arms and open checkbooks. Tonight we have raised over one million dollars from the auction alone!"

Applause and cheers roared through the auditorium. "Thank you. Thank you. Thank you," she intoned, until the din quieted. "I will now read the names of the donors in Miss Holbrooke's Inner Circle. Every family on this list has contributed at least two hundred and fifty thousand dollars to the endowment campaign. I would ask that each family stand as your name is announced to receive the thanks of the Holbrooke community. You have played a singular role in financing our school's future, and we acknowledge your generosity tonight with humble gratitude."

Patricia's voice rang out calm and commanding as she read the names on the list. She paused for the perfect interval between names to let each family savor its moment of glory. When the last family had been acknowledged, she held up her hand with dramatic effect.

"Now the big moment has arrived, although with an unexpected twist. I ask Roger and Enid Van Allen to please come to the podium."

The Van Allens rose from their seats of honor in the front row and proceeded to the stage amid thunderous applause. Roger, bent, frail, and in his late seventies, was helped up the stairs by Enid, forty-five and glamorous, a fourth wife. Patricia embraced each of them, then turned back to the microphone.

"As I know you are all aware, Roger and Enid Van Allen have pledged the astonishing sum of ten million dollars to the endowment campaign for the purpose of constructing a new building to house our Upper School."

The audience rose en masse for a standing ovation. Patricia looked out over the crowd, knowing that this was her last chance to turn back. But she wouldn't. She'd made her decision.

"Thank you, thank you," she said, indicating with a downward motion of her palms that they should resume their seats. "Now I would ask our audiovisual coordinator, Mr. Greenblatt, to please open the line to our bankers."

After a bit of earsplitting feedback, a man's voice came over the loudspeaker. "Hello? Can you hear me?"

"Yes, this is Mrs. Andover. You're on air at the Holbrooke gala. Can you please identify yourself for the audience."

"Kyle Chin with the Private Banking Group."

"Mr. Chin, you're aware that ten million dollars is slated to be transferred from the Van Allens' account into the Holbrooke endowment campaign account."

"Yes, ma'am. Say the word, and I'll make the transfer."

"I'm afraid I can't do that."

A collective gasp ripped through the crowd.

"What?" Roger Van Allen exclaimed.

Patricia cast her eyes all the way to the back of the auditorium, to the spot where James stood watching her. He'd guessed what she was about to do. He *must* have, because he immediately turned on his heel and fled. So much for their so-called love affair. Neither one of them had gotten what they bargained for, which made them even.

Patricia resumed her speech without missing a beat.

"I can't transfer the money tonight as planned for a very good reason. Every Holbrooke family should rest assured that when misfortune threatens our school, I am here to combat it. I stand vigilant to keep the school's resources, and your daughters' futures, safe from every foe. Tonight it has come to my attention that an important safe-guard put in place to protect Holbrooke's endowment account may have been compromised. Mr. Chin, I am therefore instructing you to imme-diately shut down the account so that nobody—repeat, nobody—can access it."

63

"WHAT WAS THAT? What just happened?" Hogan demanded, his words carrying loud and clear through the development office's door.

"I don't know. I never got an error message like that before," came Carmen's voice, small and tremulous.

"Try again!"

Melanie heard the keyboard clicking.

"Nothing," Carmen said. "I had it. You saw. But then it like just blipped away."

"You're trying to trick me, bitch!"

"No, I swear!"

"Do it right or you'll be sorry."

"Let me try again."

There was menace in Hogan's tone, pure terror in Carmen's. Melanie put her hand on the doorknob and glanced back over her shoulder at the empty hall. Where the *fuck* was Detective Leary?

"I don't understand. The account's offline for some reason," Carmen was saying. Then came a muffled cry, followed by the sounds of a struggle. Time had run out.

Melanie twisted the doorknob, but it refused to give. It must've locked automatically again. She flipped the safety latch on the Beretta so she didn't shoot herself by accident and, grasping the gun by its barrel, smashed it hard against the frosted window. Glass shattered, flying everywhere. She reached in to unlock the door, crying out as a knifelike shard sliced into the palm of her right hand.

When she stepped over the broken glass and flipped on the light in the office, the scene that greeted her was bizarrely calm. Carmen sat at the desk in front of the computer. Carmen didn't know Melanie and so gazed at her uncomprehendingly, neither moving nor calling out. Hogan stood behind Carmen's chair, acting as if nothing unusual were happening. But his hands were held oddly down and in front of him, concealed by the chair. Either he was hurt somehow or else he had a gun.

"Hey, Melanie, that was some entrance. Are you okay?" And Hogan smiled at her reassuringly.

"Get away from her! *Now*," Melanie said, raising her gun. *Mierda!* The safety was still on. But Hogan didn't know that.

"I don't really see where you're coming from with this," Hogan said reasonably. "There must be some misunderstanding. Carmen uncovered a scheme by Patricia Andover to steal money from the school endowment fund. She reported it to me because I'm somebody she trusts, right, Carmen?" And he moved his arm jerkily behind the chair. It was Door Number Two, the gun, for sure.

"Right," Carmen echoed hollowly.

"I only came here tonight to prevent a crime from occurring," he said.

Hogan looked Melanie steadily in the eye. He was an attractive man, with his lean face, longish dark hair, and lanky frame, and he had the gift of gab. She definitely got how he'd been able to brainwash Whitney Seward. Hell, she was almost tempted to believe him herself. But then she looked into his gray eyes, and they were cold and lifeless as the ocean in winter.

She raised her gun higher so it pointed directly at his head. "I *know* you're lying. You were there the night Whitney and Brianna died. You murdered Whitney Seward."

"That's not true. I don't believe in judging others, but those girls had drug problems. They did it to themselves." He was still standing there with a long-suffering expression on his face, ignoring the gun pointed at his head as if Melanie were some tiresome child. It was a good act, but she wasn't buying it.

"I have witnesses! Charlotte Seward will testify you stole her Oxy-Contin. And the M.E. will say you mixed it into a nice little heroin cocktail and shot Whitney up between the toes."

For the first time, anxiety flickered in Hogan's eyes, and his smooth facade began to splinter. "That's a crock of shit. Charlotte Seward is a junkie."

Blood was oozing from the cut on Melanie's hand, and she was well aware that the gun she struggled to hold steady wouldn't fire if she pulled the trigger. Yet she couldn't resist confronting this smug killer, who'd obviously bargained on being smarter than everyone else, on being too smart to get caught. Well, he'd bargained wrong.

"You can't fool me, because I know too much about you, *Bud*," Melanie said. Hogan flinched visibly at her use of that name. "That's right! I know you recruited your students to mule for your pal Jay Esposito. How much did he pay you for that, huh? To ruin those girls' lives? To *kill* Brianna Meyers? Did you watch her die, *Bud*, with heroin leaking into her stomach?"

In a flash, Hogan grabbed Carmen by the hair and yanked her to her feet, putting a gun to her head. The girl yelped in pain. In the same instant, Melanie lowered the Beretta and tried vainly to flip the safety with her blood-slicked fingers. *Shit!* She couldn't manage. She raised her gun again instantly, praying Hogan hadn't noticed. At this point, if he didn't believe she could fire, he'd surely kill *her*. Then who would rescue Carmen?

"You've got it all figured out, huh, Melanie?" As he spoke, he jabbed his gun hard into Carmen's head, and she began to whimper.

"Let her go!" Melanie commanded, brandishing the Beretta.

"Why would I do that? She knows too much about me. So do *you*, for that matter. The smartest thing I could do right now would be to kill you both and get out of this place." He made a movement toward the door. Carmen's knees buckled, and Hogan dragged her forward a few inches.

"You'd be foolish to kill us, Bud. That's just two more bodies to your name that you'll never get away with! The police know all about you."

"Bullshit."

"You don't believe me? We know you went to Puerto Rico with Whitney and Brianna on the drug run last weekend. A witness puts you eating lunch with Whitney at the hotel. You rode shotgun back to New York with them. Your job was to watch them pass the drugs out of their stomachs and then to hand the heroin-filled balloons over to Expo, am I right?"

He looked surprised.

"I *am* right," Melanie continued. "But you ran into a problem with Brianna. By the time she got back to New York, it was apparent that one of the balloons in her stomach was leaking. She got sick. Terribly, horribly sick. And she died. That's all in the autopsy report."

Hogan was watching Melanie steadily, still holding a gun to Carmen's head.

"Brianna's death came at a very bad time for you. The day before you left for Puerto Rico, Carmen Reyes had come to you in your capacity as"—Melanie raised her eyebrows in sarcasm—"*trusted adviser* and confided everything she knew about Patricia Andover's plans to embezzle from the endowment fund. I have that from another witness, a friend of Carmen's whom she confided in. Ten million dollars was slated to get transferred in tonight at the big gala, and *you* intended to steal it. Your plan was to use Carmen to skim off the money. Then you'd make a break for it, and Patricia Andover would be left holding the bag. She'd be the one the cops would come after. But the dead body of a Holbrooke girl was a major wrench in the works. You needed to come up with some other explanation for Brianna's death, to buy time until you got your hands on the ten million. What's more, you couldn't rely on Whitney the wild child to keep her mouth shut, so you needed to kill her, too. Overdose was the obvious choice. Reckless young girls, from a school with a druggie reputation. Who *wouldn't* believe it?"

"You can't prove any of this."

"The overdose plan got you thinking, though. You saw a way to keep Carmen under wraps until the gala while giving everyone a credible explanation for her absence. You'd make it look like *Carmen* supplied the drugs. You had access to some spare packets from Puerto Rico, and they were unusual, marked in Spanish. You planted some in Whitney's bedroom and another in Carmen's locker. People would draw the obvious conclusion when these unusual packets matched, assuming that Carmen had run away to escape the consequences of her crime. They had the extra added benefit of pointing the finger at Jay Esposito. In the meantime you'd gotten Whitney to lure Carmen up to her apartment, and you kidnapped her and held her until tonight."

"You've been working very hard," Hogan said.

"Naturally, things went wrong, as things often do. There was some unfortunate collateral damage. Deon Green—"

"You're giving me credit for something Jay did. Jay was a strict disciplinarian when it came to rats."

"Your use of the past tense is telling, Doctor. You *know* Esposito is dead, because *you* killed him. You tried to make it look like a suicide, but you made a critical mistake. You tracked Expo's blood out into the alley. We took a perfect lift of the footprint. I'm betting it exactly matches the Nikes you're wearing."

Hogan looked startled but then recovered quickly. "Bravo, Melanie. I'm impressed. But let's see if you can nail the extra-credit question. *Why* kill Jay?"

She thought for a moment. "It was personal. You wanted Whitney. But *she* wanted *him*."

Hogan's face went so livid that Melanie's insides lurched. He looked like he wanted to rip her apart with his bare hands. She raised her useless gun to defend herself.

"You think you're so fucking *smart,*" Hogan spit. "You don't know the half of it. I got your boy! That's right. Trevor Leonard, that fucking freak. I bashed his brains out with Jay's golf club, so it would look like Jay did the murder. But nobody's ever gonna know that, because *you* won't live to tell about it."

Trevor! A wave of nausea rushed through her. Just at that instant, Hogan lunged for Melanie, dragging Carmen with him, using her as a human shield. Melanie fumbled frantically at the Beretta's safety, diving out of Hogan's way. She hit the floor hard and grunted in pain, rolling back toward the desk, her brain intensely focused on her fingers' work. The safety finally clicked, and she sat up, finger on the trigger. Hogan and Carmen were at the threshold, shards of glass crunching beneath their feet. If Melanie fired now, she risked killing the girl.

Hogan gave a smile of pure evil. "You make a pretty target," he said, pointing the gun at Melanie's head.

64

MELANIE'S HEART was in her throat. She held her breath, waiting for the sharp report of Hogan's gun.

"If you follow me, she dies," Hogan said. The next second he and Carmen vanished through the door.

Melanie breathed out. She was shaking uncontrollably. Damn, she'd faced down killers before. You'd think it would get easier.

As their footsteps receded, she leaped to her feet, and the room went black for a second. When her vision cleared, she yanked several tissues from a box on the desk and wrapped her dripping hand. It was tough to fire a gun when your hand was slick with blood.

Melanie rushed to the door. Hogan and Carmen were just disappearing down the main staircase. She ran after them. She'd catch this lunatic before he harmed the girl. *You can run, but you can't hide, scumbag.* The route Hogan had chosen would take them all smack through the middle of the gala. That must be his plan—to fade into the crowd. She paused at the top of the stairs to be sure they were out of earshot before starting down after them. The buzz of voices drifted up to her from the floor below. Guests were streaming out of the auditorium toward the main doors of the school. Melanie glimpsed Hogan far ahead, gripping Carmen tightly by the arm and pushing her through the crowd. Nobody seemed to pay them any attention.

Melanie flew down the remaining steps, struggling to keep her prey in sight. But the minute she reached the first floor, the throng engulfed her. Even standing on her toes and craning her neck, she could no longer see Hogan. She fought her way to the exit, earning outraged stares from the power elite. Just as she was about to barrel through the red doors, somebody grabbed her from behind in a powerful grip.

"Hey!" she yelled, whirling.

"Where you going, princess? You don't like to stay put," Dan said, looking down into her eyes.

"Where'd you come from?"

"The airport. Lulu Reyes called my cell phone, said to get over here right away."

"Oh! I told her to hit redial. I thought it would call Detective Leary, but she must've done something wrong. You'll have to do."

"Gee, thanks a lot."

"Seriously! We've got to catch Hogan. He has Carmen Reyes. He's using her as a hostage."

"Any weapons?"

"I have a gun," she replied, patting her coat pocket.

"Not *you*—Hogan."

"He has one, too."

"Where'd *you* get a gun? Never mind! Which way?"

"Outside. Come on, let's go!"

Out on the sidewalk, the snow was coming down hard. Between the flakes and the horde of guests milling in front of the school, visibility was limited. Melanie scanned the block frantically.

"I don't see them!" she cried.

"Any idea where they're headed?"

"No. God, I wish I had a megaphone."

She turned around to face the well-heeled crowd and held up her hand, wrapped in blood-soaked tissues. She projected in her best courtroom voice.

"May I have your attention, please! There's been an abduction from the school. We're federal law enforcement. Did anybody see Harrison Hogan just now?"

People gasped and murmured, looking at one another in surprise.

"We need your help," she demanded.

"I saw Dr. Hogan with a girl. They were running toward Central Park," said a woman in a black satin cape.

"Me, too!" a man yelled.

"Somebody call 911 and tell the police about this!" Melanie exclaimed, and she and Dan took off at a run toward Fifth Avenue, snow whipping into their faces.

Within minutes Melanie's feet were soaked through and numb with cold. The cut on her hand stung bitterly in the harsh wind. She slipped and slid, trying desperately to match Dan's pace. At the intersection the light was against them, but Fifth Avenue was deserted in the heavy snow. They tore across the street and entered the park at Seventy-ninth Street. Snow lay thick on the path, and two fresh sets of footprints led straight ahead. In the halos cast by ornate street lamps, thick flakes blew sideways. They sprinted forward as fast as they could, following the footprints, their breath billowing up in great puffs as they ran.

The path sloped steeply upward past Cedar Hill. As she sprinted up the incline, Melanie's feet went out from under her and she fell hard, coming down on her injured hand. Dan turned to help her.

"No! Go! Help Carmen. I'll catch up," she said.

"But you're bleeding. I can see it in the snow."

"It's just a cut. *Please!* Don't worry about me."

He helped her to her feet and brushed her off. "I'll take it from here, sweetheart. Just turn around and go for backup, okay?" he said.

"Sure. But hurry, you'll lose them!"

Dan turned and bolted up the hill. Once he reached the top and disappeared from view, Melanie took right off after him. Go for backup, my ass! Who did he think he was dealing with here? The little woman? She heard sirens in the distance anyway, hoped it was for them, but she had no intention of waiting around to find out. Sweet Jesus, the boy was fast! Melanie reached the crest of the hill and sprinted across the Seventy-ninth Street Transverse, getting her second wind. Dan was nowhere to be seen.

She was alone in an eerie, magical landscape. To her right, Turtle Pond was a frozen expanse, and the lights of Central Park West shone so dimly through the snow over the Great Lawn that she might have been at sea glimpsing a distant shore. She plunged into a tunnel of dark, overhanging trees, still following the footprints. Counting Dan's, there were now three sets, and they were clearly heading toward Belvedere Castle. Did Hogan plan to murder Carmen and leave her body in the castle tower? He would be just demented enough to come up with a plan like that.

At the end of the path, Melanie emerged into a clearing. Belvedere Castle rose steeply from the ground like a Gothic apparition, its turrets draped in snow. She stumbled up shallow stone steps and across an open plaza, still following the footprints. Shadowy figures were barely visible moving on a high balcony. Melanie shaded her eyes against the driving flakes. It looked like Dan and Hogan.

Inside the castle a narrow stone staircase the width of her body spiraled to the floors above. She raced up the stairs and found herself in a rectangular room with a flagstone floor, empty except for a small display entitled "Birding in the Four Seasons." Out of breath, hurrying across to the French doors, she looked out onto the wide, flat balcony, but it was deserted. She'd gone only halfway up: Dan and Hogan must be on the highest level. She ascended the next flight slowly. Not just to catch her breath—she wanted to do reconnaissance first and make sure she had the lay of the land before she took action.

The second flight of stairs dead-ended at a narrow door, which was propped open and led directly out to the balcony. Melanie pressed herself against the curving wall into the cover of darkness, so she could look out without being seen.

She had to suppress a gasp at the sight that greeted her. They were in midconfrontation, at a complete standoff. Dan stood in firing stance, both arms outstretched, pointing his nine-millimeter at Hogan's head. But Hogan held Carmen in a death grip. He clutched her by the neck and pressed his gun to her temple.

Melanie's mind raced. There was no way for her to storm the group on the balcony. Hogan was facing the door. He'd see her the second she made her move, and when he realized he was being attacked, he'd shoot either Carmen or Dan—or her. It would only make things worse.

An iron ladder rose steeply above her head, disappearing into the hollow interior of the tower. Melanie stepped onto the first rung. But she was so unstable in the wet Manolos that she kicked them off and clambered up in stocking feet, using her toes to grasp the slick rungs as her wet coat flapped against her legs. Inside the darkened tower, a large round window looked down onto the balcony. She had a bird's-eye view of Hogan from about ten feet above his head. And what's more, she had a perfect shot.

Leaning forward against the ladder for balance, she took the Beretta from her pocket. It was ready to fire, but she was terrified to try. Carmen and Hogan stood mere inches apart. And she'd have to shoot through the glass. Did she need to compensate for that somehow? She didn't have the experience to know how the window might affect a bullet's trajectory, or even whether the bullet would penetrate the thick glass at all.

But as she hesitated, to her horror, the situation below deteriorated. Hogan's face was contorted in anger. He was shouting something at Dan, but she couldn't make out the words. He must've threatened to kill Carmen. Dan lowered his gun. Hogan turned his. He was about to shoot Dan! Melanie raised the Beretta fast, aimed, and squeezed the trigger, turning her head away as the window exploded all around her. She opened her eyes, panting in fear, and looked out to see Dan on top of Hogan, struggling to get his gun away. When the window shattered,

Dan had charged. Within seconds he flipped Hogan over on his stomach and cuffed him. Carmen sank to her knees, sobbing hysterically.

Melanie raced down the ladder and out onto the snow-covered balcony, not even stopping for her shoes.

"Did I get him?" she shouted at Dan.

"That was *you*? Jesus, you are full of surprises!"

"Is he shot?" she asked.

"I don't know." Dan hauled Hogan to his feet and inspected him. "You shot, scumbag?"

Hogan stared at them stonily, saying nothing.

Dan grinned. "*He* may be in one piece, but you sure did a job on that window."

She looked up into Dan's face, deeply relieved he hadn't been hurt. "Show a little gratitude, cowboy. I just saved your butt."

"Yeah, I know. Don't worry, I'm thinking up some excellent ways to thank you," and he winked at her, baby blues twinkling.

With that, Melanie went over and embraced Carmen Reyes, thrilled that she could finally reunite the girl with her father.

65

ON THE AFTERNOON of Christmas Eve, Melanie sat at Trevor Leonard's bedside waiting for him to wake up. Tucked in his hospital bed, with all his piercings removed, Trevor looked like the young kid he still was. The night of the gala, Detective Leary had found him in an alley a few blocks from Esposito's warehouse, half frozen and beaten within an inch of his life, and had rushed him to the hospital. Trevor's jaw was wired shut, he had three broken ribs, and several frostbitten toes. But he was alive, and the doctors expected him to make a full recovery.

The courthouse had closed early today, but not before Melanie arraigned Harrison Hogan on charges of murder and assault in furtherance of a narcotics conspiracy. Hogan faced a minimum twenty-to-life sentence, with the possibility of the death penalty if aggravating circumstances were proved. His lawyer was already talking about a plea to thirty years.

While she was in court for the Hogan arraignment, Melanie had taken the precaution of obtaining sealed warrants for the arrests of Patricia Andover and James Seward on wire-fraud charges. That takedown, along with a big press conference, was scheduled for the day after Christmas. With celebrity perps like those two, it should be a media circus, and Bernadette was so thrilled that she was flinging around words like "promotion" and "award."

Melanie had done one other thing while she was in court. She'd come here to tell Trevor about it, as well as to reassure him that Hogan would be locked up for a long time, unable to do any further harm.

Trevor's lids fluttered. He opened his blackened eyes.

"Hey," Melanie said, as he struggled to lift his head. "No, don't try to talk."

Trevor pointed to the bedside table, and Melanie picked up the water bottle that sat there, helping him drink through a straw.

"Listen, I came by to tell you how sorry I am about what happened to you," she said. "I'm really devastated, Trevor."

He motioned toward the table again, and she saw a pad and paper there. She handed it to him; he scribbled something and held it up so she could see.

"Chill out," he'd written. "My choice. I did it for Bree."

"Well, I want you to know, we got him. Hogan, I mean. It turns out he was Jay Esposito's cousin, and his right-hand man. He was recruiting Holbrooke girls for the drug operation."

"Expo?" Trevor wrote.

"Dead! Hogan murdered him."

Trevor raised his eyebrows in shock.

"I know," Melanie said. "Pretty wild, huh? *And* Hogan murdered Whitney Seward by shooting her up with heroin and OxyContin. Plus," she said, counting on her fingers, "we have him on heroin distribution resulting in the death of Brianna Meyers, assaulting you, and an embezzlement scheme at Holbrooke that I'm charging under the federal wire-fraud statute. He's looking at thirty years, minimum."

Trevor gave her a weak high five. She could tell from the tautness of his cheeks that he was fighting not to smile.

"But there's something else I came here to tell you, Trevor. Luckily, it's Christmas, and the chain of command in my office is feeling generous, because even given your stellar cooperation, getting this approved is pretty rare."

He looked at her questioningly.

"I dismissed all your charges. The ecstasy, that Internet-fraud thing—everything. *With prejudice,* so they can't be brought again. That's different from just getting sentenced to probation. It means you have a clean record. A fresh start. And I want you to make good use of it, because I see what a solid person you are. You have a lot to offer the world if you walk the straight and narrow path."

His eyes filled with tears, and they hugged.

D AN WAS WAITING outside with the engine running and the heat on.

"You told Trevor about dropping the charges?" he asked as she sank into the passenger seat, pulling her heavy coat tight around her.

"Yes. He was *very* happy. It was a nice Christmas present to be able to give him. Speaking *of*—what the heck is that in the backseat?"

There was a huge teddy bear wearing a Santa hat in the back of Dan's car.

"Well, you invited me over for dinner. I'm a little nervous about meeting Maya again, since she didn't seem too keen on me last time."

"She was *sick,* silly."

"Whatever. I'm not taking any chances. I know better than to show up empty-handed. Chicks always dig a gift."

She giggled. "Not me. I'm not materialistic like that."

"No?"

"Nope."

"Okay, then I won't give you the thing I got you."

"You got me something? *Really?* That is so sweet!"

"Yeah, but since you're not materialistic, you don't need it."

"Hey, come on, don't be that way! What is it?"

"I'm not telling."

"*Where* is it?"

He lifted his arms and gave her a million-dollar smile. "Somewhere on my person."

"Oh, you want me to pat you down? You sure?" she said.

"Yes, ma'am."

"You have no idea what you're in for."

"Bring it on, Melanie Vargas. Life's short. Let's not waste another second."